James Barnes, Carlton T. Chapman

Drake and his Yeomen

a true accounting of the character and adventures of Sir Francis Drake as told by Sir

Matthew Maunsell, his friend and follower

James Barnes, Carlton T. Chapman

Drake and his Yeomen
a true accounting of the character and adventures of Sir Francis Drake as told by Sir Matthew Maunsell, his friend and follower

ISBN/EAN: 9783337339715

Printed in Europe, USA, Canada, Australia, Japan

Cover: Foto ©Andreas Hilbeck / pixelio.de

More available books at **www.hansebooks.com**

Drake and His Yeomen

A True Accounting

of the

Character and Adventures of Sir Francis Drake

As told by Sir Matthew Maunsell, his Friend and
Follower.   Wherein also is set forth much
of the Narrator's Private History

BY

JAMES BARNES

Author of "Yankee Ships and Yankee Sailors," "For
King or Country," "A Loyal Traitor," etc.

ILLUSTRATED BY CARLTON T. CHAPMAN

New York

THE MACMILLAN COMPANY

LONDON: MACMILLAN & CO., Ltd.

1899

To EDWARD SIMMONS

WHOSE FRIENDSHIP IS WORTH HAV-
ING AND WHOSE ENCOURAGEMENT
IS WORTH REMEMBERING . . .

This Volume is Dedicated

Contents

List of Illustrations

ix

INTRODUCTION

"My dear Norman," wrote Basil Ennis to his friend, Norman Coolidge, fellow at Oxford, "I at last redeem my promise and send you the old Ms. that I told you belonged to my friends in Northamptonshire. It was found, as all these old papers *should* be found, you know, in an oak chest in the library at Highcourt — too bad that it was not just newly discovered in a secret drawer and I the discoverer; but the fact is that the existence of the paper had been known to the family for a long time, but you understand how careless some families are in matters of this character. It requires the loving and knowing ken of such grubby old bookworms as you and myself to detect the value of a possession like this. I have copied it out (a labour of love that has nearly cost me my eyesight), and submit it to you for your critical judgment. I have compared it with all the well-known published accounts of Hakluyt, Purchas, Fletcher and Pretty, and 'Drake redivivus,' and find that it agrees with most of the accepted, and perhaps throws some

light upon details that the over-cautious had ex-
cluded.   You remember how I once said that
those fine old stories were too good to have been
invented!   I have not changed it except here and
there in a sentence perhaps, and in the spelling,
which is fearful and wonderful.   As you see, it
is written quite simply, in a way; as those old
Johnnies used to write.   It is rather interesting to
see how Sir Matthew has tried at times to get away
from his own story, — I wish very often he hadn't,
— in order to make a record of historical events
and to chronicle the doings and sayings of another
man — an immortal man, whose fame will never
die, by the Lord Harry! as long as an English
heart beats in an English bosom!   Oh! brave old
Francis Drake!   Can't you see him on his sturdy
bow legs walking those steep quarter-decks, with
the light in his blue eyes as he sees the Armada
come crowding up the Channel?   And to think
that one of our armoured cruisers could send the
whole great show to the bottom (the way one might
sink floating bottles, one after another, with a rifle).
Isn't it a shame that the old days have gone!   I
suppose you will say *no;* but if you do, you don't
believe it.   But to return to the Ms.   It had no
title, and so I have suggested one; perhaps you
can help me with a better.   As you read you will
see that Sir Matthew cannot, for the sweet life of

him, keep his personal history entirely out; it will creep in, as it were, despite his determined efforts. There is a good deal of '*ego* in his *cosmos*' — witness his introduction of himself. But more anon when I see you, and we will talk over printers, etc. I have *carte blanche* to do what I like, but I wish thy counsel, friend. The old portrait you can see any time you are in this part of the country.

"Yours faithfully ever,

"BASIL ENNIS.

"P.S. Some people nowadays do not appreciate their ancestors, do they? Search the Oxford Mss.; you may find something there about this hardy old sailor."

DRAKE AND HIS YEOMEN

CHAPTER I

CONCERNING MYSELF

TRULY, if the matter should be looked into with diligence, it would be found that men's callings in life are not selected after a manner of haphazard; neither are they forced by circumstance altogether, but come more often from the effect of long inheritance. Why I should have been a sailor is plain to see, although at one time I was far from it beyond doubt, destined for something less or something greater; and this leads me to tell, even at the risk of being tiresome, a little of my birth and parentage.

My forefathers were men who had to do with ships and deep water, and their names are not unknown in the records of England; for an ancestor of mine, on my father's side, was Admiral of the North and West — Richard Childerbow, who held the post under Henry the Fourth; his daughter

married a Captain Maunsell, who commanded a
great ship; and his son, a famous mariner, was my
grandfather. I had uncles who served with Lord
John Russell in the reign of Henry the Eighth,
and my own father saw service as a young man in
the fleet of Baron Clinton, Admiral of England,
Ireland, and Aquitaine. So there must be a drop
of the brine flowing in my blood, for well do I
remember how the smell of it affected my nostrils
and how the first sight of the broad waters lifted
my heart.

I was born in troublous times, and I was destined
to live my early life feeling the effects of them.
My father, Sir John Maunsell, was of a Northampton family, well-to-do, and possessing wide acres,
although most of the estates that he inherited, and
that are now mine, at this writing, were in Ireland,
not far from the Boyne water. After leaving the
sea my father made a marriage, considered by some
beneath his quality, although the lady was of honest
parentage and comely of face and figure. By her
he had one son, [born shortly before her death,] who
was named John. But neither my half-brother nor
my father do I remember, for if I ever saw them,
it must have been while I lay in my nurse's arms,
—a sickly infant, I am told,— with apparently small
chance to live long or to make a fight of it.

I was the child of a second marriage and —

without pride — my father's lineage, which was good, as I've said, was nothing to the emblazoned records of my mother's family. She was Spanish of the greatest line in Spain, and akin to those who count themselves akin to royalty : —

Donna Maria, the only daughter of Miguel de Valdez, and a sister of Don Martinez de Valdez, an admiral afterward of King Philip, and of whom I shall tell, and a niece of Juan Martinez de Racalde, another great sailor, and of him, too, I shall speak further on.

The Maunsells were stanch Catholics, and, during the reign of Queen Mary, people of some importance, and it was at court that my father met his second wife, who was on a visit to England at the moment. Now, while again and again, we must think it strange that Spanish intrigue had gained so much power in our country, it is a fact that at the time of the King of Spain's proposals to Queen Mary the steersmen of the state in England were nobles of the Spanish court; but so much for all of this, to come back to myself once more : —

I was born on the 10th day of November, 1556, and it was on the 17th of this same month, two years later as every one knows, that Queen Mary died, and her reign had been marked by trouble for her subjects.

I was told long afterward that my father, who

was in great concern for the Catholic cause, was
one close to the ministers of the court, although he
held no position that could be named important,
and he counselled concealment of the Queen's death
for the good of the faith, but such things are hard
to keep secret, and but four hours sufficed for it
to leak out, and then both houses being informed
at once, after a momentous discussion was our
great Sovereign Queen chosen by joint resolu-
tion; and this was for the glory and good of the
nation.

Two days later she had left Hatfield, but it was
not until the third and twentieth of January that she
made her public entry through London. I speak of
this because it was that day my father died, of a
broken heart, it was said, because he knew the set
purpose of the Queen was to restore the Protestant
religion, and he observed the temper of the people.
And now the Queen soon after her coronation showed
the strength of her purpose. Though during the
reign of her sister she had declared herself a steadfast Catholic, [and it was known she had confessed
ofttimes to Cardinal Pole through fear of death,]
she had been but guiding herself as a ship in tem-
pestuous weather, to escape destruction.

The alterations now made in her councils and
her ministry and their transactions afterward, proved
that she was bent on promoting the reformation,

and the lives of the Catholics were soon destined
to be hard ones again in their turn. Those who
had no immediate landed interest or holdings found
ere long that it behooved them best to leave the
country. And so my mother, as soon as she was
able, (for her illness had been lingering, and for a
long time it left an impression on her mind,) took
first chance offered to set sail for France. She took
me with her, I being yet in the care of my foster-
mother; but I do not think that I was of much
concern to any one. From France we took a small
coasting vessel and landed at Cadiz. And on this
voyage, I have been told, I was so ill as to have
been given up more than once for dead.

With us had escaped an old servitor of the family, a person who had so improved his mind and
opportunities as to have been more of a friend and
companion to my father, than a varlet, though most
humble of origin. Selwyn Powys was this man's
name, and had he been of the cloth or born to
position, a person indeed, who would have left impression of his mind and life. I owe more to him
than I could state in short writing, for he moulded
my thoughts to take the direction of the right and
shaped my destiny by his teaching—God rest him,
I am grateful.

My first recollection is of a brilliant day, a young
companion, and a fountain in a garden filled with

sunlight and flower scents.   I saw many such days,
the fountain may be still plashing, and my companion, who is now dead, was once within arm's
reach of a throne.   For my mother had rejoined
her own people, and I was brought up as a child
among grandees and nobles, who lived at the
courts of King Philip, whose hand our maiden
Queen had spurned.   I, beyond peradventure, was
out of place in these surroundings; for, first, I discovered that I was not like my young companions;
not so much from the way they treated me or
from what I was told, as for the reason that I was
so different in my outward appearance.   Having
weathered the shoals of my early years' existence
with great difficulty, it seemed that nature was willing to reward me for so doing, for I gained in
health and strength until I was half again the size
of the others of my age, whom I encountered in
my games and play.   I spoke Spanish and knew
not but that I was a Spaniard until my eighth year;
it was then that I began to notice that my hair was
exceedingly light in color, while that of most of my
companions was black and heavy; my eyes, too,
were gray, which was unusual in Spain—I was all
English.   [And there is a prejudice against this in
other countries.]   I saw more of my good nurse
Martha and Selwyn Powys than any one else; but
there was a priest that was much with my mother

and was now attached to her retinue, a man that I
recall yet with instant recollection of the fear and
distrust in which I held him from the very first.
He was Padre Alonzo Garcia of the Order of St.
Joseph, lean and dark, with the eyes of a ferret
and the beak of a bird of prey. His voice, too,
I can recollect to this day, cautious and smooth,
modulated, and sympathetic, if need be — the
voice of the lip-server. To him I was especially
confided by my mother's orders at the time I began
to think and reason, and this I did not fancy, for up
to that time, as I say, I had been left to the charge
of Selwyn Powys and my foster-mother. Now
they kept away from me.

Well, one fine morning, when I had passed my
ninth birthday, the growing dislike, nay, hatred,
that I had formed for Padre Alonzo, took definite
shape. [How well do children know those whom
they can trust!] It happened thus wise: The holy
man had been instructing me in Latin, and I, having found out that he thought me stupid, decided to
play it thus, as my tasks would be lighter. His
duties were not easy; I was often surly with him
and would be spite-dumb in his presence. Something happened — what, I do not remember; it may
be that I tore up my written exercise, mayhap something else; be it what you will, it made the priest
angry, and he said hotly: "You English cub of a

heretic nation! had your mother not made the mistake of marrying in your cursed country, I would
have been spared the trouble of trying to teach so
dull a clod as thou art."

This would not have affected me and I would
have let it go, had it not been for the speech of Selwyn Powys, who at that moment happened to be
going by.   Pausing, he remonstrated with the Padre,
saying somewhat hotly: "Holy father, the boy is
fair and like those in his own country, but that he is
English is no reason for his being reviled — mark
ye that; nor is he of heretic birth, for such is a
lying speech without cause or reason!"

And now I recall to my mind that there were some
more words, and that I was the subject of them, and
then my mother entered.   But before she did, the
priest had said something to Powys that made him
cringe — what it was I had not caught; but at all
events, his face went white and red and white again,
while the other glared at him fiercely under his great
eyebrows and shook a threatening and triumphant
finger.   But the presence of the Marquisa — for that
was my mother's title by inheritance — put an end to
the scene; Padre Garcia took me by the arm, and
with his face all smiling led me up to her.   Would
that I could call to mind any tenderness that my
mother ever showed me; I did not know, then, that
it had been years before her dislike had permitted

her to be at ease with me. She might not have
been able to help her feelings; but I think that I
had begun by that time to notice them. Yes, verily
I believe I was often hurt by her unresponsiveness
to my caresses.

"Don Marteo will not study, and hath developed
a contrary disposition," said the Padre, with a hiss
that was soft and yet to me threatening. "He has
been subject to bad influence that should be removed,
and I will see to it."

I felt a new feeling welling into my heart; I had
often known short outbursts of temper, if things had
gone wrong with me, but now this was something
more, — an angry passion of distrust and hate. I
looked up and my eyes met his.

"I shall be gentle with him," went on the holy
man; "he shall be taught and led, by kind words, to
see his errors and to regard the truth."

But he must have read my mind and seen the
thoughts thereof, or mayhap he felt the heat of my
body, for my anger had set me all on fire: one hand
of his rested on my shoulder, and the other held my
arm. I felt his fingers closing; at first slowly, with
a pressure as if admonishing me to be silent; but
stronger it grew, even as he spoke, until the pain
was such I could hardly stand it — I thought his
nails would be meeting through my flesh! But, child
though I was, I would not for my life let him per-

ceive that I felt it, and I looked him squarely in the eyes though my sight was blurred and red spots danced across my vision.

" Be a dutiful son," said my mother, in her languid way, "and obey the holy father." To this I replied nothing, but cast a quick look round the chamber. Powys had left it, and without further word my mother did also. Scowling the priest half flung me into the depths of a great chair and strode out into the hall.

Now I think we remember events, not so much from what we did, as from how we felt at the time of doing, and this day I have marked for this reason. I followed the Padre out into the hall; he had descended but a few steps of the stair. Having no warning of my coming, he was unprepared, and I struck him with all my small strength full in the face ! It could not have hurt him much, but he whirled and caught me, and the first thing I knew I was dangling head downward over the marble court below.

But the priest did not seem to be angry, he laughed softly to himself, — the cruellest, most bitter laugh, God grant I shall ever hear (I heard it once again) ; it was the laugh of one who enjoys the suffering of others — the inquisitor, not only calloused but delighted at the quivering of anguished flesh. He must have been strong in his sinews, for after shaking me, — and this time I believe I did let forth a cry, — he lifted me over and laid me down on the stairway. I was helpless to move, the whole place seemed swimming, the great arch overhead swaying and unfolding like the main course of a galleon! But soon I was to witness something. A voice spoke above me and there stood Selwyn Powys!

"What have you been doing to the boy? what have ye done to my young master?" cried he, and his voice grated and croaked.

"Hanging him by the heels for the benefit of his manners, as I will hang thee for the benefit of thy soul," said the priest, warningly. "Come, thou hast betrayed thyself! Betray thy companions and escape the thumb-screws, though by St. Jago I promise thy neck shall feel the steel! Come, heretic!" he snarled. "Speak, I command thee."

Now Selwyn Powys was not a young man, nor was he, to appearance, one of much bulk or strength. But I came to know the build of such in after days and to judge them at a glance. Small men perhaps, but with thick necks and big shoulders, sturdy limbed, with legs somewhat bowed — the men for lifting and heaving on the ropes — I learned to know them. There came a fierce, strange sound, half groan, half curse, and he was at the priest's lean throat! There came another sound, short and horrid, like the breaking of a bone, as they swayed over the stone railing, and then with a quick heave and a thrust, the priest's body shot out and fell. Down it went like a sack of grain, down on the marble steps at the foot of the landing.

I had closed my eyes as I saw the figure in the cassock disappear, and now through the half-open lids I could see that Selwyn was bending over me. He was panting hard and praying, but after ascertaining that I was not much hurt he glanced about him with a gesture and look of sudden fear. Then he picked me up in his arms as if I weighed nothing at all and carried me back to the room where I took my lessons from the priest. I had really been made faint by fright, and there was no dissembling in my weakness. But now I am going to record a strange thing: Though, after a lapse of time, we met in close companionship under circumstances unusual, Selwyn Powys never learned from my lips that I had seen him attempt to do a man to death!

Although the fall and scuffling must have made some noise, no one had appeared, and this is right easily understood, for the staircase is at the end of a long corridor. We had few servitors and no guests. Powys, as soon as I could lift my head, stood me upon my feet and brushed my clothes with his hand, as a nurse might treat a child that had tripped and fallen. At the same time he straightened out the lacing of his doublet that almost had been torn apart in the struggle; this done, and no one yet appearing, he took me by the arm and together we passed into another room and down a narrow staircase into the garden, where he began to talk to me about the flowers, for he was a gardener of no mean merit. I could not display much interest; but he did not remark upon it, and we were thus employed when there came a cry, and one of the maidservants rushed forth, calling in great anguish for Selwyn to return, and that Padre Alonzo had been killed. We hurried back into the palace and found that they had carried the body into one of the rooms in the lower floor and placed it on a bed. My mother was there with some of the females, and breathlessly one of them informed us that a man had been sent down into the town to fetch a surgeon.

"Is he dead?" questioned my mother of Powys. There was no mark on the priest's thin face, but he lay there like an effigy, still and white. His heavy cowl had broke the force of his fall and prevented his pate from being cracked. But the great crucifix that dangled about his neck had been broken, and what was left of it lay on his breast. "Is he dead?" asked my mother again, and Powys, with his face as white as alabaster, laid his ear against the other's heart.

"No, Donna Marquisa!" he said; "he lives! It is no doubt that the holy man suffered from a vertigo and fell o'er the balustrade."

There came a slight movement from the figure upon the couch, and Father Alonzo's deep-set eyes opened. There was sense in them! his lips quivered as if he was trying to frame words that would not come — his mind was alert, but his body for the time was dead and useless. Such malignancy never have I seen as that with which he regarded Powys. The latter shrank back fearsomely. Before many minutes the leech had arrived, and he pronounced that Padre Alonzo would live, but that his body might remain dead, for his backbone had been injured — and that affects the powers which govern action.

When this verdict had been reached, once more the priest's lips moved, but no sound came forth. It was plain that he could hear what passed, and that he was endeavoring to frame words without result. There was nothing to be done, and I would not have lifted a finger, so I slipped away. When I left the chamber I found Powys in the hallway. He grasped me in his arms and kissed me on the forehead. Then he picked up a long cloak from a chair, went out the door, and that was the last I saw of Master Powys for many long months.

In the evening some of the priest's sombre-clad

companions came and carried him away bodily on their shoulders, [still lying upon the couch where he had been placed,] and it was a long time before I set eyes on him either; but of this there is more to come, that shall be told in due order.

CHAPTER II

THE MYSTERIOUS BEGGAR

THE disappearance of my old friend of course excited comment and questioning at first, and then when the surprise was over all became known. Padre Alonzo's speech had returned to him and he had denounced Master Powys, not only as a man who had intended to do murder, but as a heretic and unbeliever, which was much worse. Great search was made for him; but months went by and there came no word, or inkling of his whereabouts, and no one spoke his name in my hearing. As the Padre lay warped and twisted at his monastery, he bothered me no more, and I resumed my studies under the care of a young Jesuit who, although possessing an able mind, was of indolent habit and allowed my own will to work its way; so without much trouble we managed to pass the time. But I made progress, nevertheless, and was, I dare say, as much advanced in studies as most boys of my age. I spoke French fairly, Spanish with a pure accent, I knew Latin and Greek (the latter not much). But I was satisfactory.

My mother had forbade either Powys or my nurse speaking to me in English; nevertheless I had picked up not a little knowledge of my native tongue from hearing them use it (my mother spoke it with difficulty and detested it heartily), but now all this was changed. My new instructor was a wise man in some ways, a Frenchman by birth, and he had lived some time in London during the reign of Queen Mary. So it was his advice that I should learn to speak what might be of some use to me, and we began to talk and read in the language which by all rights was my inheritance. But I soon surpassed him, for I had the means of practice that he had not. My foster-mother's tongue being now unloosened by permission,—for she had never learned to well master the Spanish lingo,—I made a great progress. In fact, I would search her out at all times, and as she loved me as were I her own and as I loved her, deep grew the affection between us. The Marquisa I saw less and less of; for although she had many admirers (I had met plenty of great people who are of no moment in this telling), there had been no favorite suitor until at this time, when Don Pedro de Vertendonna, an exceedingly haughty and handsome man, aspired for her hand. They said that in all Spain there were but three richer men. Sooth, he was bedight with jewels and gold and a brave sight to see! But he scarcely ever took

c

notice of me and regretted doubtless my existence with all his heart. *Digito Monstrari*, I was a reminder he did not like.

*   *   *   *   *   *   *   *

After the marriage, which was celebrated with great pomp in the big cathedral at Cadiz, near which, I might here say, lay the castle and estate at which we lived, we all moved to Valliera, and I came to reside at the palace of my stepfather.

I was now in my thirteenth year, large and strong, with the tendency to be so rough in my sport that my boy companions, who were few (but exceedingly noble), avoided me, and I was often complained of, lectured, and punished. This led me into a somewhat solitary manner. I can say of a truth that I did not know much happiness in those days. But when I was not at books, I was consumed with a fierce desire for action and adventure. My exercise with the sword (for it were part of my education) was a great delight; my wrist was strong and my eye quick. The old guardsman who instructed me often cried out with pleasure; but this alone did not give me sufficient outlet. One of the old servants of the house had been a seafarer and had sailed in the Spanish Main, and many a long yarn did he spin for me, and many a night did I lie awake thinking them over. He made me a little gallease that I used to sail to wonderful far countries in the fountain. But

imaginings alone did not fill out my nature; I delighted to climb to the topmost branches of a tall
poplar tree that lifted high above the others in the
grove, and I made my way up the sheer face
of the great wall that surrounded the garden, with
nothing but the crevices to help me. By means
of a vine I clomb from the edge of this wall
where it joined the battlements, to the window
of a little apartment next my own. There was not
a corner nor a secret passage (and the place was full
of them) that was not known to me. The wall to
which I referred looked over a narrow street, to the
north. Now the houses of the poor encroach upon
those of the mighty in Spain, and a hovel may be
but a stone's throw from the postern gate of a
grandee. Well, I stood upon the wall one day, with
a sheer fall of twenty feet below me, and looked down
into this alley. Off at the corner I could perceive
some children playing, brown skinned, half naked,
and despised ones; but happy for all of it, and I
longed to be with them, for I was, of a truth, though
neglected, a prisoner confined to bounds, except for
the times that I left under escort with a priest or
instructor at my side. O! How I hated all of
them!

From watching the playing children my glance wandered nearer, and I saw seated in the warm sunlight
at the foot of the wall, what was so common a sight

in Spain, that it did not hold my attention for even an instant. A beggar, a mere bundle of rags, sat there with a crutch beside him. Though there were but few passers-by on this lonely street, his hand was outstretched, alms-asking. He was so fair beneath me, that it was easy for me to obey the promptings of a whim, and taking a small coin from my pocket, I leaned over and dropped it so that it fell into his palm. Then I drew back; but I heard a voice say plainly in weak, muffled tones : —

"Thanks, thanks! from a poor beggar who is both blind and deaf."

Looking over the wall again, I saw a strange sight. The cripple — for that he appeared to be also — was turning his head slowly from left to right. He had pushed up the bandage on his forehead a little, and from his attitude I perceived that he was both looking and listening, and was perplexed at hearing no footfall and perceiving no one. That he had thus betrayed himself was easily seen, but I cared not for that; there was amusement in the prank, and I detached some loose mortar from the top of the wall and poured it down upon his head. This disclosed my position; with a quick glance he looked upward, and his eyes met mine, and then it was my turn to betray astonishment. I knew those eyes! (And here let me state that it is this part of the face that has to be hidden if one wishes to avoid recognition. The eyes tell tales, and it will always be so.'

Selwyn Powys sat there in the sun beneath me! Whether he had recognized me, or not, was not plain at first; but all doubt was soon removed — I was on the point of addressing him when he spoke my name. So glad was I to see him that I was tempted to make a leap of it at the risk of my legs. I cried out shrilly that I knew him. But, raising his hands and lowering his eyes, and the bandage at the same time, he cautioned me to silence. Then he went on as if crooning to himself (speaking in Spanish) and told me much in few words.

He had seen me before, and now I remembered that once, when accompanied by Martha, I had seen her stop and speak a few words to a blind beggar on the corner as she gave him alms.

"Young master," he went on, "despite how I appear, it fareth well with me and with thee also — that I know; but no happiness will come to thee in this land, or from the life here about thee. Thou shouldst go to thy father's folk in England, and it will be so," he went on. "Here thou art out of place."

"Then take me, Selwyn Powys," I replied in English, "I will go with thee."

He started at hearing me address him thus, but did not glance up. Now as I lay prone on top of the wall my figure was all but concealed; but to my sorrow and chagrin I heard my name being called in the garden. Some one was searching for me amid the shrubbery. It was my study hour and I was late.

"They call me," I said in a whisper over the wall, "but be here after dark, and we will talk more."

Some one was coming down the street, and Master Powys began to clamor for charity just as I slid down the surface of the wall, much to the detriment of my hose and my hands. There I found the servant who had been sent out to search for me, and went back with him into the castle. Even to Martha I said nothing this night of the meeting; but my mind was far astray during my lesson. I went to bed, perhaps earlier than my wont, and after Martha had looked in on me, to see if I were sleeping (a way she had of doing, and of course to all appearances I was), I waited but a few moments to don my clothes again, passed into the next room and opened the window.

The moon was high in the sky, and though not at the full, it cast soft shadows and tipped the silver leaves of the poplar. I could see the reflection of the tireless little fountain, without which no Spanish garden is a garden. Above the wall I could see the lights twinkling in the town, and the air was so still that I could hear the low throbbing notes of a theorbo, where some gallant serenaded his mistress. I could almost detect the words of his song, although from what direction it came I knew not. But I had other business on this night than listening to music or gazing at the scenery, and slipping out of the window, I grasped the vine, and was soon on the wall. Thinking it better to observe caution, I crawled forward on my hands and knees. At last I reached the place where my old friend had been seated, and craning my neck looked down. No one was there, the street was empty; but at the corner rose a house of some pretension above the low, white buildings. Before it stood a figure, and then I saw where the music came from, for the singer was picking away at his great lute, and evidently directing his voice at a window on the second floor; but no one appeared, and he shouldered the theorbo after the manner of an itinerant musician and walked directly toward me. When he got very close he flung his instrument into position again, and trying the strings lightly as if setting them atune, he paused directly under where I lay, and in the same key in which he was playing, he hummed a few words.

"Are you waiting, friend, are you waiting?" he asked in Spanish. (Tra la, boom boom, went the lute.) There was no use to tell me who the singer was; for as he stepped out of the shadow of the wall into the full moonlight, it was Master

Powys and no other. I would have recognized his
sturdy legs if nothing else; but I would never have
known him as the beggar of the morning; though his
troubadour habiliments were not glaringly new, yet he
might have passed for a wandering minstrel in fair
circumstances. We talked in whispers, and Selwyn
played a running obligato. But I could see that he
felt there was some risk in this sort of thing by
the way in which he glanced up and down the street.

While he talked, I got the outline of strange
things. He had been to England, having smuggled
himself on board a Biscayan coaster that set sail
from Barcelona (boom, boom, tra la), and he had
returned to Spain some three or four months previous; since which time he had been endeavoring
to see me upon a mission, he said, of the greatest
importance (tra la la, boom, boom); but what it was
he would not tell me that night, but would reserve
for some other. "And now," said he, changing the
tempo, "young master, we must meet where we
can talk in a way we cannot here, for I must com-
mune with thy inward thoughts and self, and speak
to thee of things that can only be arrived at through
close converse." Then he went on to tell me that
Martha could be trusted, and that had I not met
him in the manner that I have related, she was to
have arranged it. "But now," he said, stopping
his playing in his earnestness, "it is better to

assume that she knows nothing; there will be naught to conceal between you, and no suspicions may be formed." Then he called my attention and asked if I knew of a heavy iron-studded gate that, half hid by a clump of rose bushes, led through the wall at the farther angle.

"Yes, but there is no key," said I, "and I have never known it to be open, nor does it open on the street."

"I know that well," he replied, "and if there had been one anywhere within the reach, it would have been found; so we must get around that. Can you see me where I stand?"

"Beyond doubt," said I, "most readily."

"I am holding something," said he, in reply. "Could you catch it if I should toss it you?"

"Try me," said I.

Gently he tossed something up to me, and I caught it even in that bad light, without a mishap. It was soft and pliable.

"Now listen," went on Selwyn Powys. "What you hold in your hand is wax, and with it you can get the impression of the inside of the big lock to the gate. Martha has tried to do so, but her fingers are too big to press the wax into the niches, and the keys that we have made fit not, or at least so badly that they are useless." Then in a few words he directed me how to mould the various interior parts

and to make note of them so that when put together the complete form of the key could be
gathered.

I was for sliding down the wall to him with the
assistance of a rope, but to this he would not listen,
as being dangerous and sure of ultimate discovery.
Then added he: "We must talk together at
length and be unobserved for this purpose." So I
made my way through the flower beds and the little
maze to the gate, and following his directions as to
keeping the wax warm by holding it in my hands
and wetting it after sticking it upon my finger, I
succeeded in getting several misshapen lumps, and
carried them back to him on a stone as he directed,
so as to avoid destroying the shape by handling,
and because the moulds kept better and entire when
cold. I had to exercise some caution in getting
them to the top of the wall, and not a little care in
dropping them into his hat and remembering the
parts of the lock from which they came. We were
once interrupted by the approach of a party of rev-
ellers, and for a long time it looked as if Selwyn
would have to desist from his plotting and turn
minstrel again for their benefit; but after some coarse
bantering they went their ways, and the rest of the
wax was delivered in safety.

With a parting injunction to be guarded and to
be on the lookout the next evening, Master Powys

left.   As I crawled in at the window, [my passage
hid by the thick leaves of the vine,] I heard the
throbbing of his theorbo down the street.

Now it may be thought that I was over young to
be indulging in this sort of business, and my only
answer to that is doubtless this was so ; but I
was older than my years, and though inexperienced
in the ways of the world at large, confident of myself and was resourceful to some extent for the very
reason of my mode of life.   For I had been de-
pending on no one else during the years that most
children rely upon others.   Had the young priest
who had taken me in charge been less lazy and
more desirous of influence, I doubt not that he
might have gained some hold over me ; but as it
was, he simply existed and counted for neither
one thing nor the other.   Having caught him once
in a falsehood, I had lost respect for him, and you
know what this means with young people.

It was impossible for any one to leave the cas-
tello after nightfall, for watches were kept at the big
gates, and no one, servant or otherwise, left without
permission from the guardian, except it were on
business for the Don or at his command.   At
some time in the past this old keep must have stood
out well from the town that had grown around it,
for it was built after the fashion of the old feudal
fortresses.   The castle proper was still surrounded

by a moat, and the portcullis was still in existence. The garden had been a recent addition, and by recent I mean made during the last one hundred and fifty years.

That day was one that tried my spirit — I could scarce wait for nightfall. The young Padre Francisco was exacting of me, and for the first time betrayed that some force lay beneath his placid exterior; but he found me at least willing to listen to his lecture, though my mind wandered sadly and I was taken to task for inattention. After I had crept into bed, this time with my clothes on, — for I feared Martha's curiosity no longer (although according to arrangements I had told her nothing), — some one entered. Thinking it was Martha coming in on her usual visit of inspection, I breathed slowly and regularly with my eyes closed, and then I opened them, for I felt that whosoever it was had not left the room and was bending over me — watching. Above me stood my mother! It was the first time that I could remember that she had come in to see me.

"Marteo," she said gently, in tone that was new to her, — "Marteo," and she bent as if to put her lips to mine. I turned my head and shrank back into the bed coverings. I am glad to state that the reason I did so was because of the sudden knowledge that I had everything on but my shoes, and not from any disdain of her tenderness. But she must have taken it that way, for I heard the door close; and although I waited, listening for her footsteps, and deep in my heart longing for her, she did not return, and never again was this visit repeated. My poor mother! she was one of those people who enjoy life but at odd moments, and then intensely, and suffer during the most part of their existence.

Well, I reached the appointed spot on the wall and lay there for a few minutes before I saw any one, and then it was a gray Friar who came waddling along with his cowl over his head and his arms thrust into his wide sleeves. Soon came a hail in my direction.

"And who art thou?" I asked, though of course I knew.

"Father Selwyn," was the reply, "who wouldst talk with thee. Here, my son, take this." And he threw the end of a slight cord over the wall. I caught it and drew up a heavy key almost the length of my forearm.

"Now," said Selwyn Powys, dropping for the nonce the tone he had used, "hasten to the gate, and when the moon is hidden behind the big middle tower unlock the bolt and open the door."

So, all impatient, I did as I was told; I passed through the garden, found the gate, and inserting the key as soon as the time came, I tried to turn it. It grated, but would not move. Then, placing my foot against the side, I strained with all my might, and slowly it gave way. Again it required all my strength to move it upon its hinges. It groaned and moved; I put my hand forward and my heart sank. There was another door inside! But as soon as I had pushed the first one open [so that the dim light entered the archway] I perceived that the sizes of the locks were much the same, but there were two huge bolts securing it. Trying the key once more, I found it unlocked the inner door; then, using it as a lever, I slid back the iron bars. This door pushed through the other way I perceived, after trying it several times, and I slowly opened it; the hinges gave a hollow grumble at first; then it swung wide of its own accord.

I peered past. Behind me the garden was flooded with moonlight; but before me there was nothing but jet blackness, and then I heard a hollow rapping sound, and a damp air crept past me that chilled my limbs.

It was a fortunate thing that I felt my way before taking a step — I might have come to grief had I not used diligence. The passageway, into which this second door led, began with a straight descent of six steps, and I went down them much after the fashion of a person who, unable to swim, enters deep water. At last I found that level ground was before me, and sounding with my foot as I advanced, my heart beating loudly, I pushed ahead. The knocking continued growing louder, and I came to the foot of another stone staircase. It had appeared that I had unlocked enough doors, but this was the last.

"Try the key," said a distant voice behind the obstruction. I found the keyhole and pushed the door open.

I came out into another garden, and the dim moonlight seemed brilliant after the darkness. Selwyn Powys was there alone, and I threw my arms about his neck. For a full minute after the embrace we stood there looking at one another. Then Selwyn said, "Come," and turned. Before us rose a well-built structure of gray stone, and holding my hand, he conducted me into the building by what was evidently a rear entrance. We came into a room sparsely furnished and dimly lighted by a sputtering dip. He placed me on a chair, and drawing up nearly opposite me, he began to submit me to a course of questions.

It did seem odd that, after having told me that he had come from England at the risk of his life to find me, he should be concerned, not for my liberty or my happiness, but for my spiritual welfare. For, after asking me concerning the teach-

ings to which I had been subjected, and if I loved
the Pope, he began to sift me to find the condition
of my soul. Earnestly, indeed, did he talk, and
from a condition of surprise and disappointment I
caught the infection.

When I went back to the castle through the hidden passage, I had much to think about; of course I
was puzzled. To be short, for five or six nights
this continued. Perhaps I was a willing convert,
or perhaps I had seen enough of the ways of
popery. At any rate, after a week I had imbibed
enough heretic doctrines to bring me to the stake,
and before a month had gone by I was a member
of a little congregation that met secretly at midnight in the cellar of this house and worshipped at
a risk that was fearful to contemplate. Some well-
known people did I meet at these gatherings, one
very aged man who had been a pupil of Melanchthon,
and another, who had been a close companion of
Lefebre. The Reformation was making long strides
in France, but it had not dared to raise its head
in Spain; nor methinks will it ever gain foothold
there, so strong are the powers that work against
it.

It had become so much a matter of course for me
to indulge in these nocturnal excursions that I took
them as a matter of granted. I had almost worn a
pathway through the vines by means of my frequent

comings and goings, and soon the great key turned the locks easily from constant practice.

Months went by. I was the very youngest that appeared at the meetings, and *certe* I was but a listener ; and I began to wonder what was expected of me and why I had been reckoned of so much importance by Selwyn Powys. One day I knew, and as he told it tersely I can tell it best in his words.

We had left the cellar, where there had been a somewhat larger attendance than usual, and he stopped me in the garden.

"Young master," said he, "I know now that young as thou art, thou hast embraced the truth and that the new spirit is born within thee, and I do not fear that it will be driven out ; and so I will tell thee something of thyself and why I have been so cautious in my dealings. Thy half-brother in England is dead, and to thee belong the estates and possessions of the family. Thou art Sir Matthew Maunsell of Highcourt and art entitled to take place of a baronet in Free England, and there thou must go right shortly. And strong in thy new faith thou wilt find everything ready to thy hand : a royal welcome, good friends, and, praise God, liberty !"

I was all on fire at once ; for it was daily growing harder for me to dissemble, I hated the acting of the part, and the excitement of the evening excursions had died away.

Powys promised me that all arrangements would be made as soon as possible, and that Martha and I would be provided with means to reach some seaport where he would join us, and then: Ho! for distant England! But the programme that we arranged so easily was to be interrupted. I had not seen my mother, except once or twice, since the night that she had come to my bedside, and Martha informed me the day after the speech of Powys's that I have recorded, that a great event had happened for the house of Vertendonna, and that an heir had been born to my stepfather — not such a babe as I had been, but one strong and lusty with lungs like a clarion-player, for I could hear the cries of the strange little voice when I entered the apartment where the babe was being shown to the members of the household and family.

My mother was an exceedingly sick woman, though; there was much concern for her, and no one was permitted to see her but her attendants. I did not look upon her face until the next morning, and then she lay cold and white, and for the first time, to all appearance, supremely happy, in the great high bed, with the gold and crimson canopy. Candles burned beside her, some priests were chanting the requiem, and I stood awed, and silent, and untearful in the presence of death. I mourned sincerely at the funeral, and for the few days following

was moody and unhappy and more neglected than
ever.   In fact, I was not considered at all, and had
Powys learned what I knew subsequently, much that
happened could have been avoided.   Assuredly most
people thereabouts would never have missed me,
and my stepfather doubtless would have considered
my departure good riddance.

Powys condoled with me in my loss, and put off
on account of it making the final arrangements for
our flight; but under his direction I now broached
the subject to Martha, and she appeared to be well
informed.   She also told me more of my family and
more of herself.   She was not young, but in the prime
of womanhood, and she was to marry Selwyn as soon
as they had arrived in England.   She expressed the
hope (and it was odd to hear her do so) that neither
she nor he would ever have to leave my service, and
she made me promise this — which I did on my
heart.   Martha told me that my father's sister, who
had married a Scotch lord, was still Romish and a
lady in waiting to Mary, the wife of the King of
France, and who afterwards styled herself the Queen
of the Scots.   She described to me the scenery of
England and was as eager to return there as I was
to go.   Every night I dreamed of it.

CHAPTER III

THE BLACK ORDER

PADRE FRANCISCO had paid little attention to me since the death of my mother, and I had been left to my own devices absolutely, and this had given Martha and myself much time for talking. But the priest appeared one evening, shortly after darkness had set in, with a request that I should accompany him upon a matter of importance. Now this was the night that preceded the one that had been settled upon for our escape! Martha and I were to pack up a few belongings and leaving by the secret entrance to meet Selwyn, who would have horses ready. It had been the intention to ride all night to some place where we could take ship before we could be apprehended.

The priest's request was a strange one, and he did not enlighten me as to his intentions. It was clear that he had made some arrangement, however; for, as we went out of the great entrance, — he having close grasp of my hand, — he spoke to a black Friar, who turned and accompanied us, the warder at the gate

bowing low as we passed. We walked a long way
in a direction that was new to me, and passing before
a great church, followed close along an unbroken wall
and entered a low, sombre building with narrow windows that were heavily barred. I had not asked a
question of my conductors on the journey, but no
sooner were we admitted (after some knocking and
words) than I began to feel a sense of fear. The
corridor was but dimly lighted, and here and there
stood whispering groups of priests in the black habit
of the one who had accompanied us. I would have
stayed close by the young Padre, for even he seemed
like a friend among these frightening strangers; but
telling me to remain where I was, he shook his
hand free from mine that would have held him, and
disappeared. No one spoke to me, no one even
approached me, and my pride tempted me not to
show my feelings, but to affect an attitude of uncon-
cern; and thus I stood with my arms folded, out-
wardly possessed, but with my heart beating and
hammering against my ribs. Soon my tutor returned, and leading me down the corridor, he conducted me into a room lit by a few tapers burning
before a great crucifix, almost life size, that hung
over a draped altar. Another door opened, and the
crooked figure of a man dressed in the same black
gown as the others, with the cowl drawn over the
head, tottered up to us. I say tottered, though it

were better to use the word "shuffled"; his feet
dragged heavily, and he only kept himself from falling
forward by the help of a stout staff grasped in both
hands. When quite close he stopped and pushed
back the cowl. I recognized the ferret eyes and the
hooked beak of Padre Alonzo! The picture of
him as I had seen him last, came to me; but all that
was human had faded from his face; the temples
were sunken and there was scarcely enough flesh to
cover the outlines of the skull. His shaven head
made the resemblance to death more frightful, and I
could not control a start of horror. Formerly he
had been a tall man; but now he appeared bent to
half his height.

"You know me, you remember me?" he asked
in the flat cracked voice of a hunchback.

"I do," I replied, and I spoke his name.

"'Tis well," said he. "We will delay no longer
—follow!" and we fell in behind him as he worked
his way toward an entrance, the door of which had
been thrown wide open. It closed behind us with
a heavy, echoing report, and there we were in a long
room filled with objects that were strange to me.
But I cannot even now remember or describe them
clearly. There were utensils of wood and iron,
wheels and ropes and several long bars hung down
from the ceiling. Seated on either side of a great
throne-like chair were five horrible beings whose

heads turned with one accord as we came in. Beneath their cowls their faces were hid by long black masks with slits for eyeholes. They rose without a word and remained standing until the deformed priest had seated himself on the great centre throne. The mystery, the silence, and the horror gained such possession of me that it took great effort to prevent myself from screaming as one might in the foul clutches of a wicked dream. Padre Francisco, who stood near me, was affected also. I could see that, from his drawn face and his lips that moved in the ejaculatory prayer.

Padre Alonzo's hand sought a cord that hung beside the chair in which he sat. In response to a pull a solemn muffled bell rang somewhere and a door at the farther end of the chamber opened. Two figures in black hose and doublets, with masks — black also — hiding their visages, came in, dragging between them the half-dressed figure of a man. He was tightly bound with cords so that his shoulders almost met behind him, his head was hung back loosely; but even before I saw his pale blood-streaked face I knew it was Selwyn Powys. I would have cried out then, of a surety, had not one of the black-robed council, who had risen a step before me, closed my mouth with his hand, at the same time shielding me from my poor friend's sight.

" Thou hast denied that thou knew me, or that I know thy name!" hissed Padre Alonzo, leaning forward. "We have a witness here to confront thee with." With that the black-robed captor whirled me suddenly about, and Selwyn Powys looked me in the eyes. His countenance had undergone a dreadful change. It was waxen, with deep lines down his cheeks; the white upper garment that he wore was red from wrist to elbow. With an effort he straightened his knees and stood firmly.

"Yea," he said, endeavoring to speak aloud. "Thou hast spoken right; I am the one who made thee what thou art, but who did the work badly, as all can see. But Satan will accomplish what I failed to do, and thy misshapen soul shall be tortured as thy body hath been."

I fain believe that the chief inquisitor would have felled him with his staff had he possessed the strength, and perhaps Powys hoped that he would do so, for he inclined his head as if eager to receive a blow, but none fell. Instead, the judge leaned forward, and, pointing with his trembling, bony finger, spoke a word I could not catch. At this Padre Francisco stepped out boldly.

"Holy Father," he cried, "I beg of thee to allow this young boy to retire. He is not fit for such scenes; I beg of thee," he repeated.

"And for thyself, thou speakest also," hissed the devil-hearted one, for such he must have been. "No, both shall stay."

"Shall he have no time to recant?" asked a deep voice from behind one of the masks. At this Powys spoke again.

"Recant!" cried he. "Listen well, and you may hear every fibre of my body cry out against thee and thy teachings, against all thy deviltries and idolatries! The last flutter of my heart will praise the new faith and its meanings; the faith that will rise to confound false doctrine and evil thought!" The misshapen priest stamped his foot and half rose. Again he pointed. There came a sound of scuffling feet and Selwyn Powys's voice saying in English:—

"Have courage, Sir Matthew! Fear not; have confidence, and be faithful!" A heavy chain dropped on the stone floor. I heard the creaking of a rope, the room whirled about me, and I fell senseless, made so by God's mercy who protecteth His children.

And thus did the soul of my master, beloved friend, and faithful servitor go out in anguish, as many souls have departed before and since.

When my senses came back to me, I was in the open air, being carried in some one's arms, and it was some moments before I could tell the why or

wherefore of such procedure, and then I saw that
it was the young priest and a stranger who had hold
of me. My brain wandered sadly as if in a
fever. I must have been a heavy burden, but they
carried me thus into the castle and placed me upon
my couch. There I remained for five days, and
when I did grow strong enough to raise my head,
my mind was like that of a child but two years old;
the names of things had left me, and all my recollec-
tions returned but slowly: it was over a year before
I could recall the happenings of this night. Faithful Martha Warrell never learned what I could
tell, though, poor, broken-hearted creature, she
suspected all of it. Selwyn Powys had disappeared,
and granting that to be a fact, he was as good as
dead in Spain.

How or where they had found him is more than
I know, but several others of the little congregation
with whom I worshipped were missing; for the
Spanish inquisition, like some great monster that
lurks beneath a nation, as a devil-fish does beneath
the water, thrusts its arms in all directions, and woe
betide the unlucky mortal that is once within its
clutches.

Martha tended me faithfully during my illness.
Hardly for an instant did she leave my side, and as
soon as I was able to be about, she told me that a
great change was to come over my affairs. She did

not have to go into deep explanations, for I accepted the news that I was going to go upon a journey with the indifferent delight of a child, and as before my experience in the torture chamber I had been advanced for my age, my brain had now gone backward: I was a dolt and a dullard. This fact did not seem to excite much comment from my stepfather's adherents, and mayhap Martha was the only one that noticed it, and it but increased her devotion. At all events, one morning we drove away from the castle, she and I, and I caught a glimpse of the Don, a handsome figure, to be sure, in his black and silver mourning, standing at the great gate surrounded by some of his friends. I sat there in the coach, with my head on Martha's shoulder, not caring where I went, and he watched me go, with a smile on his lips, not caring either. I was somewhat of a joke, I dare say, with his relations. I had become familiar with great names a-plenty, and knew many faces to fit to them; but every one knows how it is with proud people: they seldom concern themselves with others whom they regard as dependents or pensioners of their acquaintances. Martha told me that we were going to embark at Cadiz for Flanders, and that all this had been brought about by my Aunt Katharine, who was then in France. I cannot tell where we landed, but I think it L'Orient, and thence we went inland, having been met by a courier, and I was taken to the chateau at which Lady Katharine Taliaferro (born Maunsell and twice widowed) was stopping.

CHAPTER IV

ENGLAND

I HAD been much wasted by my illness, but had grown so tall, that I no doubt appeared unprepossessing and feeble in body, as I was certainly dulled in mind. The only thing that I craved deeply was sleep and solitude, and this I soon got plenty of; for after four or five attempts to draw me out and ascertain my aptitude and temper, my aunt decided that I had neither one nor the other, and again I settled down to a life that could not possibly harm any one and did no end of good to me, in that every day I gained health and strength. Nothing was said to me about the fact which Selwyn Powys had appraised me of; namely, that I was the heir of some property, and a baronet by right of descent. I was not forced to study or to exert myself in any measure; I simply existed healthily. Without any reluctance I had gone back to the going through with the outward forms of the religion which my aunt professed, and there was no hypocrisy here, for at this time I would have worshipped a golden image or a clay one, so far as any effect of doing so would have had upon my mental consciousness. Perhaps Lady Katharine regretted the bargain she had made and the burden she assumed in sending for me; perhaps she had but hoped to use me as a tool to further her own designs and found me what she wished.

*   *   *   *   *   *   *   *

I remember the gleam of interest that awakened in me at the news that we were at last going to England, and I date from this day the complete recovery of my mental powers. Yes, well do I recall how it seemed when I was on the ship midway across the Channel! I was watching the waters dancing and leaping, — for we were in the midst of the chop, and every one was ill but myself and the crew, — yes, and as I looked out, a heavy veil seemed to lift; I drew a long breath and gazed down at myself. It was the wakening from partial sleep; I realized who I was, where I had been, and to what I was going. I was Sir Matthew Maunsell, aged sixteen, a Protestant, by the grace of God, and all the old courage that had marked me in my very early days returned. The ship, a small craft of five and thirty tons, was bound for Dundee in Scotland, and most of the sailors were Scotsmen or French. But it was a long time before they saw the northland. Well do I remember the storm that sprang up and how, through

"We could not fight against such head winds and so bad a sea."

the terror of it, though I was sometimes frightened,
I rejoiced in keeping the deck, [though bidden by
the captain to go below,] once or twice hauling
away lustily on a rope with the crew. But there
was naught for it; we could not fight against such
head winds and so bad a sea. We sprang a leak
and were forced, against the will of all on board, I
take it, to put in for the coast of England. By the
narrowest chance we managed to make the harbor
of Portsmouth, and there came to anchor in the
midst of a great fleet of vessels that lay riding to
long cables. To the dismay of every one, but especially to some gentry whose countenances and
methods of speech showed them to be offsprings of
the Church, we were informed by the captain that
the condition of the vessel precluded all idea of proceeding farther, as the hull had been strained from
stem to stern-post, and it required constant pumping
to keep her afloat even in water that was fairly still.
I remember well my aunt's consternation at this up-
shot; but still she was not in as bad position as some
of the others, who spoke no English and whose appearance told tales on them. There were plenty of
Romanists in England, and of course with them she
had held communication. She was English in appearance, and as she had intended to proceed from
Scotland to London at some future day, she decided
that it would be best not to wait on the odd chance

of getting a vessel north, but to go ashore and make
her way to her friends: Martha and myself and a
young Jesuit, who was her private confessor, were to
accompany her.   I did not know that her mission
was one that every one would have praised for its
disinterestedness.   She had left the service of Queen
Mary some three years previously; but when the latter
had been defeated by Earl Murray at Langside, she
would have joined her if she could, and after Mary
had landed at Workington in Cumberland, she had
made the attempt.   Now that the Queen's imprisonment seemed to promise to be long, nothing would
do but she must join her, and this she did and remained to the last.   All else aside, and despite the
fact that my feeling toward her is perforce not
kindly, I grant that she was a faithful soul and honest
and steadfast according to her limitations.   But this
is digressing.   It seems to me that I have written a
great deal and not told all that I might or half that
I would like to; but I was saying they were very
much upset on board the *Sagita*, all except myself
and Martha.   She was the first to discover that a
change had come over me.   I cannot explain, nor
have I met any one who ever hath had another such
experience; but it appeared to me as if I had
suddenly grown and recognized myself as men's
equal.   Even my hands and feet, that were large and
puppy-like, I could use to some purpose without

awkwardness —altogether it was a very marvellous
thing!

Martha had come to me, shortly after the danger
was over, when we were riding at anchor, and with
tears in her eyes and fear still filling her speech she
would have taken me to her arms. "Where hast
thou been!" she cried. "I could well punish thee
for the anguish thou hast caused me and thy aunt!"

"I have been working with the men," I replied;
"for many lives were in danger."

"You are raving!" she cried.

"Of what use was it to crawl in there," I returned,
"and lie like maggots in a nutshell, not seeing or
knowing what went on?"

And then I pointed out over the bulwarks (we
had not yet been boarded by any officer of the port).
"There is England," said I; "thy country and
mine, good Martha, and somewhere there is a place
called Highcourt in Northamptonshire, where they
wait for me, and there we will abide and be rid of
priests and popery forever."

Martha's astonishment at hearing me speak in
this fashion was so great, that, added to the weakness
she felt from the motion of the ship, she would have
fallen had she not grasped some of the rigging for
support.

"You have heard me," said I, "and this gentleman here," and I indicated the captain, who was

E

approaching us, "hath promised to set us ashore. This vessel can proceed no farther."

"Very good, Sir Matthew, 'tis well," stammered poor Martha, and she stumbled down the ladder, up which some of the passengers who had strength to move were endeavoring to crawl.

We were soon surrounded by small craft of all sorts, and a bargain was struck for one of them to set us on shore with our baggage. As we rowed in, the young priest, who was disguised in a feathered hat and a thick wattled cloak, addressed me.

"Move closer, my son," he said, "for the spray drenches thee."

"Many thanks for your kindness," I returned; "a few drops of salt water can harm nothing, and moreover I am not 'thy son,' but Sir Matthew Maunsell, of England, and thou wouldst call me heretic and unbeliever, and I rejoice thereat."

There came a squeal from my aunt, and she nearly had a confusion of blood to the brain on the instant. My speech had deprived her of words, and she gasped, with her arms stretched out straight in front of her, and her fingers working like a player on the harp. The priest turned white, and Martha Warrell looked frightened. I think, poor woman, she imagined I was possessed of a devil, or under a spell of witchcraft, and truly the new-born feeling of

strength and self-dependence was like to it. I have
seen such things take place in a measure, when men
have overcome by their own unaided strength some
long-feared enemy, and have gauged themselves
anew and found that their standard of themselves
had been too slight. This seemeth to increase the
stature and to broaden the soul. I had spoken in
French, and the priest replied in the same.

"Have a care of thy speech," said he, in a whisper. "The Saints guard us from trouble! watch
thy tongue!" He glanced anxiously at the wherrymen who were pulling on the after-thwart. They
understood nothing; but seeing what consternation
I had set them all in, I did refrain, and in silence we
reached the shore, Lady Katharine glaring at me,
after she had recovered, so fiercely that it was most
comical. We went to an inn, secured the best
rooms the place afforded, and once there, with the
door locked, how her ladyship did rake me! I was
"a snake that she had guarded in her bosom"; I
was "a limb of Satan"; I was everything that she
could think of that was ungenerous; and from imprecations which availed her nothing she fell to tears,
and as a last resort turned me over to the priest,
who attempted to reason with me. It was to no
avail; I had declared my true colors, and I stood by
them. Of course that they were afraid of me I soon
saw; however, I had no intentions of betraying them,

and assured them of the fact; but the situation was uncomfortable, and though they probably exaggerated their fears to themselves, there may have been some danger. Lady Katharine had passed us all off as Protestants escaping from persecution, and an English innkeeper did not like to have it known that he had papists for guests, even if parts of the kingdom were filled with them.

The teachings of the sect of Jesuits lead to perfection in the arts of dissembling and subterfuge, and untruths count for little in what they consider good cause. For instance, the priest, after perceiving that he could not convince me, pretended to agree with some of my views. But I saw through the deception, and told him so; then he gave over and let me go, with something that might have been taken for a malediction. I left the inn for a ramble, filled with the desire to be alone, and of course wended my way to the water front.

There were vessels unloading and loading, bound some for distant ports, and one or two for harbors along the shore — coastwise traders. I began to wonder for what purpose Lady Katharine had brought me with her, and I learned subsequently that she had destined me to play a part that would have been unrighteous and unprofitable, for it was for me to profess the "new faith" with my lips and prove my rights to the title and estates of my father, but at the same time keep my heart in allegiance to the cause of Rome, and give my soul to the keeping of the young priest, who was to be my companion, and play a part also. I might here state that there was much of this going on in England, under-currents of plotting and counter-plotting wonderful to relate. But my frank declaration had upset this deep design, and they were sore distressed what to do. But what they did, nevertheless, was surprising.

CHAPTER V

DESERTED

I RETURNED to the inn after an absence of perhaps two hours, feeling lonely, but still held up by my strange new sense of liberty. I knocked on the door, and there came no response, and then I opened it. The room was empty! The four great boxes that Lady Katharine had brought off from the ship were missing, and my heart began to beat faster and faster. What could be the meaning of this? A servant passed by, and I called him up and asked him. The fellow was a blockhead, who knew nothing but that the people I inquired for had left the inn; so I sought out the landlord. He was a surly, cross-grained mountain of flesh, who listened to me with a leer, and when I had finished laughed loudly.

"Oho!" quoth he, "but thou tellst a great tale! Body o' me! but thou art handy with words. But to be forewarned is a good thing! I was told what was to come, and thy mistress left this for thee if

thou shouldst return, and she trusteth that in thy
next place thou wilt serve with more diligence and
honesty."

He extended toward me a few coins, and I struck
them out of his hand.

"Thou lying knave," I cried, "know that I am
a baronet of England, Sir Matthew Maunsell of
Highcourt, and I will not brook such speech to
me."

"That for thee, Sir Matthew!" was the reply,
and he caught me a tremendous blow with the side
of his foot, and I fairly left the floor. As I started
to rise he gave me the swift boot again, this time so
cleverly that I went through the doorway and tumbled out into the mud of the street. I would have
returned to the attack as soon as I had gathered myself together, had he not slammed the door in my
face. I vowed vengeance against that man (and one
day I had it, and 'twas worth rejoicing in — and they
say witnessing), but he was too much for me then.

Muddy and sore, I retraced my path to the ships.
There was one of perhaps fifty tons out in mid-
stream, hoisting up her mainsail. The creaking of
the blocks and the flapping of the great canvas could
be heard on shore; a wherry was rowing out to her,
and in it I perceived some figures. Before the vessel had gained headway the small boat was alongside;
two women were helped over the bulwarks, and even

at the distance I recognized Martha's portly figure and my aunt's slim one!

To be deserted is one of the most deplorable of feelings in human life; the heart sinks and the brain sickens; that Martha should have deliberately left me was ruinous to my belief in women! but poor good creature, I wronged her — as I afterward found out. Had I been able to swim, I might have jumped into the water, so bent was I upon joining them; but as that was impossible, my spirits gave way, hailing them was out of question, and I sank down on some ship timbers that were on the shore, and bitterly did I weep.

Somebody touched me on the shoulder while I was still sobbing, and looking up I perceived that it was an old man in a worn black velvet suit. He had a kindly face, and his white beard flowed over his powerful chest.

"What is wrong? what is wrong?" he asked kindly. "Can I do aught for thee, young gentleman?"

I looked over the water. The coaster was but of a speck in the distance, carrying the wind just abaft the beam and making fine running.

"My friends have left me," said I, pointing out the ship. "They are in that vessel yonder!" — which, by the way, was a race-built craft and must have been a fast sailer.

"But thou canst soon follow them," replied the old man, kindly. "She is bound for London, and there are several vessels that will sail from here within the next day that will take thee thither."

I had dried my tears, for my pride was again coming to my rescue, and I stood up. "I doubt if I would desire to be with them," said I.

Now I do not think that I am very revengeful in character, yet I may have inherited from the Spanish side a tendency to remember and to satisfy old scores; but my feelings were so bitter against the Jesuit, (who had Lady Katharine completely in his power,) that I would like to have followed them for one reason at least, and that was to tell who they were and watch the consequence, whatever that might be.

The Ridolphi plot, and the plan to assassinate our good Sovereign Queen, was just then being unravelled by Cecil Fitz William (of course I did not, then, know of this); it would have fared ill with any counter-reformers who were found new-come to England and mixing in with the retainers of the Scottish Queen.

"Did your friends leave no word?" asked the kind voice of the old man again.

"None," I replied; "and moreover I do not think that I care to follow."

"Art thou not a stranger here?" was the next question.

"Yes, and alone, kind sir."

He put his hand on my shoulder.

"Prithee, listen," said he. "You see the low white house yonder. It is mine, and my name is Thomas Blandford; if I can do aught for thee, remember it and do not hesitate to come to me."

"It is very kind of thee," I replied, "and I shall not forget, good sir, your offer." And saying this, I made as if to walk away. I had not yet grown used to the position of being pitied, and I desired to be alone.

"Give me thy name," said my unknown friend, taking a few steps toward me, "so I can leave word that I will see thee." So I gave it him, thanking him again, and I knew that he was standing watching me as I walked away. I might state that I had not added my title, seeing that it produced no effect on the landlord, who had put into practice *hoc deposuit potentes* with a vengeance. From anger and fright I fell to self-pity. The deplorable situation in which I was placed became more and more plain during the next hour, for I grew hungry.

I had in a small pouch in my doublet one gold piece of Spain, and around my neck a chain and locket of gold that I had worn ever since I could remember. These, and the clothes I stood in, were

my only possessions, as my changes of linen and
so forth were in the big box with Martha's belongings.   I was soon compelled to search for food, so I
entered a seaman's tavern, and throwing my gold piece
down on a table, called for it.   It was a rather for-
bidding place that I chanced upon; there were several
rather villanous persons sitting back in the shadow.
They surveyed me with interest, and the servant,
when he came to wait upon me, went over and
spoke to them; but I got some food which warmed
me, and I paid for a bed, which left me but little
money; being badly cheated in the prices.   As
I sat there thinking matters over (I had entirely
forgot that I was so young), I reasoned that everything depended upon myself, and yet that it was impossible for me to accomplish anything without
assistance, and my mind turned to the gentleman
who had spoken to me in the afternoon.   I decided
to call upon Mr. Blandford and tell him my story —
so I sallied forth.   It had grown dark, and at first
I was not sure of my way, but at last I found it,
and was walking along, thinking of my plight, when
suddenly I was grasped from behind; the cry that
I would have uttered was stifled in my throat by
a strong grasp of my wizen, and I was carried
bodily up a dark alley and into a building that I
knew was a stable from the smell.   There were two
robbers, and one held me while the other despoiled

me of my doublet and searched me thoroughly.   I
struggled, of course, and used my feet and hands to
such good purpose that the rascal who was holding
me flung me back angrily, and my head striking a
wooden post, I knew no more.

*   *   *   *   *   *   *   *

CHAPTER VI

NEW FRIENDS

A FEELING of intense cold came with my senses, and sitting upright with difficulty, I found out the condition I was in: I had nothing on but my shirt; the locket was gone from around my neck, and I lay shivering in a stall half filled with straw. The one next to me was occupied by a horse, for I could hear the thumping of hoofs. I was so miserable and sick that I wished I were dead, and yet it appeared as if I were dreaming, and I fain would have cried aloud for Martha to come and waken me and hold my hand. When I got to my feet I was dizzy; it was so dark that I had to feel my way, and I stumbled around, bringing up on one occasion against the flanks of the old horse, but I could not find the door nor anything to guide me. From whimpering I began weeping, and from weeping I fell to shouting for help, my terror adding strength to my voice, and my voice increasing my terror. All at once I heard the sound of a latch, and out of the darkness some one speaking.

"Who is it making all the noise?" inquired a man, in half-frightened tones.   It was on the tip of my tongue to say, "Sir Matthew Maunsell of Highcourt," but I refrained, and answered, shivering, for I was no longer in tears: —

"I have been robbed and almost murdered; pray help me."

Another voice broke in here with: "It is a boy, and not a woman!   Come hither, lad.   Giles, you lazybones, go fetch a lanthorn; the poor lad is in trouble."

I stumbled into the last speaker before I saw who it was, and I was laid hold of and led up a short flight of steps; then I saw that it was a fat, elderly dame who had me by the shoulder.   An instant later a big man appeared with a taper shaded by his fingers, and we walked down a hallway and entered a low-ceilinged room.   I must have cut a sorry figure standing there in my shirt-tail, with my knees knocking and my teeth chattering.

"He's hurted, poor lad," the woman said. "Here, Giles, fetch a cloth and some water." There was a cut over my forehead that had bled a little.   "And he's most froze, too," went on the good woman, who was herself not clad for a winter's night.   "Here into bed with you."   And she picked me up in her arms and heaved me over into a great bed stuffed with soft shavings that was still warm from where she and her spouse had been lying. As she made me snug she asked me a number of questions, and I told her that I was a stranger in the town, having just come off a ship and was on my way to see Mr. Blandford, when I had been waylaid and robbed. The good, kindly soul tied up my head, and as I had not rested, it seemed to me for days, drowsiness came over me, the warmth was grateful to my aching bones, and I fell asleep. I do not suppose that the good couple kept a midnight vigil on my account; but when I awakened I was alone in the bed, and it required a great effort for me to remember what had taken place. There was a smell of cooking, which I discovered, and a savory dish of tripe and onions was steaming upon a rough table near the fire.

I had been conscious of the odor for some time, and had been dreaming that I was hungry; now I was sure of it. Very soon my hostess appeared.

"Oh, you're awake, lad," was her greeting. "See, I have some clothes for thee." She laid upon the foot of the bed some rough worsted hose much darned, a shirt, and a leather doublet. As the thieves had even taken my shoes, she had produced a heavy pair with wooden soles. All this toggery had seen service, and when I had donned it I might have passed for an apprentice boy, were it not for the whiteness of my hands. The woman looked at them as she drew up a rough, three-legged stool, and bidding me sit down, placed herself opposite me, with her fat elbows resting on the table and her good-natured chin supported upon her entwined fingers.

So fixedly did she regard me, that I did not raise my eyes, but made a worthy feeding. When I looked up she would say, " Eat some more," and I would go on. The door opened, and the goodman entered; he had on a great leather apron and leaned a whip-stock against the door-post. The woman rose and went to him.

" Think'st thou he is not like? " she said, pointing at me. The man shook his head.

" I see it not," he returned.

" But I say he is," went on the woman, "all but the hands."

" Have it so, have it so! " said the man.

The woman approached me then and tilted my face up to hers. "Thou art like our son," she said, "who left us a year ago this Whitsuntide. Where wert thou born? "

" In London," said I.

" And thy father's name? "

I reasoned that there was no use of exploiting myself, and I had no clear recollection what I had said the night before, so I answered her questions again as shortly and truthfully as I could (except I laid no claim to title); but she interrupted me two or three times to give me a resounding kiss on the forehead — a motherly buss that betrayed her kindly heart. She would not hear of my leaving, but I promised to return after the call upon Mr. Blandford, that morning, and make report. My visit was a fruitless one, I found that the old gentleman lived after the manner of a person in easy circumstances; but the servant who opened the door for me must have regarded me as suspicious, for he told me that his master was away, so I returned to the mews where my new-found friends lived, and the comfort of having found them such was great. Dame Truman was awaiting me, and Giles, who made his living by doing carting along the water front, appearing at noonday, I accompanied him back to his labor.

The day following this I worked driving the horse and helping load timbers, and won Truman's good opinion by my effort. He was a man of few words, honest of speech and mind, and completely beneath the thumb of his goodwife. They had made a couch for me in a small closet adjoining their room, with a little window that opened out into the alley.

I found that their son, who was three years older than I, but into whose shoes I had fitted, had been tempted on board a ship bound whither

F

they knew not, and that was the last seen of him.

I did not call upon Mr. Blandford now for three or four days, and then when I did so, I was informed that he had left for Plymouth to be gone a fortnight. So I worked on, happy and contented in my labor; my hands were white no longer, and my muscles and sinews grew strong and sturdy. I had discovered little more that was new about my friends, for there was little to discover, and they found out not much more about me, except that I was a scholar and could both read and write. But there was small chance to exercise my learning; we went to bed shortly after nightfall and were up betimes in the morning, and this was a fine life for a tall lad of sixteen.

But a strong temptation was growing up in my bosom. After a few weeks of this sort of existence, never could I see a ship getting up her anchor but I wished to be on board her. I talked to the sailor-men who lounged about the jetties, and great was the consternation of good Giles Truman when he found me deep in converse with a bearded mariner from the port of St. Sabastine, who spoke a mixture of French and Spanish — a vile and outlandish tongue that Giles considered it ill for a man to know. I had discovered also, by this time, that Mr. Blandford was a merchant shipowner

given to good works, who had retired from the sea
possessed of some affluence — made, it was whispered,
in the slave trade. I had never clapped eyes on
him, however, since that first day and had got it in
my head that he did not wish to see me for some
reason, not knowing that after his return from Plymouth he had gone out on a long voyage of business
that had taken him into the Mediterranean.

I had fallen so quietly into this new life of mine
that all of its strangeness had disappeared; I was
like to any young lad who worked for his living out of
doors, except that I was taller than most; after I had
trounced the bully of the inn yard at "The Crowing
Cock," I had quite a following among the young
fellows who played at games of strength and swiftness in the few hours they had free from labor.
I learned to swim the first time I was in water over
my head and could pull an oar with any of the
wherrymen. I made one short sail in a lugger to a
neighboring port and back, and true to my temptation was about the shipping as much as possible.
Besides this I served Giles Truman faithfully and
well; as if I had been his own son I served him.
Now and then he would give me a bit of money
with a warning, "Not to lose it at chuck fardhen"
— but I never saw more than sixpence. Dame
Truman always treated me with respect that tran-
scended e'enmost her affection, for I would read to

her every scrap of print I could lay hand to, and my scholarship was a constant source of wonder to the good soul. I was a fortnight's mystery to the neighbors, and then they spoke of me as " Giles Truman's lad Matt" and treated me as such thereafter. Thus a year went by and I was getting to chafe more and more at the even life that I was leading and be more drawn than ever by the sight of a departing ship. Not a word did I hear from my aunt or any of my family. I did not wish to think of them, I despised them so, from the treatment I had received; but what I was then doing could not last, I knew; there would come a day when I would step out of the harness that had begun to gall me. There was always a demand for a willing lad on shipboard.

One fine morning I was leading the old horse, [hauling a load of baled goods to a gallease that was moored alongside of the stone dock,] when I saw a tall man in velvet clothes talking to another, evidently a seafarer from his costume and general cut. I recognized my friend, Mr. Blandford, in the tall man, and as it was a cold day, he had over his shoulders a heavy fur cloak with a huge clasp of silver that fastened it at the throat.

As I went by him, a strong gust of wind blew in from the sea, the silver clasps became unhooked, and the cloak was whirled off before he could grasp it. It would surely have gone overboard had I not

been there; I handed it to him, and he thanked
me.

"Thou art spry, lad," he said, with a laugh.
"Salt water does not improve otter fur, and here is
a coin for thee."

"Thank thee no, good sir," I returned.   "'Twas
my good fortune to be of such slight service.   Do
you not remember the lad that you spoke to,
when you found him weeping yonder a twelfth
month ago?"

"Body o' me," he returned, "but 'tis the same;
thou art changed," and of a truth I was.

He asked me how I came to be in this employment, and I told him my story.   In explanation
of his absence he informed me that he had been
detained longer than he expected to have been in
Morocco, and he requested me to come and see
him the following evening.   I promised this and
adhered to it, although Dame Truman murmured
at my going out so late, and just after nightfall I
knocked at his door.

I was received in a spacious but comfortable room,
and Mr. Blandford, who had risen upon my entrance, showed me, with a display of manner, to a
seat before the fireplace.   He did not begin to
speak at once, but sat there looking at me
fixedly; and as I had been taught to observe silence
in the presence of my elders, I did not open the

conversation. All at once he began with a statement.

"You're a Romanist," said he.

"You are mistaken," I returned, "or you have
been misinformed — I am Protestant."

"Very good," said he; "art glad of it.   I have
been both."

"The same holds true," said I, "for myself also."

Mr. Blandford looked at me curiously. "You
have had some education, eh? Do you write?"
and then he added, "Art sure thou art no Catholic?"

"I am Protestant," I replied; "but I am a fair
scribe in Latin, French, and Spanish."

"Oh! you speak Spanish?" he exclaimed.

"Yes," said I, "as if 'twere my native tongue."
At that he asked me a few questions in the language, spoken badly, and I replied. I have discovered that when people, who have a leaning
toward knowledge, possess the smattering of a
tongue other than their own, they will exercise it
upon every opportunity and will not be kept from
it by any amount of stumbling at the outset; so the
rest of our talk was in Spanish. And in this
language we discussed the religious condition of our
minds principally, and then suddenly my friend
made a proposition to me that was so foreign to
our subject that I feared for an instant that his
mind had left him.

There was an expedition being formed, he said, to carry out a project which interested him greatly. Some ships were to sail from Plymouth on a cruise into the Spanish Main. Had I any leanings toward adventure? According to this recounting it can be seen that I had indulged in some upon my own account—I told him I had.

"There is a position," he said, "open to a young man qualified for it, gifted in languages; and if you care to take it in consideration, I will speak a word to the right people."

Without hesitation I declared my willingness, nay, my wild eagerness, to go, even if it were to set sail in the next hour—indeed, I was like to a hungry man told of a feast. As I had suspected, he had considered me much older than my years, supposing that I was at least nineteen. There was no reason for me to enlighten him, I thought, and before I left, a bargain was struck. I had promised to accompany him when he next went to Plymouth, which was to be within a week.

Dame Truman was waiting up for me when I returned. She asked no question, but at once hurried me off to bed as if the lateness of the hour was scandalous. In the four or five days that followed everything went on as heretofore. I did not think it would be necessary to tell the Trumans as yet of my planned departure. But I am glad to say that when I did leave, I did not desert them without explaining. The good woman was in tears at once when she heard tell of my determination; but Truman said nothing — perhaps he could think of nothing to say, or he was a philosopher mayhap, for all I know.

Mr. Blandford had persisted in my taking from him some money and had made necessary purchases in the way of clothing and some extras, which I enclosed in a canvas bag. Thursday morning we set sail; I had left the good dame weeping in the doorway of the little house in the alley, inconsolable that I had refused to take a small hoard of silver that she had tried to slip into my bundle, for of course I had refused to accept a farthing, though my heart was dull at leaving the kind old folks. Mr. Blandford had to call me twice before I stirred — I confess frankly that there was a lump in my throat.

Once free of the land, the sailor habit of the old gentleman returned to him. He began a ceaseless pacing of the deck, and his replies to my questions were so curt, that I went forward to where the crew were sitting and made friends with a fine young sailor who had a scar the width of your finger slashed across his face. And about it he told me a marvellous story in which a woman (an Indian Princess, he informed me), a Portuguese adventurer, himself, a knife, and a bag of gold figured prominently, and all became entangled after a wonderful fashion. I slept upon a little shelf in the after part of the ship that night. The next morning we made Plymouth Hoe.

Going on shore with my patron, we proceeded to an inn named "The Bell and Anchor," and as we entered the tap-room four or five bronze-faced men left a table in the corner and came forward with hearty but respectful greetings. I was presented to the company and made my best court bow.

CHAPTER VII

WHEREIN I JOIN THE TREASURE-SEEKERS

AS every one whom I met at this gathering has much to do with the real tale that I set out to relate, when I took up my pen in the first place, and as it is my intention to record the doings and sayings of a great man who was there present, I shall tell of the company and in short fashion describe its members; especially the one whose name and character tinges most of what I shall write hereinafter.

"I have great pleasure," said my patron, while he pointed me out, "in bringing here with me a young man whom I think can be of service to us all, and who is anxious to cast in his lot with the rest and to take what comes. I must say that despite his youth he is a scholar of no mean order, and I take it also that he has the making of a sailor in him," and with this he presented me to the gentlemen of the company, speaking their names, although at the moment he had forgotten to mention my own.

The first to extend hand was Captain Francis

Drake, then followed John Drake, a captain also, and his brother Joseph; the others were Master John Oxenham, Ellis Hixon, and two young men named Christopher Nichols and William Fletcher. As I sat down with them, a cup of sack was placed before me; they pledged me, and I responded, feeling much set up at the attention. Mr. Blandford and Captain Francis Drake were talking in low tones at the table's head, and I thought from the way both were glancing at me, [although I made believe not to notice it,] that I was the subject of their speech. Suddenly the Captain catching my eye smiled and said in a pleasant, ringing tone: —

"Young sir, we are right glad to have you with us, and I speak for the company;" again my health was drunk, and every one appeared to be in a pleasantly eager frame of mind. I was soon lost, however, in the general conversation that followed, knowing nothing about the matters upon which they touched; but I observed them all closely; especially was I interested in Captain Francis.

While not, strictly speaking, handsome, he had that peculiar attraction that is even more marked in men than grace or distinction. Energy and force showed in his eye and speech; he had a high, broad forehead, a strong mouth, scarcely hid by a thick ruddy beard; his shoulders were of great breadth, and every line of him stood for strength and natural force. Some people may talk loud, yet never be heard or listened to; this man had the gift of calling attention to his slightest utterance without an effort; while he spoke, the others were quiet, and his word seemed to decide any question in dispute. After spending a good part of the day together we went back to the shore at sunset; there one of the younger men sent a hail out across the water in the direction where lay two sea-going vessels close together.

A boat left the side of the larger craft, and taking us all on board, we were rowed out from the pier head. We placed Captain John Drake, with Masters Nichols and Fletcher, on board the smaller craft as we passed; the rest of us clambered over the side of the one that lay farther out. I had noticed that the name of the craft we first visited had been the *Swan*, and I heard one of the company refer to the other as the *Dragon*. There was a great deal of difference in the size, the latter being seventy-three tons in burthen, and the former but five and twenty. The decks sloped so that until one learned the trick, it was hard to keep proper footing; they were much littered about also with cordage and bales and boxes. The rigging, too, was slack, and some of the running gear had been removed to make room for new. It was plain that they did not intend to sail for some time to come. Captain

Francis turned to me after we had been a few minutes aboard and noticed that I was still standing with my bag under my arm, not having the least idea what was expected of me, or how to set about any duties that might be mine — I was in fact half heart-sick.

"Go down the ladder here, lad," he said, "and sing out for Farley; and when he comes tell him who you are, and that I say he is to find some place for you to stow your belongings and to sleep — and by the same speaking I don't know who you are yourself," he added.

So I told him my name plainly, informing him that my father, who had come from Northampton, was dead, and that I had lived in Spain and France with relatives.

"I will hear more about you at a later day," said Captain Drake, and then he stopped himself. "Maunsell, Maunsell!" repeated he; "there was an officer of that name with me when I served with Hawkins, — Alleyn Maunsell; he was on board the *Minion*, and fought well against the Spaniards at De Ulua."

"I know naught of him, sir," I replied; "for I know but little of my family or if he might belong to it."

As he did not seem desirous to renew the talk, I went below, and sang out lustily for "Farley," the way I had heard an officer shout on the *Sagita*.

Presently a short, squat figure scrambled up from somewhere; and whether it was boy or man I could not tell.

"Aye, aye, sir!" said a shrill, cracked voice. "Did you call? Who passed the word for me?"

"I did," I replied. "Captain Drake's orders are that you shall find me a place to sleep and stow my bag."

With that, the little man—for I perceived that he was well along in years—picked up my belongings, and I followed him down another ladder to a deck that was scarcely five feet in head room, and here he pointed me out a sort of shelf wedged in between two deck beams, with a rough locker underneath.

"The last left," he said, "and you're in great luck to get it."

As soon as I deposited my dunnage I once more went up on deck, and the Captain seeing me, ordered me to come with him to his cabin, and set me to work at once copying out long lists of ship's articles. He spoke rather well of the neatness of my writing, saying that he had appointed me "Ship's Scrivener and Interpreter." (My! but I was set up over it.) From that day henceforth until our sailing I was busily employed.

The object of our voyage was kept somewhat quiet; but it must have been known and talked about, for how could so many people who surely

knew of our destination keep it a secret? Captain
Drake, himself, I must confess, was great at talk,
and used very often big words and great promises;
but as he intended to fulfil every one and boasted
of nothing that he left unfulfilled, even this failing
of his waged but little against his character; and
maybe, also, his youth and remarkable self-reliance
might well account for it. From Master Nichols
I learned something of the birth and early life of
this great man and leader, whose chronicler I now
become, in part, and of whose friendship I have been
so proud.

There has been much discussion as to the fact of
his parentage being low or humble. In my mind it
makes no matter. If he did not win for himself the
right to a coat of arms, and make up for lack of ped-
igree, no man ever did. His forefathers had lived
in Devonshire. He was the son of Edmund Drake,
and was born near South Tavistock. During
the reign of Henry the Eighth, Edmund Drake,
embracing the Protestant religion, was obliged
with all his family to fly that part of the country.
So he retired into Kent, and there he lived, in the
hull of a ship; and in this strange abiding-place
many of his children were brought up, among them
the man who was to be the greatest sailor of England. While Edward the Sixth was on the throne the
elder Drake earned his bread by reading prayers to

the sailors.   He was ordained a deacon, and afterward made Vicar of the Church of Upmore, on the
Medway.   But he was extremely poor, and the
living scarcely provided food and clothing for his
offspring; so his son Francis was indentured to a
neighbor of his, who was master of a trading bark.
The boy's industry was so great that when his
master died he left him his little vessel as a legacy,
and Drake, although but a lad, carried on his own
business.

He had made one voyage in deep water with
Captain Lovell, and had grown to dislike the Spaniards because this expedition suffered at their hands;
so he had joined forces with Sir John Hawkins,
after selling his bark and putting in all of his fortune
into helping outfit this unfortunate undertaking.
Alas! all of the bold seamen who took part in the
enterprise lost their money, and many lives were
sacrificed, as every one remembers, on that event-
ful day at San Juan de Ulua, where Drake had
succeeded in saving his ship from the wrath and
treachery of the Spaniards by what I call good headwork.   Farther on in this volume I intend to relate
how this happened, in the words of an eyewitness.
Now as this had taken place scarcely four years
previous to the time at which I am now writing,
the desire for revenge was still keen in the Captain's mind.   Of a certainty England was not then

at war with Spain, and friendly relations were kept
up 'twixt both courts; but many respectable subjects of our good Queen — men like Mr. Blandford,
for instance, of worth and standing — were found
who would lend their assistance in adventure, and
placed their purses at young Captain Drake's disposal.

I listened with great attention to Philip Nichols,
whose story I have thus shortened above, and
I did not know, then, that the narrator was a
preacher, for he resembled in habit and talk the rest
of the young fortune-hunters of good birth, — in
part, soldiers, sailors, and gamblers, — who attached
themselves, their swords, fortunes, and brains to the
personal following of Francis Drake.

On the 20th of May I made record that we had
received on board the frames of three small pinnaces that had been so cleverly built that they
could be put together in short order if occasion
demanded. I also remember setting down that our
complement and crew were complete, numbering
seventy-three, men and boys; and I do not think
that, with the exception of Farley, there was a man-
jack of us over thirty-five years of age. Everything
had been placed on board by the third and twentieth
of May, and this day all the crew worked like spiders
setting up the lower rigging. In the gray of the
next morning, with a fair wind, we got up our

G

anchors, and the *Dragon* leading, we made out to sea.

And now let us be truthful: despite the fact that we had two preachers with us and began the day with prayer, we were pirates every one, from the lob-lolly boy and the scrivener to the captain, except that we did not prey upon our own countrymen, and aimed only at the Spanish.

No one could sail with Captain Francis Drake without becoming a seaman; there were few idlers on board either ship. I well remember the talking that we all got in the cabin from the Captain one day, and there was none who would discount his words by word or look, though he employed mighty strong figures of speech.

"I rule now," he said, "and any one who gain-says me or disobeys my orders shall get short shrift of it." And he went on to tell, then, what he was going to do and how much treasure he ex-pected to recover. From his talk I began to gather the opinion that one Englishman was worth ten Spaniards, and of a truth I found little to contro-vert it in my after adventures.

CHAPTER VIII

SUCH wonderful weather I have scarcely ever seen as that we enjoyed from the day of sailing until we sighted land, which was the eighth and twentieth of June. All hands crowded on deck, and great was the excitement as the wooded headland loomed clearer and clearer. It was the island of Guadeloupe, but we held on our course and passed between it and Dominica, the Captain knowing well his ground; and ten days later we came to the exact place that he had intended to make, and where we were to prepare for the carrying out of his designs.

He had been here before, and conned the ship to her anchorage, displaying the most absolute knowledge of currents and soundings, but the work had just begun. We were in the midst of the Spanish cruising grounds, and time was precious.

The bay in which we lay was of exceeding beauty. Captain Drake had well named it Port Pheasant, for there was a great abundance of that fine fowl.

The great wooded hills rose straight from the water's edge, and the narrow entrance could scarcely be marked; the surface was calm as a pond, and even at great depth the bottom could be seen, so clear was the water. We dropped anchor and furled sail. Captain Drake called away the dingey, and with his brother John, Oxenham, myself, and four sailors, we put in for shore. The island appeared to be uninhabited, but just as we set foot on the sand John Drake cried out, "See there!" and pointed to the north. A thin column of smoke like the drift from a fog-bank hung amid the branches of the trees. At once we pushed off again to the ships and returned with the large boat filled with men, this time armed and ready for attack. A path overgrown with vines and bushes led up to the smoke, but there was no sign of a living thing. Right cautiously indeed did we move until we came out into a clearing, and there saw that the fire that had caused our uneasiness was in the body of a great tree that lay upon the ground. It had charred it for a length of mayhap thirty feet, and was burning without flame after the way of damp peat. How long it had thus existed was hard to tell — a fortnight or more doubtless. But what now met our eyes was a large leaden plate nailed to the trunk of a stripped pine. The Captain tore it down, and as we crowded about we found that it bore an inscription addressed to none other than himself.

"Ho!" cried he. "Here's news! and small comfort!" After his brother had seen it, it was handed me, and I read as follows:—

CAPTAIN DRAKE: If you fortune to come to this port, make haste away! For the Spaniards that you had with you here last year, have bewrayed the place and taken away all that you left here. I depart hence, this present 7th of July, 1572.

Your very loving friend,
JOHN GARRET.

"So Master Garret is still afloat," quoth the Captain. "Well, if the dons have took everything, they will not return, and for that matter neither will honest John. We are safe from being troubled. Here we rest!"

So we went back to the ships, where the carpenter was employed in breaking out the frames of the pinnaces from the hold and casting loose the larger timbers from their lashings on deck. John Drake was set on the beach to lay out a fort, and the crew worked getting the frames overboard, in order to set about putting them together on shore. For three days we labored.

I had made great friends with a young man, a gentleman's son, Master Christopher Ceely, and

he and I were sitting in the shade of a sail that had
been spread to keep off the heat of the sun one
afternoon, when suddenly one of the men, who was
working at something aloft, shouted out and pointed
to the mouth of the harbor.

There, coming slowly in, was a large bark followed by a caravel that was Spanish at a glance,
and a smaller vessel just to be seen astern of her,
with one mast and a great mainsail,—a rig that was
surely Spanish also.

A few of the crew were at work in the waist of
the ship. The other men were on the beach with
most of the people at this moment, including the
Captain and both his brothers.

The *Swan* lay farther south and off-shore, and
on board of her out of her crew of twenty-six there
was but one man; [there were probably eight of us
on board the *Dragon*.] The approach of the vessels
had been hidden by the headland; but now it
looked as if we had been caught in a trap, as they
surely would be within gunshot before our crew
could possibly be got on board. The shout that
Ceely and I both gave had called the attention of
the men in the waist, and one of them running
forward discharged a culverin that awoke the echoes
of the hill and stopped the work ashore.

Immediately there was a great confusion. The
little boat that had brought them from the ship

would not hold the entire party, having made several trips, and there appeared to be some controversy who should get into it, one man taking hold of the gunwale, — for she had been left high and dry on the beach by the fall of the tide, — then another man would push him away, and the result was that it appeared as if none would come to our assistance. Ceely, knowing more about such matters, and being of higher rank than the carpenter, had taken command of our ship, and we had loaded all the guns in the broadside as quickly as possible.

The bark that led the incoming vessels had hauled her wind as if waiting for the others to come up with her, or as if doubtful of what best to do. The single man left as anchor-watch on board the *Swan* had displayed good judgment in a measure, for he had severed the cable with the blow of an axe, and the little vessel was now drifting nearer in the direction of her consort. All at once I heard a voice shout from shoreward. The quarter-boat, loaded down within a finger's reach of foundering, was approaching; but the hail had not come from her, but from the water nearer to us, and looking over the side, I perceived a man swimming, and almost a half musquet-shot away were two others. Never have I seen before or since a human being go through the water the way this man made headway.

It almost boiled under his chin as he took his great full arm strokes.

"Hoist up the flag," he cried, "and get out the nettings!"

Then I perceived that it was the Captain himself, who had run down on a little sandspit, [being some distance from the launching party,] and had taken the shortest way to get on board his vessel. In order to be less hampered he had cast aside his clothing, and thus he clambered over the rail, glistening wet, panting and shouting in one breath. Now I have seen many men standing as God made them, but never such a one as this. The muscles of his back and shoulders were tremendous; he may not have been the largest man aboard ship, but as you saw him standing there you would have sworn he could have taken any two of the crew and torn them to pieces. But he was as unconscious as if he had on a full suit of armor, and running up the slope of the quarterdeck to the top of the stern castle he measured the distance of the strange vessels, and that of our approaching boat. She had fourteen men in her; but the flag had now climbed to the reach of the halyards, and a sudden puff of air tossed it out. A small ensign was shown above the taffrail at the same instant, on board the leading stranger.

"English, by Saint George!" exclaimed the Captain. "I thought from the way she acted she was neither French nor Spanish." Then he roared down the transom for Farley to lay out his best embroidered doublet.

It was a minute or more before the other swimmers, who proved to be Master Hixon and Joseph Drake, clambered over the sides. Some time after their arrival, the loaded shore-boat made fast to the gangway and the excited men tumbled inboard. In order that we should not be caught napping, the crew was sent to stations, and their movements were directed by Drake, who, with the assistance of Farley, was robing himself on the quarterdeck.

All eyes were fixed on the stranger who was making in close, shortening sail, and was soon within speaking distance. A man mounted the railing and proclaimed in good English that his ship was the *Lion*, of the Isle of Wight, that her captain's name was James Ranse, and that it was he speaking. Drake's return to this was an order to anchor at some distance and come on board at once.

But not until all three had dropped their anchors was our warlike attitude changed, and then a small boat from the *Lion* was seen approaching, and Captain Drake and the rest of the gentlemen went down to the gangway to receive our visitor. He was a little hairy man, with pock-marked features, dressed in a gorgeously braided cape-coat and a huge feathered hat; [spoils of war, I afterwards found out,] a beautiful Toledo blade with a jewelled hilt hung at his side. He saluted us as he stepped on deck, accompanied by a tall, fair-haired man, and he accepted pleasantly Captain Drake's invitation to partake of a glass of wine. As our leader included us also, we all followed and were presented by name in turn to the gorgeous little sailor, who told us, with his eyes twinkling, that the cruising-grounds were fruitful, the spoils were rich. With his little bark of but sixty tons he had made several fine prizes, among them being the two vessels that accompanied him; the caravel he had named the *Lioness*, and the little sloop the *Whelp*.

"I have several men with me who have served with you," he said, "and my leftenant, now in command of the *Lioness*, was with you in the *Minion*." He turned, and indicating me with his hand, added, "He has the same name as this young gentleman, — Maunsell, — and his first name is Alleyn."

"Oh, I know him well," Drake responded, — "a fine and gallant sailor, and mayhap a kinsman of our young friend."

I had told nothing of my story to any one on board the *Dragon*, so I merely acquiesced to the suggestion with a nod of the head. A few minutes later Captain Drake sent me ashore in the shallop to inform his brother John, who had now appeared upon the shore, having returned from his hunting-trip. I also took with me as many men as I could, to help the rest in putting the finishing touches to the pinnaces. The single man aboard the *Swan* had again done well, for when she had drifted to a point just astern of us, he had let go of her spare anchor, and she was riding there in safety. He proved afterward to have been John Oxenham, who, having been ailing, had been left on board. That night we got all three pinnaces into the water.

The next day we stretched the sail and divided the crews of both the *Swan* and the *Dragon* to make the complements of the small boats. There had been a conference going on between Captain Ranse and our Captain and his brother, most of the day, and by evening they had reached a conclusion. We were informed upon our joining the ship that Ranse and his company were to become adventurers with us under some arrangement of shares.

On the 20th day of July we set sail, I being attached to the first pinnace, which was in command of Drake himself, Captain Ranse being given the command of the three ships and the caravel.

Everything had been done with the utmost care, the outfitting of the pinnaces being looked after by Drake himself. I may say it without false modesty, that the Captain had taken a strong fancy to me, not only for the reason that I was always with him and apparently a glutton for work, but for the reason, also, that I was not behindhand in feats of strength or agility, despite, as I say, my youth. My few months of hard work had wondrously improved my figure; I was growing up to my hands and feet, and there were not over five of the whole company who were taller than I. For two days we sailed along easily, and I heard much speculation indulged in as to our probable destination; but Drake kept his own counsel, and sat there in the stern sheets, his blue eyes dancing with a strange light, and a smile continually on his lips. The prospect of danger or adventure, to him, acted like a refreshing draught. The worst possible torture that he could have undergone would have been luxurious confinement, with nothing to do. I was sitting close by him, when he bent toward me, at the same time saying, in a low voice: —

"We're bound for Nombre de Dios, and I'm going to give you something to look at, lad; aye, and as much gold and silver as your broad young shoulders can carry."

He gave me a playful pinch that almost made me wince, and then laughed quietly to himself. The third day our kindly wind died down, and we took to the oars, at which we labored in turn for ten hours. Drake, in his eagerness, showed no mercy on his men. If they showed any signs of failing, he cajoled and bantered them into their extreme effort, and though we were the largest and heaviest pinnace, he kept us in the lead, and we overtook and passed the ships that had outsailed us.

*   *   *   *   *   *   *   *

Late in the evening we headed for an island for which our leader had been looking; known as the Island of Pinas, and we rowed along the sandy beach for about half a league before we came to a promontory beyond which the Captain said we would find a snug harbor. It was as he proclaimed. But, as we came about the point, all eager to land and stretch our limbs, we saw that there were two vessels — small galleys with one mast — moored close to the shore. Laying back on our oars, we made for them; and using caution, boarded them without our approach being observed. We found the crew, who were all negroes, with the exception of one man, busy at their evening meal. Great was their surprise.

I addressed them in Spanish, proclaiming that we did not intend to harm them, and the Captain selecting two of the most intelligent, I began to question them, for we had found out that they had come from the town of Nombre de Dios, which is but four or five days' good sailing to the westward. The news that we learned was not encouraging. These negroes, who were all slaves, stated that, owing to the warfare that was being waged between the Spaniards and a race of warlike people, half-black and half-Indian, the town was exceedingly well prepared for defence and guarded at all points. Now as the Captain had been counting upon their apathy and general indolence for a complete surprise, this disturbed him, and he swore roundly. But it made no possible difference in his determination; for but a few minutes later I heard him declaring in a loud voice that he had just found out that the time was most propitious for descent on the Spanish stronghold, as they had allowed their defences to become useless from neglect. This was but to encourage those about him, and yet it evinced his character also. The harder a thing was to do, the easier, the way he looked at it with his sanguine mind, because it required greater effort and completer preparation, and at this he was past master.

CHAPTER IX

THE vessels under Ranse came in early in the morning; another conference was held while the men were given an hour's run on shore with orders to assemble at the call of a trumpet. I had accompanied the Captain on board the *Lion,* and this was the first time that I had been on board any of Ranse's ships. A big man with a grizzled iron-gray beard came forward and greeted us most cordially.

"Well met indeed," cried Drake, in reply, "and here is some one who may prove to be a kinsman of yours, no doubt." He presented me by name, calling the big man 'Alleyn Maunsell,' and as we shook hands he remarked upon our resemblance to one another.

Mr. Maunsell laid his heavy hand upon my shoulder. "Thy father's name, lad?" he asked. I told him, and he led me to one side, where he asked me one question after another quickly, and all the time his eyes were searching my face as if

he were trying to see the workings of my mind.
I told him that I was a Protestant of course, although
I did not know then the entire meaning or comfort
of deep religious thought and had yet to learn it.
When I had finished, and we were all alone, — for
the Captain had gone below, — the big man threw
his arms about me and kissed me on the forehead.

"Beyond doubt thou art my nephew!" he exclaimed, and then held me off at arm's length and
surveyed me over again.   I did not know then, that
at this first recognition all his castles of hope had
tumbled into dust; but it was so.   It had been
reported that I had died in Spain, and I, alone,
stood between him and the estates and titles.   Everything had been made ready for him to enter into
possession of both upon his return to England.

The conference in the cabin lasted for hours, and
must have been quite stormy, although I know not
exactly what passed; but I could hear the Captain's
voice ringing out every now and then like the report
of a culverin, and all the time my uncle and myself
were busily employed learning of one another, and
from this we came to speak of Drake.

"There have been hard stories told of him," said
my Uncle Alleyn, as I shall now call him, "but
believe them not.   I was with him at Ulua, when
we both served under Hawkins; hast heard of the
affair?"

"But by name," I replied; "I know naught of the circumstances."

"I was on board the *Minion*," quoth my uncle, "and know whereof I speak, for the whole thing passed beneath my eyes, and contrary to Hawkins's opinion Captain Drake acted with both wisdom and bravery."

"Wilt thou tell me of it?" I asked.

"I am not much at yarn spinning," he responded; "but I have a true document in my possession, written by Hawkins himself, and I will lend it to you. It tells shortly and in clear words of our doings, and much better than I could," he added, "in my own poor way, for I am no scholar. But he does small justice to your Captain."

This promise he redeemed, and I shall tell of it hereafter as it is well in the province of this narrative. Our talk was interrupted by the Captain appearing on deck, with his arm slipt through that of Ranse in friendly fashion. Whatever may have been the points he had insisted upon, he must have carried them all, for he was in a good humor and smiling.

My uncle, advancing, proclaimed that our relationship had been assured, at which Drake laughed and shook hands with both of us, and Ranse did the same.

Cunning power did Captain Francis Drake pos-

sess over men when they had once given in to
the sway of his spirit, for the commander of the
Lion was apparently in his power.   He acted as
if on one of his own vessels, called for the ship's
trumpeter, and bidding him to mount the forecastle there to blow a certain call.   At the sound
we could see the men joining together on the shore,
so bidding farewell to my uncle, I entered the
shallop with the Captain, and we rowed off to the
large pinnace.

It was noon of the next day before we set
sail, the shallop having been ordered to be one of
our little fleet, thus making four vessels.   Captain
Ranse was left behind with the ships and the prisoners; but we took a draft of twenty of his men
with us, he being ordered to land the prisoners on
the mainland, where they could either join the Cim-
meroons, as the warlike freemen were called; or,
if they preferred to remain as slaves, proceed to
Nombre de Dios through the wilderness, a journey
of great difficulty and hardships that would con-
sume a month; so they could not possibly bear
information of our approach.

There were fifty-three of our men from the *Swan*
and the *Pacha*, [for thus Captain Drake had renamed
the *Dragon* for a reason of his own].   Thus the
whole expedition numbered seventy-four, all told,
including our commander.   The three pinnaces had

been named the *Minion*, the *Eion*, and the *Lion*;
the shallop was referred to as such, but she was
almost the size of our own craft.

Every one was in high spirits, and with a fair
wind and smooth water we bore away to the westward, and long before nightfall the island had
sunk below the horizon. So we sailed on until on
the fifth day when we were about five and twenty
leagues from the Island of Pinas; here we landed
on another island that had a low, sandy beach, upon
which we drew up the pinnaces, and so close were
we to the trees that we moored them to the trunks,
so that the tide currents, which ran swift here,
should not sweep them away. It was in the cool
of the morning, and the air was filled with a chattering and calling of the awakening birds and
beasts.

The boxes and arm chests were carried on shore
and broken open, and as I had made a list of everything they contained under the Captain's direction,
who looked out for everything, I may well state
that nothing had been forgotten, the armament of
the force consisting of the following : —

There were six targets, six fire pikes, twelve
pikes, twenty-four muskets and calivers, sixteen
bows of the best selected English yew, six partizans,
and two drums, and two trumpets. No one wore
armor except the Captain, who had on a light

corslet, and more than this I have never seen him
wear. Some of the men had steel head-pieces, but
the most of them had but their leather doublets
and studded belts for protection. The bowmen
had been selected before the expedition had left
England on account of their expertness; yet Drake
had found time to make sailors of them also, but
the bow is essentially a weapon for land fighting.

The Captain sifted the men into shape, and the
party was divided into three detachments: one
under charge of his brother John, who had Oxenham with him as second in command; the other
was given to Ellis Hixon and Joseph Drake;
and the third was commanded by Drake himself.
Hour after hour we were drilled in the hot sun
up and down the beach, — the drummers practis-
ing their marches, and the trumpeters their calls,
awakening the echoes of the forest and silencing
the shrieks of the brilliantly plumaged parrots and
other birds that fluttered in the tree-tops. The
sun was beating down with such a fierce heat before
noon, that we were compelled to give over and
sought the shelter of the shaded woods, and there
we ate the first meal we had that day and refreshed
ourselves with the cooling waters from a spring. I
could not get the strange happening of the day
before out of my head, and I regretted bitterly that
my uncle was not with us, for I now knew that I

was not alone in the world and I felt sure that I had discovered a trusty friend and benefactor. I had little time to think over my future affairs, however; there was too much to do in the present that occupied my mind.

In the afternoon we were called to attention, and everything was again inspected to see that nothing had been displaced; then, shoving off the pinnaces, we set sail in a southwesterly direction.

CHAPTER X

A S we skirted the mainland, I could see that the Captain was keeping a sharp lookout. In the whole company there were but two there who had ever sailed these waters, and the rest of us were green hands, who knew little of what was before. Not a sign of a habitation had we seen nor the figure of a human being. All at once Drake arose and, shading his eyes from the glare of the setting sun, pointed.

"There lies the river," he said, and he ordered the steersman to head nearer into shore.

For a long time we could discern no difference in the line of the coast, which seemed an unbroken stretch of green down to the water's edge; but at last we saw a break, and, as we came in close, we perceived that a little river there debouched into the sea. How the Captain could have remembered all his bearings and recognized the landmarks is more than I can understand; but he had a peculiar gift for this, and I have never known him to forget a face, a name, or a locality, and this is one of

the powers of leadership. Passing the mouth of
the river, we held on so close inshore that we missed
several reefs as if by miracle, and dusk still found us
on our course. All at once one of the men in the
bow cried out that he saw a light, and sure enough
there it was straight ahead; but how far off might
be hard to state. Orders were given to drop our
anchors, and for an hour or more we waited for
darkness to set in. And dark indeed it was, for the
clouds hid the wonderful display of stars that glow
in this latitude with wonderful brilliance, and the
moon would not rise until shortly before daybreak.

The light that we had seen had now disappeared,
and there was nothing to guide us. But the little
Minion raised her anchor and pushed out ahead;
the other pinnaces and the shallop were made fast
astern with stout ropes so that they would keep in
line, and if one grounded, the other could assist her
in getting off again. Word having been passed for
strict silence, we crept ahead under the oars, listening between every stroke for the sound of the lapping of the waves against the shore, which was our
only way of keeping in our course. It may have
been two leagues that we traversed thus, feeling our
way, and then suddenly the word was whispered back
from the *Minion* for the anchors to be lowered
quietly. We were evidently at the mouth of a bay
or harbor, and straining our eyes we could perceive

dimly, the form of a headland rising against the sky. Once or twice distant lights appeared to flash beyond the point. Drake placed his hands upon my knee as I sat next to him, half shivering, for the air was cold.

"There lies the town, master scholar," he said, "and no mistaking; enough treasure is hidden there to make us all rich men."

That there was any danger in our reaching for it never seemed to enter his mind. He was smiling quietly as a joker doeth to himself. Then he ordered all hands to rest as easily as they might, so that they would be fresh for the work that lay ahead of them, and with that laid him down. But I do not think that any felt the least temptation to indulge in sleep. They were all whispering and consulting one with another, and I, going forward in order to give the Captain more room to stretch out, heard some of the talk. As I have said, they were all young men, and darkness and long waiting dampen the ardor, especially if the air be chilled.

"They say that the town yonder be as big as Plymouth," quoth a young fellow whose teeth were chattering in his head.

"And full, no doubt, of armed men well prepared," put in another. "I like not the job. I would that I were in the tap-room of the Bell and Anchor."

"I would be satisfied," spoke up the third, "if I had the deck of a ship under my feet, for of a truth I like not this land fighting."

"Craven hearts!" spoke up a gruff voice, "if you had not stomach for such business, why should you embark in it? Regard the Captain; he sleeps tranquilly."

It appeared thus as the man said; but it was not so, for Drake had overheard all that was passing, and as yet said naught; but such a strange thing is fear that it increases with suspense until it may gain the mastery of brave men. To my amazement, I overheard a whisper close at hand from some one in the darkness that I could not recognize, proposing that they should take possession of the pinnace, and, willy-nilly, set her bow to the northward and give up an enterprise so full of peril. Now I must confess that I would have welcomed such a departure; for my own courage, which was that of entire ignorance, was oozing from me. The man who had reproved the early speakers held his peace, and the fiercesome gabble increased. It needed but a little to inflame it into loud speech and action.

I heard voices, too, coming from the other boats that lay close by us, and as I learned afterward their crews had grown into the same state, but much worse.

A faint gray streak appeared in the east, the

Captain stirred himself, and standing up gave a short loud laugh, the very sound of which strengthened my heart.

"Ho! my brave lads," he cried heartily. "Here cometh the dawn, and now prepare for it. I'll warrant you that every man shall have an ingot of gold on each shoulder and a pouch full of jewels in his belt before nightfall. On board the *Lion* there!" he shouted to the nearest pinnace. "Brother mine, stir out your men! Come, my brave bullies! Get up that anchor and get out your oars! I'll wager my share 'gainst a pewter tankard, the Spaniards are all asleep."

These words had marvellous effect, they nipped the whisperings and closed the seditious mouths. The men, who were in another moment at the point of joining in a mutiny, were stirred into action. A sound as if it were a sigh of relief came from the whole crew, a few laughed eagerly. Then a tall figure arose in the stern sheets of the *Lion*, that had drawn up alongside.

"Let us pray to God," said a high-pitched, melodious voice. It was young Fletcher, the minister. The men bowed their heads, and there in the darkness he made a fervent prayer, asking for the protection of the Almighty, and begging for success. When he sat down, out tossed the great oars, and everywhere I could hear the jingle of steel and the sharp twanging as the archers tested their bowstrings. It did not appear to be the same company that a few minutes since had been on the verge of cowardice. But I have noticed that most all strong men, who are used to carrying arms, will be willing to fight if they trust their leader and see that he counteth not the odds against him.

CHAPTER XI

WITH strong, full strokes, the *Minion* leading, the little fleet passed the headland and entered the bay. The gray light broadened, and a pale silver disk crept up out of the sea. It was not the dawn, but the rising moon that bewitched the water astern of us into a dancing, shimmering wake. It would be a full hour before day would begin, but in the spreading light objects were plainly visible; the roll of the heavy oars, as the men lay back at them, must have raised some disturbance and been a warning of our approach had any one been listening for it. And right ahead of us we could discern a ship, there were active figures moving on board of her; she was slowly turning, and we could make out that she was creeping up to her anchor. We had been sighted!

There was no use of further caution. Drake began to encourage the rowers, and the other men turned in their seats and began to assist them. A man in the bow shouted at top voice : —

"Mark lads! See there! she's sending a boat to shore to warn the town!"

True enough, a little shallop with five men in it could be seen leaving the vessel's side, and now our efforts were increased to intercept them. They had a longer way to go than we, for we were nearly in, but our strokes were redoubled. The other pinnaces caught up abreast us, and it became a grand race; for mayhap the success or failure of the expedition depended upon our speed. We were almost within bowshot of them, and three or four of the archers had selected their arrows, when the boat gave over, and putting across the bay made for the opposite shore. Even then it was a question whether we could get in, before a messenger would make his way round on foot.

The town could now be clearly seen, and I was surprised at the size of it. Numberless white houses rose tier upon tier, and above the roofs lifted the spires of two good-sized churches. There was something that appeared to be a fort crowning the top of a hill, and on the water front was a battery of cannon placed on a platform and covering the approach to the wharves. But not a sound came from the place. As Drake had said, the Spaniards were all asleep! We stopped rowing as we came near shore, the men boated their oars, allowing the headway of the pinnace to carry us onward.

All hands began buckling on their swords, adjusting
their targets ; and the fusiliers, snapping their flint
and steel, ignited their matches — I remember how
strange the smoke smelled to me. We struck
against the side of the wooden platform with a jar,
and at the same moment a frightened face peered
over the bulwarks. It was a Spanish sentry, who
had just been aroused from his slumber.

An archer let fly at him, but the arrow glanced
from his helmet, and with a howl he disappeared.
The three other pinnaces landed about the same
time, within a stone's throw of us, and the crews
jumped ashore as our men scaled the walls of the
battery.

Not a soul was there to receive us ! Drake calmed
all confusion, and sending me to tell his brother to
form his party on the beach and await further orders,
he set all about him to work tumbling the cannon
into the water. They accomplished this without
much ado, and soon all ran out of the fort and
came to the place where the men under Hixon and
John Drake were drawn up in line.

Up to this time there had not been a sound from
the town, but now we heard a sudden shout; a
drum began rolling, and then another answered it.
The trumpets began to blow from the hill, the bells
in the towers of the two churches started an alarm-
ing clangor, and from the noise of people shouting

and the lights appearing in the windows, we could
see that the place was gathering itself to resist
attack. The men-at-arms were being called together, but they were in great confusion, and there
was no time to be lost if this surprise was to be
taken advantage of. Drake hurried down the line
of men, here and there touching one on the shoulder,
bidding him to step out. Calling for his brother
Joseph, he bade him take charge of them and guard
the pinnaces against the return of the party. As
had been prearranged, he, at the head of his division, started at once for the Plaza, while his brother
and John Oxenham led their party around a great
white building to enter the square from the eastward.

Up the main street we went, Drake ambling in
advance and waving his sword about his head.

"Shout, ye knaves!" he cried, setting the
example. "Rip your throats! Don't save your
pipes!" And at his bidding, tearing and roaring,
we surged along, the trumpeter in our rear, who
was a fair one, executing flourishes and grace notes
until one might have thought we were accompanied
by a band of musicians. The drummer left with
the other party was pounding away, and thus we
entered the Plaza at the same moment they had
debouched from the side street, and we greeted
one another like madmen with fiercer shouts than

before. But Drake did not stop; knowing of the existence of the fort, straight up the hill we went and tumbled into the earthworks, the men now laughing and shouting, and each one making good for ten so far as his lungs went.

The fort was not entirely completed and was un-armed; so leaving the spare trumpeter there to tarry for a minute, we turned back once more into the Plaza, I sticking close at the Captain's heels. There we saw the fire-pikes of the other party moving up toward us. The inhabitants were pouring from out of the houses; some were shouting that the Maroons were upon them, and all were hastening, [a fair majority half naked,] heading pell mell with one accord for the southern entrance to the town, which was known as the Panama gate.

On the corner of the main street was the big house of the Governor, and here the Spaniards made the first stand. We could see the glint of armor, and the red darts of the burning matches standing back in the shadow. They outnumbered us five to one; but it counted for nothing.

" Have at them, lads," shouted Drake, fiercely. And, head down, he rushed forward like a fierce young bull, without waiting to see whether we were following him or not; but we were there close be-hind. I saw the flash and heard the roar in front of me, and the trumpeter, who was charging and

blowing at the same time, went over in a heap, and I
on top of him. I scrambled to my feet; but the
poor man lay there, shot through the breast.

The second party now came charging to our relief, and just as I joined in the fight where the cutting and slashing were going on, the Spaniards, seeing
the reënforcements, and I dare say imagining that we
were an army and not a handful, threw down their
weapons and did some grand running in all directions; most of them heading for the same big gate
out of which the populace was streaming. Five or
six sailors were after them, and Drake called for the
trumpeter to bring them back. I told him that the
poor fellow was probably dead, at which he turned
to me, and leaning on me slightly, said: —

"Thy legs are good and long, boy; stretch after
them and fetch them back with thee."

And so alone, I started in the wake of the flying
ones and their pursuers. I had almost caught up
to them, when a man in a great steel casque stepped
out of a doorway, and made at me, sword in one
hand and dagger in the other. I was running so
fast that I would have been spiked upon his point,
when there came a whistling sound in my ear, and
an arrow that could not have missed me by a hair's
breadth caught him through the throat, just above
the gorget. Backwards he fell with a clatter, and I
leaped over him. I have no doubt that the shaft

I

had been aimed at me by one of the Oxenham
party, who mistook me for a fleeing Spaniard.   My
close escape had one good effect, however, for I
doubled my speed and soon caught the party of
sailors, who were like to be cut to pieces had they
gone much farther.

They were surprised, indeed, when they found
that they were alone, imagining that the rest of
the party were at their backs.   These men were
mad with blood-thirst.   They had slain several of
the fugitives and wounded many more, and their
blades were red and dripping.   I myself felt now,
for the first time, this elation, the wild unreasoning
desire to kill, and there is no stronger potent force
in any animal than this in man, when once it is
aroused.   But orders had been given them, they
were men who were accustomed to obey, and while
I dare say they demurred, they turned about and
followed me to where the Captain and the rest of
the company were waiting.   Several of the men
appeared to have slight wounds, but none seriously
except the trumpeter aforesaid, who was as good as
done for.   The poor fellow had sounded his last
call.

I saw Captain Drake leaning against one of the
arches of the doorway of the big house before which
the Spaniards had made their stand.   No sooner
did he clap eyes on me than he beckoned.

"Come hither, Master Maunsell," he said, "and talk to these rascals. I can make neither head nor tail of their lingo."

Two pikemen stood in front of him, each holding a weak-kneed prisoner. Though I was so out of breath I could hardly speak, I interpreted the Captain's questions, which were in short as follows: —

"Where were the *recuas* or mule trains from Panama unloaded? Where was the precious metal stored? and where did the Governor keep his treasures of gems and coined metal, and if they didn't tell, how they would like to die?"

The younger man said nothing, but the elder, who, I take it, was a mulatto, told us to follow him, and Drake, bidding him lead on, called off five or six of us by name, and we went down a narrow passageway, at the end of which we found a heavy wooden door sealed and bolted. With the aid of a large stone we broke it open, and one of the pikemen with a torch being sent for, we entered the cellar of the Governor's house, and there we were all stricken speechless, for the vault ran the full length of the building, which was nigh seventy feet, and in the centre was a pile of silver bars that I am willing to swear was twelve feet in height and ten in breadth! Some of the men picked two of them up and placed them on their shoulders, and from what they afterward said, and from what I judge, each large bar weighed between thirty-five and forty pounds! Thus at a rough guess there must have been some three hundred and sixty tons of silver waiting for the fleet that was soon expected to fetch it to Spain. It was more than enough to have sent our little fleet to the bottom, and probably the bulk of it dismayed the Captain or made him think it cheap, for he ordered the men not to burden themselves with it, and forcing the prisoner down upon his knees, he placed a dagger at his throat and swore to kill him if he did not tell where the gold and jewels were at once. The poor man could not understand a word of English, so I came to both his and the Captain's assistance.

"Where are the Governor's treasures of gold and gems?" I asked.

"In the stone treasure house by the water front, noble Señor," he responded. "The big white building near the wooden fort. They were removed there three days ago," and he began to babble for mercy and protection.

When we emerged into the air again, we found that the dawn had chased away the moonlight, and each instant it was growing brighter. The red eastern sky showed us that the sun would soon be up. One of the church bells was still ringing lustily, bugles were blowing and drums rolling down the side streets, Spanish soldiers could be seen hastening

and gathering together; nothing but their own confusion protected us. Calling to his brother John,
the Captain directed him to take a party and proceed to the treasure house, break into it, and carry
away the contents, and make off to the pinnaces,
while with his handful he endeavored to hold the
Plaza.

Hardly had they left us, when one of them came
running back, crying that the pinnaces were attacked
and were in danger of being taken. This was cheer-
less news; but Drake put it aside as if it amounted
to naught.

"Where is John Oxenham?"

"Here am I," replied that bold sailor, "at thy
bidding."

"Make haste to the boats and tell my brother
that all goes well with us, and bid him hold them
at all hazards, and then come back to me and make
report."

Oxenham started off hot foot down the hill and disappeared. A few great drops of rain had begun to fall,
and the Captain, giving a glance at the sky, muttered
a curse beneath his breath, and, calling us to follow,
he started toward the treasure house, where he had
sent the first party. But before we had gone many
paces the heavens seemed to open, and such a
sheet of water poured down upon us that it was fain
to wash the clothes off our backs. In an instant the

street became a brook running ankle deep; never could I imagine that such a downpour ever would take place. It was like attempting to walk beneath the outlet of a wier. Instantly the matches were put out, and by the time we reached the treasure house, where we found the rest of the party sheltered beneath the veranda, all of our powder was wet and our bowstrings soaked and useless. Thus, indeed, it was a fine turn of affairs! We had nothing now but cold steel to depend upon; to step out from our shelter was as good as getting drowned, and we were not certain as to whether our boats had been captured or not. All looked at the Captain. He appeared undisturbed, and was quietly washing some blood off his hands at a stream of water from an eaves-spout. — By St. George, I admired him!

His brother reported to him as he stood there that he had been all round the treasure house, and there appeared to be no doorway or entrance; the windows were too small to allow the passage of a man's body, and were heavily barred at that.

" Then we must break through," said the Captain, cheerfully. " Come, let us start at it."

It was easier to say so, than to do it; for the walls, judging from the depths of the embrasures, were four feet and more in thickness. We had no tools but our weapons, and it was folly to break them, in merely scratching the stone.

"Where in the name of Heaven is the prisoner?" cried Drake, testily; "there must be a secret entrance." We looked about.

In the confusion, the trembling old man had escaped, unless he had been drowned in the street. And now the men began to murmur. One said that he had been told by a negro, who spoke English, that over one hundred and fifty men had been added to the garrison but the day before, and that as soon as the Spaniards knew how few we were, and where we were hiding, we would be eaten up man for man.

"To the boats! to the boats!" cried some. And let me state for these, that some of them had been doing the boldest fighting. I think they felt that, despite Mr. Fletcher's prayer, the Lord was not on our side in the venture. The rain was now ceasing, and as was usual in this climate, it bore all indications of soon clearing away. The Captain turned. I have never heard him curse at his men, but he was near to it this time.

"Oh, you cowards!" he cried. "Here I have brought you to the mouth of the world's treasure house, and almost within your grasp are riches enough to buy us all a kingdom; if you go away empty-handed, whose fault is it? Not mine! that brought you here, but yours for leaving it when it was in your grasp! Are you such poltroons that you are afraid of a wetting? We have yet our swords! By the powers, I'll stay here and carve my way to a fortune — who's with me?"

One of the fusiliers cast down his musket with a clang, and, drawing his short sword, stepped out.

"I am with you, sir," he said, "until death shall find us."

"And so am I," said I, stepping close also.

Young Ceely followed.

The Captain put his arm about my shoulder, and leaned upon me somewhat heavily. His face was pale and his lips pressed tight together.

"And now, who's next?" he asked.

With one accord they all stepped forward this time, and the Captain smiled.

"Then back to the Plaza!" cried he; "and, John, you take four men and search the rear of this building for an entrance, and if you find it, send me a messenger."

With this, he lifted his arm from my shoulder and stepped out into the street. The rain had ceased, the sun was now shining brightly, and the sandy soil had drunk up the water like a sponge.

The Captain had taken but three or four strides when I saw him waver. He put forth his sword as if to steady himself, and then with a faint groan he fell in a heap to the ground. I was the first to reach him.

The high leather boots that he wore had prevented us from knowing that he had been wounded, but the right one was full of blood to the top, and as we lifted him it poured out in a stream, showing how great must have been his suffering and how badly he was hurt. His brother John placed a silver flask of cordial to his lips, and he raised his head after a sip.

"Let me have your dirk," he said faintly.

Ceely handed him his, and with it he cut away the boot leg, and there exposed a gaping shot wound. He had been hit in the first volley over an hour before, but had said nothing. Taking a scarf from around his neck, — for he would allow no one to minister to him, — he bound it round his thigh and with great effort stood erect.

"'Tis naught but a scratch," he said. "Come now and follow me."

But with their leader wounded, the idea of a fight had left the men's minds. One or two others who had received slight hurts showed signs of distress also. The Captain started up the hill, but again fell backwards, fainting from his weakness. It was all up now. He was picked up bodily on the shoulders of four men, and all turned and hastened, regardless of orders, about the corner of the building in the direction of the pinnaces. As I looked back toward the Plaza it seemed to me that it was swarming with men-at-arms, and it was with a lift of my heart that I perceived the pinnaces were still safe on the shore with a guard deployed before them.

Drake had revived again and was protesting weakly against leaving, and had he possessed more strength, he would have fought to carry his point, I doubt not.

"Sir, your life is worth more to us than all the treasures," said the huge sailor who was supporting his shoulders. "We are not empty handed either." I looked about and saw that the two men who had gone into the treasure vault with us must have disregarded the Captain's order, or returned there again, for each one had a bar of silver. Two or three of the men, as it was proved afterward, had found time to enter some of the houses, and one had secured a golden crucifix that weighed almost a pound. The black man who spoke English had asked if he might make one of our party also, and had been well received.

Hastily we shoved off, and taking a count of our numbers, we found that we were but one man short, and he was the trumpeter, whose body we had not found time to fetch away. As there was little wind, we were forced to take the oars, and we perceived that the small galleon that we had first discovered was trying to make an offing, but finding this impossible, her crew deserted to another small boat, and we took her and found that her hold was filled with casks of wine.

We placed a crew aboard her with John Drake in charge, and succeeded in working her out of the harbor, and then under orders of our leader, who had strengthened sufficiently to give all directions, we landed upon a little island just outside the entrance of the bay. It was called the Isla de Bastimentos, where were the public vegetable gardens and poultry yards. We had a fine breakfast of roasted fowl, yams, and fruits, and the surgeon found time to attend to the needs of the wounded. To the relief of all, he found the Captain to be in no serious condition, but I wondered what next was to be done. I wished that my uncle had been with us, for I was not ashamed at all of the way I had behaved.

CHAPTER XII

AN EXCHANGE OF COURTESIES

THE Spaniard is a strange individual, and self-deception with him has grown to be so much a part of national character that it can be reckoned upon of a surety. If he has the last word, he has won the debate, no matter his logic, and if he has dealt the last blow, he has won the fight and congratulates himself accordingly; but the last word may be an epithet, and the last blow a gesticulation. Nevertheless, he will vaunt himself as though both were conclusive evidence of prowess. I say this because it has so often come under my own observation. When we were well out of gunshot of the town, and about the time we were boarding the wine-ship, the Spaniards, after a great deal of drumming and trumpeting, had succeeded in gathering a large force on the water front, and had mounted one of the cannon that we had displaced. Thereupon they had fired a shot that had fallen midway between us and the shore, and upon this circumstance they always boasted that they had driven us from Nombre de Dios at the point of the sword, and claimed a great victory. They are welcome to the satisfaction of believing it so, but I think had it not been for the downpour of rain, we would have held the town with our handful, barring, of course, our Captain having been wounded.

For two days, now, we stayed upon the island, and we lived like lords of high degree. The Spaniards' fowls were of excellent flavor, and the vast garden furnished fresh vegetables, so that after our hardships we were like to grow fat and wax proud and indolent. The wounded were recovering with wonderful quickness, and the Captain himself was able to be up and to hobble about. The negro to whom I referred, and who had joined himself to our party in the town, proved to be a man of superior mind and attainments. His face showed intelligence, and though black, he was good to look upon — a strong, comely man, straight backed and deep chested. His name was Diego, and Drake had attached him to his own person as body-servant, and decked him out bravely in some clothes taken on board the wine-ship. I will have much to say of this fine fellow hereafter, for he proved to be a godsend to us in more ways than one. He spoke fairly, Spanish, English, and Portuguese.

On the second day, one of the lookouts — for we had not remitted precautions against being taken by surprise — announced that a boat was coming around the point flying a flag of truce, and evidently hailing from the town. So the Captain turned out the guard, and we went down to the shore to meet it. Scarcely had the bow grated on the sand than there stepped forth a tall man, with dark features and a long black beard, who lifted his feathered hat gallantly, advancing at the same time in a friendly and frank manner with a gracious greeting on his lips. He was clad in a slashed doublet of crimson silk embroidered with gold, and the hilt of his long sword, and his dagger also, glittered with gems. He was in great contrast to our leader in his spun cloth and buff leather. But Drake responded in proper manner to the salute, and we, all 'standing by,' in ship fashion, doffed in our turn — it was a strange sight. I acted as an interpreter, and requested that Don Jose de Farina, as he named himself, would accompany us to the tent that we had erected on shore, and where refreshments were being prepared. The crew that had rowed the boat were rather for staying in it, but under Drake's orders they were taken ashore, and our men were told to supply them with all that they could drink or eat, and this was done to such good purpose that when they left it appeared as if it was their intention to traverse the Spanish Main before weathering the point.

But to get back to the story: Don Jose disclaimed any knowledge of English, and perhaps in that he was truthful, but if he had understood, he must have been amused and been a fair dissembler, for Drake unburdened himself after this fashion to me as we walked up the beach, he leaning on my arm : —

"It is evident," quoth he aloud, "what is this bearded coxcomb's business! It is to ascertain our force and condition. But notwithstanding, we shall not be outdone in politeness of manner, nor in formality of reception, as he may reckon our power in proportion to our courtesy." So every time that the Don bowed and scraped we did likewise, and this with such gravity that he was soon at home, and we were bandying smooth speeches and elaborate wishes, as were they balls in a tennis court. Once seated beneath the shade of the awnings, Don Jose stated the purpose of his visit. It was, according to his words, made at the request of the Governor of the town, in order to inquire if " El Capitan Drake " was the same officer, as some of the town-folk alleged, who had visited the parts during the last two years and had always treated his prisoners so kindly. As Drake expressed the pleasure that it gave him to have any Spaniard as his guest upon no matter what occasion, the Don went on to tell that His Excellency the Governor desired to know

if there was anything that he could supply him
with, and that His Excellency had great concern at
hearing that so courteous a gentleman and so kind
a friend had been wounded.   Upon my soul, when
I translated this to the company, I was afraid that
they would burst into guffawing, so transparent
were the words.   The Captain's eyes twinkled merrily as he replied, extending his thanks to the Governor for his courteous wishes.   His wound he
made light of, but his gratitude much, and the Spaniard appeared pleased, and said so at length.

"At the first alarm," went on Don Jose, "and
before our brave men had driven the sleep from
their eyelids and recovered from the surprise into
which your sudden visit had thrown them, it was
feared that you were French, and the consternation
that you perceived was resultant, but when we
found out that you were English, and that it was
the redoubtable El Capitan with whose name they
were familiar, that was amongst them, their fear
subsided, for they knew that whatever happened to
their treasure, — and treasure will always tempt men
of spirit to acquire it," he added politely, — "their
persons were safe from cruelty, their women from
rapine, and their town from the torch." |

"And how did you first find out that we were
not French?" inquired Drake, with great gravity
of demeanor.

"From your arrows," returned the Don. "A weapon used to good effect only by your country-men. And this leads me to inquire, if I may venture to do so, and be not too bold, whether these arrows are poisoned, as they have wounded many, and we should like to know the proper treatment to be accorded them."

When I asked this question in English, we all grinned, but the Don made believe to pass it by.

"Pray tell His Excellency the Governor," observed the Captain, "that Francis Drake makes obeisance, and states that Englishmen do not use poisoned weapons, and the wounds should be treated as though made with the cleanest of Toledo. And tell His Excellency also," he said, "that I am grateful from my heart for his wishes and offers of supplies, but," and he waved his hand out over the flowering gardens, "we trespass upon him already, and there is nothing lacking to our good comfort."

Don Jose let his eye wander over the scene. A short distance away some of our men were roasting His Excellency's fat fowls, and a group in the shade of the tree were sporting about a cask of His Excellency's wine, so there was some cause for the contentment at least. But had it all been all ordered for our special benefit, Don Jose could not have been more gracious, and so he expressed himself. Oh, I laugh now as I think of it; even the

K

polite irony of Drake's next speech did not discon-
cert him.

"It would be unfair," said Drake, smiling and
addressing us all, "to allow this good gentleman to
depart in perplexity as to our intentions, and" (this
to me) "I desire you, Master Maunsell, to decorate my words, and to spice what I am about to say,
so that it will not be bitter, but yet take heed to
plainly state what are our intentions; and now for
it—" With that he set me a hard task, and I often
had to cast about for proper phrasing. But leaving
out the spice and the garlands, this is what Drake
said: "Let the Governor, your master, hold open
his eyes; take heed and make all due preparations
and all health to him. But, as God has lent me
life and leave, I mean to reap some of the harvest
that has been wrenched from the earth and that is
being sent to Spain to trouble all the people thereof,
for it is by force that it is garnered, by force it is
held, and by force must it be taken." And then
he went on to say that long before England or
Spain were known, the gold was in the mountains
and the precious metals lay hid under the ground,
the jewels existed, the wealth was there for the finding and keeping, and that all this meant power, and
belonged to him who could hold and guard it; it
differed from crops or commerce in that it was
neither sown, nurtured, made, or fashioned by the

hand of man, and thus it was the property of the one who possessed it simply, and who had the strength and desire to make it all his own by force of arms, and guard it thus also.

I do not claim that the logic was complete, or even that the point was taken well, but it was a frank confession that we were after gold and silver, and considered our desires sufficient license, and it was honest speech and boldly said.   I had some difficulty in framing parts, so as not to jar upon the Spaniard's feelings, for it is easier to dress a lie to suit the fancy than to make truth appear attractive. But naught disturbed the Governor's messenger; and now the repast being made ready, we sat down about the table and drank healths and made toasts, as were we all of one mind and of single purpose. The Captain sent for some men who sang fairly some carols, young Ceely obliged with a French chanson, at which the Don expressed delight, and applauded; but all the time he would steal glances beneath the awning in order to take in as much as he could of our numbers and armament.   And he saw a great deal too, a fine show, I can warrant; for the Spanish sailors had been sent well loaded back to their boat, and for an hour or more our men had been passing and repassing, apparently at drill, by a narrow opening in the woods.   Each time the lines would be differently arranged, and this was done by changing

helmets and headgear in secret, and putting fresh
men upon the company flanks, so that even it appeared to my eyes as though we numbered some two
hundred odd, and we afterwards found that we were
reported by Don Jose as being of twice that force.
When it came time for him to depart, we all arose
and escorted him to his shallop, and there Drake
took from around his own neck a gold chain with a
small jewelled pendant, and forced it upon him,
despite the Spaniard's protestations.

"I may get the bauble back some day," he
laughingly remarked to us, ere the Don, still bowing
and scraping, was out of earshot. "The world is
a small place."

Some wonderful rowing was done, as I before
stated, by the crew, and the emissary's scarlet
doublet must have suffered a severe drenching ere
he reached Nombre de Dios.

We had some hearty laughter that night, and not
a little trouble with our own men when we came
to shut them off from their supply of wine. Mix
many sailors with much drink, and there generally
will follow some sudden fermentations. That I
have observed to hold true at home and abroad.

It was late before we sought sleep; for Drake,
who had dropped his fine manners and had become
the adventurous sailorman again, was full of carrying out his threat of relieving the Governor of his

superabundance of possessions. Oh, what a wonderful man this was! A thing planned with him was as good as done! He reckoned neither cost nor danger. He counted not odds nor difficulties, and yet shrewdness and well-defined method lay underneath his scheming, and he had us all on fire with his talk, until the prospect of inaction — were it in paradise even — would have seemed distasteful. Our fingers itched for the hilt of our weapons, and our blades were eager to leap from their scabbards. Yes, and each one of us saw himself a master of riches, and the envied of all beholders. Diego, the negro, had been admitted to this council; and he had been plied with questions to some purpose. He spoke English, as I have said, after a fashion, and his answers were clear and trustworthy. He informed our leader that the Maroons already held his name in reverence, which is another name for fear perhaps, and he claimed that if he would be allowed to make advances to them and to open up communications by extending mutual aid, we could obtain enough gold and silver to load our vessels, and supplies also sufficient for our homeward voyage. He proposed nothing less than a plan to seize the treasure boats as they voyaged down the Chargres River, and thus obtain the gathered products of the mines. This latter plan caught Drake's attention, and he determined to carry it out

if possible.   The next morning he informed us that
he had slept over it, that he had made arrangements
that he thought would work to a successful issue.
Calling the company together, we embarked from
the Island of Bastamentos with the wine-ship in the
van and headed for the Island of Pinas, but Ellis
Hixon and Drake's young brother were detached
in the *Eion* to reconnoitre the Chargres and to land
Diego, who was to act as our emissary with the Maroons.   The rest of us proceeded eastward to join
Captain Ranse, who was awaiting our return, and
who probably thought by this time that we were
killed or held prisoners, for his surprise upon seeing
us was plain.   He had enough of our companionship and was keen to embark for England before he
lost what he had already.   He regarded our safety
as miraculous, and wrote Captain Drake down as a
hairbrain for proposing any further expeditions —
of this I am certain.   But there was much more to
happen ere we saw home.

CHAPTER XIII

RAKE and Ranse conversed but little after the interview they held immediately upon our return. Our Captain had, to all evidences, spoken his mind in regard to the other's lack of spirit, and both being obstinate, there was no reconciliation. I was enjoying a new sensation now, for the Captain had taken it into his head to learn Spanish, he having known only a few words up to this time; and never did any tutor have such a pupil! He went at his lessons fiercely, and would bellow out the parts of a verb as if he was giving orders that he was glad to free his mind of. He learned to speak fluently enough before we parted company for any length of time; but he would always talk at top lung when using a foreign speech.

The pinnace hove in sight one evening at sunset; and Ranse, as if afraid we might attempt to detain him, bade us a hasty farewell, and crowded on all sail to get away from the island. Hixon's men reported good news from their expedition, and Drake said, on hearing it: "We tarry here no longer, my masters! If we can take a city one day, and be thanked for it, surely there be others that will deliver themselves for the knocking." So we sailed off, all five vessels, to the westward, and made the Island of San Barnardo, that I heard said was but a few leagues from the capital of the Spanish Main.

One thing rejoiced me exceedingly. I had feared that my Uncle Alleyn would have left us when Captain Ranse did; but what was my delighted surprise to see him — for I knew his stalwart figure at a glance — on board the *Swan*; and as soon as we had anchored he came on board the *Pacha* with the other officers and the Captain's two brothers, and I had a long-wished-for chance to talk with him.

"Ranse and I parted company for good reasons," said he. "I was under no obligations to him of the smallest, neither was I bound to his service by any paper, but could come and go as I pleased. Therefore, being of a jealous temper, he was glad to be rid of me, and welcomed the chance to buy my share of the profits at a price that will well repay him. Mind you this, my son, the man that now leads us is of no common mould, and he has gifts that come direct from God. Granted that we follow him without fear, he will bring us safely through, and we will see England, rich men all of us."

Then he spoke of the chances of my coming into my own, — that is, the property that of right I should inherit from my father, — and he told me that the money I might make from my share in this voyage would help me push my claims, even better than his patronage. It was for the purpose of gaining this for himself that he had embarked with Ranse. The Maunsell estates, he also informed me, were much impoverished and in sad need of care and fostering.

My heart warmed to him as he talked, and we had but half finished our discourse when he had to return to his ship.

Swords were out, and all fell to whispering, but this time without fear.

No sooner had night fallen than it was 'up anchor, and hoist sail,' and, helped by a favoring breeze, we crept down the coast and into the very harbor of Cartagena. There, near the entrance, we seized a small frigate without much trouble, for she had but one aged man on watch, and the rest of her people ashore. From the old sailor we gleaned some important information. First, that the news of our being on the coasts was all abroad. A pinnace had arrived from Nombre de Dios, and all the shipping had been warped in under the castle guns, where they were safe from us for the time being at least. But Captain Drake aired his newly gained knowledge of Spanish to some purpose; for he shot such a broadside of straight questioning and bad grammar, primed with fierce looks, into the Spaniard, that, of his own will, he offered us the information that there was a large vessel, all on the point of sailing for Seville, anchored just inside the point, to the southward. As the little frigate contained naught of much value, we left her and made off to find the new quarry. Bells and cannon were sounding from the town, but they affrighted none of us, although no doubt the Spaniards were in a terrible turmoil, as is their usual wont upon such occasions.

The old man had not lied. We found the ship, boarded her, and took her after a short fight, in which they lost two lives, and we had some blood drawn. Then, while we could yet take advantage of the darkness, we endeavored to get her out to sea. But it was gray of dawn before we succeeded, and, in the meantime, with drums and trumpets, the Spanish force, to the number of three hundred horse and foot, had gathered on the beach just beyond bowshot. They fired upon us without effect, and we vouchsafed no reply, which I daresay hurt them more than if we had killed a few of them, as they are quite as chary of their pride as their persons.

This same morning, as we lay off the mouth of the harbor, we caught two small frigates entering; they also hailed from Nombre de Dios, and

on one we found a message from our good friend
the Governor, telling that: " El Capitan Drake had
been at Nombre de Dios, had taken the town, and
had it not been that he was hurt by some blessed
shot, by all likelihood he had sacked it; that he
was still upon the coast, and that they should
therefore carefully prepare for him."   After reading it our leader gave it back to the messenger, with
a kindly laugh, and set him on shore with all the
prisoners we had taken.   Then we headed for the
San Barnardo Islands with our prizes, and in a se-
questered bay, where we were nearly screened from
the sea, we dropped anchor.

CHAPTER XIV

ROGER TRUMAN AND THOMAS MOONE

IT was a fine day but rather warm, and we still were lying in our hiding-place. I was making out a list of things worth keeping, that we had found on board the captured craft, when I heard a laugh that caused me to raise my head. There stood a good-looking sailor lad, who I remembered had joined us from Ranse's crew (deserted, to be plain spoken). He was all a-grin over something that one of the men had said about an object that he held in his hand. It was a leather headstall such as the Spanish muleteers like to decorate and place upon their animals.

"No!" he chuckled, "it is not for thee — but for an honest old gray horse that belongeth to my old father in Portsmouth — lay claim to it, and forsooth we will buffet for possession, and if I lose, thou canst have it to wear as beseemeth thy features and reasoning."

With that a stout man, much the elder, stepped forward, a ring was formed in the waist of the ship,

and there followed as pretty a game of fisticuffs as
I had e'er witnessed; but so evenly were they
matched that they might still be at it, had not one
of the sailors parted them, and, seeing I was watching, appealed to me to decide the winner. The
shorter man was perhaps the worse blown of the
twain, but both were good-natured.

"Well," said I, "seeing that the tall man had it
first, and hath a reason for holding it, and the will
to fight, to him I give it, and what might his name
be?"

"Roger Truman," panted the young fellow,
"son of Giles Truman, carter of Portsmouth, and
this is for our old horse —"

"Whose name is Dray," I interrupted.

"The same!" exclaimed the youth. "Pray,
good sir, how knew you so?"

"I know both of thy honest parents," I returned,
"and, when home again, see that thou serve them
as faithfully as old Dray hath done." With that I
concluded and made believe to return to my writing that was spread out on the slope of the taffrail.
I watched, out of the tail of my eye, to see how the
lad would take it, and he would have come to the
mast to speak with me had not some orders been
given him just then that sent him and his fellows
scampering aloft. Before evening, however, I had a
chance to talk with Roger Truman, and knew

after a few words that I had found a friend worth having, for he shed tears when I told him my story and spoke of his mother and how she mourned him.

Yes, it is a small world, after all, as our Captain once remarked, and the saying was doubtless trite, before they knew of a truth, how big the world was. I thought of the kindness that the two good people had shown me, for the sake of this same wandering lad that I had met by the merest chance in this far country. But he was better off than I was, for he had welcome and a home to return to, which I had not. Thus was I moralizing, when the Captain and Diego, the black man, came from the cabin and began talking earnestly. Diego was, as I have before hinted, a noble fellow in more ways than one; he had a carriage to his head and shoulders I have never seen the equal of at court. His features were chiselled and cut clean like a white man's, he was never obsequious or fawning; in fact, from Drake alone did he take orders, and although he performed in a measure the duties of a body-servant, he was both companion, confidant, and counsellor to our leader. I doubt not that it was true that he had the blood of some royal line in him as he claimed.

Drake, seeing me standing near, called me to him and told me the gist of what had passed. Diego had once more been referring to our alliance

with the Maroons, and had urged that, as the Spaniards were all on watch afloat, looking for our coming at any time and well prepared for it, we should
abandon the coast and strike inland, where we could
profit by the panic into which they fell upon being
taken by surprise.   This meant, of course, a complete change in all our plans, but it promised great
reward if we could ever escape with the plunder we
might gain.   The big ships were well-nigh useless
for this purpose, as the river shallows prevented
them from entering any stream except the largest.
But the pinnaces were just what were needed,
granted that we had them fully manned.

Now a sailor is never hot to turn soldier; he
dislikes the very name, he wishes to have his vessel
near him at all events and in all cases, for to him
she is a citadel and stronghold of defence, and, if
necessary to retreat, she goes with him.   Thus, in
a sailor's life, there is an element that enters not
into that of a soldier, and to have the former think
and act after the manner of the latter, you must
burn his ships behind him.   Our Captain knew
most men as if he had charts of their minds, and
above all, he knew the thoughts and methods of
mariners.   So, having decided upon what was best
to be done, he called no council, but went about, in
his own way, to accomplish his end.

I was an eye and ear witness to a strange meeting,

and can make record of what he told Thomas
Moone, our carpenter, late that night, — such a
brave, fearless fellow this Thomas! — I was in the
cabin when he was sent for, and at the Captain's
orders, there I stayed and listened to all that was
said.

Moone, being duly announced by the cabin boy,
entered.

"Now, Master Moone," says Drake, "first swear
that thou believest what I tell thee, and that thou
wilt obey me." And the carpenter thereat makes
solemn oath. "Then answer me some questions
before I charge thee with my will."

"Aye, sir, I am ready," saith the carpenter.

"My brother commands the *Swan,* but who
owneth her, — knowest thou that?"

"It is said none less than thyself, Captain."

"By my troth, that is fact," says Drake. "Every
stick and every stanchion. It would grieve my
brother to give her up."

"Most assuredly it would, sir."

"It would cause him pain if told to sink her?"

"Sir, beyond all manner of doubt it would."
Thomas Moone stole a glance at me, but I, not
knowing anything, was as puzzled as he, and eke I
showed it.

"'Twould pain me to give such orders to him,
but she must be sunk."

"But she is new, well built, and in good trim," quoth Moone. "I implore you not; she is quick and handy! I pray you, Captain, spare her!"

"Much as I hate to see my own brother and his crew bereaved of their vessel, she must go. I can do what I like with mine own, and 'tis for the good of all. In thy chest thou wilt find a long spike-auger. The *Swan* must sink before noon to-morrow, and slowly. And mark this, no one must know but the three who are here present."

"I will get my throat cut if I am found at such business," and Thomas drew a sigh — not of fear, but of regret.

"That risk must thou take at my bidding, but regard thy oath when thy throat troubleth thee."

The Captain smiled, and Moone stepped nearer.

"She will lie on the bottom before noonday," he said earnestly.

"Three holes will suffice," returned the Captain. "And now hie thee forward with God's blessing."

I knew better than to speak, unless I was spoken to, after the carpenter left us, and so, without having the mystery explained, I wished the Captain a good night and went up on deck, where I was wont to sleep, covered up with a sail-cloth to keep out the soaking dew, for it was hot in the 'tween-decks. But little rest came to my eyelids that night. I could see the trim little *Swan* where she lay anchored a cable's-length from us, all unmindful of her coming fate, and nearby, also, the prizes that we had taken — then eight in number. That they were to be disposed of, also, I did not doubt; and from the present my mind went roaming back into the past. I thought of what a strange life I had had, of my boyhood in Spain, of how suddenly I had grown to be a man, and from what had come all the strange self-reliance and the independent spirit that I felt in my bosom. And to what was I tending? I can now, looking back again, attribute much of my nature to the fact that I had been so often and so long alone, that I had learned to think and reason out things at a time when most boys are frolicking, or asking questions of their elders. And I think that my independence and love of adventure was due to my splendid health, my knowledge of my size and strength, and the idea that much was expected of me. But I had been fortunate also, in finding friends — first Mr. Blandford and the Trumans, then my captain and my uncle, and now Roger Truman. Yes, it was a small world.

CHAPTER XV

THE CAPTAIN'S PLOT

WHAT I have now to set down is like unto some plays that I wot of, both amusing and serious, comedy and tragedy interwoven ; at least it appeared so at the time, for I myself was filled with mingled emotions this day, to be sure. Hardly was the sun up when the Captain called away the jolly-boat, and setting but two men at the oars, put out for the *Swan* that lay two or three cable's-lengths distant. At his request I went with him.

As we neared the vessel's side, against which the little waves rippled and chuckled merrily, the Captain stood up and, seeing John Drake looking over the rail, he addressed him thus : —

" Ho ! brother mine, come out with me a-fishing. I know a spot, hearkee, not far from hence, where lies such a school of dainty monsters as would tempt thy eye and appetite. Come off with me, for the love of fair sport and good angling."

I saw him carefully measure, as he spoke, the

way the vessel sat in the water, and a frown, followed by a bright sparkle of the eye and a half-hid
smile, crossed his face. (On the peak of the forecastle was Thomas Moone, talking with some of the
crew ; good Thomas was evidently in the middle of
a yarn of some kind, for all were laughing.) John
Drake at first demurred, on plea of work to be done,
but upon the invitation being repeated, he turned
to order his own boat, saying with small grace that
he would follow us, but that he "was a poor angler
and a killjoy at such sport."

At this moment I saw the *Swan* clearly settle at
least two or three inches, for I had marked a line
on one of her strakes to measure by. Captain
Francis noticed this also, and again his eye twinkled, but he gave the order for the two sailors to
pull ahead, and we passed under the bows of the
smitten craft. As we did so, the Captain looked up,
and when he had acknowledged the salute of the
crew, he asked very casually and in a careless tone
this question : —

"What aileth your vessel, lads, she sets so deep
this morning?"

At this they looked over the side, and there arose
a great exclaiming. A man (who afterwards proved
to be the steward) jumped down into the waist and
hastened to descend the ladder of the mid-hatch.
In a moment he appeared with his hair all on end,

his face as white as a lady's kerchief, and his mouth like a cavern.

"We're sinking!" he yelled. "Man the pumps! The water in the hold is up to my middle! Man the pumps!"

Now there was a great hullaballoo! I thought I heard the Captain chuckle to himself as his brother John came running forward and in a half-frightened voice began shouting over the bulwarks.

"Some mishap has befallen us, and we've sprung a leak!" he called. "I pray you to allow me to stay until we find out what has taken place, and get the vessel dry, for it cannot be of much account."

But it was of much account, and cunningly must Moone have done the scuttling. There was no bubbling or noise, and despite the fact that all labored at the pumps, the crew from the pinnace helping, — for we went on board at once, — the water gained. Captain Francis now appeared as if he had altered his mind entirely, and encouraged the fellows at the pumps and bade his brother also keep up his spirits. But every time he passed me, he would give me a poke in the ribs or a playful buffet with his elbow, although his face was solemn as a grave-digger's. Well, to be short, by great exertions we kept the *Swan* afloat and no more; but at three o' the clock in the afternoon John Drake saw that further work was useless, and gave over in despair.

"What shall we do?" he asked the Captain. "The water gains, and our men weaken!"

"Let her sink," was the reply. "She is surely bewitched, and 'tis best to let her go ere she drowns all of you; and now let us turn to, and save what we can from the fishes."

So all hands, except a few who were kept pumping, began to break out the upper hold and to get everything of value overboard into the boats. At this they made great progress; from the first, most of them had seen that the vessel was doomed. That our Captain had an exceeding warm heart and was touched by his brother's sorrow, was evident, for as they stood apart he spoke to him thus, quietly:—

"Brother," he said, "take command of the *Pacha*; she is a larger and finer ship, and to you I give her, against the time that we capture a better, that will be thine for the asking."

John Drake was so overcome that he could scarce reply, but placing his arm about the Captain's shoulder he gave him a hug like a schoolboy, which spoke more than words could. After the *Swan* had been well stripped, she was set fire to and sank blazing in the still water, half hid in a cloud of vapor. Not even did her masts show, for the anchorage, though close to shore, was nigh fifteen fathoms deep.

This same day did we put the torch to all the

prizes except two; these were sent out with all sail set, and helms lashed amidships, to go whither they wished or the wind might waft them, and to be picked up or be sunk as fate might decree.

And thus did Captain Drake persuade the Spanish that he had abandoned these waters and had left their shores for good and all. But not so. Taking advantage of the half moonlight, we crowded into the pinnaces, and followed by the *Pacha*, deep laden with our spoil; thus we made out from the bay and headed into the Gulf of Darien, intending to make a landing on the main coast and then — what? No one really knew but Captain Francis, Diego, and myself, so I thought, but there was one other — my Uncle Alleyn, who told me in secret that he had fathomed the Captain's plot and heartily approved of it. But he declared also that no other would have dared to think of it, or having dared, to put it into practice.

We sighted one day, as we followed the trend of the coast, a tall two-topped mountain rising against the sky, and it was without doubt what our Captain had been on the lookout for, as he then ordered us to follow him more closely, and after a few leagues of rather ticklish sailing, he signalled from the pinnace to close up, and we entered a land-locked harbor much like the one that we had dropped anchor in at the Isle of the Pheasants.

There we found a clearing on the larboard hand as
we came in, and unloading the *Pacha* until there
was little left but her skin, she was warped close to
shore and vines and trailing foliage entwined in her
rigging.   Under the direction of Diego some of the
crew busied themselves building huts out of palm
leaves, while others set up forges, baking-ovens,
and storehouses in which to keep our treasure and
supplies.   This was all happening during the season
known as the Great Rains, and verily I believe I
have never seen such a continued downpour or
more drenching storms excepting the memorable
one at Nombre de Dios; but now it was every day
the same, although we had some bright weather
between times and employed it in fishing, hunting,
playing at games such as bowls and the like, and
at the first all kept in fine health.

The fact was held from the men that five months
must ensue before we could attempt our inland
raid, as, to Drake's chagrin, the Maroons (with
whom we had made friends) informed us that the
mule trains did not move until the advent of the
dry season, when the rivers were less like the raging
torrents that they were during the rains.

The Captain had not counted on this, or else he
would not have been in such a hurry to burn his
ships, I am sure, and no doubt he was in a quandary
what to do to keep his men busy, for that is per-

force necessary in any community, big or small, afloat or ashore. Otherwise there will be mischief after the manner of human flesh, quarrels, gaming, drunkenness, or disease. So, before a fortnight had passed, at the risk of betraying to the Spaniards that " El Capitan," whom they so dreaded (and admired of course), was still with them, Drake started on a cruise with two of the pinnaces, and while he was gone we shifted everything, but a little that we hid and buried, back into the *Pacha* and the other craft, and moved our camp some leagues to the westward, where we landed at the mouth of a river that we called the Diego, after our black companion. Here a fort was built, the boats concealed again, and another little village completed. I have always thought that this was a bad move, as the first place was by all odds the healthier — but it is easy to reason backwards, and I may be wrong.

After some time, when we had everything in our new quarters in shipshape order, the Captain again appeared with two prizes laden with supplies and fresh beef, and also some sugar and a few pearls. He said that he had put the Spanish on the wrong scent by appearing to the east of Cartagena, and he had been up the Magdalena River, and plundered a good part of the province of Neuva Reyna, finding enough there to support an army in the storehouses. Strange to say, although he had met with some opposition, he had not lost a man ! My uncle, who had accompanied him, had a deal to say of the fine headwork that our leader had displayed, but he felt more assured of one thing. If God had not had the whole of them under his special care, they would have met with disaster more than once. I had been rather unhappy at being left out of this expedition, but had been so busy that I had found little time to brood over it. Now again we began to grow indolent; for another two weeks nothing was done but eat and sleep.

CHAPTER XVI

MY UNCLE'S TALE

DURING these pleasant days, while we were refreshing our bodies and souls with liberty and freedom, I asked my uncle a question in regard to the writing of Sir John Hawkins, to which he had once referred; and one day, as we lay beneath the shadow of a grove of great palm trees, he handed me the following that I transcribed and kept a copy of. It was written by Sir John himself, in a very legible script.

It seems that Hawkins, with a little fleet of three vessels, the *Jesus* of Lubec, the *Minion*, on board of which was my uncle, and the *Judith*,—the last under command of Francis Drake,—had been on a trading expedition into the Spanish Main, but, having met with misfortune, and being hard put to it from bad weather and failing supplies, he was compelled to seek port and succor. Finding himself at the mouth of the harbor of San Juan de Ulua, and being honest in his intentions (the open maurauding of the English had not then begun, it might be stated), he considered it safe to enter, as ships of one friendly nation might, the ports of another. But before he did so, he negotiated with the Governor for permission, and everything was arranged in a manner that appeared satisfactory. So in he sailed, and anchored close to a little island, upon which he landed a few guns and built a small fort. Perhaps this showeth that he suspected some treachery, but it was more of a precaution than a menace. While there, the long-expected Spanish fleet arrived from Cadiz and Seville, and, seeing that the English were in the harbor, they anchored outside the entrance. Another conference was held with the Viceroy, and a second agreement was entered into, Hawkins explaining that his mission was peaceful, his desires just, and his situation forced upon him against his will. The Spanish admiral (all bows and smiles) had kindly promised to do all in his power to help him, and to further his departure.

All this my Uncle Alleyn explained to me in a few words, for he was a man of short speech; and then he bade me read what Hawkins had writ, for the reason that it had been already printed in England, and, though it contained one serious error, that he would correct; it told how it happened that English sailors (and our Captain especially) had come to prey upon the Spanish commerce as of a right. Here follows what Sir John hath written over his own name, transcribed truly as aforesaid;

and all this had taken place but five years before the
time proper of which I am now writing.

"At the end of three days," began the paper,
"the treaty was concluded, and the fleet (viz. the
Spanish) entered the port, the two fleets saluting one
another, according to custom. We then labored
two days to place the English by themselves and
the Spaniards by themselves; the captains and the
seamen, on each side, promising all friendly offices
to each other; which as faithfully as it was meant
on our parts, was as treacherously designed on
theirs; for they had furnished themselves from the
continent with a supply of a thousand men, and had
formed a design of falling upon us, on all sides at
once, on the twenty-third of September, at noon.

"The same morning, the time fixed for the execu-
tion of their villany being then near at hand, we
began to discover some appearances of it, such as
shifting of arms from one ship to the other, planting
and levelling of their cannon from their ships toward
the Island, where our men had the guard, companies
of men moving to and fro, more than their common
occupations required, and many other circumstances
which gave us a vehement suspicion. We, therefore, sent to the Viceroy (the same who had
signed the agreement) to enquire what this meant.
He immediately sent strict orders to remove all
the cause of suspicion, and assured us that he,

on the faith of a Viceroy, would be our defence against all treachery. This answer not being, however, satisfactory, we were suspecting a great number of men to be hid, in a large ship of nine hundred tun, which was moored next to the *Minion*, we sent the master of the *Jesus*, who could speak Spanish, again to the Viceroy, and desired to be informed of the truth. The Viceroy, seeing he now could conceal his treachery no longer, detained our Master, and, causing the trumpet to be sounded, the Spaniards set upon us, on all sides, at once. Our men on shore, being dismayed at the unexpected onset, fled, and endeavored to recover their ships; but the Spaniards landed their men in such numbers, on all sides, that very few of them got on board of the *Jesus*, the rest being slain, without quarter. The great ship, which had about three hundred men privately put on board, fell immediately on board the *Minion*; but in the time we had the suspicion of the treachery, which was not above half an hour, she had loosened her fastenings to the shore, and so, escaping this first brunt, got out of the harbor. Upon this, the great ship, with two others, set upon the *Jesus*; but she, likewise, with great difficulty, and the loss of many of her men, got out to sea.

" No sooner were the *Jesus* and the *Minion* got about two ships' length from the Spanish fleet, than

the fight began to be so warm on all sides, that, in
less than an hour the Spanish Admiral was supposed
to be sunk, the Vice-Admiral burnt, and another
of their chief ships believed to be sunk, so that they,
from their vessels, could not do us much harm.

"The cannon on the Island was, in the meantime, fallen into the hands of the Spaniards; and it
was with them they now chiefly gauled us. The
masts, yards, and rigging of the *Jesus* were so shattered, that we had now no hopes left of carrying
her off. With this cannon, likewise, they sunk our
small ships. We, therefore, resolved to place the
Minion in such manner that the *Jesus* might lie between her and the shore, and be, as it were, a fence
to secure her from the enemy's cannon till night,
when we determined to take what provisions and
necessaries we could out of the *Jesus*, and then leave
her.

"While we were thus consulting, and endeavoring
to place the *Minion* out of danger of the shot from
the shore, the Spaniards set fire to two great ships,
and let them drive down toward us. Upon this,
the men on board the *Minion*, without either the
Captain's or master's consent, set sail in such hurry
and confusion, that it was not without great difficulty that I was received on board.

"Most of the men which were left alive in the
Jesus, made shift to follow the *Minion* in a small

boat; but the rest, who could not get into the boat, were left to the mercy of the Spaniards. Thus the *Minion*, with only one small bark of fifty tuns — the *Judith* — escaped the treachery of the Spaniards; but the same night the *Judith*, likewise, forsook us. We were now left alone with only two anchors and two cables, our ship so damaged that it was as much as we could do to keep her above water, and a great number of us with very little provisions. We were, besides, divided in opinion what to do. Some were for yielding to the Spaniards; others chose rather to submit to the mercy of the savages; and again, others thought it more eligible to keep to the sea, tho' with so scanty allowance of victuals as would hardly suffice to keep us alive.

" In this miserable plight we ranged an unknown sea for fourteen days, till extreme famine obliged us to seek for land. So great was our misery that hides were reckoned good food. Rats, cats, mice, and dogs, — none escaped us that we could lay our hands on; parrots and monkeys were our dainties. In this condition we came to land on the eighth of October, at the bottom of the Bay of Mexico, in three and twenty degrees and a half, where we hoped to have found inhabitants of the Spaniards, relief of victuals, and a proper place to repair our ship; but we found everything just contrary to our expectation. Neither inhabitants, nor provisions, nor a haven for the relief of our ship. Many of our men, nevertheless, being worn out with hunger, desired to be set on shore, to which I consented.

"Of about two hundred souls we then were, one hundred chose to seek their fortune on land, on which they were set, with great difficulty; and with the remainder, after having watered, I again submitted to the mercy of the seas, and set sail on the sixteenth of October."

So wrote John Hawkins. I had read this aloud, and my Uncle Alleyn had listened attentively to all of it.

"Now," said he, "I was on board the *Minion*, as I have told thee, and I know two things. First, that the *Judith* did not desert us, but having had her stern post and steering gear shot clean away, she was compelled to drive before the wind, unmanageable and hopeless, until a new rudder was made and new gear rove, which, on account of the weather, took the best part of four days. Then, of course, there was no use in searching for us in the *Minion*; we had disappeared to the southward. Secondly, Drake, like a true, loyal soul, cruised for a week, constantly on the lookout, ere he departed for England. Every one who had aught to do with that expedition was ruined. It cost many lives and much suffering that is not yet over. Rotting in dungeons, or slaving at the galley sweeps, are

M

scores of English who were honest traders and guilty of no crime whatsoever. Canst thou blame us now that we seek to regain our own and get revenged?" My uncle threw both his hands above his head.

"Curse them! curse them one and all!" he cried. "There is a long score to pay, and some day, God willing, it will be paid — paid in so much blood as will tinge the sea waves and color the sands o' the shore. Aye, lad, we will live to see it — praise God once more!"

The change in my uncle's manner of speech had come so quickly that I was startled; for, until his outburst, he had been talking in the quiet way that was usual with him, and now, having concluded, he sank into silence.

I did not disturb him for some time, and then I could no longer curb my curiosity.

"How did you get to England?" I asked half-fearsomely.

"I was one of the poor devils who were thrust ashore," he said. "That is, to be honest, I chose to go, for the reason that I loved well some of the men whom Hawkins put out of the ship, for they had little choice in the matter."

But now, as my uncle's tale would fill a volume, I will tell it as I wrote it out for Master Purchas, the chronicler (who hath published the story), and he hath told me that it was confirmed by the account he had of one Miles Philips (hereinafter mentioned). The tale took up all the evening, and lasted far into the night, so I have shortened it and tell it in my own words. But this is not trusting to my memory, as I wrote the main part out at the time, and Alleyn Maunsell said it was clear and true. But to go on with the story that is not mine, but his, and thus return to the adventures of those whom Hawkins set ashore to the mercies of the Spanish and Indian savages.

When they left the *Minion*, my uncle said they numbered one hundred and fourteen souls, weakened by starving and disease. One boat, not being able to get on shore, two of the men were drowned, and the rest got a mile thro' the sea to the shore as well as they could. Some died in two hours' space with too abundant drinking of fresh water; others were swollen exceedingly with salt water, and from eating fruits they found; a shower of rain, also, leaving them not one thread dry. It was as if heaven had pursued the sea's challenge without, and partly hunger, and partly the water and fruits of the earth within their bowels, had conspired against this unhappy crew.

The Chicbemici Indian savages added their inhumanity, killing eight of their company in the first onset; but they yielding, having neither weapons

nor heart to resist, the savages perceiving them
not to be their Spanish enemies, pointed them to the
port of Panuco.   So they divided themselves into
two companies, one going westward, among whom
was Miles Philips ; and the other northward, among
whom was David Ingram, who both came afterward
to England.

After the stinging of flies, deaths by Indians, and
manifold miseries, the western company got to
Panuco, where the Governor stripped them of the
little which they had, and deprived them of their
liberty, calling them "English dogs and Lutheran
Heretics."   When they desired the assistance of
their surgeons for such as the Indians had wounded
by the way, he answered, they should have no other
surgeon but the hangman.   After four days he
sent for them out of the prison, and with many new
halters (with which they were in expectation of suffering), he bound and sent them to Mexico, ninety
leagues distant, with a great guard of Indians.   If
some of their keepers used them mercifully, the
others would knock them down, and cry, " March,
march, English dogs, Lutherans, enemies of God."

After their coming to Mexico many died, but
the rest had kind usage in the hospital.   Thence
they were carried to Tescuco to be used as slaves,
where by the means of one, Robert Sweeting (son
of an Englishman by a Spanish woman), they met

with great assistance from the Indians, or else had all perished.

After this they were put to the Spaniards, as servants, and were allowed the means to get something for themselves, till they became a prey to the hellish Inquisition, which seized their goods and persons, and shut them asunder, in dungeons, for a year and a half. By frequent examinations, they endeavored to pump something out of them, in matters of faith, and not being able (the prisoners craving mercy, as men who came into that country by stress of weather), nevertheless, the Spaniards put them to the rack, to extort confession that way, which made some betray their own lives. After solemn proclamation that all might come to this sight, they were brought in fools' coats, with ropes about their necks, and candles in their hands, to the scaffold. George Rively (my uncle's great friend), Peter Monfrie, and Cornelius an Irishman, were burnt, others condemned to two hundred or three hundred blows on horseback with long whips and to serve in the galleys, six, eight, or ten years; others to serve in the monasteries, in the St. Benito (or fools' coats) divers years, of which Philips was one. The whipping was cruelly executed on Good Friday, two criers going before and proclaiming, "Behold these English Lutherans, Dogs, Enemies of God!" the inquisitors themselves, and their familiars crying: "Strike! lay on those English Heretics, Lutherans, God's Enemies." They were remanded to prison, all bloody and swollen, in order to be sent to Spain, to perform the rest of their martyrdom. It was while in this prison that my uncle met with deliverance.

Of the daring escape that gave him his freedom, he made light; but it was accomplished with the aid of a woman, who loved him of course, and I verily believe that in his heart he returned the affection, though she was a half-Indian (the mistress of the gaoler) and a worshipper of idols. When he had returned to England (having been placed on board a Huguenot vessel that appeared off the Mexican coast, through the aid of this woman, who cut away his chains and brought him to the vessel in a canoe), he was penniless, and broken in health and spirit; destitute of means to feed himself, or to push his claim to his brother's (my father's) estates. Now, since I had appeared, he was truly in a worse position; he had no hope or future, nothing but his sword, he being more of a soldier than a sailor-man.

Once only at the end of the recounting had I asked a question. "What became of the rest of your comrades?" I queried.

"God alone knows," he answered; "they may all be dead. I wot not. Or they may be all slaving

and suffering, which is worse.   But there will be a
justice and a retribution on the heads of their
oppressors, and if I am but a humble instrument
in the performance of such, Heaven give me the
strength of ten, for I owe them blows without
number.   This very day should England be at
open war with Spain !   Ask any sailor, ask any one
but the faint hearts who have got the ear of our
good Queen, to our shame be it."

After this I felt no longer any pricking of con-
science when we took any Spanish treasure, and
truly up to this time it seemed as if we had God
with us, as my uncle said.   For some nights I
dreamed of those poor fellows, captive and forlorn,[1]
and the memory of that dreadful day (which seemed

---

[1] It is interesting indeed to follow out their fate, and it worked out that,
" Philips, and the rest, having served their times, had their fool's coats hung up
in the chief church.   The rest married there (in Mexico) ; but Philips escaped a
second imprisonment, and, after many travels in the country, and dangers in Spain,
returned to England, in 1582.

" Job Hortop, another of this company, with some others, were also sent prisoners into Spain, by the Viceroy, with Don Joan de Valesco de Varre, Admiral
and General of the Spanish fleet.   Offering to make their escape, they were discovered, and severely stocked : then imprisoned a year in the Contretation House,
in Sevil, but breaking prison were taken, and by the Inquisition sentenced : Robert
Barret and John Gilbert, to be burnt ; Job Hortop and John Bone to the Gallies
for ten years, and after that to perpetual imprisonment.   Others were adjudged to
the Gallies, some eight, some five years.   Hortop served twelve years, in hunger,
thirst, cold and stripes, and after four years imprisonment, in his fool's coat, was
redeemed to the service of Hernando de Soria, from whom, after three years service
more, he stole away, and landed at Portsmouth in December 1590, after three and
twenty years miserable bondage." — *Purcbas.*

to have been in another age and life) when Selwyn Powys stood before the Inquisitors and died for telling the truth, would come to me; then I shuddered, but was glad I had grown so quickly from a boy to be a man. I understood better than before why Drake and his yeomen felt that they had a right to prey on the Spaniards' commerce and take their treasure where'er they found it.

CHAPTER XVII

THE Captain, now having time to spare, took up with me again his lessons in the Spanish, and despite a strong accent (that never left him, by the bye), he was soon able to converse well enough for all his purposes. Henceforth he interviewed the prisoners himself, and he was great at it; I verily believe that he could perceive a lie forming in a man's mind in time to nail the same on his lips; the glance of those light blue eyes of his would go through some poor trembling devil as were they rays from a burning-glass. His own people knew this well and never sought to deceive him — woe betide the unlucky knave he caught in a falsehood.

One day the crew (such as were not employed at repainting the pinnaces) were indulging in some sports of the green, wrestling, running, and merry-making; amongst other games, a half-dozen stout fellows were toying with a round shot on the sward near the water's edge. Young Roger Truman was no bad hand at this, and as the Captain and the rest of us were watching, the men were eager in their attempt to outvie each other. It came Roger's turn again, and he made a manful hoist.

"Come, young Master Scrivener," cried Drake, clapping me on the shoulder, "there is a lusty youth, younger than thou art." (Roger was older than I, as I have said, but he did not appear so.) "Come, see what thou canst do at such brave pitch and toss." With that he shoved me forward, and I being really keen to play was nothing loath. So I took up the shot.

"Well done!" cried every one at my first attempt, for I had bested them all by half-a-yard at least.

"Well done, indeed!" echoed the Captain, laughing. "So steering a pen has not hurt thy muscles. That yon is a fair put for a stripling."

"I will wager a ducat that there is none of the company can beat Master Maunsell's mark," spoke up John Oxenham (and I could have loved him for so saying, being puffed with pride).

"And I will wager the same," put in Ellis Hixon, hefting the ball in his hands.

The crew had stopped their sport, and all gathered near, as men will when their elders or superiors take up a game with them. I could see that I had not hurt my reputation by my display of strength. No one had spoken, and, boylike, I drew a long breath and filled my lungs, as if to say, " Beat it who can." Then I looked about the ring, like a champion at a fair. My uncle gazed at me proudly.

" I will take the wager and add five ducats more," quoth the Captain, very quietly, " that there is one here who can exceed it by a foot."

" Done, sir," says Hixon, who had just had a try and failed most wofully in his approaching.

Now we all looked about us, and who should stand forth but the Captain himself? We were all astonished, never dreaming that he would conde-scend to child's play ; but he measured the distance with his eye, and then picked the round shot out of the grass with his fingers as one might a hen's egg from a nest, gingerly, as if he feared to break it. Then, clasping it with both hands, the way the game is played, he gave a short swing betwixt his knees, and hove it out. Such a shout as went up! the shot cleared the bough of a tree overhead and plumped into the waters of the bay! There were strong men there present who could not have equalled it in two heaves. He had beaten me by three yards easy. We let out a huzza that startled every parrot on the hillside into squawking and squalling, but the Captain brushed his hands to-gether, smiled, and walked off to his tent. But he was well pleased with himself all day, refusing to take Ellis's wager, on the ground that he discountenanced gaming and that he had failed in his attempt, which was to beat me by a foot, whereas he had exceeded this, through misjudgment, and beaten me by nine.   I, seeing that he was in such good fetter, made bold to ask a favor of him, and that was nothing less than to take me with him on the next expedition of the pinnaces.   But he would promise me nothing, and said that if he left me behind, it was for a reason.   Now I did not know what this might mean, and when three days later he started off again with the same boats as before, I was disconsolate, for I was not included in the number chosen to accompany him.   Of course I could say nothing, but I was heart-broken, and sulked for a day like a bad-tempered child.   I did not learn the reason for this overlooking of me until later.   It was all my Uncle Alleyn's doing, but he had not set about it in order to thwart or to annoy me, but because he did not wish me to be exposed to unnecessary danger.

My poor uncle was soul-vexed at this time, and somehow imagined himself possessed of a devil (as I afterward learned).   He had dreams in which he had seen himself leaving me to the harsh mercies of an overpowering enemy, and again of hearing that I was dead, and rejoicing thereat.   Both of these things would have been contrary to his nature, but being a simple soul, he thought himself tempted of Satan. This goes to show what stuff dreams are in general,

for in them we often act as we never would in real life
— God be praised for it! I take small stock in
visions, anyway, although I know wiser men than I
who do. At all events he had craved as a boon
from the Captain that I should be left behind. But
as a sop to my feelings I had been appointed second
in command of the camp, John Drake being made
Governor of Fort Diego.

I gnawed my fingers, however, when I saw the
pinnaces vanish about the point, my uncle having
waved his hand to me as the head sails caught the
wind.

For three or four days thereafter, I was in an
exceeding bad humor, and John Drake's company
was not of the kind to dispel it. He was a good
enough sailor, but not clever; a slow-spoken, even-
tempered man, with a large body and a silly smile.
His brother could wrap him about his finger;
nevertheless, he had the Drake courage when
aroused.

And now comes the task of recounting some
doings that I am sorry for, at least for the part
I played in them.

CHAPTER XVIII

W E were sitting in front of our tent (five days or such a matter after the others bade us farewell), and, having worked myself out of my distemper, to while the time away, I was asking Master Drake some questions in navigation, and he, in his heavy manner, was trying to enlighten me. I had already learned all the knots and splices, and might have proved a competent sailor-man of the lowest class; but of higher seamanship I knew little or nothing.

Teacher and pupil were becoming interested as the hour went on, and pictures of myself giving orders from the quarterdeck filled me, when suddenly there came the sound of some one coming at a great pace through the bushes, and a man burst into the open. Seeing us, he stopped short, and then approaching, saluted; but he was so out of breath that, for about the space of a minute, he could not talk, and stood there panting. At last he found words,

and they were to say that while he was in the crown
of cocoanut palm, he looked over the tops of the
trees and had seen a large Spanish frigate, with little
wind carrying her, heading south about four miles
offshore.

"Then tell all hands to keep out of sight, close
to cover, and she may pass by us unheeding and
unmolested," quoth Master Drake.

The man made as if to say something, and then
held his peace. It was evident that he had expected
no such orders.

"You speak as if we were rabbits, and she a ger-
falcon," said I, interrupting him when I had no
call to — "are we in fear of her?"

John Drake paid no attention to me, which was
right of him, in the man's presence, but bade the
sailor forthwith to call all the men quietly together
at the fort, and not to show themselves at the
water's edge. The fellow looked angry, and was off,
but at no such speed, I noticed, as he had used in
his approach.

"Why not put out in the two small boats, sir,
and take her? there is but little wind," I suggested,
mayhap with some arrogance.

The Governor turned, and I saw that he was in
a fine rage and containing himself with effort.

"Happily I should say that it is none of thy affair," quoth he. "But allowing for thy youth, I

make answer: it is my brother's orders that we leave not this bay in any craft during his absence."

Our friendly talk was broken up thus suddenly, and, on the plea of something to look after, the Governor betook himself to another part of the fortification. The crew were beginning to gather at the gate by this time, and they stood about, talking, evidently taking it hard that they were not allowed to set out against the Spaniard. Including John Drake and myself, the garrison numbered sixteen. But it was more than ample for the purpose, as, according to orders, the maroons kept to their camp some leagues back in the country, and we kept to ours.

The next day at sunrise we proceeded on foot to the first landing place that we had made in the bay to the southwest of us, in order to bring up some of the supplies and the shallop we had left concealed there. It was a hard journey, for the trees and vines grew close to the banks, every foot impeding us. Were it not for the rivers, and the path the maroons keep open, the interior of this country, I might state, would be well-nigh impassable to travellers.

It was high noon when we arrived at the clearing, — it having taken us seven hours for the eight miles! After we had eaten, we set to work discovering the shallop, and unearthing the needed supplies. It was late, but we took things easy to return after dark. As soon as we had placed everything on board, we hid the rest again, and were about to shove off, when one of the men (there were nine of them with us) pointed out to the open water, and there, but a half mile off shore, drifting slowly along, her great mainsail banging and clattering against the mast, was a large frigate deep laden, — probably the one that had been sighted on the yesterday. It was John Smith, the armorer, who had first seen her, a brave fellow and a leader with the others; but now the crew were all quarreling among themselves, each claiming that he had made the discovery. I looked at John Drake, and his brow was drawn in perplexity. But, after thinking a moment, while we all watched, not knowing what was coming, he ordered the men out of the shallop, and told them to draw her back in the bushes. There arose outright grumbles at this, and Robert Minicy, a boatswain's mate, came up to me; he was a man with a reputation for dare-deviltry that he took every occasion to sustain (he lost his life a few years later, because he would not run, and chose to face a squadron of horse single handed), — as I say, this man, coming up, put his face close to mine, and spoke hoarsely: —

"Take us out, sir," he begged; "'tis as easy as guessing to take yon vessel. We have two firelocks

N

here; but them aside, there are enough of us to board her bare fisted."

I savored that the man's breath was heavy with liquor, but he was alert, and his eye clear; the rest of the crew were likewise all eager, and more than likely for the same reason. Unknown to the Governor or myself, while searching for the supplies they had tapped a half-barrel of wine and unearthed a bottle of brandy. But I did not notice then that the drink headed them at all. No sooner ashore than one of the men began to load the heavier musket, making a great to-do over it.

John Smith, the armorer, had taken Minicy to one side, and they were chattering like two gossips in the kiln-hole; anon they would look over at me and then at John Drake, who stood with his arms folded, leaning against a tree. His gaze was fixed on the vessel, that was plainly to be seen through the leaves of the trees. The rest of the men had their eyes glued on her also, and were muttering in whispers. All at once Smith gave the boatswain a clap on the shoulder as if they had decided upon a plan, and Minicy approached me again. He pulled his leather cap off his tousled red pash and saluted respectfully.

"Will you speak for us to Captain Drake, sir," said he. "We want just a word, and we'll bring in that ship and have her holystoned and rechristened to

his worship's taste, ere dark.   Good sooth, 'tis lur-
ing to see her hanging there like a maid at the stile
who waits for a whistle."

"Speak for yourself," said I.   "I'm one with
you."

The Governor turned his head.   "What's this
I hear?" asked he, with his brows lowered.

Minicy again saluted, but I saw his eyes sparkle
and his teeth gleam in his beard.   He did not hesitate, but came to the point boldly.

"The men would like to take the Spaniard, sir,"
.:e said, pointing; "she's ripe for us."

Now the rest of the crew stepped forward and
stood about most eagerly; the mutterings rose
louder.   John Drake shot a look around him, and
his speech came quick this time.

"Clamor your tongues — not a word more!" he
growled.   "I've had my say; keep low all of you,
and let her clear the point."   Minicy was silent,
and all might have gone well had not Drake added
a few words to his speech.   "No one would like to
set foot aboard her more than I," he concluded,
"but there are reasons."   With that he cast a look
at me as if desiring my help.   The boatswain saw it.

"Master Maunsell will lead us, sir," he cried, ere
I could put in a word.

"How's this!" answered the Governor, whirling
on me.   "How durst thou speak with these stretch-

hemps behind my back, sirrah! art thou of the same kidney and bold for the same reason?" He glowered at me, but my blood ran hot to my temples.

"Prithee, hold easy," quoth I. "I said I would go with them; that is naught but truth. What lets us from doing so?"

The vision of making a prize on our own account and thus evening up matters with the pinnaces tempted me, as did the sight of the Spaniard, heaving lazily up and down on the long, sweeping seas and but a mile from our hiding place. As John Drake said nothing, I went on, but still hotly:—

"The reasons you spoke of held to the other harbor, and not to this."

"Oh, if Captain Francis were but here," spoke one of the men (I think it was the armorer).

The Governor stroked his hairy chin with both hands; he was wavering, any could see.

"We can take her," I cried. "What say ye, lads?"

I believe the foolish fellows would have cheered (which would have been a fine thing to do under the order of things, would it not?), but Captain John raised his hand and turned furiously on them.

"Hold, hold! you hot heads!" he cried; "would you betray us all, and spoil our chances?"

"We can take her, God bless your worship," said Minicy, in a thick whisper, as if clinching the argument by repeating my words. "We can take her," echoed the crew, crowding yet closer.

Then the boatswain (who had the gift of apt speech) parted the leaves of the bushes and stretched out his hand. The frigate was about to weather the point. As she swayed gently from side to side a long silken streamer on her mizzen swung out with a flutter of color and caught the rays of the setting sun. "See how she wafts to us," he cried; "she challenges like a maid at a kissing game. Aye! Good sooth, she would wanton with us; she is ours for the catching. Shall we let such a prize slip our fingers, eh? are we old men? is our blood cold?" He stood there watching and his lips moving.

Truly it did appear as if the vessel had beckoned. Then she rounded the point, and the trees hid her from sight. No one moved; all eyes were on Captain John. His face was pale and his gaze was on the ground; he stroked his beard with his fingers all aquiver.

"He did say the other harbor," quoth he half to himself; then he raised his head and saw the vessel was gone.

Now 'tis a curious thing in human nature that while a thing is yet in our sight we often will not move to possess it, nor do we seem to value our opportunity. But let it once go by, and then (often too late) we will strive to regain by hard work what

might have been ours for the reaching.   Perhaps
our imagining addeth to temptation.

"Tumble that stuff out of the boat!" roared
John Drake, suddenly, as if he had just awakened
from sleep.   "Out with it! overboard with it! fall
to, my bullies!   How now!   let's see who's the
ablest."   His voice had a sound like to his brother's.
I could not help but notice it.

The men fell down the bank and attacked the
shallop as if they would tear her to pieces.   The
Captain turned to me.

"We can be up with her before darkness sets in,"
he said, "and make anchorage here for the night;
yea, methinks ere the tide turns."

Where he was dallying before, he was all eager
now, and he began directing the crew where to
place the clutter that they were heaving out like
madmen, grunting and cursing, and not a few laughing.   Somehow I did not like it; there was lacking
the determined order with which Captain Francis
would have done it.   Every man was working for
himself and making a holiday game of the matter;
it took some stern words at last from Captain
John to stop the horse play, but they had put all on
shore in one-tenth the time they had loaded her,
and then all piling in at once they weighted her
down so much that to save our lives we could not
stir her nose out of the sand.   When the order was

given to lighten her, four men in the stern jumped
overboard, and as the water was deep, of course they
went head under, and one (being no swimmer) was
like to be drowned ere we fished him out. I never
saw such confusion ; if it were not such serious business, I could have grown sore laughing.

"Steady ! steady, you jolt-heads ! " cried Captain
John ; "what has hold of you ? are ye all bewitched !
Steady, every mother's son ; bear a good hand
now ! " And then he ripped out the first oath I had
ever heard fall from his lips ; for at last they managed to push us off, which they did with such a
vengeance that the Captain, who was standing up,
was launched backward in the stern sheets, and his
long sword, catching beneath a thwart, the blade
was broken off about eight inches from the point.
The fellows who had done such lusty shoving were
all in a heap in the bow, and the men on the after-
thwart were red with mirth, and only kept from guffawing outright by the sight of the Captain's angry
face. It was a fine way to start off to do any fighting, and a fine array we made when you come to
think of it. Counting up, we had : one broken
rapier, two firelocks, and a dirk (the last belonging
to me). But after much shoving and sifting down,
some order was made out of the chaos, and the oars
were shipped in a very ragged fashion. Then we
pulled away for the mouth of the harbor.

CHAPTER XIX

WE PAY THE PIPER

THE shallop was a fast-rowing craft, despite her bluff bows and her heavy load, and in ten minutes we had rounded the point, and there was the frigate, less than a mile away down the coast, almost becalmed.

The men, when they saw how near she was, began to chuckle and wager as to her cargo, but I suggested to Captain John that it might be well to prepare some plan if we were really going to board her; and he agreed, as it was evident from a slight commotion on her decks that we had been sighted. The helm had been put down, and with the little way she carried, her head pointed out to sea. John Drake had not spoken for the last few minutes, and now when he turned to answer me, I saw that his face wore a worried look.

"Master Maunsell, don't think I'm the one to blench at this time," said he, in a low tone, "but by my troth, I like it not as we have begun it. With our men sober and well armed I'd fear naught,

—but now—" And he bit his words off short, as if afraid to say more.

" We cannot turn back," I rejoined.

" No," said he; " I see no way for it but to go ahead."

We were speaking in whispers.

" How will we arm the men?" I asked.

" God knows — there're the boat stretchers — I've seen them used before. A curse on me for being a fool! — The drunken spawn!" he suddenly broke out, as a man missed his stroke and went over backward. " Steady there, and mind your work, you clumsy tike!"

I looked closely at the men. They were more serious than they were a few moments since, and those at the oars had sweated some of the spirit out of them. I noticed one of the fusileers in the bow ramming down a charge in his musket, and I could almost have sworn that it was the same fellow I had seen loading his piece ashore; but there was no time to remark upon it, for the Captain began to address the men by name, telling them to loosen the stretchers and prepare to use them as cudgels. At the same time he told them that he was going to board at the stern, and hurriedly gave out their stations.

We were within hailing distance of the Spaniards, and I looked out across the water. The man at the helm was calmly gazing back at us, and four or five heads appeared above the taffrail. Just at this instant a puff of wind struck the vessel's sails, and she moved away from us. One of the lads in the bows began to curse, but a word from the Captain silenced him.

"Hail them, Master Maunsell! Hail them, sir!" cried Captain John. "Stand up and bid them heave to and surrender! By the great Harry, don't let them slip us!"

I rose to my feet in obedience — one thing had struck me forcibly: the men on board the frigate had shown no signs of fright. It took two or three swallows before I found my voice. I feared me it had gone down my throat to stay, till at last I managed to shout in Spanish (in the loudest tones I could muster) a summons to heave to and give over.

There was no reply. The man at the helm still looked at us in silence. Captain Drake was roused now; something had to be done, and that quickly.

"Give way at the oars, my bullies!" he shouted, and again his voice sounded like his brother's. "Give way, and we'll have at them. Now, my bawcock in the bow there, take good aim with the caliver and bowl over yon scroyle at the helm — his blood be on his own head, and not on ours!"

The same fellow whom I saw doing the loading laid his cheek down to the stock and fired, and as

he did so, ere the smoke had hid things, I gave a
cry of horror. For the man's head went off his
shoulders like an earthen pot all into flinders! His
piece had burst in the breech; his body fell back
amid the rowers. Whether he hit the Spaniard I
never learned, for at that minute so many things
happened.

A single port in the frigate's stern dropped with
a vicious clatter, and there was the grinning mouth
of a demi-cannon gorming out at us. But the
mouth was soon hidden by a burst of flame and
smoke; then came a sudden shock, as if we had
struck a reef, and I was hurled back in the bottom
of the shallop, feeling as if my left arm had been
torn from its socket! But my senses had not left
me, and, with a struggle, I got up on my knees.
As long as I live I shall never forget that sight!
Close to me lay the Captain grasping a dreadful
wound in his breast that showed his ribs, another
man, dead and mangled, lay on the mid-thwart, and
three others, tossed hither and thither, were groaning and bloody; but four of the boat's crew had escaped that fell discharge. It was, beyond doubt, a
lucky thing for us that the breeze had now fresh-
ened, and that the frigate was skipping away before it;
for a score of calivers were let go at us as we lay there
helpless, but they were bad shots at the distance,
their balls scattered harmlessly about in the water.

Robert Minicy was one of the fortunates who were left unscathed; standing up in the bows, he began shaking his fists at the retreating craft, calling all on board cowards, and daring them to return and fight. Thank God they did not, or we all might have met a worse fate than had already befallen us. The vessel was full of Spanish soldiers; I could see the glitter of casques and salets! They had lured us handsomely to our destruction.

But there was no use cursing our enemies, or bemoaning our misfortunes; we had reaped our own sowing, that was all there was to it. I called the boatswain to order (and to his senses), and despite the pain in my left arm — that was gashed and maimed with a splinter from the boat's gunwale — we all began to do what we could for the wounded, and strove to see if we could not save ourselves into the bargain, for the shallop was riddled like a sieve, and was leaking badly. But I could stand little exertion, and all at once I fell back weak from loss of blood, and deathly sick all through me.

After Minicy had tied up my arm and given me a pull out of a brandy bottle (that had been part cause of all the trouble), I felt better and managed to sit upright; then I turned and bent over our wounded leader (poor Captain John! it needed but half an eye to see that he was done for). I called his name; his lips moved, and at last he spoke.

"We well boggled it," he murmured faintly. "What will my brother say?" and then he drew a long breath. "'Twas all my foolishness," he said, looking up at me.

"No — I say it was my fault, sir," I answered.

"You had youth for excuse, and the men had rum," he returned weakly — "I had neither." Then again he drew his breath, this time not so easily. "O Lord, my strength and my Redeemer, forgive my sins, and receive my. soul," he said out loud, and died thus bravely like a Christian gentleman. There he lay, with his eyes wide open, staring up at the darkening sky.

I remember directing Minicy with another man to get out the oars and to make for shore, bidding the rest, who were able, set to bailing. With that all went black, and for the second time I fainted; my last thought was: "There is naught to be done — this is death and the end of it."

CHAPTER XX

DARK DAYS

THE sound of the keel grating on the sand was my next recollection, and a babble of voices. A torch was flaring over my head, and some one was trying to lift me.

"He's alive," cried Robert Minicy, whose face I knew, as I opened my eyes. "He's alive, but hurted sore; lend a hand, you gaping louts, and get him out of this. Yes, we've been time-passing with the Spaniards, but it's no place to tell o't."

We were off Fort Diego, and I must have lain insensible for hours. I was carried into the tent, and, weak and sick, there fell asleep at last.

The events of the five succeeding days can be told in a few words. In the morning we buried the bodies of the Governor and the three others (one poor lad having died of his wounds during the night), and to add to my distress, I found myself in command of the fort, with a pretty tale to tell Captain Drake upon his return. The only person we had on the expedition that knew aught of surgery was away with the pinnaces, and our wounded men were not doing well; my arm troubled me more than a little, and for a long time showed no sign of healing. The men began to grow despondent and sick for home; they declared among themselves that a blight was on us and that we would never see old England more. As best I could, I tried to keep them busy, but sometimes I was on the point of despairing, when day after day passed and there was no sign of the Captain. Another man died, and was buried with the rest — the gloom settled deeper upon us.

But at last one evening the welcome sight of the missing vessels met our eyes, rounding the point with (as usual) two prizes following in their wake.

But there were no cheers to welcome them. Leaning on Minicy's shoulder, I went down to the shore to meet them. They hailed as they approached, but I was too weak to shout an answer, and held silence until the Captain set foot on land. They had seen that something was amiss, and I was almost bewraying my extreme youth, and greeting them with a flood of childish tears.

" Where is my brother? " asked the Captain, anxiously.

" Dead," said I. " Alas, sir, dead !" And all atremble I told the story, while I was conscious

that they were standing close, and that my Uncle
Alleyn had slipped his arm about me and kept me
on my feet.

"And he went out and led you on such a venture?" asked the Captain, with a cold set face, when
I had paused.

"'Twas little fault of his, sir," I replied.   "We
would have it so; I urged him on."

"But he had his orders."

The Captain turned to his brother Joseph (who
was defeatured with grief) and the other officers:
"'Tis a lesson, my masters, in obedience," said
he, "and showeth the penalty of rash conduct.
Hixon, back with you at once, and bring Ashmead
here to me."

Then anxiously he asked after the wounded, as
he sent off the small boat to hurry the surgeon
ashore from the pinnace.

Now, it might seem strange to hear Francis
Drake decry rashness or daring, as he was the most
venturesome man surely that ever dandled a sword.
But then, I remember that he was always sure of his
own mind, and never went off half primed in anything he undertook.   My uncle related that, on
this last excursion, he had only succeeded in quell-
ing something like a mutiny, by a display of personal recklessness but short of madness, going
ashore alone and beating about with his rapier on

one occasion to convince the rest that the ambush they feared was imaginary.

It seemed cold hearted, the way that he had taken the dire news I had to tell. Nevertheless, I must set down something that proves he sorrowed deeply. Early the next morning I was up before most of the camp was stirring; from the door of my tent I could see the little knoll where our dead lay in their new-made graves — alas, the mounds were soon to grow in number! There stood the Captain bareheaded. Suddenly, he dropped upon his knees, and, turning his face to the sky, he prayed most fervently. Then he walked back to his canopy, and, as he passed, I saw he had been weeping. But he never mentioned his brother's name thereafter; and soon we had so much to think of close to us, that our sorry adventure was forgotten in the shadow of the great and impending disaster that threatened our existence.

*   *   *   *   *   *   *   *

Thinking it all over now, the wonderful thing to me is that we ever held together during the weeks that followed, and I make claim that the only reason we did so was because our leader had the God-given grace and power that no other man would have in like occasion, and that his word was law, and the tone of his voice meant hope. Not once during the darkest hour did he show a sign of faltering, never

o

did the firm look leave his face. The men who
lived, lived through him, the men who dared, did
so because he bade them, and those who feared held
back their fears and stifled their groaning that he
might not know or hear them. I have seen more
than one man about to die, brighten and gather all
his wits with cheerfulness, as one sure of his just
reward, when the Captain had knelt beside him.

But this is forecasting. What means it?

Fever, disease, and death, hopeless sickness and
endless suffering; for a murrain was upon us! Up to
now everything had failed, despite our risks and our
leader's promises; we had made no treasure (scarce
ten pounds per man), we had burnt our best ships
and thrown our prizes to the winds, and now the
very land itself turned against us, and out of the
ground rose the strangling enemy, that turns a strong
man into a saffron skeleton and warns him with the
dread *vomito negro* that his end is close upon him.

It was January of the year 1573 (three weeks
after the return of the pinnace) that the plague
broke out, and it came so suddenly that it was like
unto the effects of a draught of poison taken by all
hands. Eight men died within three days after the
first signs of illness, and before the week was out
no less than thirty-one were down with it, among
them being John Smith, Roger Truman, and some
of our best seamen. I nursed Roger myself

(thinking of what I owed to his mother, and because he was a likely lad who had stuff in him), but it looked black indeed; no one knew who would be the next·to go. It was prayers to God in the morning that we might be spared, and prayers that we might be relieved of our suffering ere nightfall, and then further prayers at the grave side. Joseph Drake fell ill (I can see him now as he lay in the Captain's arms, breathing his last); and when he had expired, the Captain called Ashmead, the surgeon, and taking him to one side, he told him how important it was that something should be found out in regard to the seat of the trouble and where lay the organs most affected. (Francis Drake himself was no mean leech, I can tell you, and had some knowledge of anatomy.) So his brother's body was given over to the knife, and what they found I wot not, but the next day the surgeon died and we buried him.

At this time the Maroons brought to us the news that the plate fleet (that was to carry the treasure over to Spain) had arrived at Nombre de Dios. To some this meant little, but to others, much; as it turned their thoughts to other things than thinking of death, and without doubt gave them spirit to throw off fear, that is an open gate to mortal sickness. The Captain sent out a pinnace to see if the news was true, and it appeared as if the plague was

spending its force. In three days the expedition
returned with a captured frigate, taken with supplies on its way to the Spanish fleet, and on board
among the prisoners was an officer of the govern-
ment from Tolou, and a woman with a very beautiful little girl nine or ten years of age. The word
of the Maroons was confirmed about the arrival of
the convoy, or at least part of them, at Nombre de
Dios.

To see Captain Drake when he heard all this
was a sight to make one marvel. At once he called
a council of the officers and gentlemen and was so
sanguine that his manner was e'enmost gay. But I
think that it was in a measure assumed, to hearten
the rest of us.

"Our voyage is well-nigh made now," said he;
"we have but to turn soldiers and strike across
country, capture the mule trains, and make good
our escape; then we are rich men, every mother's
son of us."

"Rich men!" what words those are to tempt poor
human mortals with. I could see our adventurers
prick up their ears and hearken to the same old
song; even my Uncle Alleyn, whose hopes of late
had been at the lowest ebb, stopped his despairing
talk and grew once more to take faith.

But when we had mustered all hands, it was found
that there were, out of the seventy-three fine fellows

that had sailed that morning from Plymouth, only twenty-four capable of wielding a sword, and but eighteen strong enough to undertake the venture of going so many leagues inland with any chance of keeping afoot. The rest were yet ill, ailing, weak, or dead. There were twenty-eight graves now on the hillock!

My being so let down from my wound mayhap kept the fever from laying hold of me (I noticed that it took the strongest first and spared the very ones who seemed ripe for it). Roger Truman was recovering; John Smith, the armorer, was very ill, as were Master Ceely and Fletcher, but all three recovered. Minicy, who boasted that there "never was a fever that could touch his blood," escaped the penalty for his big talk, but many a strong, brave-spirited man died miserably, raving of England and home, prating of some woman, or shouting defiance of some enemy.

But enough of this sad recital. I have endeavored to shorten it in the telling, but even now I cannot think of those days without a shudder.

＊　　＊　　＊　　＊　　＊　　＊　　＊　　＊

On Shrove Tuesday, February the third, our allies, the Maroons, came to the fort under leadership of their chief, a straight-haired, black man named Pedro. With him were thirty picked warriors, almost naked, armed with spears, and bows and arrows.   They appeared to be honest, cleanly folk, much better than mere savages; and this they proved in every way, being easily subject to discipline, willing to assume tasks without a murmur, and the finest woodcraftsmen I have ever seen.

In the afternoon Captain Drake, with his eighteen followers, bade farewell to us, and under the guidance of Pedro and his forces started to the westward through the forest.   Ellis Hixon was left in charge of the camp with its garrison of twenty-seven, of whom twenty-one were too ill to be of much account.   Besides, it took some of the able-bodied to guard the prisoners who were gathered together in the hulk of the frigate that we had dismantled, and I was placed there to look after them, with four men to help me; but there was hardly need for so many, as the Spanish common sailors, if you treat them kindly and feed them well, prove the most docile captives in the world.

I would that I could record of my own knowledge the adventures of the inland expedition, but I did not grieve so sorely this time at being left behind, for I was yet scarcely able to use my arm, and subject to fits of dizziness, especially after exertion in the heat of the sun.   My uncle had bade me farewell in a troubled state of mind.   If he could, he would have stayed with us, — on my account, I am sure, — for he deemed me a sicker man than

really I was. His nature was much like a woman's;
he had all a woman's softness and depth of devotion, and the affection that had grown up between
us was heartfelt and unfeigned. He was father and
brother and mother to me. I had vowed that,
no matter what happened, we would never be
parted if I could help it.

Days went by, and there came no news. Every
morning we hoped to see our men appear on the
trail from the west, joyous and successful, laden
with gold and silver. But nothing happened; the
great forest might have swallowed them.

CHAPTER XXI

THE LADY WITH THE PEARLS

THE Tolou official, who was our unwilling guest, proved to be a Captain Don Lopez de Serrano, an officer of the army, and at first I had thought that the lady who had been on board the frigate, and thus unfortunately had found herself a prisoner, was his wife, and the little girl his daughter. I had given over the cabin to their use, and bunked in the little round-house on the deck forward of the main mast; the crew, during the daytime, had the run of the forward part of the vessel, and the lady and gentleman had the after decks to themselves. I, not wishing to intrude upon them, held aloof entirely. For many days the lady, who was tall and strikingly handsome, had been in deep grief, and I could not but respect the attitude of Don Lopez, who was, to all appearances, courteous and kindly, and who did everything in his power, apparently, to comfort and sustain her.

I cared mighty little for my own position and

pitied them both heartily, and this was one reason why I had no communication with them.

One evening, when the air was growing cooler, I sat upon the steps leading to the after galleries of the frigate, thinking, it must be confessed, deeply about myself, wondering, as I often did, what was going to become of me. Would my uncle be able to make good his word, and would I be rich when I returned to England? What would I do with my riches, and, forsooth, would I be happy if I got them? It was all a riddle that was beyond my solving. I was in the hands of God, and He had watched over me thus far as if He had, in His wisdom, destined me for some purpose. From the present I went back into the past. In my mind's eye I could see an old walled garden in Spain, and a poor little lonely lad who used to listen to the tales of the old sailor sitting by the fountain in the garden; how he had longed for freedom and adventure. I could scarce believe that I was the same person. I thought of Selwyn Powys and drew a long breath. I frowned as I thought of my aunt and Martha Warrell (who, I judged, had played me false), and then I remembered my mother; and I could see her again as she lay on the great bed, still and white amid the crimson and gold.

Suddenly I caught the sound of voices close by, speaking in Spanish. Looking up, I saw that Don

Lopez and the lady were leaning against the rail of the deck above, with their backs to me. Thus evidently they had not observed my presence.

"No, Donna Maria" (I started as I heard the name), "there is naught to be gained by disclosing your identity, and no chance of being ransomed," the Don was saying. "These English are ill-bred swine, but they consider themselves above brigands, tho' by the saints there is no difference. They will give us our liberty when they see fit and no sooner. I know this Captain Drake, and would rejoice to see him swing, but his men are above bribing."

"But this lank, callow youth who appears to be in command of the guard," responded the lady; "think'st not that his eyes would open at sight of a single pearl the size of a malaga grape; ay, and the promise of another like it should he set us on shore within two leagues of Nombre de Dios? Sooth! I have with me enough to buy each man who guards us a ship of his own, and the tall youth a castle into the bargain."

"Hush, I pray you!" put in the officer. "Did they know what they had overlooked, the fact of your being a woman would not protect you an instant. We had best take heed that we arouse not suspicion. Do you carry the jewels with you?" he asked.

"No," was the response; "at least, but a few of

them; the English submitted me to no indignity, though they searched my cabin."

"I wish that I had given you the locket that they took from me, then," responded the officer. "'Twas blessed by the Pope, and had a fine topaz in the framing."

"But think ye not if these men knew that they held the wife and daughter of the Governor as prisoners, that they would speedily try to obtain ransom for their deliverance?"

"I think that they would consider the risks too great, Donna Maria. We had assured ourselves that they had abandoned the coasts, and here they are, hiding within scenting distance of us, waiting for the mule trains to deliver to the plate ships. That's the game, I will swear to 't."

"I have half a mind to try the tall young officer with the light hair," said the lady.

"Donna Maria, I warn you," cried the Spaniard; "he is a thief like the rest of them. Where have you the treasure?"

"In a safe place. It might be well to try a few blandishments on the young man; a smile or two —a glance, eh?"

"More precious than pearls, my lady; why waste them on a junk-head?"

He leaned close and whispered something to his companion; she drew back.

"Sir, your gallant speech is too warm; I like it not, nor your humor — presume no more, sir."

Her tones were angry, and I could see that she was affronted; but the Don was in no measure put out.

"You give me less credit than I deserve," he laughed. "'Twas but my admiration speaking. Hush! hold!"

He had suddenly stopped himself, and I felt that he was pointing down at me, although I could not see him. Some whispering followed, and then Don Lopez's voice spoke menacingly in Spanish.

"Hark ye, on the steps below. I hold a knife over your head, and am going to drop it; mark, on the count 'three,' — one, two — "

I never moved a muscle, but sat as I had done before, leaning back on my elbows, and gazing out over the rail.

"He did not understand us," spoke up the woman; "he speaks no Spanish. Oh, I pray you — "

"This heavy block would crack his pate," interrupted the man. "We could swear 'twas accident."

"No, no, I beseech you! He took no notice of us. He is a kind-looking lad, if stupid. Set down the block, Don Lopez. Here comes my little daughter. Set it down, or I will point the finger! Yea, by Our Lady! that I will, if you dare."

They spoke in breathing whispers. It took some control to act as if nothing was happening that concerned me, but I had myself in hand, and then, suddenly giving a sneeze, I shifted my position, and, rising, walked forward, stretching my arms over my head as if to shake off the stiffness. I did not turn until I reached the gangway, and then, first glancing aloft, I let my eye travel back to the quarterdeck. There was Don Lopez replacing a great iron block (that would have crushed my head like an egg) on the fiferail.

"I will keep my eye on you, my bucko," said I to myself, as I climbed the break of the forecastle.

So they were not husband and wife, and she was the Governor's lady, and there was much treasure on board undiscovered. Somehow, thinking it o'er, I was glad that the rest of the crew did not know what I did.

The fair Spaniard and her little daughter had walked aft, leaving Don Lopez leaning with folded arms against the mast; before he moved he looked furtively about him, and, seeing that I was watching, he hurried down the ladder out of sight.

*   *   *   *   *   *   *   *

Late in the evening it came on to blow; the wind howled through the dismantled rigging like a great warlock, and the hulk tossed uneasily from side to side. Thinking that we might be dragging our

anchor, I crept out of my bunk, and went on
deck.

I could see the black masses of the tree-tops
swaying against the star-lit sky, and the sound of
their moaning, mingled with the lapping of the
water against the vessel's side, and the waves on
the shore, was like to the rush of a mighty river.
The lone man on guard at the gangway was fast
asleep, but as all the prisoners were safe under
hatches, I did not think it meet to waken him, and
let him rest. What the Spanish lady had said of
her keen desire to get away from this place to her
own people came to my mind. I wished from my
heart that it was in my power to help her. But
what could I do? I was quite as much of a prisoner as she was. If Captain Drake did not return,
none of us might ever see freedom. Ellis Hixon
and I had held talk that day, and he was low in his
mind over our affairs. The men, who were recovering from their illness, were grumbling and
bemoaning their fate. Surely, to be saved from
death only to be taken prisoners in our turn by
the Spanish would be a hard lot. I shuddered
as I recalled my uncle's tale of the burnings and
lashes.

There was a faint light glowing from the transom in the quarterdeck, showing that some one
was still awake in the cabin. As I noticed this

I saw a figure come with great stealth up the after ladder.

Now, the cabin of the frigate was divided into two apartments, separated by a heavy bulkhead in which there was a sliding door; the ladder led down into the forward one, and the other took up the whole of the after part of the ship. It was in the larger that the lady and her little daughter were then quartered; Don Lopez occupying the other at the foot of the ladder, as I afterward found out.

Keeping well hid behind the corner of the round-house, I watched the skulking figure. It was a man, I made out, crawling stealthily on his hands and knees; he looked down into the waist, most cautious like, and, seeing that the sentry slept, away he went on all fours until he was over the transom from which came the light. I perceived him tip himself on his elbows and gaze down, watching intently. At first I was sorely tempted to hail him, and ask him what he was after; it seemed to be, at least, a small spying business — this playing Peeping Tom; but, thinking that it were better to catch him red handed ere he had a chance to hide, I walked quietly toward the ladder. Just then the light below went out, and it was all pitch dark; but I had reached the coaming of the hatch, and, knowing my way, I approached the spot where the figure had been lying; I leaned down to lay hold of the fellow with one hand, at the same time drawing my dagger with the other. But my fingers closed on air; and yet I could have made oath that I would have grasped him by the throat! Hurriedly I felt about in all directions, and then, following the bulwarks closely with my foot, I searched every portion of the deck. It was deserted; I was all alone!

It was passing strange, and my heart began beating wildly. Men fear most what they least understand, and I stood on guard as if I might expect a blow from the unseen at any moment. Then gathering my wits I went down to the waist and woke the sentry. He was all scandalized at being thus caught napping, but I stopped his excuses and told him to follow and help me in the search. As we went up the ladder I thought I saw a figure cross the deck again in stooping posture, and I was sure I heard some hasty steps. But the man declared he saw and heard nothing.

"Lord protect us!" he said. "Ghosts! your honor, ghosts, and no less; they say the hill ashore yonder is full o' them, and then why not the ships? Oh, 'tis bad omen! I'll see my old father in Plymouth never more. We're sure acurst."

I said nothing then, but hurried down to the cabin held by Don Lopez; putting in my head I could hear him snoring as were he one of the seven;

coming up again, the man met me, and recommenced his whimpering.

"Close your head, you geck," said I, "and back to your post with you, and mark! no more sleeping, or you'll taste the rope ere morning! —'Twas the Spanish officer."

With that I went into the round-house and sat down to think. It is no pleasant thing to have a ghost for a neighbor on land, but 'tis much worse on shipboard, and I knew that if the sentry told his tale, the men would be for leaving, and would be malingering to be set on shore. I could not go to sleep, try my best, and after tossing for an hour I got up and crawled out to the air. The man on guard must have been very bad o' sight, for I passed him on the opposite side of the deck and went up the starboard ladder to the quarterdeck and crawled again to the hatchway. It was my intention to list if Don Lopez was still snoring, but, as I thrust my face o'er the coaming, I drew back quickly, for I had almost come in collision with another! and there we lay staring into each other's eyes at but hand's-breadth distance. It was the Spaniard! and I almost upset my kettle on the spot, by addressing him in his own tongue and asking what he was up to. But he spoke first.

"Morrow," said he.

"Good-morrow," said I

"No sleep," he grunted, "hot — hot," and he began fanning himself with the luff of a big silk kerchief he held in his hand. He had reached the end of his tether in English, and there we sat, I at the top of the ladder, and he a few steps below me. It was e'enmost embarrassing. But one thing — I had laid my ghost handsomely, and I began to smile. The Don stopped his flutter of the kerchief (for he must have perceived that the air was cool), and glancing in my face he said "Morrow" again and went down to his cabin. I arose and began to wonder in what manner he had first concealed himself; he had been very foxy, to say the least.

Suddenly I heard a noise from the lower deck, and looking down, I saw the sentry on his knees babbling in prayer; the poor carl had seen me for the first time and had taken me for the ghost. Going to him, I stayed his fears and, relieving him of his halberd, I sent him below, resolving to stand guard myself till morning. Then, I reasoned, I would tell Hixon what had occurred and place the Spaniard in close confinement, for I doubt not he was up to some mischief. I felt that the lady and her daughter were now doubly entitled to my protection, and my pity grew for them.

The child was most beautiful to look at, with her great black eyes so like her mother's, and her mass

of raven hair that hung down to her waist; and then
the lady had saved my life, or had done her best to,
and I forgave her calling me "lank and callow,"
although it rankled a bit; I dare say I was both.

Day dawned at last, and when the relief appeared,
I surrendered my post and speedily sought sleep.

CHAPTER XXII

A VENTURE AND ADVENTURE

I WAS awakened the next morning by the sound of voices and the smell of cooking from the galley. It was evident I had overslept, and should be on deck. So I hastened into my clothes.

"He's here again, sir," said one of the sailors, as I stepped out into the bright sunshine. "He's here again, and all agrin for his breakfast."

At first I did not get the meaning of his speech, and was about to ask, when the man pointed out over the bows at the still, clear water. Following the direction, I could see the dark green length of a huge shark lying motionless almost in the same spot where he had been discovered a week before. Every morning and evening he had put in his visit, waiting for the slop from the galley or hoping, perhaps, that some luckless wight would take a venturesome swim. The sailors had tried to catch him, with ill success, he was ware of tricks, and when near the vessel kept at such distance below the surface that no arrow could reach him. But the water was so transparent on still days, that his little wicked eyes could be seen, as he cocked them up at us. The men had named him Beelzebub, and truly he looked to be a retainer of the Evil One, sent to keep our track. But I had other things to think of than sharks or devils; a plan had been forming in my mind, that, if possible, I meant to carry out that very day.

I had called away the jolly-boat, intending to row ashore to the fort and consult with Hixon, whose advice I needed, and whilst the men were fetching alongside, I stood in the gangway, watching a brilliant butterfly that was flickering in and out of the slackened rigging; at last, it settled on one of the ratlines over head, shining like a great opal. Looking up at it from the quarter-deck was the Spanish officer. As I noticed him, he slipped his glance, and gazed thoughtfully out to sea. Our strange encounter of the night came to my mind. I disliked the man the more I saw of him, and he had reason to dislike me. Doubtless he must have known I had watched him.

Just then Donna Maria came running up from below, and a look at her face was enough to show that something was amiss. She was exceeding pale, and her hands, all a tremble, were clasped over her heart. As soon as she saw Don Lopez she came to him hurriedly and grasped him by the arm.

"They are gone! the pearls have been stolen!"
she cried, in tones that could be heard over the
ship. "The thieves! the villains! they have stolen
them!"

The officer, turning quickly, tried to calm her with
some words I could not catch, and whilst talking led
her away out of earshot. But from the lady's gestures and the way she looked down at me, I could
see that I had been referred to in his speech. Twice
he restrained her when she would have left him and
stepped forward (I feel sure would have spoken,
and I stood waiting her address), but Don Lopez
was whispering earnestly in her ear, and before long
she appeared to be under the influence of his words,
for she leaned her head on her clasped hands, and
burst into tears.

So the lady had been robbed! The meaning of
the night's adventure flashed clear upon me. But
I did not wish Don Lopez to suspect, as yet.

The men were ready in the small boat by this
time, and I was about to descend the ladder when
something else on the quarter-deck caught my attention. The little girl had appeared from below, and
there she stood at the hatchway, shading her eyes
from the glare of the sunlight. A pretty picture she
made, and I began to think of the anguish of the
parent who was waiting for her at Nombre de Dios,
not knowing what had become of his loved ones;

for the frigate by this time must have been long
overdue.

The brilliant butterfly had left its resting-place in
the rigging and was fluttering about the child's head ;
she grasped for it with both her hands, and the
insect as if enjoying this game of play, skimmed
across the deck and lit on the halliards of the flag-
staff at the stern, where it kept folding and spreading
its gaudy wings, as if tempting the little one to reach
for it again.   The child followed to the taffrail,
leaning far out with a cry of pleasure at seeing the
chase so near.

How it happened I cannot tell, but the first thing
I know, with a wild clutch at the swaying ropes, over
she went, and I heard a plash in the water.

Before the others could have known the meaning
of the sudden scream she gave, in two jumps I was
on the quarter-deck and in an instant more I hove
myself out, head foremost over the stern.   I saw the
little figure in the white dress struggling on the surface, but there was something else to think on—the
great shark!   It had flashed through my mind, even
in my flight through the air, that I must be quick.
When I came up I grasped the little girl ; in a few
strokes I was under the vessel's quarter.   A row of
faces lined the bulwarks, — prisoners and guards, —
and on the high poop Don Lopez was supporting the
swooning figure of Donna Maria.

"Heave me a rope!" I cried; "make haste there!
— don't stand agape — make haste!"

One of the men I could see gathering up a tangle
of loose running gear and making ready to send it
out — again I called for him to hurry.   There was
a slight current, and burdened with the struggling
child I could just stem it and no more.

A cry arose; a mingling shout in Spanish and
English, but full of words of horror and warning
that I understood too plainly.   Turning my head,
I saw but a half-cable's length away, the black lateen-
shaped fin!

There was a plash, and the rope fell almost about
my shoulders.   Taking a firm hold, I gave it a turn
about my waist, singing out for them to heave away,
and they began to draw me in — we were up to the
frigate's side again.   I feared to look round, and
using all my strength I lifted the little girl clear of
the water.   It seemed as if my arm would be torn
loose from my body as the strain came upon it,
and I knew my old wound had opened; but hope
rose in my heart.   A sailor had jumped down into
the chains, and his hand was almost touching the
little girl — in another instant she would be safe.
Suddenly the man's face turned gray with horror.

"God's love! look to your legs!" he cried.
I looked down just in time to see the shark's white
belly flash as he turned to take me in!   The great

jaws, with their rows of pointed teeth, were wide apart, and he was coming upward with a rush that would carry him free of the surface. I thought my time had come, but in a wild effort to get clear I kicked out with both feet and threw myself with all my force away from the vessel's side. So great was the swiftness with which the monster had attacked, that he leaped full a third his length into the air, and so narrowly had he missed me that I rasped against his great, ugly body in its descent; the blow threw my hold from the rope, and I fell with the little girl back into the waves. But to my joy I saw the jolly-boat rounding the frigate's stern.

A wild scream had mingled with the hoarse shouts of the crew, who now appeared to be in greater confusion than before, and directly above us I saw the Spanish mother stretching out her arms. Don Lopez was restraining her, or she would have jumped and joined us. As I had released the rope, the end of it had been drawn inboard, and there I was helpless and so exhausted I could not frame a word; and then my marrow chilled with fright, as I heard again the cry of warning, and knew that the shark was coming up once more. The little girl had began to cry and had clasped her arms about my neck. Suddenly, as I looked down watching for the next attack, I felt a tug at the back of my leather doublet. A man who had kept a cooler head than the rest had leaned out

over the frigate's rail and had hooked onto me with
the beak of a halberd — it was Thomas Moone the
carpenter.   But just as he began to lift I saw the
white flash beneath me, and knew he was too late —
the boat was four or five strokes distant and powerless
to aid me !   Men think and act quickly in dire need.
With a quick pull I snatched the halberd from the
carpenter's hands, and with the same motion drove
the great blade downward at the yawning open jaws.
It must have turned him, though it did not stop his
onslaught, for he struck me with such force that I
thought my side was stove and all my ribs crushed ;
the water swirled about me, but at that instant somebody laid hold of me, and I was drawn over the bow
into the jolly-boat.   I had not lost my senses and
held fast to my precious burden — so we both were
safe !   In the water near us floated the shaft of the
halberd, bitten clean through some three feet above
the iron.

" Marry ! but you have done for him, sir ! " said
one of the sailors, bending over me.   " Look'ee
there, sir, yarnder."

I feebly raised my head.   ' Beelzebub,' the shark,
was floundering in a mass of bloody spray and foam
scarcely two oars' length away.   The men on the
frigate — Spaniards and English, prisoners and
guards — were cheering.   I looked at the figure of
the little girl beside me and saw that she had lost

consciousness and needed help. We were at the chains, and with the aid of extended hands we were hauled on board, and with the child in my arms I stumbled up the ladder to where the trembling Donna Maria stood. She called down the blessing of the saints upon my head, she half knelt as she thanked me, and would have kissed my hand had I allowed it. Don Lopez held aloof, and followed by the mother, half weeping, half laughing, still telling her thanks and praises in Spanish, I carried my burden down to the cabin — where I called for brandy. But before it was brought the little one opened her eyes, gazed about her, and stretched out her arms to her mother. Donna Maria clasped her all wet and soaking to her bosom.

"Thank the good señor," she said. "Thank him, my precious one; tell him you will pray to our good Lady to bless and reward him." She covered the child's face with kisses. Then she turned to me again.

"I pray you keep the pearls," she said. "Would that I had given them — and would that I had more to give!"

And then it came to her that I understood no word of what she had been saying, and with eager gestures she tried to make clear her meaning. But I understood and knew more than she did, and my anger rose, for I saw that Don Lopez had accused me of the theft to cover his own evil doing. I was about to tell her, when hearing a footstep close by, I turned, and there was the Don himself standing back of me. As I looked at him, his swart visage flushed, and he turned his eyes.

"Donna Maria, I will reward the young man," he said, "should he ask for it, which is likely. Had he not best leave you?"

I fain would have sprung upon him and choked his words in his lying throat, but with great effort I restrained myself, owing to the lady's presence and the desire to save more turmoil. The men had not followed us into the cabin, and we were alone; otherwise I would have called them to lay hold of him and take him out to search him on the spot, for I did not doubt that he had the pearls on his person at that moment. I stepped between him and the door, as my feelings got the upper hold.

"Donna Maria," said I in Spanish, "I regret to inform you that yonder stands a villain and a thief. Hold, sir, I warn you! He has told you that I have taken your treasure, and I say that he has it now, and that he has robbed you. He who should be your protector has played you false!"

The surprise of both at hearing me thus address them was so great that neither spoke. The lady looked from me to the Don and back again. The

officer had turned pale this time, and his hand still
to his side as if reaching for a weapon.

"The knave lies!" he blurted.

"An' you say that again and I will string you for
the vultures," I returned. "Here; what is concealed
in your doublet? Ah! you rogue of rogues!"

With that I reached out and caught the end of
the silk kerchief that I had seen him toying with
the evening before; with a sudden twitch I drew it
forth, ere he could stop me, and a shower of great
pearls scattered about the deck.

With a cry of rage the Spaniard sprang upon
me. My wounded arm was well-nigh useless; I
was weak from the long struggle in the water, and
being unprepared, he bore me down, one hand on
my throat, so I could not cry for succor, and the
other fumbling behind him. I saw the gleam of
the small poignard as he raised it, and then Donna
Maria, with a shrill scream, caught his uplifted arm:
and this was the second time that she had saved my
life; for though the blow descended, it had been
turned and the force diminished. Hasty steps
sounded on the ladder, and two of my men ran in.
One was Thomas Moone, the other the sentry of
the night before.

It was the work of but an instant to throw my
antagonist from off me, and Moone disarmed him
with a blow of his fist. I struggled to my feet.

"Take that man forward and put the gyves on him," I ordered, hoping that the men would not notice the wealth scattered about their feet. But Moone had seen the gleaming pearls. I noticed his eyes grow large. But the other man, whose sight was not so sharp, saw nothing.

And now I was in a situation that I did not in the least enjoy. In the first place, I felt my mind was reeling and a deathly sickness was growing upon me. There was a sharp pain through my shoulder, and a warm trickle down my chest warned me that I was wounded. Calling all my spirit, I kept myself from falling and leaned against a stanchion for support. Donna Maria was regarding me with staring, frightened eyes. I could think of naught to say.

"Oh, good young sir, you are wounded," she whispered, her voice faint with terror. "What shall I do? what shall I do? Saint Joseph intercede and aid me!" and then her tone changed. "Oh, the traitor! the wicked villian!" she cried, "to think that one could be so villanous! I beg forgiveness from you, sir; but what must I do? Here, I pray you, sit you down and let me see to your hurt — I am used to wounds."

She placed the little girl in the bunk beside her, and taking me by the arm she pushed me to a great oak chair and would have opened my doublet, but

I caught sight of the scattered pearls, and my thoughts returned.

"No, madam," I said weakly, "I shall be right well looked after; I pray you first pick up your jewels."

"Nay; what are they against a life?"

"But they must not be seen; hasten; here some one comes." A step sounded on the ladder, and I heard Thomas Moone's voice saying,—

"And how fares it with Master Maunsell? No; all of ye keep out; I can attend to him. Bide ye here. I will fetch him out." With that he entered and bent over me.

"Master Moone," said I. "I wish thee to mark my words. This lady—" But what the rest of my speech was to be, the carpenter never learned; for my tongue clove to my teeth and refused to move, and I fell forward with my faint, and would have pitched headlong to the deck had not Thomas caught me in his arms and carried me into the forward cabin, that had been occupied by the Spaniard. The carpenter placed me on a couch, and examining my wound, said it was not dangerous — though deep. "A sore hurt, but not mortal — and I have sent ashore for Master Hixon," he concluded.

I think the loss of blood must have carried me off my head, for the next thing that was plain was Ellis Hixon's voice.

"How now, young friend? I hear that thou hast been indulging thy taste for adventure," he said, as I looked up. "But you are in good hands," he added. "This lady is a marvel at bandaging."

Then I saw that Donna Maria was standing at the foot of the couch.

"How fares the little señorita?" I asked.

"Donna Inez will soon be thanking you," she returned; "she is well — but you must not talk."

"Madam, will you leave us?" I interposed some-what abruptly. "I must talk to this gentleman and am forced to disobey you."

She flushed, and then without a word went into the after-cabin and closed the sliding door.

CHAPTER XXIII

HIXON made a sweeping bow as the lady left us, then he turned.

"Now say on," quoth he. "'Tis of this fair Spaniard that you wish to speak, I warrant."

"Yes, none less. And I pray you listen till I have made an end of it."

"Twang your string, Master Maunsell, and then hearken to me in turn, for though God forfend it, things are at a dule ebb with us."

So I told him of my plan. The lady was none less than the wife of the Governor of Nombre de Dios, and the little girl his daughter. We were not making war upon women, nor were we brigands to exact ransom. I proposed that we send out a small boat with a picked crew, and place our captives and their personal belongings within such distance of their home that they might reach it in safety alone on foot, trusting to their gratitude not to betray our hiding-place, or, if the Spaniards attempted to find us, relying upon the care we had taken in choosing

our seclusion. I recalled the courteous message of
the Governor, and urged that this would be a right
gallant return for it. But I said nothing about the
pearls, thinking they were safe in Donna Maria's
possession.

Ellis Hixon listened as he had promised, and
remained for some time deep in thought.

"Master Maunsell," said he at last, "methinks
there is reason in thy speech; for, gallantry to one
side, 'twould be good policy. Three weeks have
nearly flown since the departure of the Captain and
his company. If all went well, we were to hear from
him within the fortnight. No word have we had
from the Maroons, who have moved their camps I
know not whither, and if they have proved treacherous — God knows what has become of our companions. There is not a man Jack of us left that
knows aught of the science of navigation. Our
prisoners outnumber us, and supplies are dwin-
dling. 'Twould be folly to put to sea, for where
would we fetch to? If our Captain returns not,
there are two alternatives: one, to turn savages
and hide in the forests till rescued, or to become
prisoners to the Spanish, which means slavery or
worse. Now it might go easier with us, by my
troth, if we had a friend at court — in latter case.
What is your opinion in the matter?"

"You are our leader now," I murmured.

" I have command on shore, but you are in control
of the prisoners."

I saw that he wished to shift the responsibility
upon my shoulders, and I was willing to take it.

" May I have three men from the fort to follow
me in a certain enterprise ? " I asked.

" Yea, readily, and I will supply extra guards for
the frigate during your absence."

" Then I choose Robert Minicy, Roger Truman,
and Smith the armorer, they are well of their
sickness."

" You have picked the best, Master Maunsell."

" They must be the best for my purpose, Master
Hixon."

And thus was the matter concluded, and the next
day the men were sent me.

I was so much recovered that I was able to be on
my feet again, and sending a messenger to the cabin,
requested the honor of an interview with Donna
Maria. Soon I knocked on her door, and she received me graciously.

" Madam," said I, " I know how this captivity
has been preying upon your mind, and believe me
when I say that it has been a distress to me that
we have had to detain you. But if you will trust
yourself to me, I will do my best to land you and
your daughter at Nombre de Dios, or at least at
such near distance that you can reach your home

safely. This I promise to do upon the honor of a gentleman of England."

"You have been most courteous and brave, sir," she returned, "and I know the truth of an Englishman is like unto a vow made at the Holy shrine — so I do trust myself and what is dearest to me into your keeping, and may the blessed saints reward you, more than I can — for well do I know that such service as you tender cannot be priced or boughten."

The little girl had been looking up in my face as her mother spoke, and suddenly she stepped forward at a whisper from Donna Maria and extended her hand. Though she was but a child, she did this with such grace and lack of shyness, that I was the one embarrassed, and bending down I kissed her little fingers as if she had been a lady of the land.

"Oh, sir," went on Donna Maria. "I never will forget what you have done for us; your speech is like that of my countrymen. You have been in our beautiful country?"

"My mother was a Spanish lady, madam, but my father English — I have lived in Spain."

"My husband's cousin married an Englishman," said Donna Maria; "his name I have forgotten, but hers was the same as mine, and the same as my husband's — de Valdez."

"De Valdez!" cried I.

"But you knew it?" she replied, somewhat puzzled

by my exclamation. "You knew who it was you were befriending?"

"You are the wife of the Governor, I know, madam, but his name I had not been told. 'Tis one I have often heard in Spain."

When I left the cabin I was wrapped in my thoughts. I knew enough of my mother's family to feel sure that, wonderful as it may seem, the governor whose treasure house we had come so near sacking was my own blood relation! and that the little girl whom I had saved from the shark was none less than my cousin. And this I had found out without betraying myself— for what would have been the use? None, surely. But again I marvelled at the smallness of the world and wondered what was to come of it all.

Thomas Moone met me at the after-gangway. I had chosen him to be the fourth one of the crew that was to start with me on the venturesome expedition to the gates of the Spanish stronghold. We were to leave the following morning before daylight.

"Master Maunsell," said Moone, touching his cap, "the lady in the cabin told me this belonged to you, and bade me deliver it safe in your hands as soon as you were up and about."

I took the pouch he offered, and thrust it in my doublet, knowing by the very feel of it what it con-

tained.   But Thomas Moone might have been
handing me a bag of beechnuts so far as one could
tell from the expression of his face.

    *   *   *   *   *   *   *   *

We had been three days and nights sailing to the
southward down the coast — keeping so close that
at any minute we might have sought shelter in one
of the numerous harbors or inlets ; but as good
fortune had it we saw no sail.

Donna Maria and the little girl occupied a small
tent or canopy in the stern, that we had made out
of sailcloth, and they were as comfortable as our
limited quarters could make them.   The shallop
sailed well, (it was not the same in which we had
met disaster,) and I knew that we were nearing the
headland that guarded the entrance to Nombre de
Dios.   It was our plan to reach there at night, and
landing our passengers, retrace our course as speedily as might be.

What the Captain would say of the whole affair,
I did not care to think, but I determined not to let
Hixon get the blame, and to take it on myself.

Moone, who had been at the tiller, having the
trick following mine, spoke to me as we bowled
along before the northeast wind.

" Methinks, Master Maunsell," said he, gazing
over his shoulder, " that there is a blow coming eftsoon, and as to the best of my reckoning, we are but

ten leagues from the harbor, 'tis best to put in somewhere and make fast till nightfall. Mind yon clouds,
sir; there's wind in them or I miss my hazard."

I looked out to seaward and saw the great masses
of vapor standing up against the sea-line. White
and feathery they were on top, dark and cavernous
below. Higher and higher they mounted; lifting
and changing into hills and valleys, building into
mountains, and castles, and turrets, and as the sun
was setting, the edges tinged with pink and red and
the purple shadows deepened and lengthened. It was
as if we were watching the Creator at work on another
and more beautiful world.

Donna Maria, with whom I had been talking
before silence had fallen on us all, spoke at last.

"Señor," she said, "I've seen such sights before;
and though beautiful, it warns us to seek shelter. —
Mark, sir, the wind goes down, and that is sign
enough."

Even as she spoke the breeze had died away, and
the sails slatted uselessly from one side to the other.
To the west of us about a mile away was the wooded
coast, to our eyes unbroken, — and in the stillness
we could hear the thundering of the surf as it broke on
some outlying reefs. The air was full of portent.

Moone, who was a good sailor, looked at me and
shook his head.

"Best get to oars," he said; "go in and search

for a harbor; there may be an inlet where you see yon dark opening in the forest."

So we took in the sails, and getting out the heavy sweeps, turned in towards shore. We kept well to the north of the surf, where the waves crested white and angry, and running in on the tops of the surges we made good speed. At first it looked as if we were all in for a wetting, if not a capsize, for the sea was dashing with great force against the narrow beach. But it was as Moone had said; there was a narrow opening much like the one where we had first built our fort, and inside a goodly sized harbor.

But imagine our surprise when we had once entered, to see a large vessel with three masts, close to shore at the farther end! I was for turning about and putting to sea despite the threatening weather, but Robert Minicy, whose eyes were sharp as a hawk's, called out that there was something strange about the way the craft was lying.

"She's abandoned or a wrack," he said, pointing. "Mark ye her shrouds and her sails in tatters."

As we came closer, we saw that he spoke true. The ship lay stranded and high, close against the bank. Her topmasts were gone, and as if to add to the forsaken appearance, a number of large birds flew up from their perch on her after-rail.

We were close under her stern, when the carpenter gave vent to an exclamation : —

"The pest ship on the sands."

"Oddslife! she's English-built, by the Word!" he cried. "Come, let's aboard and find out the meaning of it."

The sides were too steep to clamber up, but running our shallop to the sand, we found we could reach her decks from the bank. Leaving Donna Maria and the little girl alone, we hurriedly climbed over the bulwarks.

The sight forbade long tarrying! It did not require our eyes alone to tell us that death claimed all there ahead of us. She was full of the bones of dead men! A great skeleton in a rusty breast-plate grinned at us from the foot of the mainmast, and several huddled, shrunken figures lay about on hammock cloths.

"The fever!" cried Moone; "she's a pest ship. Hold! look there!"

He pointed to the arch of the poop deck, that extended well forward, and there in red letters was painted, "Perivil of Hull."

"One of Garret's vessels," cried Minicy. "Poor luckless devils!"

There came to my mind the message writ on the leaden plate at the Isle of Pheasants. So this was the fate of one party of adventurers. What would ours be?

"God's love! let's ashore," suddenly put in Moone. "I've had enow."

I was nothing loath, for the sight, let alone the laden air, was taking me hard, but Minicy demurred.

"An have I your permission," he said to me, "I will go below and see if there is aught to be learned."

Without staying for an answer he hurried down the ladder — where I would not have gone for all the gold and silver in the mines.

We went over the side and waited on shore, and presently he appeared.

"She has been sacked," he said. "Either our friends the Maroons or the Dons have been here; she's been cleaned to the backbone like a herring."

So we left the vessel and joined Donna Maria, who had been wondering what had kept us such a time away. In a few words I told of the ship being filled with the fever, but said nothing of the dead men.

The storm was about to break over us, and we had scarce time to prepare a shelter up on the hillside (where a well-defined path led to an old camping ground) before the rain fell in ropes, and the wind rising afterwards, it blew a great gale with thunder and lightning until nearly dawn. We were glad to be on shore, for after the storm it grew so cold that we unearthed some dry wood and built a fire. But Robert Minicy did a strange bit of work that night. All alone during the storm, he had been on board the luckless *Perivil of Hull*, and unassisted he had given each poor bundle of bones a sailor's burial over the side where the water was three fathoms deep even at the ebb.

The storm cleared away at last, and before the sun was fairly up we took to the oars and rowed out of the harbor, leaving the pest ship on the sands, and beyond her we could see rising the smoke of the smouldering fire from our camping-place. There was a fine breeze outside, and spreading sails, we bore off to the south, glad to be away from the unhappy bay. Late in the afternoon we made the headland, and knew that we were at the end of our cruise; so we crept inshore and drew up on the beach. Not a league away was the Isla de Basto-mentos, and there we intended to land that night, for any one of the gardeners would take Donna de Valdez up the harbor to the town.

* * * * * * * *

"Before we part, Donna Maria," said I, "there is one thing left for me to do."

"And what is that, señor? Surely you and your brave men have done enough."

"This," I returned shortly — "to return to you your property." And I handed to her the bag of pearls.

"Nay," she cried, her voice breaking, "you must keep them; they are yours."

"Now," said I, "you make small return for the value of our service."

We were drifting in, lying on our oars, off the little collection of huts where lived the gardeners and their slaves. Our voyage was made.

The moon was shining so brightly that one could almost have read a book. Donna Maria poured the shining jewels into her lap. The men had watched me closely when I had returned them to her, and they were wondering what was coming. Quickly she picked out the largest pearl and extended it to Thomas Moone. He shook his head. Then she tried Smith the armorer; he did likewise. Robert Minicy bowed with an attempt at gallantry. So she turned to Roger Truman. The poor lad was trembling. He looked at me, and it was so pitiful that I had hard work to prevent my tongue from telling him to take it. What would the value of that pearl have meant to the old folks at Portsmouth! The lady saw him wavering, and somehow it reminded me of the way a stranger might cajole a child to take a dainty; she smiled at him and stretched forth her hand. I should have said nothing had they each accepted, for they had been laid under no agreement. But the lad closed his eyes.

"Tell her no, sir," he said appealingly.

"Master Maunsell," broke in Minicy, "prythee inform her ladyship that we ask for naught, nor

did we look for reward.   We may rob the king of
Spain, — we are common English seamen, — but
we take no largesse when we risk out lives for
women or for children.   We have as much pride as
our leaders.   Thank God for that!"

"If I may make bold," suggested Moone, "had
not the lady best set foot on shore" (our keel was
grating on the sand); "for this is scarce a safe place
for us."   He looked up the bay, where the lights
of the town twinkled in the distance.

"Hold you here," I returned, "until I fetch some
one from the huts."   So I jumped into the bushes,
and hastening forward roused out an old man, who
was at first dazed with fright and sleep.   But I succeeded in getting it into his head that a large reward
awaited him if he would convey a lady to the Governor's palace that night, and he followed me to the
shore.

Little Donna Inez was awakened, and soon her
mother and I were facing one another on the moon-
lit beach, she holding her daughter's hand.

"Señor," said Donna de Valdez, "Heaven grant
that we meet again, and that I can repay you in
some kind.   My heart is too full for mere words
now, but I will pray for you and your brave men
every night.   My husband, too, will learn from me
what it means to know and trust Englishmen.   God
grant our countries will never be at open war."

I kissed her hand; the little girl turned up her face to me.

"See, she would say farewell," said the mother; and so, bending, I kissed the little girl on her forehead.

Then I turned back to the boat. Not a word was spoken as we pushed off.

Before daylight we were under full sail up the coast.

I had not the smallest chance of ever seeing Donna Maria or her daughter again, I thought; forgetting how often it had been proved to me that the world was small.

CHAPTER XXIV

THE RETURN OF THE WANDERERS

HAD we arrived at Fort Diego two hours later than we did, we would have missed a sight that none who were witnesses of are ever likely to forget; I never shall forget it so long as I live. But to go on with the tale:— Hixon's relief at seeing us was manifest; he had done much brooding over our long absence, but even the relief he felt at our safe return did not prevent him from giving vent to his feelings of despair.

Not a sign had come from the expedition, and although the sickness was in most part over, the men were in a bad state from lack of employment and despondency. I told him of how we had found Garret's vessel stranded, a monument of disaster, and the effect did not encourage our hopes in regard to ourselves.

While we were thus discoursing there rose a great shout from a group of men gathered about one of the cook tents near the gate. Jumping to our feet, half fearing trouble, we looked up the hill. There, a half mile away, we saw the glitter of steel through

239

the leaves, and, a minute later, a band of men came
out into the open. One glance was enough.
Heaven be praised! the figure leading was no other
than the Captain! I knew him by the swing of
his shoulders, and his short, sturdy steps. Behind
him trailed his followers, and then came a few blacks
bringing up the rear, but they carried no loads, and
our men also had nothing in their hands. With a
cheer we ran to meet them, all welcome and eagerness, but as we got near we halted, and for an instant
none on either side spoke a single word. Such a
gaunt, weary-legged lot never reached a journey's
end. Many were half naked, their scratched skins
showing through the rents in their clothing; all
were limping and bare-footed, and Drake himself
had but one boot that was whole. My eye sought
for my Uncle Alleyn. I should scarcely have known
him had he not spoken. He had grown to be almost an old man; so thin and worn was he, that
his fingers were like a bird's talons, and his eyes,
sunk back in his head, gleamed like a wild man's.
The Maroons, who accompanied the force, were in
better fettle, but they too showed the effects of
hardship.

"Food for these men!" cried Drake. "How
now, my masters; we're not ghosts, and we have
need of filling. Make haste, for we're nigh
famished."

"Our meal has just been made ready in the big tent," replied Hixon.   "But thank God there is more than plenty."

"Then, let's at it," Drake replied, "and have some fetched me, too, for, by the Dragon, I'm naught but ribs and backbone."

The men made a mad rush for the tent from which came the smoke and the savor of cooking, and the Captain, with my uncle and the rest of the gentlemen, made for the headquarters, where wine and bread were set before them.   And when they had refreshed themselves, we heard their tale.

It was but a repeating of former ill-fortune.   The Maroon leader had proved faithful to his word.   He had shown them from the top of a high hill the great stretching waters of the unknown sea to the westward, and there on his bended knees did Francis Drake (when he had descended from a tall tree he had climbed, and from which both oceans were visible), make solemn vow.   It was, if God gave him strength and life, to sail with an English deck beneath him in those waters that had known heretofore but Spanish keels.

Pedro, the chief, had so won Drake's good opinion that the Captain had spent the greater part of the westward journey in endeavoring to convert him from idolatry and false doctrine, and he had been baptized to our faith.   And this was the only fruit

R

of the expedition — the saving of a soul — for
though they had found the mule trains at the point
designated by our allies, our archers had prematurely
disclosed themselves, with the result that warning
was given, a guard had been hurried out from
Panama, and our forces had to retreat empty-handed.
They had fought their way through a Spanish town,
sword in hand, and since then had wandered in the
forest, with nothing but what they could pick up on
their march to keep body and soul together.

"And now," asked Hixon, when the story had
been finished, "what is there next to do?"

"There is still Nombre de Dios," quoth Drake,
who, warmed by food and wine, was beginning to
look up again. And at this we all sat there and
gazed at one another. Out of the seventy-three
souls we were now scarcely thirty left, and these
weak and ill-found in everything. Not only was
the desire to fight killed in some, but apparently the
very desire to live — so looked they, at all events.
But the Captain smiled bravely round at us and
poured his wine. "Hark'ee all to me," he began.
"I am neither mad or cajoling you, but this voyage
will be made! yea, despite all that has gone before
— we will live to see it through. Come, lift up your
hearts, good sirs. Remember ye are Englishmen!
Two days' resting, and we are out to sea, and before
two months we are off for England! — then there

will be a merry time in Plymouth, I can promise ye
—every one with gold jingling in his pouch, and
trinkets galore for his sweetheart ! "

Lifting his goblet of wine, he pledged " Success "
the same as a man might pledge a boon companion
present at a gathering.

Again followed the strange infusion of new
spirits.   Not many minutes and we were in gay
talk, big with hope, — counting our fishes ere we
baited hook — as was our wont when Drake had
spoken.

So busy were we during the next few days (it was
a week before we were ready to sail) that I found
no chance to tell Captain Francis of what I had
done with our fair prisoner, and her absence was
not remarked until the time came for setting the
Spaniards ashore, which we did, turning Fort Diego
over to them if they chose to take it.   But, Drake
securing promise of safe escort for them from the
Maroons, they started under the command of the
treacherous Don Lopez for a Spanish stronghold
up the coast.   Drake was not pleased with my doings
in regard to freeing our hostages, I could see that, and
warned me against women and their wiles, as if he
were not the most human creature in the world and
as prone as any man to the influence of a bright eye
and a smile.   But enough of this; what I had done
had no bearing upon the success or failure of our

expedition, and was of future concern to no one but myself, and, as will be shown, my softness of heart was not wasted, nor was it forgotten either, which is more to the point.

Under the Captain's orders the frigate (where the prisoners had been) was sunk, and in the *Pacha* and pinnaces we embarked, bidding farewell to our friends, the Maroons, only for a time, as they were pledged to meet us within a fortnight down the coast in the direction of Nombre de Dios. Several who had some experience as sailors embarked with us. I was chosen to go with our leader, who had taken the *Minion* under his command. Although Pedro, the black chief, had, with fruitless effort, urged Captain Drake to proceed forthwith and attack the hacienda of a rich Spaniard, a mine owner in Veragua, Drake thought best to set out boldly against the treasure frigates that were gathering at this time in the harbor of Nombre de Dios.

On the third day as we cruised to the southwestward we sighted a sail, and as we carried a fair wind we made up to her and without any fighting worthy the name we took her. This was the beginning of the turn of the tide in our affairs. Fortune began to smile on us. The vessel proved to be a frigate late from Veragua, and she had on board some treasure and a pilot from Genoa who was willing to serve any one for reward. He promised, without

asking, to take us back to the port he had just
quitted, where there was a large frigate with over a
million in gold on board just ready to sail. So
nothing loath, back we went, and boldly sailed in
for the harbor. But they were forewarned, and
made such a show of defence with so many cannon
mounted and ready (the frigate warped in between
two great forts), that we had to give up the idea of
attack, and sailing out again we joined the other
pinnace at the place we had appointed. John
Oxenham, who was in command, had been even
more fortunate than we had been, for he had taken
such a fine new vessel that the Captain, upon seeing
her, declared she was just the one for his purpose.
So he determined to keep her and to fit her out
with cannon and culverins as a floating fortress to
which we might retreat if need be, when hard
pressed, as she was victualled for a three months'
voyage. Our little force was thus again divided,
and keeping close together we sailed down the coast
for the harbor where, as had been agreed, we were to
meet Pedro and his Maroons. But we were to have
another bit of good fortune happen us, upon which
we had not counted, ere we joined our faithful allies.

*   *   *   *   *   *   *   *

It was dusk of evening and we were but three
leagues off shore when the lookout at the masthead

of the frigate shouted down that a large vessel was in sight, up to windward, heading in, so that unless she changed her course to avoid us she would cross our bows shortly after nightfall. Soon she was in plain sight, and her conduct was such that we were puzzled to make out her purpose; certes it was not to run away, for on she came with all sail set, as if to meet us ere we could put in to shore. Gently we fanned along in the light wind, and darkness closed down when she was yet a league or more distant, but still nearing, and we could surely count the time when she would be within hailing.

The *Minion* discovered her first, and then the stranger was close aboard and taking in her mainsail to stop her headway.

" We are in for a fight," said Drake, half grinning, [we were all prepared for it, steel out and matches burning,] and he shouted for the other two vessels to close in. We were about to cheer — the way Englishmen begin any such business — when there came a hail and a loud voice spoke in French, asking if " Captain Francis Drake was in command ? "

" 'Tis a trick ! " cried the Captain, not answering, and putting down the helm we almost grated along the big ship's side.

" They are Spaniards ! " cried another voice from the stranger in French again, and with a frightened ring to it. " Spaniards ! Make ready to fire ! "

Our cannoneers had sighted their pieces, and
there might have been a pretty slaughtering had
I not jumped to my feet and cried, at top lung, —

" 'Tis Captain Drake!   Who are you?"

" Hold!" came the answer.   " Friends."

There we lay but a pike's length distance, for a
moment's silence.   Then the Captain himself took a
hand.

" I am Francis Drake," he cried, with his broad
Devonshire twang.   " What want you?"

" This is Captain William Testu of the *Fran-
coiyse de Grace*," replied the voice that had first
spoken.   " For six weeks I have been seeking you.
Do me the honor to come on board, and fear no
treachery."

With that a big man could be seen standing upon
the bulwarks, a plain mark for any of our archers
— but he feared naught, and stood stretching his
hand out to us.   Another moment and we had
drifted together and Captain Drake stepped boldly
over the stranger's side.

Everything that had been said had been heard on
board the other pinnace and the frigate, and the
marvel was that up to the first hail there had been
no shot exchanged.   Now all anxiety and in deep
wonder we lay there waiting.

CHAPTER XXV

THE RAID

IT seemed more than an hour that we waited, all anxiety to hear from the stranger, not knowing what had become of the Captain, and half in fear of his safety, but doubtless this very uncertainty made the minutes drag so.

Great, verily, was our relief when we heard Drake's voice calling to us that all was well, and asking certain of us to come on board. This we did, and were presented to the Frenchman and his officers. Down in the cabin, as we sat over our wine, we learned much of the goings on in the world from which we had been so long apart. Captain Le Testu proved to be a Huguenot (as many had correctly guessed), and he told us of the great massacre of the eve of Saint Bartholomew, a tale so horrible that we were struck at first speechless, and could but gaze at one another, and at the speaker with loud beating hearts. But when he had finished there rose a chorused groan. A bond of sympathy was formed at once between us and the little wandering band of Huguenots, a bond that was stronger than any written compact; and when Le Testu proposed that he should cast in his lot with ours there was not a dissenting voice, all welcomed him as if he were a friend and countryman.

There were thus seventy well-found sailor men added to our forces, and the terms were easy — share and share alike, in any venture that might befall. As our new friends were in need of water and supplies, we put in shore together at the place, where, true to his word, we found Pedro the Maroon in waiting, and there we lay for five days tuning up, and planning out the work ahead of us. Captain Drake, as usual with him, had his own way in all things, so there was no conflict as to design or leadership. Health and spirits had returned to us, and there were no more forebodings or doleful prophecies.

*　　*　　*　　*　　*　　*　　*　　*

I cannot conceive how it was that, during all the time that the Spaniards must have known of our being near to them, they had fitted out no expedition against us. There were rumors of such, but we saw no evidence that they wished at any time to turn aggressors. Perhaps they were too busy growing rich to take notice of our presence, or in their way — which is a national habit — had put all off to

that fleeting morrow that never comes in the Spanish calendar.   Suffice it, we were unmolested in our
retreat, and continued our preparations until everything was ready to the last detail, the men had been
picked out who were best suited for the purpose,
and the forces divided into three divisions.   There
were twenty men from Testu's ship under command
of their captain, fifteen of us under Drake, and a
band of twenty-five black men led by Pedro.   The
plan was to leave both ships with a strong guard in
the secret harbor, and, with the frigate we had taken
and the two pinnaces, proceed to the Rio Francisco
and thence inland on foot to a point on the Panama
road, not far from the big gate of Nombre de Dios,
where the trail enters the city.   Pedro knew every
lane and pathway that led through the woods, and
with his followers was to act as guide and vanguard.

When we reached the river we found that a wide
shallow prevented the frigate's entrance, so that much
against our will we were forced to leave her and push
up with our two pinnaces alone — they being
crowded to the gunwales and giving us little room
for carrying off any goods or treasures that we might
be fortunate enough to gather.

A small force of French and English was left at
the Headlands, and with a wind to help us we entered the current of the stream.   Good progress

we made and, landing in the evening, again a boat-
guard was detailed and given instruction to put out
with the pinnaces and join the frigate, but to return,
on their lives, on the fourth day and await us. I was
in great fear that I should be left behind with them,
but to my joy I was chosen to land, and declared to
myself that I would stay as close to the Captain as
a hound to his master, to be ready to obey any
order, and to win a word from him if possible.   It
took all of the next day — hard travelling — to cover
the seven leagues that lay between the river and the
highway, but at dusk the word came back that we
had reached our journey's end, and we lay down to
sleep, tired and footsore, but hopeful and confident.

Not long were we suffered to remain at rest, for
the Captain, accompanied by Pedro and Diego (who
knew every foot of ground) stirred us out, and we
were moved a mile or so to the eastward and sta-
tioned on the crest of a hill up which the trail from
the west wound its way, looking like a white ribbon
stretching below us in the bright moonlight.   On
our other hand lay the town with its two spires lifting above the trees.   I could mark where was the
Plaza and where the fort, and the roof of the governor's palace could be plainly seen, also the treasure
house down by the shore.   All was calm and peaceful;
a few lights showed here and there on the water-
front and at the big gate, out of which the populace

had hastened upon the occasion of our previous attack. A slight breeze sprung up from seaward in the early morning hours, and as we settled ourselves, and the rustle and movement ceased, we could hear a distant sound of hammering, and now and then the creaking of block and tackle showing that not all of the Spaniards were asleep.

Hixon, who lay close to me, whispered in my ear : —

"Hearken," said he. "They're at work in the shipyards, and needs must be pressing when the Dons turn night into day."

"The fleet must be near to sailing," put in my Uncle Alleyn, at my elbow. "Who can tell how many poor English shipwrights are at work down there in chains — slaves for life — and better dead than living." He went on bitterly at some length, when from the shelter of some bushes across the road a calm voice broke in upon him.

"Come, hold thy tongue and strain thy ears, friend Alleyn, for we are all listening; not to thee, or to the town, but for the sound of hoofs, and thy talk would outdin a charge of horse. So hold quiet, we beseech thee."

My uncle clapped a stopper on his tongue, for it was Captain Drake who had spoken, and for a few moments nothing was heard, and the air that had brought to us the notes from the city died

away. Suddenly from the westward came a faint
strain of music like unto the wind among guitar
strings.

"I hear bells!" said some one, off down the line,
out loud; and then followed the sound of stirring
midst the leaves, men were heard awakening others
roughly, there were mumbled curses and back talk.
A sword clinked loudly against a scabbard.

But the Captain commanded silence and threatened
the first who broke it with the halter, and all was
still as a grave once more. I could hear the beating of my own heart plainly.

But now the faint and fitful music had grown to
a chorused tinkling; a continuous chiming was welling up from the vale beneath us.

"The recuas!" whispered my uncle, teeth
a-chatter, "the mules are coming, we're on time."
He drew his fingernail along his sword-edge.

Parting the leaves about my head, I cautiously
peered forth. Ay! there they were: winding,
single file, out of woods on the slope below. At
the head rode a shrouded figure on a gray horse, and
here and there I could make out more men, some
walking, some astride the little mules. There must
have been two hundred laden animals in the long
procession. Now, as each could carry twice what a
man could, think upon the value of that convoy!

On they came! the leader had mounted the hill;

a little more and we could hear his horse's hoofs, and now he must have passed the outposts and must be well within our lines! Yet no one stirred. The man on the horse must have been asleep; his head was bowed forward, his great plumed hat hid his face, and the great cloak he wore was wrapped tightly over his shoulders. As he drew abreast of us, I heard Drake give an order in a loud whisper, as one might to a bloodhound straining in the slip leash.

"At him, my brave Bob!" said he.

A figure leapt like a beast of prey out of the bushes, full six foot clear of the ground was the leap, and the Spaniard, ere he was awake perhaps, tumbled with a smothered groan almost at my feet. Minicy was atop of him, and some one grasped the horse's bridle.

The business had been done so quickly that I could scarce believe I was not dreaming, but there was the boatswain standing above the now silent figure on the ground, and I saw him bend and wipe his dagger on the Spaniard's cloak.

"Good work, sir, eh?" he said in prideful tones, looking up at me.

But there was too much doing for reply, and I grant that just then I was filled with the horror of the suddenness of death, and half drew back. The leading mule at the halt had laid him down and, not

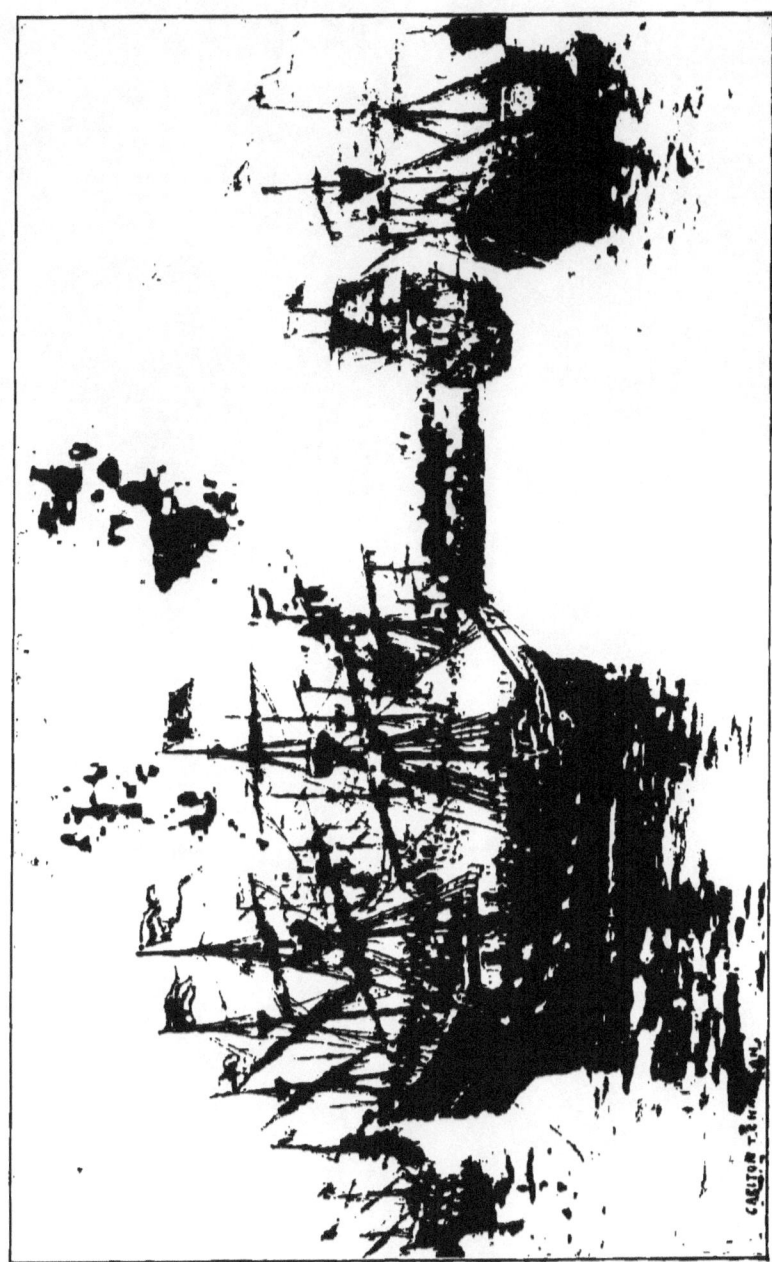

"The fight began to be warm."

knowing this was the custom, I was most surprised when the second did the same, and then with a jingling of their bells the whole long line sank to the ground. It was like witchcraft!

But all at once there came a cry followed by the crash of steel against steel, a pistol shot, and then with a rush we broke cover and ran down the line. Half way up the hill I could see a mass of struggling figures — here was some tall fighting — and with my blood running hot, I tried to get into it, but our own men outnumbered the Spaniards at this point and they were soon borne down.

"Back to the end of the train," cried Captain Drake, emerging from the crowd. "Don't let them turn away from us!"

With a few others I started down the road again at top speed, and from the hill crest I saw twenty or thirty armed men come charging up to meet us. The way was narrow; on each side rose the thick mass of shrubs and vines (in which one could not swing a weapon), and the mules blocked the centre of the trail. Turning, I shouted for assistance to meet this onslaught, for there were with me but one English archer, two Frenchmen, and four blacks. I saw it was Captain Testu who was at my side; but my cry had been heard. Coming on the jump were Drake and Oxenham, Minicy, Ceely, Diego, my uncle, and Thomas Moone. So by the time the crash came the odds were not so great against us. All of the Spaniards were on foot, with the exception of a big man who, mounted on a saddle-mule, was urging on the others from the rear. It was a confused fight that followed, and I ever marvel that I could recall so much of it to my mind.

The headmost Spaniard stumbled over a recumbent mule, and ran straight upon my point; the second, who was, to say the least, more cautious, got his bearings well, and crossed swords with Testu, who stood like a fencer, wrist up, and foot advanced. There were a few passes and nothing done, and then the men from behind us crowding up, one of them ran full tilt against the Frenchman, so that he staggered to one side, and the Spaniard, with a cry of triumph, ran him through the lungs ere he could gain his balance. Not long did he live to gloat over it. The archer let fly a shaft, at six foot distance, that went into his heart up to the goose feathers, and he fell dead. No front could be maintained; soon we were hand to hand in a long struggling line, and for half a minute I fought with one of Testu's men, ere either of us found our mistake. There was no quarter asked or given; it was cut and thrust to left and right, and wicked stabbing on the ground, and I can affirm that the Dons fought bravely. The recua guards were all picked men and ably led; but many of our fellows had joined us, and soon there were but four Spaniards left, the man on the mule and three stout fellows who stood beside him. Boldly and undismayed by our numbers they charged upon us. We were in such confusion (being mixed up with the pack animals, who were now badly frightened, and letting go their heels) that for an instant the handful beat us back.

But the Captain and Minicy forged to the front. I had been pushed to the opposite side of the road and could not get to them, but I saw the Captain cleave a swart pikeman almost to his middle, and the man on the mule at that moment rode our leader down. Now I have spoken of Drake's great strength, but what he did I should have said no mortal man could do; for as he rose he grasped the beast's forelegs and tossed him and the rider to the ground. Minicy, with that tiger spring of his, leaped across the fallen mule. I saw his dagger flash three times, and the last of our enemy was done for. If there were others we did not see them; the field was ours! We had more wealth at our command than we could count, let alone carry off. The men were befuddled with good-fortune.

Nothing but Drake's calm voice held back our lads from cheering, and naught but his influence restored order to our ranks. For a few minutes the

party was like to go to pieces, and fall to quarrelling.
The packs were torn from the animals, and a great
babble of French and English curses rose.   Quoits
and ingots of gold and silver were scattered hither
and thither on the road.   The men would pick them
up and cast them down again, searching for the
largest; some were trying to lead the animals off into
the brush, where they were stalled ere they had
gone ten feet.   But our leader was here, there, and
everywhere, cajoling, laughing, and threatening,
using the flat of his bloody sword at times, and on
one occasion tumbling a huge Frenchman to the
earth with a fist blow.   And soon he had them in
some order, and when all were listening, he por-
tioned out as much as each man could stagger with,
and forming us into line, with Pedro and Diego
leading, we made off through the forest, retracing
our journey of the night before.

For two miles we kept going, but the burdens
were too great for men to last under, and as they
had begun to lighten themselves, either by design or
because of fatigue, a halt was called, and in the land-
crab holes and at the foot of a great tree we hid
a half ton or more of treasure.

The Maroons, who had held aloof from the struggle for possession that had come nigh to undoing
us, bore their part of the burden, and we pressed
ahead, Robert Minicy carrying a loaded pack-saddle,

on his shoulders, that must have weighed more than
he did, and refusing to allow any one to help him.
The wounded, of whom we had a dozen, bore up
bravely, and I heard neither groans nor complaining
— there was but one thought in the minds of all.
The Captain's words had come true — our voyage
was made; we were rich men all!

There was a sad scene that I must tell of in this
speaking: The French captain was grievously
wounded. We had lost but one killed, and he a
black man, but Le Testu was in much suffering.
Tho' borne on a litter, he would choke up with the
blood in his throat, and at last he called Captain
Drake to him and declared that another mile would
kill him; he begged to be left behind to die in
lesser agony. At first Drake would hear naught of
it; but seeing at last that the words were true, he
gave in, and the Maroons made a hasty bower in
which we laid the poor fellow, and he was grateful.
Two of his men chose to stay with him, and Drake
promised to send back and get them all as soon as
we had reached our ship and were ready to set sail.
We left with them all the provisions we could spare,
enough for a week or more, and bidding them farewell, we pressed ahead.

It rained and stormed all that night, but we rested
not, and the next day we kept at it, although weak
and soaked, and dog tired — but no one shirked.

Our voyage was made, and each man encouraged his neighbor with cheerful words. So at last we came to the river but a furlong from the spot where we had disembarked; we threw our packs upon the bank, and sank down on our knees and gave thanks to God. But alas! all was soon black again, and our future changed to a dismal prospect. There were no pinnaces in sight, no welcome sails to greet us, and there, to our dismay, we saw in the offing beyond the headlands — five vessels — all Spanish, as plain as could be, and to all appearance waiting there on guard!

CHAPTER XXIV

THE CAPTAIN SAVES US

AT the Captain's orders we all hurried back into the bushes, and there sat us down; alas, a sorrowful party, for to all minds there was but one meaning given to the presence of the Spanish vessels — our own had been sunk or captured!

I can see it all now in my mind's eye — the deep dejection into which we had been cast, making of each man's face a tablet, on which was written anger or despair! Poor Roger Truman lay sprawling on the dank ground, his head buried in his arms, racked by silent sobs; Minicy, seated on his saddle-bags, and gray with the exhaustion of the journey and his labors — stabbing with his dagger at the earth — surly mutterings on his lips; the Frenchmen casting angry glances at our Captain, who stood leaning with one hand against a tree-trunk — the other parting the bushes while he gazed out at the Spanish sails. Beside each man as he sat there rested a fortune — quoits and ingots of gold and silver tied together, like bunches of small fagots, with rope, bowstrings and withes — and it all seemed to mock us. I would have exchanged my precious burden on the spot for a loaf of wheaten bread, for we had been on half rations all that day, and there was scarce a mouthful left apiece. We were separated by leagues and leagues of trackless forest from our supplies, with a raging river in front, and an angry enemy behind us on our trail — besides, I could fairly smell the fever rising from the swamps. Things were, as friend Hixon had once remarked before, " at a dule ebb with us." To save my life I could think of naught that could be done — it was a hard blow. I had been thinking of England, of which I had seen so little, and heard so much; I had been building to myself all the great things that were to happen when I had entered into mine own; how my Uncle Alleyn should share with me equal part in everything I had; how I should reward Moone, and Minicy, and the rest of them — Roger Truman should have a tidy coaster, and his old father, Giles, as fine a span of draught horses as could be bought for money — for, to my foolish mind, to be an English baronet meant to command all wealth untold. Now this dream was dashed, and something my Uncle Alleyn said at the very moment sent my spirits still lower, for it betrayed that, to his thinking, all hope was gone.

"My dear son," said he, in his paternal way, coming over to me, " if in after years you reach home, and by that I mean English soil, make your way to Temple Court in London, and ask for one Edmund Pattesworth, a barrister; tell him thy tale, show him this ring that I now give thee, and inform him that the key and complement of the paper that he holds—giving the warrants and title-deeds—will be found in the framing of the portrait of thy father, done by Holbein and now at Highcourt on the great staircase; and so much it resembleth thee— for thy father was but little older at the time 'twas painted — that any court would uphold thy claim on the very strength of it alone. Thou hast thy father's brow, and eyes, and coloring, and with a beard to thy chin might pass for his very self come back to life — 'twas this resemblance that first convinced me." He went on sorrowfully — "When the Spaniards take us, I shall get short shrift; and I shall be glad of it, for never will I wear chains again if I can earn death, I promise thee."

What I might have made in reply to this speech my uncle never knew, for just then the Captain turned, and his face was lit by the same fearless smile he always wore in times of danger — that smile that seemed to say, "Ho! this is nothing; trust to me, I will fetch ye through all your troubles, my children; fear naught." To me 'twas as if he spoke these very words as I looked at him. But what his lips did say was as follows : —

"List to me, all ye! The ships are rounding yonder headland, and from the set of their canvas, they are not cruising, or on the watch for us, but have come a long way, with a voyage ahead." He turned again, and then talked to us as he kept outlooking. "See!" cried he; "the foremost squares away! My brave lads, our vessels are not taken, or we would have found the Spaniards at anchor here below us!"

We had risen to our feet and saw for ourselves that the ships were standing broad off the land; then the wind freshening they came about on the other tack, and the headland hid them from sight. But something had to be done. There was no use waiting on the shore for the river to run dry, and the men's minds must be kept busy so that they would not fall to thinking of their plight.

The swift current of the stream was filled with drift-wood, — great trunks and limbs of trees, — and under the Captain's direction many of them were hauled inshore, where the water was scarce up to a man's middle. The Captain kept saying, as he encouraged us: —

"Build me a raft that will float me, and I will put out and fetch in the pinnaces; for by the Faith I cherish they are safe somewhere hidden up the coast. Methinks I know the very place," and he described it to us as if he could see the missing ves-

sels, promising the crews a raking over for failing to
be at the proper rendezvous.

After four hours' work a floating platform had
been made that would support a few men, and a
rough steering gear added by which it could be
managed. But it was a crazy affair, with only a
biscuit bag for a sail, and it appeared like to come
to pieces if it should once get in a seaway. Nothing
daunted, the Captain called for volunteers, and I fain
believe that he could have had all of us, for none I
saw held back. I begged that he might take me,
but he declared he wished but able seamen, as there
was no room for officers; so he chose John Smith,
Diego, and two Frenchmen, and we pushed the frail
craft out into the river. Before the current had
swept them out of earshot he delivered himself of
the following speech, that I well remember: —

"An it please God," said he, firmly, "that I put
my foot safely on board my frigate, I will, God willing, by one means or other, get ye all aboard, despite of all the Spaniards in the Indies."

We gave him a cheer, and watched anxiously as
the raft, now feeling both the wind and stream, swept
down to the river mouth. Ever and anon the waves
would wash it clean, so that the Captain and the crew
would be up to their armpits, and once or twice we
thought them gone. But God had them in His keeping, and once free of the tide-rips and the chop, the

raft drifted out of sight to the northward, and after a prayer for their safety, we settled down to waiting, much more content and mostly hopeful. In my heart I felt certain that Captain Francis would return. But during the afternoon a great wind rose, with much rain; and, soaked to the bone, hungry, and disconsolate, we feared the approaching night.

But rapture filled our hearts when we saw (as it was just light enough to see) the two pinnaces beating up the river, and we knew the Captain had made good his word. Even the worst grumblers now began to aver that they had always said that Drake would win us out, and that "never once had they doubted,"—and much more of the like—so that it was worth smiling at. Great was the welcome the little vessels got as they dropped anchor close inshore, and great was the joy with which we loaded them down with our heavy burdens that from being so much dross had turned into gold and silver again. At dawn of the next day we set sail.

The tale of the raft voyage I got from Smith, the armorer, and it may be told very shortly. For three leagues they were drenched with every surge, and like to die of thirst, when they saw the pinnaces pounding in the sea, trying to beat up against the wind that was urging the raft along. Then they saw the sails, that had been such welcome sights, turn and put in to land. So the raft was beached, and in the doing of it, the Captain plunged into the surf after one of the Frenchmen at great risk, else he would have drowned. The land gained, they pushed to the north, and found the pinnaces close in at anchor, with part of their crews on the beach gathered about a fire. And Drake here called on the others to follow him, and set to running toward the astonished group as if the Spaniards were at his back, nor did he answer a question put to him until they were all on board the pinnaces (thinking the rest of us were lost, and in great fright); then, after listening to the explanation of why they were so tardy, and rating them soundly, the Captain put his hand into his doublet, and bringing forth a quoit of gold, said, "Thank God, now lads our voyage is made, and safe and sound the rest are waiting." At which there was such great rejoicing that the sailors would have embraced him. But he, taking charge of the vessels, ordered up anchor, crowded on all sail and made in, as I have told, to our rescue.

The amount of our booty, added to our weight, loaded the pinnaces down well in the water, and we were glad to find the frigate, and with her we passed unmolested up the coast to the place where we had left the ships in hiding. There we found them, and right glad were the crews to see us, and their eyes bulged as they saw the treasures we had to show.

On the deck of the French ship the profits were divided, and strange to say there was no complaining. Gold and silver meant very little to Pedro, the Maroon — he had not included them in his idolatry; so Drake gave to him the old *Pacha*, and transferred his flag and belongings to the frigate. He also gave to Pedro a carved jewelled sword that had been given him by the unfortunate Le Testu, who said he had it of Admiral Coligny, who was killed in the massacre, as we all remember.

But do not think that our Captain was one to abandon a distressed companion while there was a chance to succor him. No, no! he was hot for leading a party, and with all our force retracing our trail until we had found the wounded Frenchman and his faithful sailors, and incidentally gathered in the buried treasures we had left in the forest.

But it was judged that he had already exposed himself too much, and at a meeting it was petitioned that Oxenham should lead the party and the Captain stay for once on board the ship.

I went with the ones who landed, and not a sign of life did we see (we would have lost ourselves but for Diego, the trail was so overgrown) until we heard a cry from a tree, and looking up, found one of the Frenchmen. He had a sorry tale to tell. Le Testu and his companion had been taken prisoners, and he had scarcely escaped with his life.

We looked for the hidden plunder, but our pond had been fished; the Spaniards had been beforehand with us, and we could recover but thirteen bars of silver and seven quoits of gold.   Back to the ship we went and told how the ground had been digged up, and how 'twas a wonder that the Dons had missed anything.

So there was nothing to do now, but to sail for home! We were rich men! Not a common sea scullion but could afford a ring to his finger and a twelfth month idling ashore if he chose; and as for the young gentlemen adventurers, those who were left, they had more than enow to pay their debts, and had gained a credit that might last a lifetime. No one talked of aught else but England now, and it was to our surprise we found that the Captain had determined on one more venture. Nothing more nor less than to exchange our frigate for a larger one, or capture one for a consort, and to shake off the French vessel that clung to us like a leech.   So, willy-nilly, with all sail set and pennants and ancients all flying in the wind, — a great Cross of St. George rolling at our masthead, — did we put into the mouth of the Magdalena River, and we held on past Cartagena, within plain sight of the town, and so close that we could see the crowds on the water's edge.   But no vessel came out to do us battle, and out again we went, and at the river mouth we ran across a frigate much larger than our own.

So then, Drake, on seeing her, exclaimed aloud in his joy, saying she was "a gift from Heaven." But not a gift, properly speaking; for she outnumbered us in men and firearms, and did not give over without a fight. Such was our marvellous fortune, however, that, owing to the bursting of a Spanish demi-cannon, the crew became confused, and led by the Captain and Minicy, we boarded and took her without loss of life, having but four men wounded. We sent the prisoners into Cartagena in their shallops, and with our prize made for one of our hidden coves, where we shifted cargoes and revictualled her. Drake gave the faithful pinnaces to Pedro.

Then off at last for merry England, our two vessels ballasted with gold and silver, and our hearts with feathers. It took us but twenty-three days' sailing (the finest weather one could wish for) after taking a departure from the Cape of Florida until we sighted the Isles of Scilly. Sunday, the ninth day of August, dawned fair and clear, and off over lee bow was Plymouth Hoe. Seventy-three men had sailed out but little above a year ago; thirty now returned. As we entered the harbor we could hear the bells summoning the folk to church, and down on the deck we knelt and gave thanks to God. Our voyage was made, and on this account the lives of many of us were to undergo great changes.

" We boarded and took her."

CHAPTER XXVII

THE PARTING OF THE COMPANY

MONDAY morning we were gathered about a table in the big guest room of " The Bell and Anchor," talking over the doings of the day before, and reviewing the happenings of the year gone by, as if it were a time far remote, belonging to another life and age. Surely surroundings separate us from the past more than do long years, and from the midst of strange places we can see ourselves in our past actions without being hampered by the nearness of familiar scenes. There were missing from the group, that had met there on the first occasion (when Mr. Blandford had presented me), but Drake's two brothers, who lay near one another in the far-distant graveyard on the hillside. But now the Captain, Ellis Hixon, Fletcher, and Nichols, Oxenham, Ceely, my Uncle Alleyn, and myself, were grouped about the board, and at the head sat none less than my old friend and patron, who had chanced to be in Plymouth on a visit at the time of our arrival.

Mr. Blandford was telling us how the news of

Drake being in harbor had reached the churches on
the yesternoon, and how the congregations had left
their prayers, and one minister cut short his exhort-
ing, to rush to the water front to bid us welcome
home.   Truly it had been a strange sight, and in
many ways a sad one, for we had brought back with
us a list of our forty dead, and most of them hailed
from Plymouth town.   There were widows and
orphans, childless parents, and many broken-hearted
lasses who heard the news, but the grief of these
had been swallowed up in the rejoicing of the friends
of those who had returned.   The news of our wealth
had been so multiplied that nothing there was in the
town that we might not have had for the asking.
And as success will have its own success, our fellows owned the streets and tap-rooms, and from
below us, as we sat there in the tavern, we could
hear the sound of a great carousing and the roaring
of a lusty sea chorus led by the voice of Smith the
armorer.

  "Thy lads possess the place, Captain Francis,"
laughed Mr. Blandford, "and I doubt not that if
you wished it, a fleet could be manned from this
port that would leave no shipping in the harbor,
provided that thou wouldst take command and start
for the Spanish Main again.   If our Spanish cousins
would so allow you," he added.

Captain Drake half smiled and lifted his shoulders. There had been some news told him, that was not entirely comforting, about the doings at court, and he turned to the subject that was in his mind.

"So the Spanish Minister has complained of me," he said, "and the Queen listens? 'Tis a strange world, and in royal circles it beseemeth best never to let one hand know what the other doeth. I should not be surprised if I should soon be quartered at the Tower, and I can well imagine that King Philip would admire to whistle the march to which I might walk to the block. I am not anxious for a martyrdom, my masters, nor do I wish to see our treasures turned back into the coffers of His Catholic Majesty. Therefore I crave that this very day the shareholders hold meeting, and profits be divided, and I wot not but some of it will show at Windsor Castle in a jewel or two." ('Twas an open secret that some court pin money had found its way into our expedition.) "However," Drake went on, "I know of a place where I can rest and take mine ease in safety, and as for the rest of you, no harm will come nigh you. 'Tis against me alone that the Spaniards treasure ill. Now mark me, my good friends, while I say that which is neither threat nor boasting: Some day I will singe the beard of the King of Spain in a right lawful fashion. I will have him on his knees, night and morning, invoking all

T

his saints to work my destruction. He says that I
have been a thorn in his royal flesh, but I will prove
a twisting blade in his vitals some day. — Please God
that we will all live to see it. — And I pledge the
hope it cometh soon."

At this moment there was a loud cheer from
below stairs, as if our hardy mariners in the tap-
room had heard his very words, and had set the
rafters ringing with approval.

" Thy bold fellows are with thee, Captain !
Hearken to that !" laughed Mr. Blandford. Then
he turned to me and spoke in a low tone. "What
Captain Francis says is right. I doubt not but that
he will soon be forced into hiding, for the Queen's
counsellors seem set on making a friendly feeling
between our court and that of Spain. King Philip
is sore and exceeding wroth against Drake and the
rest who have cast their net in his waters. But
sooner or later we will be at war, as the Captain
hath said, for this false state of things cannot last
long, and is unreasonable."

This speech set my Uncle Alleyn off with a slam
of his great fist on the table, and soon no one else
could make himself heard or listened to, such a roar
of imprecations and bitter words fell from my uncle's
lips. Poor man, he was the gentlest, softest-hearted
creature on earth, but a flaunt of the flag of Spain,
and he craved blood. We sat and listened, and I

fear some smiled. Mr. Blandford was aghast at the
storm that he had set loose, but Drake, as was usual
with him, took command of affairs.

"Wilt thou plead my cause from Temple Bar,
Master Maunsell?" he asked. "I owe thee thanks,
for I could not speak thus without losing my temper
or my head, and so I pledge thee. For in all sin-
cerity thy words are true."

Now my uncle was a modest man, and praise he
could not stand, so he quieted down, saying that he
was neither orator nor pleader, but one who on
occasion voiced his thoughts.

"And those of all this company," added Drake.
"So fill your cups, my masters, and we drink confusion to England's enemies."

After all were seated, Mr. Blandford asked me of
my plans, and I told him that I was going first to
Portsmouth with Roger Truman to see my old
friends, his parents, and then I told him of my
plans and prospects, and that my uncle was going
to be my sponsor, and that our hopes ran high.
Mr. Blandford related to the company how he had
found me sitting on Portsmouth quay so desolate,
and I told of my adventure with the cross-grained
landlord, and how he had treated me.

"Surely thou hast brought mine host something
from the Spanish Main," laughed Mr. Blandford
when I described how I had vowed to pay him back.

"Yes," said I, "that I have — a pair of boots, and I shall present them to him without removing them."

"Good!" cried my uncle. "Grant I shall be there to witness the presentation."

The meeting was here broken in upon by a faint knocking on the door, and when it was opened there stood Robert Minicy — and it was the first time that honest Rob was ever frightened, I am sure. He twisted his cap in his hands and looked, for all the world, like a poacher brought before a magistrate.

"Captain Drake and gentlemen," quoth he at last, his glib tongue faltering. "The men below have made me the bearer of a message, a request, and if I be too bold, forgive me. I am in hope that the Captain will be gracious."

"What is it, lad? Speak out," said Drake.

"Would you honor us by stepping below, sir, and saying a few words to us that are gathered there?" replied Minicy, gaining boldness. "'Tis the whole company, sir, met for a purpose, and your presence is most humbly asked."

"Certes," said Drake. "These gentlemen will come with me."

So downstairs we went, and, to our surprise, found the lower floor filled with our fellow-adventurers. They greeted us with cheers, and Drake was about to step forward and begin to make his address, when he saw that Thomas Moone, the carpenter, was standing on a bench, waving to the rest to be silent. As soon as the noise ceased (there was none who seemed the worse for liquor), Moone went on and spoke.

"The men whom Captain Drake brought back with him," he began, "are here gathered to do him honor. We have formed a guild, and do now declare that we shall be called 'Drake's Yeomen,' and should the Captain desire the services of me or all, he has but to pass the word, and we will follow him into battle, exile, or prison, for we have heard the words that are on the gossips' tongues. And, furthermore, all our share of profits from our voyage we place at his disposal should he have need of such; and in these words I have expressed the hearty will of all.—Have I not, lads?" He finished, and a second great cheer rose.

We all looked at Captain Francis. His eyes were swimming and his voice was a-tremble with the depth of his feeling.

"Brave lads and followers, my gallant yeomen. I am grateful to ye all; I can but thank ye. Should there a time come when I again have a deck 'neath my feet and a venture over the bows, be it a quest for gold or glory, may ye be with me then. Some heard my vow when my eyes first rested on the

great western ocean.   Again here I repeat it: God
willing, I will sail there 'neath the Cross of Saint
George, and God grant ye will be with me."

It was a short speech, but the words sank deep in
my heart as they did in every one's, and it was
Drake's farewell in a measure, for he did not address
us at any length thereafter.

When the division had been made, I was surprised and dazed at that amount which fell to me.
But what gave me greater joy was the fact that the
Captain took me by the hand as my uncle and I
went over the vessel's side, and told me that in his
house, or on his ship, there would always be a place
for me.

"I think, lad," said Francis Drake, "the sea has
bewitched thee, and that though thy acres may be
broad and the Queen make a lord of thee, some day
thou wilt be sailing again."

"Then may I sail with thee as captain," I replied; "count me one of thy yeomen, and shouldst
thou need me, — send."

With that we parted, and it was many a long
year before again I heard the Captain's trumpet
voice giving his orders or saw his eye alight at the
nearness of tall fighting.   But when I did see such
again 'twas a picture that will be a life memory —
but of all that more anon.

*   *   *   *   *   *   *   *

We stopped at Portsmouth — my uncle and I taking passage with Roger Truman and Mr. Blandford in one of the latter's coasting-vessels, and my desire to stop there proved to be one of the best gifts of good fortune that I can reckon in my life. I had spent a day and a night with the Trumans and left Roger to comfort them (trusting that Giles soon trounced some of the airs and graces out of him, but the lad was young). And I had paid my debt to the landlord and refreshed his memory by repeating his own words with slight changes, delivering my present to him with the saying: " That for thee, from Sir Matthew Maunsell," and I trust it was a lesson to him in courtesy.

But — and it seemeth wonderful that I have not plumped out with it before — the bit of good fortune was my finding of no less a person than Martha Warrell — poor Martha, grown fairly gray with worry, had come hither from London as soon as she had found the deception that my aunt had put upon her, for Lady Katharine had told her that I was already on board the vessel to which I had watched them row from the shore on that unhappy day.

Martha now kept a small stand and sold pasties to the sailors on the wharves, and there she was, neat as a bodkin, dealing out a brown pasty to a knotty-faced old sailor, who stowed it away as if it were the last one out o' port. When the good woman heard me call her name and saw me, she turned deathly white, and then with a jump she upset her stand, almost capsized her customer, and there we were in each other's arms!

That very afternoon we were all off for London, as my Uncle Alleyn was anxious to hear what Mr. Pattesworth, the lawyer, would have to say when he heard my story and Martha's. Of all unselfish people I can say that my uncle was the most gifted in self-forgetfulness. To his companionship, counsel, and watchfulness I owe more than I ever repaid, I fear.

But now for a hurried passing over of things that though of interest to me, concern myself alone, and are of no moment to any one else. So the next chapter will but chronicle a great leap of time and tell of how once more I took up the threads of my early life.

CHAPTER XXVIII

TIME PASSES

I T seems a far cry back to the old marauding days in the Spanish Main; I can scarce believe that it was I ("the lank callow youth") who survived the fights and lived through the adversities. Verily it is a long leap that I have taken in my story! So many things have happened that I am near to despairing of ever shortening them into the compass of a few words. I almost fear to take up my pen lest it run away with me and lead me to gossip of myself and my surroundings at such great length that it would be wearisome indeed for a reader to attempt to follow me. But let me try to weave a seam that will connect all that has gone before with what there is to follow. And so I make haste to plunge once more into the middle of my story.

It is the year 1587 and early in the month of April. A dreary winter it had been, with much snow and bad weather, and there was great suffering among the poor people in town and country. I had been, most of the time, in London, and if I say

it myself, who should not, had made somewhat of a
success at court. This was not due to any natural
gifts that I might have possessed, but began through
the influence of my old Captain, who was now Sir
Francis, knighted on the deck of his own vessel by
Her Majesty's gracious order. Well indeed do I
remember the day when the *Golden Hind* was warped
up the river and lay between the crowded banks off
the water gate of the Tower. A brilliant picture
the scene made, with the crowding boats bedecked
in colors and streamers and the people shouting
with one great voice as the Queen put out from
shore in her golden barge and made the vessel side.
Never had I thought our leader a graceful man, but
he bowed with the courtliness of one used to such
gatherings and proceedings, and the Queen turning
to Marchaumont asked him to give the accolade,
and this the French courtier did. With Drake's own
sword he touched him between the shoulders, and
our Captain rose " Sir Francis," but unchanged for
all of his title, and the same bold seaman that he
had ever been, as he was to prove ere many years.

I had not been on the wonderful voyage around
the globe when Captain Drake had redeemed his
vow and ploughed the western ocean with an English
keel; for the fact was, that it was just at this time
that I was coming of age, and it was necessary that
I should be in England to undertake the care of the

estates which are now mine at this writing. But alas! for my dreams of wealth, the lands were much impoverished, the old keep at Highcourt was almost crumbling to ruins, and the tenants had so long held possession of the outlying farms that it was not without difficulty that I could prove title. In order to avoid trouble and to save myself the reputation of being a hard man, I had remitted all arrears of rents, and though, at last, I had broad acres enough to ride across and call mine own, it was years before I received return more than sufficient to keep and clothe me and to support a small household that consisted of my Uncle Alleyn, Martha Warrell, and a few old servitors who had known my father.

My uncle, kind, faithful friend that he was to me, had been ailing and in bad health since our return from the Indies, yet he would have started with Drake and his adventurers when they sailed out toward the setting sun bound for the great unknown, and we may say little fearing it. I can remember this day also, for I had gone to Plymouth with my uncle, and there we had gathered almost the same company that before had sat about the board at "The Bell and Anchor." Of course there were others who were strangers to me, but Ceely and Fletcher, Mr. Blandford (hale and hearty and fourscore) and Thomas Moone, were there (honest Thomas had

now been promoted, and commanded a ship of his
own, the smallest one of the fleet).   And as the time
for parting drew near, I would fain have stowed myself away in one of the vessel's holds and bartered
my inheritance for the mere chance of sharing in the
ventures.   But Drake would hear none of it, nor,
on account of my uncle's health (he had a continuous hacking cough that troubled him), would he
allow him to be one of the company, although the
old gentleman recalled to him the compact of the
Guild, and claimed that as one of the yeomen, he
should not be denied; but, as I say, they sailed without us, and I can see them now, the fair wind waft-
ing them out, the flagship leading, — a fine sight with
her painted galleries, — and the red Cross of St.
George on her great mainsail.

It was at Plymouth that I had first met Thomas
Doughty, and I can frankly state that this man had
not impressed me, except as a glib-tongued person,
whose delightful manners and graceful speech covered a sly nature and a deceitful heart.   It is not
here place for me to touch upon the troubles that
this man brought upon the company from the outset, nor is it meet that I should express opinion as
to the fate that he met with being his just deserts or
not; 'tis all a matter of public record, and can be
read there.   It seems to me that Drake hath made
a right proper defence for his behavior, and thus I

leave it. But 'tis passing my judgment how the Captain, usually so keen in reading the minds and hearts of men, had let this one so deceive him. But if I do not take care, I shall be working myself into a controversy, and as my opinions are worth nothing, it would be wasting time.

After the rendering of the verdict by the Court of Chancery in my favor, I returned to Northamptonshire and entered into possession. My uncle was in high dudgeon over the way affairs had been mismanaged, for Highcourt, in the days of Queen Mary, had been a show place worth travelling to see; now the gardens were overrun with weeds, the great hall reeked with dampness and decay, and, sad to relate, many valued articles of furniture and such like, were missing from the places in which my uncle had remembered leaving them. But the old portrait had been found upon the staircase, and it had played a part of some importance in the trial, for, as my Uncle Alleyn said; now that I had a beard to my chin I might have sat for it myself, and my resemblance to my father had been so strong, that many of the old people who remembered him, had cried out upon first seeing me, as if I were a ghost, or he himself restored to earth again.

As time went on, and there came no news of the vessels that had followed in the track of Magellan, people 'gan to despair of ever seeing Drake or his yeomen again. Thomas Moone's ship had returned, and the tales which he had brought of head winds, storms, and wreck, ere they had fairly started, did not bring comfort to the Captain's friends, but I knew and felt an assurance in my heart that some day the good people of Plymouth would awaken to find Drake lying at anchor in the harbor; and though I held to these opinions, as the months grew into years, I could find none to hope with me. But one day it all came true, as is a matter of history, and Drake returned with such a tale to tell that even the wildest imaginings could not outdo it, and I speak true when I say that I would give five years of what remains to me of life, to have lived and gone through with their adventures; not for the reason that they returned laden with spoil and riches past all reckoning, but for the satisfaction it would have been to have had crowded into one's existence the memory of those pulsing days. It would fill a book and be a different story to tell the whole of the affair or even to recount what had happened during their absence. The chronicle of their voyage has been written and printed, but Drake had found things to be in much the same position that they were when he had returned from his first voyage. The court was in a turmoil of intrigue. My Lord Burghley, honest and great man, though he ever was, was not entirely above it, as is shown plainly in his efforts

to disrupt the expedition, and in his dealings with
the aforesaid Doughty, who was but his tool to my
mind.   Our good Queen had no easy hand to play;
for though bound at the time with the policy of the
Prime Minister, who was, as usual, anxious to avoid
an open war with Spain, she could not yet be forget-
ful of the promises of support she had made to
Drake, nor heedless of the fact that it was in a measure due to her effort and her money that the raids
and the voyages had been successful.   So it was in
part her profits that filled the holds of the vessels
that had carried the first Englishmen around the
world.   I say this because it was to all intents
openly avowed by her when she welcomed Drake
at London and made a knight of him.

It was my great sorrow that my uncle had not
lived to be a witness to this ceremony, but he had
died a week after the announcement of Drake's
safe return, and in his death I suffered a great loss,
and I found many to grieve with me — God rest
him for a kind unselfish friend !

From Drake's own lips did I hear the story that
his nephew has so well recorded in his book yclept
" Sir Francis Drake Revived," and in the recounting I learned of the fate of Diego and Robert Minicy, — how the first had suffered death by the arrows
of the savage islanders and how the latter had died
fighting a squadron of Spanish horse, singlehanded,

— by all the Powers ! — when he might have escaped
had he chose to run, but forsooth, 'twas not Robert's
way of doing things.   He had ever chosen to show
his sword's point rather than his heels.

Drake was a wealthy man now and held great influence.   He numbered among his friends the most
powerful of all the younger set that had gathered
themselves at court.   He had but to whistle and
he could have had about him gallant swords and
great fortunes at any time, and when it was again
whispered that he was at the back of an expedition
being formed, intended to proceed on a peaceful
mission to support the claims of English merchants,
he could have taken an army with him.   It was
known that all talk of a short cruise in the Bay of
Biscay or the eastern waters was but a subterfuge,
and meant another forage into King Philip's possession in the west, for it was being organized at
about the time the plate fleet would set sail for
Spain.   None less than my friend Sir Philip Sidney
(the best and bravest) offered himself, and as at this
time I was pledged to him and his fortune, — for he
and I grew dear to one another, — I urged him on.
Drake would have welcomed me, I know, and
would have been glad of my company, but Sir
Philip's rank in England, and the position he had
taken, precluded all idea of obtaining the Queen's
permission, so we were both stopped and called

back to London by royal command, on the very eve
of Sir Francis's sailing.   And this voyage, too, is a
matter of history, and recorded in prose and verse.
'Twas a strange condition of affairs — that without
being at open war, an English fleet could capture
and hold for ransom all the points that Spain then
held in the New World, for Drake took in succes-
sion Santiago and Cartagena, and many places of
minor importance, and had it not been for the fevers
that decimated his forces, he would have taken
Havana, and this done, it would have meant farewell to the vaunted Spanish influence.

When he returned this time to England, it had
begun to look as if the continued singeing of the
royal beard had at last aroused the royal mind to
a point of action.   King Philip's remonstrances to
England (most just they were, we must admit) had
been passed over so repeatedly, that the war cloud
was surely rising.   Our merchantmen, who, strange
to say, had continued to call at the ports of Spain,
began to suffer from the royal ire.   Many seamen
were held for the Inquisition or huddled to the
galleys, while vessels and cargoes were seized and
taken by force.   Soon, in all but name, a state of
war existed.   It was just at this pass that it became
certain that King Philip was making preparations
to revenge the great losses he had received.   England was waiting and counting no odds.

It seems a trite matter to recount all this, for it lives in the minds of many, but rumors were rife of the gathering of great numbers of men and ships, and it was loudly whispered that as soon as all was ready to his liking, the Spanish king would launch them forth, and descend upon our coasts.

Now during the time that all this was taking place, I, myself, had been leading an uneventful, and in all truth, an idle life, for my fortunes had improved until (had I so willed it) I might have drifted out my existence in all peace and comfort. But now and again I would be seized by the old desire for action and excitement, and the yearly change from the gay life at court to the quiet rest of the country would begin to pall upon my spirit. I had reached the age of one and thirty, I had remained unmarried, which, for some reason, was a scandal to my friends, but need not be accounted for, and if I had chronicled all that had come under my observation, some of it might be reckoned as interesting; but it has no place here, and so I let it pass.

An outline in this short fashion is but an interlude, sufficient, mayhap, to carry the reader on — if he has had patience to follow, to the point where again I tread a deck, and draw sword. Follow me to the day when I again smell powder smoke and join the yeomen and serve my old leader who was the same

bold spirit as ever — more cautious, more expe-
rienced, but the same! And how I was aroused out
of myself, was as follows: Drake I had met at
court, where now he was a favorite, and then he had
reproached me with two things: first, that I had not
taken unto myself a wife as he had, and secondly, that
he perceived that ease and comfort were like to
destroy my worth in the world, and that I was no
longer in the first blush of youth. And his words
I took to heart, so much so, that subsequently, when
I heard that once more he was to lead the expedition,
destined in all good faith this time for Spanish
coasts, I solicited from him permission to go in
e'en the humblest capacity, provided that I should
be allowed to serve in his command. To my great
joy, I received a message, the very words of which
set my veins tingling, and aroused in me the spirit
and ambition that had so long lain dormant, and I
look upon this as truly the turning-point in my
career, and if I have gained success (as certainly I
have gained happiness), to the Captain's words and
incentive given me, I lay them both. And so, with
further confidence that what I have to say is worth
listening to, and in the hope that it will be followed
(I will be pardoned for its discontinuance, I trust
also), embark once more with me.

There was no talk of anything else but war, and
to tell the truth, it was glad news. When I reached

Plymouth, the town was agog with tales of Spanish cruelty and clamorings for revenge. The streets were crowded with sailor-men, and Drake's vessels lay anchored in the harbor. The Guild was out in force. Many bronze-featured seamen did I recognize, and glad was I when the news came that the Admiral was in town (Captain now no longer), and I received orders to join his ship, brought to me by Roger Truman, who had grown to be such a huge hairy creature that I scarce knew him. He told me the old folks were alive and well.

CHAPTER XXIX

I WAS seated with Admiral Drake on the upper deck of the *Elizabeth Bonaventure*, his old flagship, a grand craft, strong as oak and iron, and built by a past master. Close to hand lay the royal vessel *Golden Lion*, of five hundred and fifty tons, now flying the flag of William Borough, the Vice-Admiral, and beyond were two tiny pinnaces the *Spy* and the *Makeshift*, in command of Captains Clifford and Bostocke. Still beyond were more vessels: among them the *Rainbow*, a new type constructed for swiftness and close sailing on the wind. She was commanded by Captain Bellingham, a brave sailor, and one up to his duties — ready and willing to fight, but cautious, sure-minded in beginning. To the eastward a large vessel was getting up her foresail in preparation of making a shift of her anchorage. Drake pointed his finger at her.

"There's the old *Dreadnaught*," said he, "and on board of her is Thomas Fenner. He's the stripe

of a sailor-man I like to have within signal distance
upon such an expedition as this is, Master Maunsell — I crave pardon, I should have said Sir
Matthew — "

I waved my hand. "Let it pass by," said I.
"Remember that I was once thy scrivener, Sir
Francis."

"Aye," was the return, "and before I had an
earthly possession save a few nailed planks, and a
sword — "

"And before you had received a certain stroke
on the shoulder," I added.

"Yes," answered Drake, pridefully, — "and now
I have land, and a castle, and might be idle."

"There have been some changes since we sailed
together, Admiral."

"Yea, and what puzzleth me is why thou didst
forsake thy calling; for if I have not been mistaken,
thou art made for a sailor-man."

"Many a time have I longed for the bound of
the deck beneath my feet, Admiral, and I have
dreamed of the wind and the rigging, and felt the
dash of the spray."

"When a man has that in his blood," said Drake,
laughing, "all the ease and pamper of court cannot
drive it hence. Honestly, 'tis pleasant to have thee
here with me again. I am treated well of Dame
Fortune. The sailing orders that I have also please

me right famously. If I had written them myself,
they could not be more to my liking. It is folly
to suppose that peace will long exist between Her
Majesty and the Spanish king, and I shall put a
stop to it — such a shilly-shally business. Truth !
we are well informed, for our spies have not been
idle if my Lord Burghley is deaf — but that aside,
what can the gathering of all the ships on the Spanish coasts mean but a descent upon our own ? And
this it is my purpose to prevent, and, God willing, I
shall do it. For I am instructed to impeach the
joining together of His Majesty's forces, that are
this moment scattered ; and hark'ee I have license
also to destroy the vessels in the Spanish havens !
We will set foot on the enemy's soil, Sir Matthew,
and carry the war into his own country."

"Hast thou written instructions on this point?"
I asked.

"Yea, and why not? Surely this is a queen's
expedition, a royal matter, and not arranged for plunder merely, 'tho' I wot not but that we may gather
some and in the performance of our duties ; otherwise," added he, "I should not have been able to
have enlisted the services of so many bold merchant-
men, for the Levanters sail without pay."

"Admiral," said I, "'tis my advice that we should
set sail immediately, for I heard it whispered ere I
left London, that Don Antonio, the Spanish Minis-

ter, was growing in favor again, and that my Lord Burghley had in contemplation changing the purpose of this fleet to an expedition against the plate ships only."

"I have received no such instructions — thanks be to God!"

"Doubtless not yet, but they are on their way; of that I'm certain."

Drake's brow grew furrowed. "And such instructions will prove to the liking of my second in command," said he. "Borough is a good sailor, but hampered too much by traditions of the royal service. As Clerk of the Ships, he has written rules for others to follow, and these he is in honor bound to keep, or else prove a nonconformer; but I fear me that we shall break several, yea — we are in danger of it." Then he paused again, and added seriously: "But what thou hast said has given me alarm — I would not for half my wealth, nay, all I now possess, receive restricting orders. If all my vessels were gathered I should up anchor now, within an hour, but there are still ten to come."

"How many wilt thou have at thy command, Admiral?" I asked.

"Sixteen ships and seven pinnaces," was the reply. "But I have warrant to impress any vessels of war to my service that I may meet with on the seas."

After some more talk, in which Drake told me of the expedition, he went below to his cabin, and I was left on deck. Truly it seemed a small force with which to descend upon the coasts of Spain, where we had been well informed they were in many ports more ships than in most of ours, and in Cadiz alone nigh to a hundred sail awaited orders; but I knew Sir Francis Drake of old. Before he was known at courts, odds had never turned him, and dangers but increased his determination. I had heard it rumored that there was some jealousy between Borough and himself. I knew that when we were once at sea Drake's will would be our only law, yet I greatly doubted if he should be allowed to put his favored plan into practice, for the news that I had told him was not mere hearsay, but gathered from trustworthy sources, and I marvelled greatly that he had received no orders countermanding those he held. I remembered, once before, how the Queen's messenger on his way to Plymouth, with papers that were to prevent Drake's sailing, had been stopped and robbed, and I had not been surprised at the time to hear that the robbers had been described as sailor-men, and I did not doubt that Drake, if he had so chosen, could have named them. I thought to myself that perhaps he might have accounted for his failure to hear from the Prime Minister in the present case. But it was not so, as I afterward found out; or at least it was not due to any plotting of his that he was not stopped.

It was the first of April, and late in the afternoon ; out in the Channel, I could see a number of white sails sweeping landward before the eastern wind, making evidently for Plymouth.   But to all appearances they were merchant ships, and as the officer of the deck had not remarked them, I said nothing, and soon one of the stewards came and told me that dinner was served in the cabin.

We were seated at the table when a quartermaster appeared at the doorway and, doffing his cap, saluted.

" A number of vessels have dropped anchor hard by us, Admiral Drake," said he, "and I am minded that they may be the Levant Company.   I could swear that the nearest is the old *Merchant Royal.*"

"Hurrah !" Drake cried.   "Let me see them head us now !"

We left our food steaming on our plates, and led by the Admiral himself, hurried up to deck.

" The Levant fleet, surely," cried the Admiral. " Here comes a boat, heading for us, and in a hurry from the way they're hitting up the stroke." Surely enough, the thrum of oars was heard, and in another moment an officer climbed the side.   He was none other than my old friend, Smith, armorer no longer, but now a captain in the merchant ser-

vice, and one who had offered himself for the undertaking.

"The Guild is gathering," cried Drake, as he
warmly grasped his hand, and in another moment
he was overwhelming him with questions. The
answers pleased him greatly: All the ships were
there, and save for a few desertions, that had taken
place at the last minute, they were armed and
equipped for service. Now as the vessels had been
built to protect themselves from the corsairs and
pirates that sailed in eastern waters, they differed
but little from Queen's ships, and needed but small
changing to turn from trade to war.

Ere midnight, every vessel of the fleet had been
informed that the orders were to sail at daybreak.
No one was allowed to go on shore, and when the
good people of Plymouth awoke next morn, save
for the coasting craft, the harbor was empty. We
were off on our voyage again. In two days after
our departure, the orders of which I had spoken
arrived, brought by a relation of Sir John Hawkins,
who had held command under Captain Wynter. In
pursuance of instructions, he had chartered a pinnace and put out after us, but he had not carried
much sail or been very intent upon his mission,
for he returned to England (with a fat prize, by the
way) and reported that Drake was beyond finding.

We met head winds for the first two days, but as

we beat about, we picked up two men-of-war of Lyme, and Drake stopping them, showed his papers, the authority of which they respected and followed us, thus bringing our forces up to twenty-five sail in all. On the evening of the eleventh, a great storm broke, and when day dawned there were but five ships in sight, so we headed for the Rock of Lisbon, where it had been agreed that we should gather should such contingency arise. It was five days before the last vessel reported, and then, in obedience to an order from the flagship, the captains came on board to hold counsel of war, as was prescribed by the Royal Navy rules, of which Admiral Borough was so close an observer. I could have told beforehand what the result would be. It reminded me of the old days on board the *Pacha*. There was but one voice heard, or at least listened to, by the Admiral, and that, needless to say, was his own. It was his plans that were to be followed, his word that was to rule, and he asked for neither advice or counsel upon the matter in hand, talking on, as if thinking aloud.

I shall never forget the look of consternation and dismay upon Borough's face as he listened. Even I, knowing the Admiral well, was somewhat taken back, for his proposition was nothing less than to sail boldly into Cadiz, put to the torch all the vessels belonging to the King of Spain that he could find there, and put to the sword all those who should oppose him.

Admiral Borough had something to say to all of this when he found room for speech, and he called attention to the fact that the harbor was guarded by the strong castle of Matagorda, and that no fleet could live beneath its guns.

" Mine can," said Drake, " and will, as you shall see, Admiral.   Is there aught else? "

" 'Tis full of the King's shipping, vessels mounting forty guns, and there is an army there on shore," urged Borough, breathlessly.   " And then the galleys, — you know how deadly galleys are in closed waters, — they would take us all — ships would be useless."

" The vessels are dismantled and unprepared, or at least made ready in the Spanish fashion," Drake returned, " and the army, as you say, is on shore, where they cannot molest us, and as for the galleys — Bah ! that for them !" he snapped his fingers.

" But the passages are dangerous and we would need a pilot.   Rashness is not leadership, Sir Francis," quoth Borough, who was the only man that had dared to raise his voice.

" I have piloted through worse passages that I knew less," returned Drake, " and despite your objections, there we go.   To your ships, gentlemen."   And this concluded the interview.

When all had left, Drake stretched his arms above his head and gave vent to a great sigh of relief, as a man does who has completed a task and eased his mind; then he laughed. "They little know us, Sir Matthew," he said, "or they would not ask such idle questions. You have sailed with me. Have I ever set hand to task and failed? Mark me this: We will give old Cadiz such a rousing show that it will make a day in Spanish history. Faith, I can see the King tearing his hair, and confounding me and the Evil One in a hodge-podge of prayer and cursing."

"Methinks he has not forgotten thy name, Sir Francis," I returned.

"No, nor do I intend he shall; and listen: I mean to give thy sword, Sir Matthew, a chance to prove if rusting at court has spoiled its temper. Ah, 'tis a pity thou hast wasted so much time in gallantry and fine speeches and fiddle-faddle."

"I was with Sir Philip at Zutphen," I returned, somewhat nettled at his words, "and there my sword was drawn."

"Yes, happily, and if reports are true, thou didst give good account of thyself, but 'twas a holiday from thy arduous labors of bending the knee and kissing the hand and trinketing," he returned, "and thou wert with soldiers."

"Then give me a chance, Admiral, to redeem

my position in thine eyes," I cried eagerly. "I shall prove I am a sailor."

"Fear not, thou shalt have it," he returned. "I have marked thee for some duties that will bring thee to notice."

There was a smile on his lips as he spake that did not gainsay his words, and again the old thrill came o'er me that I was wont to feel when fighting was ahead, and Drake was to lead us, and I do not doubt but that every yeoman of his, who had known him of yore, felt the same that night.

I began to realize that it was my old home that we were approaching. I remembered how in the days of my boyhood, when I had been part Spaniard, I had looked from the cliffs at Cadiz, down at the crowded harbor. I recalled the day when my mother had been married in the great cathedral, and also the day when I had set sail from the town with Martha Warrell on our voyage to France. It seemed to me that all our ventures in the Spanish Main were as naught compared with that ahead of us. To descend upon a city so large and powerful with such a little fleet seemed nothing short of madness, but then I recalled that the very name of Drake spelt wonders to be done, and during my watch on deck I reviewed the past and kept courage.

We were headed in, holding a steady course, and

I knew that once within sight of land there would
be no waiting.   Many brave fellows and many fine
ships would never see England again.   For it seemed
to me that we could not follow out the Captain's
plans without great loss, but as the old saying was
among Drake's yeomen, "God must be on our
side," for what really happened was little short of a
miracle indeed, as all who read or listen, know.   The
next morning we sighted land to the eastward of
the town of Lagos, and by three in the afternoon
we could see the cliffs of Cadiz.   Once more Borough came on board the flagship, and at the interview between himself and the Admiral I was not
present, but I can vouch for this, that when the
commander of the *Golden Lion* left to join his vessel,
he was in no sweet temper.

Drake was like unto a boy about to take part in
some cherished sport.   His blue eyes were dancing,
he hummed a tune beneath his breath, and once he
clapped me on the shoulder, in the old fashion of
his, and with joy in his accents, said, in a tone I so
well remember, "We have them on the hip, my
lad, and we'll have the flames dancing against the
sky to-night, and the Dons telling their beads."

But somehow I did not like what Borough had
said about the galleys.   Drake seemed to read my
mind, for he spake again: "We'll teach them a
trick or two, lad, and I doubt not that we'll convert

the Queen's officers to my way of thinking.   Pah !
Give me a wind and sailing-room enough to turn
in, and I fear not all the rowing boats that the King
of Spain can muster."

He turned and looked back at the fleet that was
gathering up in close order, according to his plan.
" Let them all stand by me," said he, " and I fear
not but what we will give Don Antonio a case of
ague that will shake him out of London."

We were now close into the mouth of the harbor,
and as we searched the headland, a puff of smoke
blew out against the face of the cliff, and then another and a third.

" The alarum guns ! " cried Drake.   " So ho, my
masters, you'll be ready for us."   With that he
descended to the waist and saw that the guns were
shotted and the men were at their posts.   Not a
sign of fear did I see visible, for, as usual, Drake
had filled every one with the invincible spirit that
belonged to him alone.   I had ceased to marvel
at it.

x

CHAPTER XXX

THE ATTACK

AS we came nearer to the mouth of the harbor, and the tall cliffs loomed broad off our bows, we could plainly see into what great consternation our approach had thrown the shipping. More alarum guns were sounded from the shore batteries, and helter-skelter the vessels lying farthest out were making sail to reach the inner harbor, beyond the point of Puntales. There was quiet water, guarded by many shoals. A mighty cutting of cables and much loss of ground tackle now began, for few waited to raise anchor in their haste.

On we came, disdaining to reply to the fire of the Matagorda that had opened on us ere we were within farthest range, and we could mark the balls falling into the water over half a mile ahead.

"'Struth! but they think to frighten us!" laughed the Admiral, at whose side I stood. "Powder and iron must be held cheap nowadays in Spain. 'Tis a woful waste, tut, tut! and were I the King I

should have the matter inquired into. But mayhap
they salute us. We will answer later."

Not a shot did we return until we were so close
that we could see the crews of the huddling vessels
hauling and pulling at the sheets and ropes, falling
over one another like boys scrambling for pennies.
Some of the larger craft were dismantled of sails and
rigging, and more than one was moored to a shear-
hulk, but their cables had been cut also, and everywhere they drifted helplessly about like wounded
water-fowl seeking a sanctuary. Drake pointed out
one of the largest, a great galleon whose sides bristled
with big cannon.

"There's a fine prize, worth rechristening!" he
said; "and by the Powers I will make thee master
of her, Sir Matthew, so thou wilt have a command
of thine own. We will give thee a trial."

It was like to his nature to speak thus, and I
thanked him as if he had handed me a present that
was, in all verity, his to give. At this moment a
cry arose from the forecastle : —

"The galleys! Here come the galleys!"

Drake mounted the rail, and I climbed up with
him. Out from the shelter of the castle and the
land batteries we could see, heading for us, the
dreaded row vessels. They made a threatening
array, with their long sweeps swinging together and
the foam gathering under each sharp fore foot.

The decks gleamed with naked steel, and lines of pikes and musquets crossed the bulwarks.

"Twelve! twelve, and none less!" cried Drake, finishing the count aloud. "Now, brother Borough, we will shatter one of thy precious precepts!" He looked back at the ship of the Vice-Admiral, and a curse broke from him as he saw that the *Golden Lion* had sighted the galleys and was holding off. "Let him look on, then!" he muttered. "Sooth! our friend is bold as a sheep — as fierce as a dormouse. I shall caution him!"

We had formed in line — four vessels — distant from each other about half bowshot, and, putting down the helm, we crossed the path of the enemy, still keeping silent, but every man standing tense and eager at the broadside pieces. So close were the galleys now that it seemed certain that some would reach us. Drake measured the distance with a glance, and then, with a trumpet voice, gave the order to fire. Following our example, every English ship burst into sheets of flame! Then how the cheering rose! The charge of the galleys crumbled — there was no excuse for missing at that range. Splinters flew, and the leaders, heaving round, backed water as if they had found a hidden shoal ahead. Before they could recover we found time to come about, and point-blank met them with the other broadside. 'Twas the same tale told again! They

waited for no more, but, plashing and struggling
madly like a school of whales driven on shallow
water, they made a wild rush for the shore.

"There!" cried Drake. "One more question is
at rest! and we will have no more skimpy galleys
built in England, but honest sailing-craft! How
terrors dissolve when we face them, Sir Matthew!
I shall be glad to see what Borough writes of
this. What say ye, my masters? Here is material
for a new chapter."

Two of the galleys had made in past the arm of
Puntales, the rest had reached the protection of the
land. Some were sinking, and nearly all were shattered. So we turned our attention to the big vessel
before referred to. The Levanters had begun to
hammer her wickedly, and despite her forty guns,
she was replying but feebly; her crew was to all
evidence not complete, and she was undermanned.
Ere long she was so galled that her flag was struck,
and the Admiral, turning to me, said cheerily : —

"Now, master, by my word, here's thy chance.
Take my boat and a half-score of men and gain possession, and, as I promised, she is thine! I am off
to head yonder vessels; 'tis a great day for England and the game is but begun !"

The boat was lowered, but by some mistake it
was one of the smaller ones, and held but five men
besides myself. The flagship was now before the

wind and running fast; there was no time to make
the change, and besides, the little shallop was like
to be dragged under. So Drake, hurrying me to
the gangway, bade me go, saying that we were sufficient for the work ahead, and ordering us to anchor
as soon as we had boarded the galleon.

"I will be back to join you," he concluded, "so
rest easy; 'tis good holding ground. We will finish
what we have begun, in the morning."

Ten hawks in a hen yard would have created less
disturbance than we had, by this time, raised in the
outer harbor. Three or four Spanish vessels were
in flames, a round dozen had been captured, and to
all appearances the others were like to sink each
other, in the wild scramble for safety. So far as I
could make out, no Queen's vessel had lost a
finger's width of paint. The Spanish cannon were
as harmless as if they had been hurling puddings.

The men pulling at the oars were laughing and
jeering. "Let us row in and take the castle," said
one.

"Faith, we might try it," added another. "And
it might please the Admiral."

"We are in fair likelihood of being taken ourselves, my lads," said I. "For yonder cometh a
galley to the rescue of our prize. Settle to your
work and stow your patter."

It was as I had told them. One of the galleys

had recovered sufficiently to observe the plight of
the big vessel, and had started on a dash to aid her.
We were so close now that I could read the name
on her stern, painted in great gold letters a foot
high. The *Argosy* she was called, and she shone
with metal work and was gay with red and yellow
colors. As we neared her, we saw a small boat put
off, and in her we counted eleven men in great haste
to leave; some were wounded. I afterward found
out that these were all she had on board — one
officer, two sailors, and the rest were artisans and
shore folk. But why were they so eager to leave
their ship? Surely, even if they had sighted us,
they must also have noticed the approach of the
galley!

Thinking it might be a ruse to lead us on, I called
for the men to stop rowing, and we drifted a minute;
but there were no signs of treachery from the forsaken craft, no movement or hail, and seeing that
we would lose her if we did not get on board quickly
and make sail (for if we dropped anchor where she
was, we would have had to fight the galley), I
ordered my fellows to give way lustily, and we
ranged alongside at her main chains. Standing up
and grasping them over my head, I was about
to order the rest to follow, when I was struck
speechless. The vessel suddenly appeared to draw
a great sigh, like some huge stricken animal! She

quivered as if my grasp had threatened and frightened her; a strange guddling sound came from her
hold. I could feel a gust of wind, like a cold
breath, blow from an open port, and then with sudden lurch she canted to larboard, and ere I could
let go the chains, she was toppling down upon us.
All her cannon broke from their lashings and roared
across the deck. It was so unearthly, and we were
so ill-prepared for anything of this sort, that it was
a wonder we did more than sit there and let the
huge vessel crush us. But I gave a shove with all
my might, and one of the bowmen, who had kept
to his oar, laid back in a heave, and we got from
under her gallery. But even then I saw that we
could not escape, and calling upon the others to
jump, I dove out, hoping to swim from under the
sinking hull, ere it should bear me down. But the
galleon must have righted somewhat, before her
decks burst open, as she plunged down, bow foremost, and nearly on an even keel. I had risen to the
surface, but the indraught of the water as she settled
was too much for me, and being almost within touching distance, down I was dragged in the whirlpool.

I held my breath and kept my senses, and soon I
was on an upward journey and kicked out lustily, but
I despaired of making it. Just as I was about to
give up, for my lungs and head were bursting, I
reached the surface where the water was yet bubbling

"The fight was now up near the entrance of the inner harbor."

and seething like a caldron. Not a trace of my boat's crew was there to be seen, but my own danger was not over, and I had my own safety to think on. Every now and then a spar or bit of planking would come shooting upward, and one big spar as it rose grazed my side, bruising my left arm and shoulder badly. Laying hold of the very piece that had come near to killing me, I paddled with my legs and free arm, and soon was out of the danger spot, upon which I breathed a prayer to God.

Nearby drifted a hulk badly shattered from our fire; she had no yards on her masts, and so far as appearances went, had been abandoned by her own people, and as yet had not been taken possession of by a prize crew. The fight was now up near the entrance of the inner harbor, where there was a great cannonading and the smoke and flames were rising. The galley that had caused me such uneasiness had turned and was crawling off to the southward. It would be sheer folly to try to swim after any of our vessels, and I determined to board the hulk; she lay with anchor down, I thought, and but a short distance from me. I was weak from my struggle, and the blow on my shoulder pained me so that I was glad to reach the vessel's gangway, where there hung a ladder, up which I struggled and almost fell upon the deck.

There was no one in sight, and everything

pointed to the idea that, like the *Argosy* (that was twice her size, by the way), she had been abandoned after a mere show of resistance. There was a pool of blood on the steps leading to the quarter-deck ; splinters and wreck were all about. She had been badly mauled by the broadsides that the Levanters had poured out on either hand as they passed.

Getting with some difficulty to my feet, I ran forward to see how the battle was going and to look for any sign of the boat's crew. The fight was waxing fiercer, and as it was growing dark, the red flames lit the shores and were reflected in the turbid waters. But I saw no sign of my unfortunate companions and did not doubt that they had been drowned, and that, poor wights, they now lay in the mud of the harbor bottom. Looking about me, I perceived that there was no Spanish vessel near, and thus considering myself safe and remembering the Admiral's promise to return, I forthwith began to explore my prize. She was about eighty tons' burthen and not new, evidently a cartel, packet, or merchant vessel — there were some newly made ports on each side in the waist, and I suppose that she was in the process of being transformed into a warship, which work we had interrupted. As I opened the door that led into the after-cabin under the break of the poop-deck, I hastily drew back — the place was full of smoke, and in the corner I could see a tongue of red flickering feebly against the deck beams. Moved by what I know not, I hastened to the mast, where I had observed a great barrel with water, and filling a steel head-piece that I found, I dashed back into the cabin. How long I fought the fire single handed I have no inkling, but at last I had it out and could breathe easy. As the smoke cleared away, there was just sufficient light coming in at the cabin windows to show that the apartment had been luxuriously furnished. There was an altar from which most of the rich trappings and cloths had been burned, two silver candlesticks, and a crucifix at the farther end. The cabin had evidently been intended for an ecclesiastic. There was the mark of the churchman everywhere visible. On the back of a chair hung a dark habit of the Order of St. Joseph, a string of heavy beads, and a rope girdle. "A floating monastery," said I to myself aloud, "and no one to attend vespers but myself." As I hurried out to the deck, intending to wash my hands and face free from the smoke and grime at the water butt, I stopped before I had taken two strides — there was the sound of rowing, a mighty churning, grinding roar of sweeps, close to hand on the starboard side. I peeped over the bulwarks. There came the Spanish galley! and as I saw her, I heard an officer give the order to cease at the oars. Back I ran into the cabin and closed the door.

CHAPTER XXXI

AT first I stood helpless, leaning against the mast that ran through the cabin, and trying to think what it would be best to do. My sword was gone (having rid myself of it in the water), but glancing about, there on the deck lay a handsome dagger with a long blade of exceeding breadth where it entered the hilt. It was plainly of Moorish workmanship, and could be trusted. Picking it up, I threw myself into an attitude of defence and awaited the attack. Just then I heard the galley strike the side of the vessel and immediately thereafter footsteps on deck. A thought suddenly crossed my mind. What use would it be to fight? I would be surely cut to pieces. Was there no way to save myself? no chance of escape? Furtively I looked round. Through the little barred window I saw that the galley had been backed in and that accounted for the time it had taken them to get alongside. I saw in the dim light that the name in big letters across her stern was *Cristobal.* The officers who stood on the after-deck might at any time look

316

into the cabin, and, although it was so near dark, they could not fail but observe me. Then where would I be? If not dead in five minutes, standing before the judges of the Black Order in a dungeon of the Inquisition, or pulling out my heart and life at the sweeps, like the poor felons chained to the cross-thwarts of the *Cristobal.* I cast about fearfully for some place to hide, and for an instant, a horrible, trembling dread came o'er me, but I threw it off, and another feeling took its place. A wild desire, this time, to end the suspense that was so sapping me, and to rush out on deck and bid them come on and taste what I might give them ere they bore me down. I wondered why they had not entered by breaking through the door to search the cabin, for it was plain that there were a half-score of men on board, but I soon perceived the reason; the galley had drawn ahead to cross the vessel's bows, and the sailors were busy passing a great rope, making ready to tow us in to shore. Soon I could see we were in motion, and then my heart gave a leap, for some one fumbled at the door lock (I have forgotten to state I had slipped the bolt). A few curses in Spanish showed that whoever it was, was more in a temper than suspicious, and then I heard a commanding voice say : —

"Hasten below, some one of you ; the door is locked, and they must have descended the ladder."

"So," thought I to myself, "there is another entrance to this rat trap, it behooves me to find it and make ready, or at least to do something more than stand here with my eyes popping." I was about to step forward when I felt the deck jump under my feet and then followed a thump and more curses from directly beneath me.

"Caramba! there is something on top the hatch, and I've lost a finger," grunted a rough voice. "Come, one of you dogs, and help me. Hey! bring a light!"

The sudden movement had put me off my balance, and stretching forth my hand to steady myself I grasped the great oaken chair and in doing so laid hold of the monk's habit that was thrown across it. An idea flashed across my brain, and with it came a faint ray of hope. It was but the work of an instant to thrust the dagger in my belt and to struggle into the heavy cassock that covered me from head to foot. I pulled the cowl over my face and quickly tied the rope girdle about my waist. Just as I picked up the rosary, the hatch was flung upward with great violence, and a swart face appeared in a circle of light that welled up from below. I dropped upon my knees and began to mumble some Latin; what, I cannot call to mind.

A man of large stature, carrying a lanthorn, climbed up the hatchway, and I bowed my head toward him as if expecting my death stroke on the instant, but the man leaned forward.

"Padre," said he, "we are thy friends. Fear naught."

"Ye are not English?" I asked, feigning great terror, and still keeping on my knees.

"No, we are sons of Spain. Thou art safe. St. Jago has heard thy prayers."

I mumbled more Latin, and the man turned and called down to some one below.

"One of the holy Fathers is still on board," cried he. "He took us for dogs of English."

"Peace, my son," I answered. "I was ready to die if need be."

Eftsoon two other men appeared, and one going to the door, unlocked it and admitted a fourth. He proved to be an officer; but, like the rest, he treated me with reverence.

"Courage, courage, Padre," said he. "Where are thy companions?"

"Gone in a boat," I answered; for how else could they have gone, unless they had flown or made a swim for it, which, peradventure, was not like to be the case.

"And thou chosest to stand by the ship! Sooth, thou shouldst have been a captain and not a priest," said the officer. "Would that all our men showed such devotion!"

"Thou art the captain of the galley *Cristobal*, señor. Is it not so? Have I not seen thee?" I made return.

"I am the second in command, Padre."

"Wilt thou set me on shore at once, good sir, and take possession here, for I must make report of what has befallen," I ventured, hoping that I might escape ere they found out the imposture I was playing.

"That, with pleasure, as soon as possible, Padre; but we have need of thee on the galley; our captain lies there grievously wounded — the only one that suffered harm, and that by a chance shot — a curse on the head of him who fired it!"

I pondered a moment. It was a position that had been forced upon me, but I blenched at the thought of carrying it so far as to pretend to shrive a dying man. It revolted me. And should I be discovered, my fate would be one to shudder at.

"Come," went on the young officer, "let us make haste, for our brother needs the rites and services of the Church."

Out on deck we went, I loosening my girdle and preparing to leap overboard, hoping in the darkness and confusion to escape, or at least, if caught, to perish fighting. The flames from the burning Spanish ships lit the sky to the north and east, but how it had fared with our vessels I could not tell. The galley was working in toward the city, and there was a great fog of cannon smoke hanging over the water and stenching the air, and one's hearing was assailed by a turmoil of shouts, drums, and bell-ringing, enough to free the whole coast of witches.

I was hanging back, having noticed that there was now a small boat at the gangway, when some one hailed from the galley.

"Drop anchor where you are, señor," was the order. "We are safe under the castle."

Looking up, I could see the black mass of the cliff and a flash ever and anon as the Matagorda continued winging useless shots out into the darkness. We let go a spare anchor and hove up short. This done, the officer turned to me.

"Into the boat, Padre," he said quietly, and then lifting up his voice, he called: "On board the *Cristobal!* — How fares it with Captain Madrazo? — We have a priest here."

The answer that came back made hope grow in my heart.

"He has yielded the spirit. He is dead, sir — you are too late."

"God rest his soul," said the officer, piously crossing himself, and I replied with a fervent "amen" and mumbled more Latin that was nevertheless a prayer.

Y

"We were, alas, too late," said the officer, when he had waited apparently for me to finish.

"Too late," I repeated, "alas, too late!—And now wilt thou crave permission that I may be landed, señor? for there is much for me to do." What it was I could not have told for the life of me. I had formed no plan, but hoped to reach such a point that I might swim off to our ships if any were left atop the water. "I must see the Bishop," I added at last, seeing he paused. "Ask the officer who has control, for leave to set me on shore and I will bless thee."

"There is no one to crave leave of but myself," was the return I had expected. (I had touched his pride.) "I am only too glad to grant it, Padre; pray for Spain, for this is a black hour for the faith and for the King."

Saying this, he ordered the men below in the small boat to haul in and to obey my wishes as to where I should be landed, and to return at once. And as I went over the side he asked for my blessing, saying that there would be "more fighting"; and I blessed him from the depth of my heart.

When the boat had landed me, I found myself at the foot of a crowded street filled with townsfolk and soldiery. Every one was talking to no end, and running to and fro to no purpose, some declaring that the place would be sacked, that the

English would land ere morning. Many people I saw laden down with their household goods and treasures, and crying to all to save themselves and escape now. I have always held that though the Spaniards are brave at times in a way, when once on the run there is no rallying them. Had Drake the force to land that night, Cadiz would have been his; for there were rumors spreading that our fleet was of eighty sail, instead of less than a third that number, and that the whole of the army of Flanders was with us. But to return to myself.

It seemed to me that every one I met could see through my disguise, had he taken pains to look, and from time to time, cold chills passed through my marrow; my feet I could scarce keep from running, and I kept looking for a hiding-place — gripping tight my dagger beneath my gown and fearing a challenge every minute. But no one paid heed to me, and turning from one street to another (as I kept away from the water-front the crowds grew less), I soon found myself in an open plaza that I knew was in the richest portion of the town; for I saw the surrounding palaces and hard by the lifting towers of the cathedral. The cannonading had ceased, and, save for the flares that lit the harbor below, and a hoarse murmur of voices that came up on the breeze, the place looked to be deserted; yet I dared not sit me down, but continued walking — bending my

steps to the wharves again and hoping to find a
place where I could slip happily unseen into the
water, or secure a boat in which I might put out and
seek the fleet. As I turned away from the broad
avenue, all at once I heard the sound of hoofs and
the rumble of wheels, and looking round I perceived
a great coach, with lamps blazing, with one man
driving and no outriders, coming toward me at a
furious pace. I noticed that the great vehicle was
swaying from side to side like a Dutchman in a seaway, and I saw that the front wheel was canted
badly and swung loosely on the axle. As it clat-
tered past, the driver cut the horses a swinge with
his whip; they gave a mad leap forward, and as if
brought down by a shot, one of the leaders tumbled
headlong, the wheel flew off at the same instant,
narrowly missing bowling me over like a ninepin,
and with a crash the coach lurched over on its side!
The driver pitched forward into the road and lay
there senseless, and the horses plunging and struggling started to drag the wreck down the dim-lighted
avenue. I had been so startled at the swiftness with
which the whole affair had taken place that I had
remained crowded against the wall where I had
jumped to avoid the beasts' heels, when I heard a
woman's scream, and at the door of the coach, the
glass of which had been shattered, appeared a frightened face!

Instantly I sprang out and, dashing forward, I grasped the leaders' heads, for the fallen animal had gained his legs, and, using all my strength, I brought them to a halt. But they were still rearing and plunging, and I feared to drop them and go to the help of the lady imprisoned in the coach. But soon the door pushed open, and a tall figure in a long silk cloak stepped out. As she came trembling toward me, I saw it was a young girl, whose pallor and fright could not conceal her great beauty, that the darkness could not hide from sight. Her mass of raven black hair had become unfastened and streamed about her shoulders, and her dark eyes were big with terror.

"Oh, good Father!" she cried, "what shall I do! I fear that my mother, who is with me, is surely killed, Padre; and our servant Miguel is dead. Where shall I go for help? tell me, what shall I do?"

I could not tell her, for I was in as great a quandary as she was, and I was casting about for something to say, when the coachman lifted himself on his elbow and gave a hollow groan. The young lady instantly ran to him, but before she could assist him, he arose and staggered upright. I saw that the fellow was still dazed, but that his senses were coming to him, and so I called him by the name I had heard the young lady use, and bade him take my place and hold the horses. He obeyed, still rubbing his cracked pate, and I went back to where the señorita was standing half in, half out of the carriage.

"Can I be of help, my fair — daughter," I added hurriedly, just checking myself in the middle of my best court bow.

"Thank thee kindly, Padre," the young lady returned over her shoulder. "My mother seems unhurt, she had but fainted. — It is a priest of the Order of St. Joseph, who stopped the horses and saved our lives," she continued, talking to some one inside the coach. "Stay, he will help thee out. This ends our journey; we must turn back to the palace; the coach is broken. But, thank God, none of us is killed."

I hastened forward, and with some little difficulty I helped a tall, handsome woman to crawl forth and alight. As the rays from the coach lamp fell upon her face, I started. It was the Lady of the Pearls — a little stouter, but still beautiful. But none other, Donna Maria de Valdez! I knew her at a glance. In my astonishment, and before I could control myself, I had exclaimed her name.

"You know me, Padre?" asked Donna Maria, as she still held my hand.

"A long time ago, I once saw thee — in another life."

"Thy voice is familiar — what name art thou known by?"

"Father Marteo."

She repeated the name while the young lady stood by and watched us. Suddenly at the foot of the street there appeared a number of torches flaring in moving lines, and I saw that they were carried by marching men, and that they were nearing, for the tapping of a drum could be plainly heard.

Miguel the servant called out from where he was standing, "Here come foot-soldiers! they may be the English! I pray thee hasten, madam; the Padre will see thee to a place of shelter whilst I save the horses."

"Fear not, madam," I interposed, "they are not English, but I am at thy service if thou wilt accept such escort as I offer."

"Oh, could we but go on," said Donna Maria, wringing her shapely hands. "If we could but right the coach and leave the city."

"We might try," said I, "if one of you fair ladies could see to the horses so the man might help me."

I had dropped my priestly manner and thought no more of my disguise, forgetting all in the strangeness of the adventure.

"I will hold them," said the young girl, stepping boldly forward and taking the place of Miguel, who, at a word, returned to me and asked what he should

do.   Showing him where the missing wheel had
lodged, we rolled it up.

"But how, good Father, shall we set it in its place?"
he asked.

"Make ready with it and stand by handsomely,"
I returned.   "I am going to lift the coach!"

I have heard of such straining as I put my back
to shortening men's lives.   So far as I know, it has
not hampered mine as yet.   But I have made no
such heft before nor since.   But the wheel went
on.

"And how shall we keep the wheel on the axle,
Padre?" questioned Miguel.   "The pin is missing; 'twas that doubtless which first caused the
trouble."

"Go to the horses' heads, my son," said I, not
answering; and as soon as he had left I drew the
dagger from inside my gown, and slipping the point
into the slot where the pin had been, I drove it
home, and with a twist broke the blade short off.
I turned and saw that Donna Maria was watching.
The cowl had fallen back from my head, and she
gazed straight at me.

"Thou art no priest!" she said; "who art thou?"

The drum was almost upon us, and the tramping
of the soldiers' feet rang on the stones; another
twenty paces and they would be abreast of us.   I
cast my die.

"I am an Englishman whose life is forfeit," said I, quickly. "For the sake of any of his countrymen who may have served thee —"

"Draw up thy hood," said Donna Maria, quickly. "Make haste — draw up thy hood!"

CHAPTER XXXII

OLD FRIENDS

AT the head of the approaching band of foot-soldiers rode a man on a prancing black charger. He was evidently an officer of some rank, for the trappings of the saddle and bridle reins were resplendent with gold and silver, and the huge spurs he wore jingled like a chime of bells. Seeing the coach drawn up by the wayside and the two ladies standing by the open door, he approached, and lifting the great plumed hat, made a sweeping bow. It was evident that at first he had not recognized the little party, for an expression of surprise crossed his face as he came near, and I saw a flash of anger in Donna Maria's eyes as she regarded him. As soon as the man spoke, I knew him, and there came back to me the day when, save for her interference, his dagger would have cut this tale exceeding short. It was Don Lopez, and that he had not improved his standing in the lady's eyes was evident from the manner in which she received his speech.

"Ah, Donna Maria," said he, smiling and showing his handsome teeth. "Have the English driven thee from Cadiz? Art thou in great fear, that thou shouldst take thy departure so suddenly?"

The lady looked at him scornfully. "Thou knowest well, Don Lopez, that I am not the kind that fears mere rumors. I am called away to Valliera by the illness of a relative, and when your men have passed, I should like well to proceed, for time presses."

We were by this time surrounded by a crowd of soldiers, torch-bearers, and a rabble of town's folk, who elbowed up about us, eager to hear what was passing, the flickering light reflecting from 'their gorming faces. The officer cleared a space by backing his horse and swinging about him with the flat of his sword. At the same time he was ordering the procession to take up the march, saying that he would join them.

"And do you travel alone when making so far a journey?" went on Don Lopez; "thou shouldst have an escort surely."

"Padre Marteo is with me," said Donna Maria, indicating me with a glance.

"So, thy confessor! But thou shouldst have a guard, or at least a good sword at thy disposal. There are many soldiers and rough-mannered folk to be met with on the road. Would that I were not on such pressing business and I would give thee safe conduct."

"We need none," answered Donna Maria, coldly, "and at Lagos I meet my brother."

The officer did not appear to be at all put out, but turning to the young lady, he leaned forward in his saddle and spoke, half to her. "And art thou going to rob us of Donna Inez, the fairest flower of Cadiz?" he said gallantly. "Stay with us, I pray thee, señorita. Thou wilt be missed when the Duke reviews his victorious forces on the morrow."

"Victorious!" exclaimed Donna Maria. "Have we then gained a victory?"

"We have driven the English from the bay, sunk most of their ships, and ere noon to-morrow we will have their crews and leaders paraded through our streets in chains."

Donna Maria cast a swift glance at me. I felt my heart sink at the officer's words. Had Drake at last paid the penalty of his rashness? Had his self-confidence wrought his destruction? How the Vice-Admiral would vaunt himself! The dangers of my position were now increased tenfold. If it were true that our forces had been defeated, or were even compelled to withdraw from the waters, my plight would be a sorry one, for I felt certain that in broad daylight my disguise would betray me, if merely for the fact that my heavy sea-boots kept peeping from below the hem of my monk's habit, and that my head lacked the shaven tonsure of the priest. I had in my doublet but a few pieces of money, and they were English — sufficient in themselves to cast me into prison, should I try to spend them. But I had forgotten what I knew of the Spanish character; I failed to remember that a report of victory with them is the usual way of introducing news of sore defeat.

"Heaven grant that what thou hast told is true," said Donna Maria, replying after a pause to the officer's last words. "There must have been brave fighting, for I have seen the English with their swords drawn, and it is abroad that Admiral Drake, who scorched us so in the western seas, now leads them."

"Pah!" cried the officer, waving his hand. "We will see him with a Spanish rope hanging above his head, unless the Bishop desires to reason with him in the cell."

I shuddered as I thought of our brave leader meeting such a fate, and I remembered the horror of the hour that I had spent before the black-gowned tribunal when I was a child; but it was evident that Donna Maria wished to enter little into this, for she spoke abruptly.

"We must be going on, Don Lopez," she said. "We must no longer detain you."

The officer slid from his horse, and slipping the

bridle through his arm, with a show of gallantry, opened the coach door and giving his hand, first to Donna Maria, then to the young lady, helped them in. I stood there, not knowing what to do, and hoping that the deep shadow of the cowl hid my features, so that Don Lopez might not recognize me. Donna Maria leaned forward.

"Come, Padre Marteo; we must be pushing on." She made a motion for me to enter, and I stepped past the Don, who had not considered me worthy the slightest regard, I take it, and closed the door. He stepped to the window.

"I hope," said he, "that I may sometime win a gracious look or word. May I deserve it is my hourly prayer." He pressed the lady's hand to his lips, then making a sweeping bow, he mounted his horse and cantered up the street just as Miguel touched our leaders with his whip and the heavy coach took motion. Donna Maria thrust her head out of the window.

"Drive fast," she said, "and avoid the crowded streets. Go out the eastern gate!"

We rumbled on at an ever increasing pace. I knew not where our destination might be, nor did I much care. I had found the only comfort of one in such stress as mine, and that was — friends. It was a strange position, sitting there in the darkness with I knew not what before me. It was like dreaming, but Donna Maria broke the silence, speaking at first with effort.

"So Fate has, at last, good sir, given me chance to repay thy kindness to me when I was in distress. I have almost prayed for such a day, for, believe me, it is not true that women are most prone to forget such things, and it rejoiceth me that in some measure I can repay the debt I owe thee."

"But the payment is out of all seeming, and I can see in what danger your generosity will place you both. So I pray thee, madam, consider me not at all in the matter, and set me down outside the city, where, mayhap, I can work my way to a place of safety. I speak your language well, and know the manners of the country."

"Say no more in this fashion, sir," Donna Maria cried, "but give me time to think, to use my woman's wit. I fain would believe that I see the way clear to bring matters to a safe conclusion." Then the tones of her voice changed, and she leaned forward and touched me gently. "Dost thou know who is sitting here beside me?" she asked.

"I have half guessed, madam," I replied, "but time that has dealt so lightly with thee, has wrought wondrous changes elsewhere."

"Inez," said Donna Maria, turning to the young girl, "rememberest thou the kind gentleman who plunged into the water and drew thee forth when we were held prisoners by the English, and who returned us to our home? We have often spoken of it."

"Indeed, I do, madre, and I remember how we landed and how he and his men refused the pearls, and all of it."

Somehow the musical tones of the voice thrilled me through and through. They had in them that peculiar quality, the very sound of which, falling from a woman's tongue, toucheth a man's heart.

"The young man who rendered us such service sits here with us. He saved our lives, and now I believe that his is in our keeping. We shall not betray the trust."

"Indeed, we shall not, madre; if we answer with our own." Her tones trembled as she spoke, and my heart leaped faster.

"But I cannot accept such chance of sacrifice," I cried. "And thinking coolly, I see no way but for us to part company, and so I entreat that I should leave you."

"That thou shalt not," cried the young girl, warmly. "Let me prove now how great are the thanks that I owe to thee; as a woman I can tell thee; I could not voice my gratitude as a child! Stay!" she added suddenly. "An idea has come to me, that put in practice will solve our quandary:

In the big box that we are bringing to my uncle is the uniform of a commandant of Horse. 'Twould fit the señor bravely, methinks."

"Wouldst thou turn from priest to soldier?" asked Donna Maria, half laughing. "Thy beard and features fit best to the latter."

"More than willingly," said I, "for I confess that my heart and mind are given more to the sword than my appearance to the cassock. But who will I appear to be? and what part will I play? and is not this risking much also?"

"Nothing is easier," interposed Donna Maria, answering all my questions at once. "Thou wilt be a distant relation of ours, an officer of the King, who has volunteered to conduct us on our journey."

"And whither may that be?" I questioned.

"To our castle at Valliera," was the answer. "But at Lagos I meet my brother, Don Vincent de Valdez."

"Valliera! De Valdez! As a boy I lived there on the estates of Vertendonna, the lord of whom married my mother after my father's death. She was a De Valdez."

"Tell me thy story!" said Donna Maria, breathlessly. And sitting there in the darkness I told them what the reader already knows, except that I passed quickly over the years that I had spent since I had last seen them, and that I had employed in

z

making chess moves in the game that the Queen played at court.

When I had finished the lady took my hand. "Thou knowest well, señor, what the ties of kinship and the claims of hospitality mean here in Spain. My husband is dead, but his brother shall hear what you have to tell, and be assured that he will be as one of us, and that his life and fortune will be at thy disposal."

It was growing daylight, and we were on a wide, level road that skirted the Northern Inlet not many miles beyond Port St. Mary.

"We are nearing the hostelry where we change horses," said Donna Maria, peering out of the window, "and there we will have the box brought in, and thou canst make thy shift of habit."

"Had we best not take Miguel into the secret?" I asked, "for what will he think at my sudden change of calling?"

"Miguel is a good servant," put in Donna Maria, "and good servants in Spain hear and see nothing, so perhaps it might be best that thou shouldst doff thy disguise now; surely a country innkeeper would not recognize that thou wert English."

It was quite daylight now, and I had thrown back my hood, for it was hot. Donna Inez looked at me with a half smile in her eyes.

" I fear that others might see the difference," she said; "for, if I may be pardoned the liberty, such light hair and beard are seldom seen in Spain."

I blushed, I must confess, to the very roots of the hair she had referred to, which in those days, before the gray had invaded it, was the color of corn in reaping time. Donna Maria also looked at me and laughed. "We can soon change that, methinks," she said, blushing herself, and then she added: "I am sure my cousin will be discreet."

I slipped out of the coarse woollen gown, and was glad to free myself of its heavy folds, but the clothes that I wore were bedraggled and yet damp from my plunge in the bay, and I was glad of the prospect of getting into dry ones. Somehow a great elation was growing in my breast! The glamour of the adventure filled me with a joy I could scarce keep from expressing, and the presence of my fair companions was a strong incentive to the elevation of my spirits.

" Here we are, at last," exclaimed Donna Maria; and as she spoke the horses turned, and we drew up into the courtyard of a wayside inn. At Donna Maria's suggestion I had muffled up my face in a kerchief as were I suffering from an aching tooth, and, followed by a servant bearing a big box, we entered and called for rooms. Once in my own apartment, that luckily boasted of a mirror, I dis-

missed the man, closed the door, and blocked the
keyhole; then I unwrapped a small package that
Donna Maria had taken from her travelling-pouch
and had slipped into my hand.   I remembered,
also, the few words she had whispered in my ear,
and I could not help but smile.   Opening the long
box, the first thing that met my eyes was a handsome Toledo blade lying at top of some fine suits
of clothing; there were a doublet of embroidered
velvet, and trunks and hose of silk.   Even a small
Spanish hat with a jewelled buckle and a plume was
there, and long boots of a quality we never see in
England.   As I laid out all this bravery, I was as
pleased as a young girl who gazed at a new satin
gown, for men are vain creatures, after all!   Then
once more I looked in the mirror and drew my face
awry.

In half an hour, had any one been listening at the
keyhole, they might have heard some laughter, but
it was checked by loud knocking, and a voice exclaiming that the ladies were awaiting me at breakfast.

＊   ＊   ＊   ＊   ＊   ＊   ＊   ＊

When the ladies left the inn to reënter their
coach, at which were four fresh horses, they were
accompanied by a cavalier with jet-black hair and a
beard like a raven's wing.   I had learned the secret
of how Donna Maria's glossy locks still kept their
pristine color!

"And what do you think of it?" I asked.

"To be truthful," returned Donna Maria, "I liked thee better as thou wert before."

"Thou wouldst scarcely know the 'lank, callow youth' now," I returned, remembering the words she had once applied to me.

"No," she answered, "that I would not."

"Is it an improvement?" I asked, turning to Donna Inez.

She said nothing, but gazed out of the window.

CHAPTER XXXIII

AN ANCIENT ENEMY

THE gentleman who met us at Lagos was not the brother of Donna Maria, as I had been led to expect, but a brother of her late husband, Governor De Valdez, our "kind friend" of Nombre de Dios, and thus, of course, he was a first cousin of my mother's, and this we found out after a minute's talk in which I told him of my family.

But there had been one thing agreed upon, between the ladies and myself, before we had arrived at Lagos, and that was that we would tell Don Vincent but part of the story, and to him it was confided that I was lately come from the West Indies, that I was of truth more English than Spanish, and that I was, of course, a Protestant. He was also told that if my identity should be discovered, my life would be in danger; but one thing they let out no inkling of, and that was that I was one of the marauders that had fallen on the coast.

Don Vincent was a well-mannered, mild-eyed little man, more scholar than soldier, and after hearing the tale of his sister-in-law, and on top of that my own story, he insisted upon embracing me and acknowledged our relationship with warmth. He gave me welcome in the Spanish fashion — everything he had was mine to command, and I had "but to voice my wishes." He promised to see that in some way I reached England after the excitement that attended the unexpected English raid had died away. What a strange people are these Spanish! The Grandees are proud, ambitious, but indolent, and the common folk, in the main, are happy and comfort-loving, craving plenty of food and sleep, cherishing music, dancing, and gay colors. But what great things has this nation done! And how these people have spread their language o'er the world! But this is again a digression, and I must pick up the severed threads of my story.

My mind was in a strange condition, and my heart was also, for certain reasons, as it may be guessed. I was in great anxiety to find out what had become of my companions, and as I dwelt more upon the subject, I could not believe that Sir Francis had met with such dire misfortune as had been represented. I reasoned that I had been too ready in accepting as true what Don Lopez had told us; but as we had pressed ahead through the country, we had found no news to controvert it; in fact, in many places we bore the first tidings of the attack

and the "victory," and Donna Maria seemed to
take a special pride in telling of the defeat of the
English.   But she did not do this to hurt my feelings — not at all ; she did it because it rejoiced her
that her countrymen should have shown such prowess.   Before we had reached Lagos we had much
opportunity for talking, and I learned why it was
that Donna Maria had been so anxious to depart
from Cadiz.   The illness of her relative was an
invention of the moment.   It was to escape the
attentions of Don Lopez that she had undertaken
the journey.   This gentleman had brought great
pressure to bear in the furtherance of his suit for
the hand of the wealthiest widow in Spain.   He
was a nephew of the Bishop, and a favorite with the
King.   I believe, had it not been for the affair of
the pearls, he might have succeeded in gaining
favor in the lady's eyes, but this matter he could
not explain away, do his best.   And he had used
no little wit in order to accomplish the end, explaining that he had taken the jewels from the place
where, forsooth ! I had hidden them, after having
watched me abstract them from the cabin, so I owed
him another grudge in addition to the debt that I
hoped to pay some day, if fate threw us together.

I have recorded the fact that my mind was disturbed, and I repeat the statement also, in regard
to my heart, for Donna Inez's eyes had played

havoc with my feelings. I had found little opportunity to converse with her at any length, but when
she did speak, it was always to the point and with
great sense. She had a pretty wit also, and this, in
addition to her voice, which, as I have told, possessed that strange quality of thrilling, her beauty
was such that the regarder's eyes found new changes
every instant, and, silent or speaking, I could scarce
keep mine from her face; and the fact that she
would look at me from time to time as if I were
amusing, nettled me, and I would grow painfully
conscious of the change in my appearance, and
could not help feeling that I was not appearing at
my best, so sometimes there intervened long silences,
in which, I dare say, we all did much thinking.

During that part of the journey in which Don
Vincent was with us, I found little opportunity to
talk with the ladies, for the Don absorbed my conversation, or at least he insisted upon my absorbing
his, and he was chattering away when we reached
Valliera.

I was now in the country which I had grown
familiar with as a boy, and I remembered often having seen from the castle of my step-father the towers
of the one belonging to the De Valdez, and also
the great shape of the monasteries, which stood out
against the sunset sky beyond the houses. We
were a mile or two from the town, and the country

about us stretched almost bare and uninhabited to the sea-cliffs, except where to the westward rose Sagres Castle and the home of the monks of St. Vincent. We had passed small bands of soldiers upon almost every mile of the road, and, as we rode into the castle yard, we were saluted by a guard of a half-score or so, and we could see a company drilling on the wide plain beyond — the setting sun striking bright reflections from their pikes and armor. All along it had been made no secret that these forces were gathering and being made ready against the day when King Philip should let loose his mighty fleets upon our coasts. But that he had been forestalled for some time, at least, was made evident by something that happened the first night that I spent at the De Valdez castle, and in this happening, was introduced again, a man who had a great bearing upon the trending of my youth, and whom I had never expected to see alive or dead in all the world.

I had at last found opportunity to talk with Donna Inez, for I had perceived her standing alone upon the terrace that looked down over the small but well-kept garden, and whether it was the evening which was exceedingly beautiful with a lingering twilight, or the depth of my own feelings, I was moved to speak more warmly than I had intended. After reminding her of the first day that we had met and telling her that there was a recollection of our parting that would never leave me, I drew the picture of the beautiful little child that had so taken hold of a lad's heart, and now she was a woman and I a man!

"Ah, yes, but I was then a child, and children's gratitude seeks expression in their own way. But I pray thee, sir, now allow us to repay thee by helping thee escape from danger, and do not make it harder for us. When thou goest, it is to another life and land, and thy warm words are wasted. We shall never see each other again, and our countries will soon be at war, which should make us enemies."

"I crave pardon if I have spoken too boldly," I returned; "I but voiced the feelings that have swayed me for the last three days."

"For the last three days," she repeated, with a laugh, "and one day more."

"And why but one day? I perchance, might have said for fourteen years."

"Because, señor, we have found out that there is a boat sailing from the anchorage beneath the cape on the morrow, and the longer that thou stayest here, the greater is thy danger."

"I am willing to risk the danger," I returned, "and stay on till the next boat, or the next."

"No," she replied, "that we will hear none of; we must part."

I was about to urge her to state reasons, and to plead my own cause more warmly, when her mother appeared upon the terrace, followed by Don Vincent and a figure so strange that at first I could not tell if it belonged to a man or woman, but as they approached, I saw that it was a priest of the Black Order, and my heart sank as I perceived the hooked nose and the sharp black eyes of Padre Alonzo, my old enemy, peering out from under the shadow of the cowl! This man had always the effect upon me of some noxious reptile of which I stood in fear —fear that I felt would not leave me until I had stamped out his existence and rid the earth of him. Long ago I had discovered that he could read the thoughts of people from the very expressions of their faces and the wording of their speech, and now he was gazing at me.

"Don Marteo," said Donna Maria, "the Padre has just brought us news that has come by water, a boat having reached here from Port St. Mary." She spoke as if the news was sad, and she wished to prepare my mind. "Tell us," she added turning to the priest.

I shuddered as the old demon began to talk, for as his voice sounded in my ears it brought back that unhappy day when I stood before him and might have betrayed my friend to death if I had opened lips. "The Saints bring down destruction on the

English!" he exclaimed. "They have put back the Great Reckoning until I doubt if I shall live to see it."

"How so?" I asked, scarcely able to control my voice.

The priest looked at me, half smiling. "They have burnt twenty-seven fine vessels belonging to the King, sunk five galleys and threescore of merchant-men, destroyed almost two hundred thousand ducats' worth of valuable supplies, and have escaped," he went on, "without the loss of a ship!" And he paused here as if he were about to say more, and then stopped. I could feel his eyes searching my face, which was turned toward the light, and I know not whether I quailed or faltered, but my words came slowly, while all waited to hear what I might say.

"And what will the King do now?" I asked. "Such news as this must cause him anguish."

"What he will do is not for us to say," returned Padre Alonzo. "Much as we desire to know." He said nothing more.

Now the news the priest had brought of course had given me great joy, and yet I must confess that I felt a sympathy for my kind host and my benefactress, for I could see how greatly they were cast down, and yet strangely enough I perceived, also, that they had feared that I would have betrayed my-

self by some false expression or by too much elation
upon the receipt of the news. I considered, nevertheless, that I had avoided this with cleverness, but
whether I had done so or not remained to be seen.

As the darkness was falling we reëntered the
castle; I was anxious now to get a chance to speak
with Donna Maria or Don Vincent, for it did not
appear at all likely that any vessel would sail from
the Cape when it was known that Drake's fleet was
sailing unhampered in the waters, and I held that
it might be a good plan for me to set out in quest
of the Admiral in a small boat, even if I had to go
alone. Then, as I thought over this, I remembered
having heard Drake say (not in a meeting of the
officers, but to me and Master Ceely), that if successful at Cadiz, it was his intention to seize Cape
St. Vincent and hold it as a place of rendezvous for
a stronger fleet to be sent from England! It appeared
from the Spanish account that he had been more successful than even he had dreamed of, and, as I knew
him to be a man who altered not his plans without
a reason, or unless compelled to, I said to myself
that I had gained a fortunate position, for here I
was on the very ground and in advance of him.

All these thoughts were in my mind during the
evening, as we sat about the big fire in the castle
hall. I had joined absently in the conversation,
and from time to time I had looked up to see the

priest's eyes resting upon me. His misshapen form sank back into the depths of a huge armchair, and his long bony fingers kept stretching out of his wide sleeves, like talons, as he talked; but the voice that I remembered as so discordant had grown soft and mellow, and he turned his attention to me at least a score of times, and showed without rudeness great curiosity as to my past. He had been informed that I was "acquainted well in the ports of the Spanish Main." "Did I by any chance know Father Juan Gonzales at Cartagena, and surely I must have heard of the great work that Padre Tomacito Reno had done amongst the Indians." And there was much more of this examining done by him. To all outward showing the questions were kindly put, but I was puzzled often to answer them, and it kept my wits working not to betray myself. In her way Donna Maria endeavored to put him off and to come to my assistance. I could see that both she and the señorita were growing worried. At last, to our relief, the frightful priest arose and bade us farewell. As he spoke to me, I thought I discovered a wickedly triumphant gleam of menace in his eye. I returned the glance as blandly as I could, and I had chance to observe him closer than I had done heretofore. He was grown scarcely older, and his face had the same drawn and sunken expression of a skull. In fact, were it not for the eyes, that gleamed in the hollow sockets, the thin sharp nose, and the lips firm and pale, that hid the cavernous jaw, Padre Alonzo's face was a living, speaking death-mask. I reasoned that he would never grow old, and that he would stay as he was till he crumbled like some old shrouded figure in an ancient tomb.

Knowing that if Admiral Drake made good his intentions, he would not stop at half measures, it suddenly crossed my mind that fate had placed me again in position to return the kind service of my friends; for if he ever succeeded in effecting a landing, he would surely march upon the surrounding castles on the Cape in order to satisfy that peculiar greed of the English sailor-man and soldier that demands substantial reminders of his successes, and thus I might be able to protect the property of my friends from being levied on. Was it my duty, thought I, to enlighten them or not? I pondered this over for some time and decided that I was not warranted in so doing, and it would be expecting too much for them to keep it quiet.

After the priest's departure, I inquired about him without stating that I knew anything of his name or doings, and I found that he was one of the most feared and hated men in Western Spain. He seldom did anything without a motive, and it was rumored that he knew secrets of the King and Cardinal before they knew the secrets of each other. Aye, and that he knew what moves the Pope would make even before that much-advised potentate knew himself. It was seldom that he called upon any of the nobles that lived near Valliera, and his appearing at Valdez to give my friends welcome, had been a great surprise. But the reason for it was not kept long in doubt.

The apartment that had been assigned to me was on the ground floor in a square tower that rose at the corner of the moat. It was at the end of a long, loop-holed passageway, flagged with heavy stones. I had fallen asleep, and mayhap it was an hour after midnight, when I was awakened by the sound of some one stirring in my room, and voices near by, talking in whispers. I leaned out from the bed and stretched my hand to reach the corner where I had placed my sword. It was not there, and with a start I sat bolt upright and asked loudly into the pitch darkness, who it was that had entered, and what was the business he might be on. The sound of heavy footsteps came from the corridor, and before I could gain my speech or find a weapon, I was borne backward by three or four strong arms, and my hands were pinioned ere I could strike a blow. When a torch was brought, the room appeared to be filled with figures draped in long black gowns that I so well remembered. Their faces,

too, were hidden by black masks. But they were
not all priests, for I was sure that I had felt that
one, at least, wore armor. I was not even given
time to dress; bound as I was, I was hurried out
into the passageway, and there one of the coarse
black frocks was thrown across my shoulders, en-
veloping me to the feet, and I was led forward into
the big hall. There was a strange sight. The
terrified servants were standing behind a row of
pikemen. The place was alight with torches, and
in the flickering light I saw something that caused
my heart to sink. On the broad stone staircase
stood Don Vincent, pinioned and helpless, and beside him were Donna Maria and my dear señorita,
pale with fright. It needed but half a glance to
show that they were prisoners also. Ere I could
speak, I was hurried out.

How far we travelled that night I know not, but
with two hideous guards in a jolting coach, it appeared to me that I was driven miles, and then,
with my eyesight stoppered by the heavy gown
they had thrown about my head, I was pushed out
and led up a stairway into a building of some kind.
I heard a great door clang behind me, then up
another stairway, spiral in form this time, I was half
dragged, half led; another door was opened, and I
was thrust forward into a small, round cell. Then
came a crash of iron locks, and I was left alone.

CHAPTER XXXIV

THE WALLED GARDEN

IN my miserable situation, I was like to have given way to my grief and deep despair, but there was too much to think of to waste time in lamentations. But what distress and suffering were brought upon my friends! Yes, I could see that it was through me, and for me, all this had fallen upon them, and I wondered how it had come about that I should have been suspected, or on what grounds I had been seized. To the questions that I had put to my captors during the hour just ended, I had gained no reply, nor would they tell me what they intended doing, or where taking me. If it was inland, I had indeed small hope of rescue or escape, and my fate was as good as sealed. But Englishmen do not receive the blows of Fate with humility; it is their constant effort to wrest the bludgeon from her hands, and I determined first to find out my whereabouts, then to set myself free, if it were possible, and to proceed to rescue those who were suffering for me; but all my plans for the near future were inter-

rupted by a necessity for action in the present. The
cords that bound my wrists had been drawn so tight
that they were causing me the intensest agony, and
I endeavored to free myself from their cruel pressure. Save for the gown that had been thrown
around me, I was thinly clad, and I had no knife
or weapon. Getting to my feet, I felt around the
wall of the apartment. It was circular and of
smooth stone, but where the door entered there
was a sharp edge where the stone joined a wooden
framework; back against this I leaned, and in the
way a Scotchman scratches his back, and not without some effort, did I succeed in wearing away one
of the knots that bound my hands. This loosened,
the others gave, and soon I had all free.

I had thought that by this time it should be daylight, but I looked in vain for any window, and felt
about with hands extended for any opening, and
was discomforted. But after a time I perceived a
faint glow from overhead, and brighter it grew, until
I saw that there was, perhaps nine feet from the
floor, a narrow window scarcely the width of my
hand. Twice I tried to reach it and failed. On
the third jump I succeeded, and as I was about
drawing myself up, there came a sound of a key
being inserted in the door, and I was forced to drop
down on a straw pallet, where I lay with my hands
behind me, feigning to be asleep. Two men entered

quietly, each with his face hid behind the masks. I heard but four whispered words, and they were spoken in a tone of great vexation.

"His beard is black," snarled the taller of the two.

"Hush!" cautioned the other, pushing the first forward. "Try." The man approached, and kneeling beside me, shook me roughly, at the same time he placed his mouth close to my ear and said in English, with a touch of Spanish accent.

"A message from Admiral Drake! Arise, quickly!"

Like a flash I saw through the ruse. Opening my eyes, as if yet dazed, I stared about me. "What do you want?" said I in Spanish. "Who are you?"

"A message from Drake," repeated the man again, and his eyes almost burned through the slits in his mask.

"I do not understand," returned I in Spanish. "Who are ye? You will answer for this treatment of me to the King and the Cardinal!" The men stood there silently while I looked up at them. That their attempt to surprise me had failed, had hugely disconcerted them.

"We are acting under orders," said one at last.

"The orders of Padre Alonzo," said I.

"Whose else?"

"The orders of Don Lopez de Serano, mayhap,"

and at this both men started, and at a sign from one they drew together out into the hall and quickly closed the door, and there they must have stood whispering, for it was a few minutes before I heard again their footsteps. I jumped once more to the window and caught it cleverly, and, using all my strength, I drew myself up, and when I could look out, I dropped down again from sheer surprise. I was in the town that I had known so well as a boy, and I had looked across the street over the high stone wall into the gardens of Vertendonna! There was the fountain flashing in the morning sun, and there was the poplar tree that used to be so hard to climb. I remembered how I had interviewed Selwyn Powys from the top of this very wall beneath me, and I recalled the big key that locked the gateway, and the underground passage, and all of it. Once more I made the window and looked out. There were figures in the garden now, and looking closely, I perceived that they were two women and a man walking down the shrub-bordered path toward the fountain. As they came out into the open and the branches no longer hid them, I almost lost my hold again, for the two ladies were Donna Maria and her daughter, and the man who stood beside them was none other than Don Lopez! They were speaking earnestly, but of course they were too far off for me to hear the slightest sound; but I could see

that the Don was excited, while the ladies stood calm
and apparently defiant. Suddenly the Spaniard
turned upon his heel and walked quickly away,
plainly in a temper, and Donna Maria, clasping
Inez in her arms, sank onto one of the stone
benches near the fountain. I dropped down to the
floor to think, and was sitting there reasoning what
it might mean, when again the lock was heard to
turn and one of my jailers reappeared.

"Follow me," said he, and twisting the cord
around my wrists, I arose and followed him. We
went down the spiral staircase that led to the tower
in which I had been confined, and turning from the
broad hallway, we descended another and entered a
room on the ground floor, the barred windows of
which looked out into the garden, a patch, perhaps,
some sixty odd feet square. But I knew where I
was now! It was in this very room that Powys
and I had held our meetings, and there was the
door in the wall from which led the steps to the
underground passageway beneath the street. From
being a heretic stronghold, the place had been
turned into a secret prison maintained by the Black
Order, who had such places scattered through Spain
and eke through France. I looked closely around
the room; a small door half ajar led into another
apartment, and stepping there on tiptoe I looked in.
It was a store-chamber of some kind, filled with

odds and ends, stripped, perhaps, from luckless
persons who had lodged in the building. There
was a collection of old clothing, doublets, capes, and
hosiery hanging from the nail, and in the corner
stood a sheaf of swords and rapiers, some of foreign
make. I took down an armful of clothes and seiz-
ing one of the weapons, I dashed back into the
room. There was no time to wait. It was evident
that I had been left there alone for a short time
only, waiting, perhaps, for some one to make ready
to receive or to visit me. Time was precious. I
did not even try to don the things that I had taken.
With arms full, I tried the door leading toward the
garden with my knee. To my surprise and delight
it opened, for one would be as much a prisoner
there as anywhere, as the walls were twenty feet in
height, and the only gateway blocked, apparently,
on the other side by solid stone, but I knew where
we had always kept the key, and dropping my
bundle for the nonce, I felt arm's length beneath
the stone doorstep, and drew forth from its resting-
place of many years, the ponderous bit of iron.
With it, fearsomely I hastened to the gate, and, un-
locking it, there were the stone steps that led down
into the darkness! I had brought my bundle with
me, and shutting the door, though I could not see
clearly what I was doing, I managed to get into
some of the clothes. Then I unlocked the further

doors, and half fearing the sunlight again, I inserted
the key into the last keyhole. In another moment
I would be in the garden, and unless they had left,
I would be in the presence of Donna Maria and her
daughter. Breathing a prayer that I might find
them, I stepped forth. They were not there! I
paused and looked about me. The garden was not
in the same well-kept condition that I remembered
it in the old days; the weeds choked the flower-beds
and the grass grew in spots in the paths. But yet
the sight brought back to me vividly the hours of
my lonely childhood, albeit everything now seemed
to be on a much smaller scale than of yore.

But I did not pause long to think over these
things. Throwing the key behind a bush, I strode
forward, and as I neared the fountain I perceived
the ladies walking up the path toward the castle.
I flew after them, and, hearing my hasty footsteps,
they turned as if expecting trouble. I think that
both would have cried out in their surprise at seeing
me, if I had not cautioned them, finger on lip, and
we stepped aside into a recess in the hedge.

"Thank the merciful God!" exclaimed Donna
Maria; "we never expected to see thee again."
She wrung my hand while Inez stood there, her face
pale as she leaned against her mother, and her beautiful eyes fixed upon my face.

"I never expected to be seen by any one but

that monster priest and the executioners," I returned. "But I have escaped by means of secret knowledge I have of this place, for here I lived as a boy, and in the room overhead in the castle my mother died. But tell me, how fares it with you, and what does it mean, this arrest and your detention?"

"It means," responded Donna Maria, "that Don Lopez is a villain, trebly dyed."

"True," said I, "but that explains nothing."

"Well," continued the good lady, speaking quickly, "to be short, the whole city of Cadiz has been searched for an English spy in the garb of a priest, who had been allowed to land from one of the vessels, helped by one of the officers of the galley *Cristobal*; the officer has been shot."

I started. "Poor fellow," said I; "alas, but there is one brave sailor less for us to fight."

"Now," went on Donna Maria, "Don Lopez remembered meeting a priest answering the description, with us, and, knowing our destination, he evaded your vessels and reached here by water before we had arrived, and told the wizard at St. Vincent. Padre Alonzo, from whom one can conceal nothing, surprised you into betraying yourself last evening, to such an extent that you are now a suspect, and thus you have been taken, and we, also, for harboring you. We are prisoners, and forbidden to leave this castle, which at present belongs to the Bishop of Cadiz."

"A murrain on me for having brought you to this!" I cried. "Is there no way for you to be relieved? Let me avow myself. I will say that you know nothing; you shall not suffer for me."

"Hold," cried Donna Maria, "you go too fast! There is more to tell; they know not who you are, for your appearance tallies not with the description of the spy. We have said that we met you at the inn, that the priest left us at the city gate, and that he had imposed upon us so well that we thought we must have known him. We have denied that we suspected him, but now grant that it may have been the Englishman. As to yourself, Don Vincent has sworn you are his cousin, and we have sworn we knew you well and last saw you at Bastamentos, where you had rendered the Governor, my husband, such signal service that he could never mention your name without a prayer for your welfare. Which is true," she added, and then went on: "What you are doing here, we could not tell them, leaving that to you to explain. But they scent something strange in the affair, and Alonzo, the black wolf, stops at no half measures. Oh, señor, it rejoiceth us to see thee alive!"

"What of Miguel?" I asked. "Can he be trusted?" Donna Maria paused. "They have put Miguel to the torture; he has told them naught. Servants are not expected to know everything."

Donna Inez, who had been looking from her mother to me anxiously, now spoke.

"They were to have examined you," said she, "this morning. That villanous Lopez has just left us to be present, he said, at your undoing. What dreadful things he threatened! Is it wise to stand here where any one might find us? Is there no hiding-place where we can go?"

"I know a score of such places in the castle," I returned, "for there is not a secret passageway I have not explored. I know them like a rat knows a hayrick."

"Then let us in," said Donna Maria, "for Don Lopez may soon return, and if found here, we are lost — all of us."

"Walk boldly in then, turn to the room on the right, and I will follow as if guarding you."

The ladies did as I bade them. Unnoticed we went into the castle, and down the great hall at the farther end I saw two pikemen guarding the entrance that gave upon the street; but they were looking out, with their backs to us, and saw nothing. We entered the room on the left, that was a small one, through which it was necessary to pass to reach the chapel. I knew of a secret stairway opening

from a closet that led to the state chamber overhead, and it was here that I intended to conceal
myself until nightfall, or until some provision could
be made for my escape. I was hoping to gain time
enough to speak at greater length and in some security
to the ladies before seeking seclusion, but it was not
to be. We had closed the door, and I had placed
myself in a position and attitude to hear if any one
should approach, when I heard the sentry challenge
some one at the door, who answered hotly : —

" A curse on thee for a fool ! Don't you know
me, fellow ? Call out the guard ; a most important
prisoner has escaped ! "

A trumpet flourished, and voices and hurrying
feet sounded along the corridors.

" Lose no time ! escape ! Hide yourself ! " cried
the señorita.

I entered the closet where the secret door was
hid in the wainscoting, asking the ladies to meet me
there after dusk, and, in the meantime, if possible,
to procure me some food. Then I kissed my dear
young lady's hand and disappeared.

CHAPTER XXXV

I T was musty and close, and as I sat there in the great rat-hole, I had much to think on. In the assistance that Donna Maria and Inez could give me from the outside lay my strong hope of salvation, for I could not have stirred abroad by daylight without being questioned or recognized, and taken. If my fellow-prisoners should be compelled to leave, I should be in a sorry plight! I might live, for a time, like a ghost, haunting the secret passages of the castle (the ones that I had explored as a boy), but a ghost is not supposed to eat or drink, and in my search to stave off hunger and thirst I would be in continual danger.

Time passed slowly in darkness. I awoke after a short sleep and could not have told if it had lasted five minutes or five hours. But there was a tapping at the wainscoting, and, listening, I perceived that it was the signal that we had agreed upon, so I opened the panel and found Donna Inez there alone. She was trembling from head to foot.

"Oh, señor," she said, "I am in such fright. My mother has disappeared; I cannot find her.

She left me an hour ago with one of the Black
Robes. Has she been here? Oh! they will never
dare to lay harsh hands on her; where has she
gone?" She clutched my shoulders fiercely.
"Why did we ever see thee?" she half sobbed.
"Why didst thou not leave us?"

I saw now my duty clearly. I could right all the
wrong that I had brought upon them. How they
had suffered for me!

"There is one thing that I can do to help matters
now," said I, "and that I shall take upon myself
right speedily." I stepped toward the door of the
antechamber that opened out to the hall.

"Stop," cried Inez, clutching me again. "There
is a sentry there; he has been placed to guard me.
I am held prisoner in this room."

"Do not make it hard for me," returned I; "you
will soon be free, and Donna Maria also. I have
brought all this cloud upon thee both and on thy
uncle, and I shall soon disperse it."

"But think of it! they will torture thee, they will
roast thee at slow fires! They will not dare to do
more than to threaten or imprison us. But think
of thy fate."

"I have naught to tremble at. A man must die;
we die but once."

I drew my sword and laid hold of the great han-
dle of the door, but she still clung to me.

"If you die fighting, what will become of us," she cried; "who will explain? how will they believe? You are spoken of as 'the mysterious spy'; they believe there is a great heretic plot throughout Spain and that you are part of it, and they think we also hold the key to it. They will discover all!"

"But," said I, "if I tell them naught but truth, though people say strange things in torture, trust me; all their fires, and ropes, and irons will not force a lie from me. Pray let me pass."

Donna Inez had placed her back against the door; the tall candle on the table cast a feeble, flickering light, but it shone full upon her face. "It is the truth we fear also," returned she, hoarsely. "We are Protestants!"

I paused. Now I knew something I had not fathomed before; yet why had they not told me?

"Spain is no place for you then. Here you cannot live," said I. "Listen; in England, my home, there is freedom. We must escape together, you must come with me; I shall live for you always. I have loved you, it seems to me, since you were a little child; will you give me hope?"

"You speak as if we were not, at this instant, in very danger of our lives, yet what shall we do? what shall we do?" She almost broke down in her despair.

I heard a halberd staff ring on the stones out in the hall-way. Inez had heard it also.

"Back with you to your hiding-place," she whispered quickly. "Go! For if you are found, you seal the fate of every one of us. Go, hide!"

"I cannot leave you," I returned.

"Stay," she returned, "and send me to the rack."

I shuddered, and she pointed to the secret door that was partly open; obeying her, I entered, and closed it after me. I listened my very best, but I could make out no voices, not a sound, but I heard the great door open and close twice plainly. All the time I was in a storm of thought. Every minute that I stayed in the castle threatened the lives that I would have given mine own life to save. As long as I remained a mystery, nothing could be proved. I reasoned that my captors were not certain if I was English or not. But it would not take long for them to find it out, for my dark hair and beard were every hour returning more to their natural color; delay added greatly to my danger. If I could get away from the castle, I might reach the coast and wait there for the sight of an English flag. I might never see my loved one again though, and I kept halting in my mind as to what might be best for all concerned. At last I decided that night to enter the garden, which now was shrouded with the gloom of evening, climb the wall

at the old point where I used to climb it as a
boy (the only spot where its surface was assailable),
and make off on foot to the sea-cliffs at the
south.

I opened the panel, and was stepping forth when
I saw that the candle was yet burning, guttering
slowly down, on the table beside the great armchair. I could not tell the hour, but seeing that
the place looked empty, I stealthily crossed the
room, reasoning that more than likely all hands
in the castle were asleep. Suddenly I paused, for
there came a steady scratching sound from some
place close about me. It was not the gnawing of
a rat, it was not the sound of insects, and yet it
was familiar to my ears. What could it be? I
listened, standing where I was, with every cord
in my body like a harp-string. At last I knew
it to be the sound of a pen on crisp parchment,
and I looked down at the table that was within
six feet of me. I could see a white bony hand
writing with nervous, jerky strokes — just a hand
and nothing more!

All the fear that I had ever felt in my life was
nothing to what I endured that instant. I was
cold all through me with the sudden horror. I
caught my breath as my heart gave a leap at last, a
floor-board creaked; a head peered round the chair.
Padre Alonzo and I gazed in each other's eyes!

For a full minute we never moved a lid. Then he spoke, and I felt with a thrill of triumph that his voice had fear in it, and my courage all came back to me.

"Who art thou?" he asked in his hollowest, cracked tone. I saw that he had recognized me as the fugitive, though he wished not to show it.

"One who wouldst speak with thee," I returned, "and one thou knowest well."

"Say on," he returned; "but be short, or I will call the guard here at the door. How did he let thee enter —"

"There is no guard there," I returned, venturing. "Who am I but the prisoner that escaped you yesterday, come in to ask for hearing? I have much to tell that it might be well for you to hear. I know, you but labor for the good of the Cause and for the King; you are making a mistake — have you forgotten me?"

"Say on, my son; if I have erred in my zeal, I shall make fair reparation." His courage was returning also. "Who art thou that comest so mysteriously, imposes upon ladies and claims relationship, and leads so many who know nothing of thee to take thee into their secrets and confidence? — thy name!"

"I am Sir Matthew Maunsell — one of Drake's officers!" (It was in my mind to kill him in a

moment, and I cared not how I spake.) " Now,"
said I, " dost thou wish to know more ? "

The Padre could not reply ; his lips moved and
his breath whistled in his throat. His trembling
hands stole out toward the tall candlestick as if
to seize it for a weapon or dash it upon the floor,
in hopes of calling in a servant. I reached it first
and placed it so far away he could not touch it.

" Dost thou remember Selwyn Powys ? " I asked.
" Nod thy head and lie not ! Answer, or I will
let my point into your body." I could already
imagine it rattling among his bones. I wondered
would he bleed ! " Nod or shake thy head," I
concluded, and with my eyesight growing crimson, I placed the sword at his heart — how my
fingers itched to drive it home ! Padre Alonzo
nodded.

" I am the boy who heard him curse thee ere
thou racked his body. Has the curse come true ? "
I asked, leaning close. " It has ! Meet thy end !"

Ere I could draw back my hand for the thrust,
the hideous priest fell forward, and his great shaven
head struck the oaken table with a noise like a falling block on deck. I waited for him to move again,
and I would have stabbed him. But he lay there
where he fell. I touched him and drew back my
hand — it was like fingering a skeleton. No breath
came from his body, his eyes were open and glazed.

I picked up the paper he had been writing when he had first turned and had seen me — his pen had just left the signing of it. The paper read : —

"To the Guardian-Commandant at Valliera : —

"*Greeting :* Take care of the two ladies that are brought to you with these instructions, and obey the orders and wishes of the messenger who accompanies them. This will be rewarded by the King, and must be respected by any to whom it may be shown.

"Alonzo.

"Saint Joseph watch over thee."

I slipped the paper into my doublet, and picking up the priest's body, that seemed to weigh no more than that of a child of ten, I walked to the secret passage, and bundling it in, I closed the panel. Then blowing out the candle, I looked into the hall. No one was in sight but a sentry fast asleep, as might have been expected, guarding the big gate. I might have slipped out and got away; there in the courtyard stood four horses saddled and ready, — two I saw had panniers, — but I did not run. I walked up to the sentry, passed him, and turning as if entering from the street, I shook him by the shoulder.

"Awake !" said I. "I have orders from Padre Alonzo. Now look alive, and I shall not report thy sleeping. Where is thy captain ? "

"Do you mean Don Lopez, my officer ? "

"No, don't disturb him," I returned. "Where is the captain of the guard?"

"In the little room to the left; he sleeps there on a couch."

"Go, waken him."

"Yes, my capitan."

The sleepy officer appeared.

"Where are the two ladies De Valdez and the Don Vincent kept?"

"In the big state chamber, under guard, señor. Without orders I dare not. Don Vincent is held in the monastery or the castle."

"Here are your orders, given to me by Padre Alonzo at the fortress of Chagres. I am to transfer the prisoners."

"Chagres! how comes he there?"

"Who can tell where he may be now or at any time?" I returned. "Is he a plain mortal man like unto us?"

"No, indeed, that he is not," returned the officer, handing back the paper that he had taken to the fire to examine.

CHAPTER XXXVI

AS we rode away from the old Vertendonna castle, I felt more as if I were dreaming than waking. But I had learned a few things, in the hours just passed, and one thing was that when women's wits are sharpened by danger, it is nigh impossible to trap them into betraying themselves. I had had no time to prepare either Donna Maria or my dear young lady for my coming, and yet they did not do so much as exchange a look when they had seen who was to be their guardian. Not till we were well out into the open country did any of us speak a word, and then it was Donna Maria who first betrayed her curiosity.

"Explain this miracle, señor," she entreated. "One minute we are in fear of the Inquisition for befriending thee, and the next thou art coming to our rescue as if thou wert a member of the King's private council or the Pope's legate; and whither now with us? Explain it all."

"Madam," I returned, "it has been God's will

that has made me an instrument of his gracious mercy and judgment."

"Which may be true," returned the lady, "but tells us nothing."

So I began and rehearsed the tale as I have told it, and when I came to Padre Alonzo's falling forward on the table, killed as I thought from sheer fright and terror (thus saving me the trouble of putting him out of the way), Donna Maria interrupted me.

"All this has happened before," she said. "He does not die — he will never die! Some say he is an hundred; he but swoons and stays insensible for days. He himself tells that his body has been dead for years! Who has ever seen him eat? who knows if he sleeps or drinks?"

"He is dead this time beyond peradventure," said I, "and needs no more feeding or slumber. He will trouble us no more!"

I was about going on with my story, when we heard the clatter of hoofs ahead, and I could see (for the sun was just rising) a body of horsemen come galloping toward us in a cloud of dust. As they neared they hauled rein and waited by the roadside. But thinking it best, we did not halt or hold back. I told the ladies to press boldly on, and forthwith an officer rode out to meet us.

"Halt! Whither goest thou?" he cried, hailing me from a distance.

"To the monastery of Valliera, near Sagres Castle," I returned.

"Under whose orders, señor?"

"Padre Alonzo's. I am taking thither these ladies, who have been placed in my keeping." With that I showed him the passport, and he saluted humbly.

"It is strange," quoth he. "We were to act as thy escort. Are we then so late?"

"Your tardiness demands explaining. I expected to be met with, ere this on the road."

"I crave pardon, señor; there has been some mistake. I am sorry; but 'tis no fault of mine."

With that the officer gave orders to his horsemen, and they fell in behind us, he taking up a position by my side. I could talk no more now to my companions, and my brain was turning over what it would best behoove me to say and do. But I was interrupted in my planning.

"What is the meaning of all this mystery, señor?" asked the officer in a half whisper. "Don Vincent de Valdez is now in confinement at the castle, and, if I mistake not, I know these ladies also — I have been at court."

"Thy curiosity is not proof of thy experience,"

I answered. "Ask nothing and obey orders is my advice to one who seeks advancement."

"And whose orders do I obey — thine, sir? You speak with much authority."

"Mine and Padre Alonzo's — the King and the Church. Say no more, sir, and thou wilt render better service to both."

With that he hushed and sulked somewhat, and I had time to gather my thoughts again.

The paper I possessed meant all in all to me. With it I meant to work a few plans to successful issue, and I decided upon two designs. If one promised badly, the other would be left.

Imprimis, I would ask the Commandant for a boat to take my party to Lagos, and I would demand the immediate custody of Don Vincent. Once on the water, I would seek for the Admiral, who, I suspected, was not far off the coast. Finding him, I should give the ladies choice of sailing as our guests, or returning to Cadiz safely, where they might seek protection with their powerful friends or find a hiding-place. I hoped, and the idea made my heart bound, that I might do such good reasoning with Inez that she might choose to go with me, to share my all, — my life, my name, and ever my devoted love; and I fell to flattering myself that in this I would succeed. But one false move on my side, one mistake on the part of the ladies, and all would be lost! At the thought of it I shivered as if a sneaping cold wind had reached my marrow.

We rode up to the monastery, that was well fortified and filled with more soldiers than monks, and the guard turned out to meet us. I asked for the guardian, to whom the paper was properly addressed.

An old soldier, grizzled and gray, — a commandant of foot, — came forward from a doorway. He read Padre Alonzo's writing, and bowed as he returned it.

"Command my service, señor," he said; "I will obey."

Here was one after my heart; I knew the manner of a man under authority, and I spoke with sharp decision: —

"A boat, then, to start from the bay three miles from here; have it made ready; send on a messenger, and bring also the prisoner who has been sent to Sagres."

"The latter shall be done at once, señor, but a boat! no, 'tis impossible! There are none but shallops, and besides, it is rumored that the English lie out but a few miles to the eastward. They landed at Lagos, but were driven back to their ships — praise to the saints! — with great slaughter — a splendid victory for our brave forces."

I did not smile, but I might well have done so, for it was true in part. The Admiral had landed to attack the town, but, finding the place too strong, he had retired without the loss of so much as an arrow or a man hit, but with some plunder, nathless, gathered up at a rich church.

"I do not fear the English," I rejoined. "A boat must be found."

"It is impossible, señor."

He was so firm that I saw that he was right, and forthwith fell back on my second plan.

"Have you a coach and four horses?" I asked. "I must proceed by land, then."

"Yes, señor, a fine one and good cattle."

"Have it made ready at once; despatch an order for the delivery of Don Vincent de Valdez from the castle over yonder, and spare no pains to make haste. Padre Alonzo wished me to enjoin that upon you — haste."

"I will endeavor to please his Worship," said the old Commandant, as he wrote out an order and sent it off by a soldier. "You will also require an escort, señor. Is there any one you wish?"

"I will take the young officer who came here with me and two men," said I, seeing that to deny the need might cause suspicion.

The ladies had descended from their horses, and I ushered them into the shelter of a large room on

the west of the great tower entrance. I longed for
a chance to speak with them; the room was full of
guards, but I took the risk of not being understood.

"Donna Maria," said I, "the paper I hold is a
wonder-maker. At Lagos I shall attempt to do
what I failed in here — to gain a small vessel, and
put to sea; we may find Drake, for he is not many
leagues away, methinks. If so" — I lowered my
voice — "wilt come to England with me? There
I can prove to you how deep is the love I bear — "

"Señor, the Commandant ordered me make report
to thee." I turned; it was the young officer who
had interrupted me, but I had to control my feelings.

"Yes, thou art to accompany these ladies to
Lagos, and to guard them safely," I returned.

"And to whom do we deliver them, when once
we get there?"

"Again thy curiosity, young sir! 'Twill work
thy undoing surely. But I will answer thee; softly,
to the most powerful man 'twixt there and Cadiz."

"Then thou must mean the Duke! the strongest
of Padre Alonzo's enemies!" The young man had
pronounced this last in a half whisper in my ear.
"I have been at court, and know of things that
these carls here know naught of. But 'tis most
strange," he concluded.

"Never mind thy opinions; stand by my orders," I returned, wondering who "the Duke" was,

and wishing the young coxcomb a thousand miles away.

Just then a soldier approached, and touched his rusty salet.

"Señor, the Commandant desires to speak with thee — a matter of importance."

"To me?"

"Yes, señor."

I turned; there were words burning my tongue to say, but a number of soldiers were listening now. I could not speak to the ladies, nor could I reply to the glance that I caught from Inez's eyes.

"I will take care of them," put in my young feather-top. "Trust them with me."

"Then be on guard," said I, and followed the messenger out of the room.

As we passed through the courtyard, I saw waiting there a fine coach and four big black horses; the hostlers were just making the last strap fast.

In a room on the second floor the Commandant was waiting; he was alone but for a curious figure that lay back in a chair. The old officer looked exceeding grave.

"Listen, señor, to this tale," he said, extending his hand to the occupant of the chair. "Go on," he added fiercely, "and if thou liest, Heaven help thee."

It was a barelegged, barefooted old man who sat there panting; a crooked staff leaned against his

knees, and he could scarce breathe from either pain
or weariness, although an empty wineglass at his
elbow showed there had been some attempt made
to revive him. He lifted his hand, but could utter
no words at first.

"This fellow was found crawling up the road from
the cliffs," said the Commandant, "but a few moments
since. He claims to have seen a large fleet lying in
the little deserted bay where he gathers cockles; he
says men were landing — armed men from boats."

"The love of Mary; 'tis truth!" said the old
man, faintly. "I am lame and nigh fourscore. I
made all haste."

"If he says true, it must be the English," quoth
the Commandant.

"They came out of the fog like spectres. I ran
till I could run no longer, then I crawled." The
old fisherman, for such he was, could hardly say
another word, his hand reached for the wineglass.
I was about to pour him more, when a loud cry
sounded through the great stone halls of the monastery, then followed a great running to and fro,
then the door burst open, and a soldier, his hair on
end, charged in.

"Señors!" he cried, "there is a strange body of
men filling the plain to seaward. The men who
brought the prisoner from the castle first sighted
them; they say they are the English!"

The old Commandant looked at me. " What are we to do ? " asked he, faintly. " We must send word into the town ! "

" What folly ! " I exclaimed ; " let us be sure before shooting. Let us keep cool and find out ; let us behave like soldiers, like wise men, and not like children ! " I would have made a speech at great length, for I knew that every minute's delay would help matters. But another soldier now appeared at the door.

" We can see them from the turret ! " he cried, " and another company has appeared in the rear of the castle ! "

" Come," said the Commandant, " we will look into this. But as you say, let us observe caution and keep cool heads."

It required but a glance even at that distance, but one look at the marching line, for me to know it. Sir Francis and his Yeomen and no others !

" Fudge ! " said I, " are they not a company or two of the King's foot-soldiers ? What are we alarmed at ? "

I looked over the edge of the tower into the courtyard. It was empty ; the coach had gone ! Off down the highway, on the road to Lagos and the eastward, rose a cloud of dust.

Drake had landed, but too late for me !

CHAPTER XXXVII

THE CAPTURE OF THE CAPE

I WAS stunned by the discovery. And there and then I learned that it is best at times to trust a cautious imbecile than an over-zealous rattlepate; for the young officer, no doubt thinking that he had received final orders from me, had made off with his charges without further consultation, hoping, mayhap, in his miserable hare-brained head, to further his ambitions toward progress at the court. Truly, as I turned, my sinking heart must have shown in my face. The Commandant grasped me by the arm, as I leaned back against the parapet.

"What hast thou discovered?" he asked. "Are they the English?"

"I know not," said I, my senses coming to me slowly. "Mayhap they are."

"We had best send a messenger back to the town to warn them! They will hurry out reinforcements to us; what say you? The garrison there should be forewarned," urged the Commandant.

"How many men have we here?" I asked.

"Fourscore, or such a matter," he replied. "And they must now be at their stations; the word was passed, though we could not find the trumpeter."

Again I looked down into the courtyard. The big gate was closed and the place was deserted, save for a half-befuddled pikeman who was trying to buckle on his breastplate. But as I looked at the gate I saw a man on horseback ride up and thunder loudly upon it with the hilt of his heavy sword.

"Let me in!" he cried loudly. "A message for the Governor! an important message — open here!"

"Send some one down and admit this fellow," ordered the Commandant.

"Hold!" said I, "it may be but a ruse to gain admittance. Prithee, let us use caution. I have it, señor, — I'll go and speak to this loud shouter, and if he comes from the town, or from Padre Alonzo, I would be like to know him, and we can use him as a messenger to convey the tidings that a suspicious body of men has appeared on the plain from the southward." With that I hurried down the stone steps and ran across the courtyard. The upper half of the big gate was but an open space crossed by great iron bars. A ledge for archers or musketeers to stand on ran just below. Mounting this, I looked out through the grill.

"What do you wish?" asked I.

"What do I wish?" he repeated. "What has happened here? Where are the warders and why are the gates closed? Who is in charge?"

"Not so many questions, my fine fellow," I replied, "and not one till you have answered mine first. What is it you wish, and who are you from?"

"I am from Padre Alonzo," he replied, "and I have an important message for the Commandant Governor; I tell you detain me no longer!"

"How is the old Padre wizard?" I asked. "Give me his message."

"His Worship was found half dead, thrust in a hole in the chantry, so they tell — with what truth I know not. He is in a bad way, but has sent me here with this paper."

"Give it me," I replied. "I'm as much Governor here as any one."

The man handed me a missive written on a bit of twisted paper. Rising on his stirrups he thrust it through the bars and endeavored to look above the barrier, but it was much too high, and he sank back in the saddle. I had read the paper by this time and thrust it into my bosom.

"Now," said I, "thy questions shall be answered. Ride back at top speed and tell thy worshipful and aged bag of bones, that we know naught here of any escaped prisoner, and that as for ladies, this is a mon-

astery, so we know naught of them. As to what is
going on, this is the Duke's birthday. Tell him we
celebrate it with all due rejoicing; we have broached
three casks of wine and are about to broach another,
and inform him with our respects that we intend to
have some music and mayhap fire off some cannon
in the Duke's honor. So, now, hie thee off quickly.
With all due respect, inform His Reverence that we
enjoy ourselves. Away with thee!"

Whether the man thought that I was crazy, or
that we were all mad drunk, I do not know, but he
turned his horse, and, digging in his spurs, he
pounded the road on his way back to the town, that
was distant less than two leagues from the castle.
Quickly I returned and climbed the stairway to the
tower. I could see that most of the men had taken
their stations at the loopholes and embrasures, powder and ball had been dealt out for the callivers and
culverins, and matches were smoking. But there
was a lack of certainty in the whole proceeding; no
positive orders had been issued; they knew not
where they stood. The Commandant greeted me
at the head of the stairway.

"The message," he asked, "what was it?"

"It was but an order," I replied, "requesting us
not to forget that to-day is the Duke's birthday."

"Ho, ho!" cried the Commandant, raising his eyebrows till they disappeared beneath his vizor, "he

must have changed his mind in the near past.   But
a short time ago a man who shouted for the Duke
hereabouts would have had his tongue made ac-
quaint with the bowstring.   'Tis passing strange,
señor, this change of heart!"

I had not known the depth of hatred that existed
between the cousin of the King and the wizard priest,
but now I saw that the countryside must have been
divided, and the people were only waiting to join the
forces of the more powerful.   It was just by fortune
that I chanced upon making this explanation of affairs to the messenger, guided by the remarks of the
young officer who had driven off with the coach.   But
it was the one thing that had explained matters best.
I hastened now to change the subject of our speech.

"Where," said I, looking out through the battlements, "where are the foot-soldiers that have caused
us all this uneasiness?"

Indeed, where were they?   They had disappeared;
but I did not know that a slight hollow sank in the
wide plain and lay directly between us and Sagres
Castle, that rose, a huge pile of stone and mortar,
but a half-mile to the westward of us on the edge
of the cliff.

Before any one could speak, out of this hollow
rose a line of heads, and without warning a shower
of arrows came hurtling through the air: one passed
between my body and elbow!   We had been stand-

ing out boldly on the tower top and made a good
target, but only one of us was struck, and he the
Commandant, who fell back, grasping an arrow that
had transfixed his shoulder! A volley was fired
through the loopholes of the monastery, but there
came no answer, and just as the smoke cleared away,
we heard the great castle replying.

The movement on our front had been but a feint.
The real attack was upon Sagres, that had been taken
front and rear and well surprised. No one but Drake
would have dared to risk his followers and himself
in that bold way! I watched that fight, and I can
vouch for it that it was a desperate one. I saw the
Admiral lead the men up that covered way where
the cannon were discharged but a few feet above
their heads, and they passed unscathed. I saw him
in the shelter of the angle formed by the square
tower and the round one, direct the piling of the
fagots against the oaken door. From my point of
vantage I could see how he had placed his bowmen
and divided up his men with the firelocks. And
when the big gate burned and crashed away, I could
see his figure jump forward with his sword aloft,
leading the other swords and pikes that closed in
after him. A fine view I had of that fight, and it
was one, I say, to be remembered. In a few minutes after the entrance had been made, the flag came
down, and what had been reckoned upon as one of

the strongest castles of old Spain had fallen before
the assault of a few handfuls of English sailor-men,
led by a leader who knew how such things should
be done. The fort known as Avelera was now out-
flanked on its undefended side, and it surrendered
also.

Then we could see the forces marshalling upon
the plain, and that they were about to attack our
stronghold was made evident. But owing to a
strange set of circumstances, this attack never took
place, and why? Because *I* surrendered it! That
is the plain statement of the matter. At all events,
let me tell how. After the poor Commandant had
given over the charge to me, entreating that I
should defend the place to the last drop of my
blood, I reasoned with him, and at last he came
to my way of thinking. What use was there in
fighting?—all knew that we were brave! I should
obtain permission for us and our men to march
back with honor to the town, and allow the English to take possession!

I laugh as I sit here and think of it,—of how
I stepped out with the flag of truce, and astonished every man of the company by calling him
by name! "Ho! Bellingham! Ho! Clifford!
Ho! Bostwicke!" I can yet feel how my bones
cracked when Drake, all powder smoke and grime,
clipped me in his arms as soon as I avowed myself.

"Well!" cried he, "I shall have thee hung at the yardarm for a witch! I leave thee at sea to take charge of a vessel, and, by my word, thou meetest me the first thing on land and givest me a castle! Verily, had I more men like unto this one, I had but to scatter them about and we would take the kingdom piecemeal."

Somehow, despite all the kind things that were said to me and the many welcoming pressures of the hand, I could not respond with joyance. I thought of a four-horse coach that was now leagues and leagues away on the road to Lagos. I thought of a slender figure leaning back on the cushioned seat, or looking out of the window with dark, wondering eyes. My heart, I knew, had left me, but there was my duty yet to be done, for was I not one of the Guild again? And so I once more strove to win for myself those coveted words of praise that the Admiral so seldom now let fall. I tried to forget, also, the great thing that worried me, but as the flames leaped high that night (for we put the castle, the monastery, and two adjoining towers to the torch), it seemed to me that I was burning up my hopes in the great fires. As we put out from land, they were still smouldering. Farewell to Spain!

What did Padre Alonzo think now of his mysterious prisoner? I was rather glad if he had lived to learn what had happened; it seemed to me that the revenge was more complete than if his scrawny body had been destroyed.

I never found out one thing that I would have liked to: did my message about the Duke's birthday prevent him from sending out to help at the celebration? Many people have wondered why the fortified monastery at Valliera surrendered without a blow. I have now told the world the truth of it.

*   *   *   *   *   *   *   *

I related my story to Sir Francis when once we got to sea, and he listened without a word of interruption to the very end of it. When I had finished, he made but one comment.

"Thou hast had a week like a night in a legend," he laughed, "and I wonder that thou hast any head left; it is plain where thy heart lies. Now," said he, "regard me, for the once, as a prophet. This young lady thou shalt see again, for Spain and England are not so far apart, and we will win such safety for an Englishman that — like unto the days of the Romans, that Saint Paul speaks of when he said, 'I am a Roman,' and they feared to touch him — thou wilt say, 'I am English,' and walk anywhere in safety. Would that I were so sure of winning success as thou art of finding happiness." Then he went on to speak about the troubles he had had with Borough, and how the latter had hindered all his doings as much as he could by his constant remonstrances and cautions. "But," said Drake, "see what I have done; I have swept St. Vincent — the most important cape of Spain! It is free for the landing of an English army; we could go there and take possession at any moment. I have crippled the King's hand until he can no longer wield a weapon. Faith! will we ever forget the floating fires at Cadiz? two days' fighting and I lose no men killed! And now what should I be doing? Some say off for home, to be cast into prison, maybe, for exceeding authority and breaking rules writ for old ladies by the clerk of the ships! And they will tell us that we are not yet at war with Spain! And Mendoza will have interviews with the Queen, but I know a salve that works wonders. 'Od's love! I'm going to bring back with me so much gold that every man who opens his mouth to complain may be gagged with it. 'Tis strange how hard it is to talk with a mouthful of gold smothering the tongue!"

He finished this long speech, and I knew that it was but a preamble to something that was to follow.

"Where is Admiral Borough?" I asked. Drake frowned.

"He is under arrest aboard his ship," he replied. "I sent him there. And now," said he, "Sir Mat-

thew, I intend to ask a favor of thee. Wilt thou
go to England in charge of a vessel that I will give
thee? and there wilt thou say that thou hast come
from Drake? Gain the ear of the Queen, tell her
what I have done, and bid her help me, for I must
have help; and besides, I need a friend at court.
Mark me, this I shall not forget."

And so it came to pass that in a small vessel, my
first command, I put off for England, and by the
time that I arrived there I was all English again;
my beard and hair were their natural color, so that
I was forced no longer to explain, and I told no one
my tale. Faithfully did I represent the Admiral's
cause, but when he returned he brought with him
above two hundred and forty thousand pounds, and
that spoke for him also, so that he fell not in royal
favor. But what cared I for my share of this profit?
I had gained and lost more than I could value in
words and figures. And Drake one day, when we
sat at table, almost angered me when he replied
to the assembled company, who twitted me upon
my vacant look, —

"Sir Matthew's castles are in England, my masters, but his heart is down in Spain."

CHAPTER XXXVIII

YEAR had gone by; it was 1588, July, and much had happened. It was worth not a little to me to have had an admiral for a tutor, and during all this time, after Drake's return, I had been studying to become a better sailor-man and a more knowing captain under his direction. I was madly eager for work on the water! Not a person in England now, who could read or had ears to hear with, but knew of the great fleet which Philip had prepared to send against us.

Shall England ever forget the day when the hills were crowned with the dark smoke of the beacon fires, and the news spread from port to port that the Spaniards had been sighted down the Channel? Shall I cease to remember how I heard the news? Shall I ever forget my first sight of the Armada, as it came crowding on, travelling with vanguard and rearguard, flankers and guiders, like an army on the march? As far as the eye could see it was nothing but ships, ships, ships! Huge galleons, towering two decks above any that England could show, big vessels that were up in the hundreds of tons, galleasses loaded with men-at-arms, urcas crowded with beasts of burden and cannon for field and siege. There were one hundred and fourteen sail in that mighty fleet! But all this is a forecast; let me hark back a bit.

What a trouble we had had during the months and weeks previous to the meeting with the enemy! With Sir Francis's plans well devised, his forces fairly organized, we had been held in check, gallied, and delayed by the powers at court. Frobisher, Hawkins, and Fenner, all of whom I knew well, had agreed to the Admiral's designs. We knew that the Spanish fleets lay disrupted somewhere on the coast of Spain. They would have fallen prey to us, had we been given the orders for which we prayed. But no, we had hung in port, or made short excursions to the southward and eastward, fettered by a few written words that the powers then directing matters sent down to us, and by this I do not mean to reflect upon the Queen. She gave her gracious help. We had men aplenty in the big fleets, but victuals were scarce, supplies were lacking. What did my Lord Howard write from Plymouth to my Lord Burghley? "My good lord, there is here the gallantest company of captains, soldiers, and mariners that ever were seen in England. It were a pity that they should lack meat when they are so desirous to spend their lives in

Her Majesty's service." At one time the jealousies and bickerings had ceased, the game had appeared to be in sight, and we had set sail from Ushant, heading south, and this time the weather and not man, had headed us, and we were forced back to Plymouth again. It was then that the news reached us that the Armada was off the Lizard, and they had us on the hip. So we come to the day.

Now it was true that Drake was playing at bowls with Lord Howard, Sir Robert Southwell, Captain Fenner, and George Raymond, and I was standing by marking the tally, and was first to see Flemming come leaping the fence like a hurdler, and charging o'er the lawn. Breathlessly he told us that the Spanish had been sighted, and that a pinnace had just sailed in with the all-important news. It would be hard to imagine how much this meant! They had us where we had hoped to have had them! We were inshore and to leeward. To my mind, as I first grasped the news, we were surely trapped. Now follow; there has been much confusion in the reports and tales of what occurred when the news was brought, but I can see Sir Francis standing there, balancing a ball upon the tips of his fingers, as he turns and says to my Lord Howard : —

"Come, come, my lord, let's to the game and finish it. The score is even. There's time to beat the Spaniards after."

Hearty old Raymond slapped his thigh and burst into a roar of laughter, but the speech had strengthened all of us.

"To your ships, gentlemen," ordered Lord Howard, and we hastened to the shore, where there was a great turmoil and uproar. I rowed off to my own little vessel of one hundred and forty tons. She was a craft, by the way, loaned to the Queen by old Mr. Blandford, and outfitted at my expense. With me, besides a very able crew of Devon men, were three members of the Guild, — Roger Truman, who was my boatswain; Parker, who was but a lad with us in the western seas; and another smart young sailor whose name I disremember. The rest of the yeomen were with Drake aboard the old *Revenge*.

Lord Harry! how we worked that night, for many of the vessels had to be warped beyond the point, and even when we had got there it was a dead beat to windward and hard work to keep off the land. Had there not been sailors at the ropes and captains at the helms, many a good craft would have left her bones ashore. But when day dawned the deed had been done. We were beyond the Eddystone, and ere long, and to the southward, I saw the sight that I have written of at the beginning of this chapter. There lay the great Armada! They say that Medina-Sidonia had thought us

safely locked in Plymouth, and that such good seamen as Admiral de Recalde and Don Pedro de
Valdez (who, by the way, was my uncle) supposed
that we had come from the northward, or at least
from Portsmouth.　But, wherever we came from,
they must have seen that we were ready to meet
our enemy.　It seemed that they regarded us at
first with marked disdain, for they allowed us to sail
down the coast, across their line, and to reach a position that — had they known it — was the very one
for which we had been praying.　To describe the
various tactics or the formations employed in making the great fight that filled the following days, is
not my province.　I had my own little vessel to
look after, my own position to fulfil, and it is what
I saw the Admiral do, and what I did myself, that I
shall tell on.

Drake has dismissed the battle of Sunday, the
21st, with but few words, and I have heard him in
speaking of it claim that it was "but passing cannon shot."　However, it was a lively interchange,
and in the course of it I met with an adventure.

My little *Sparhawk* could be handled like a
shallop, and I found no difficulty in sailing in and
out, even among our own vessels.　But the cannon
we carried were so light of metal that it was out of
question for me to fight at long range, and it was
all I could do to keep my men from running too

close to the flanks of the enemy, where their numbers might have swamped us. I was somewhere in
advance, when there came a sudden cloud of sul-
phurous smoke and the dull report from the midst
of the Spanish fleet, that hailed, to them, some
great calamity. I saw the *San Salvador*, one of the
largest of the southern squadron, drop back in
flames — and how we English made for her! But
the Spanish rallied in such force that we did not
succeed in laying her aboard. I had got in so
close, however, that had I been of larger force, I
could have taken her! In fact, it was in my mind
to take the tall risk, when I perceived that it was
not to be.

Four great ships were bearing down to the injured craft's assistance. Her two upper decks had
been blown out. She was afire at the stern, but the
men were working gallantly to extinguish the flame,
and she was worth saving. Truman had called my
attention to a small boat that had shoved off from
the side of the *San Salvador* a moment before we
neared. The wind caught it and wafted it away to
leeward. I could see that it contained some people
of importance, for a silken flag floated at the bow,
and a tall man in a great plumed hat stood in the
stern sheets, urging the men at the oars. So I put
our helm hard down, and, judging the distance
well, saw that I could reach the boat before the

Spanish ship could pick it up. Foot by foot we
gained on it.   The men had run forward to the
bows and were swinging loose a demi-cannon, preparing to sink the shallop should it not surrender.
One of the on-coming Spanish vessels had swung
off to prevent us carrying out our purpose.   It was
a question if she would not head us.   The man at
the helm looked up at me.

"We can run her down," said he, "and bear
away, sir."

I ran forward and hung o'er the forecastle rail.
Nearer we came and nearer.   The men in the small
boat were mad with terror now.   Some of the rowers dropped their oars and raised their hands.
Those in the stern sheets half stood up, as if about
to jump, and then at that instant I perceived, alack!
that at least two of the party gathered there were
women!   The tall officer had unsheathed his sword
and stood on guard as if he might expect to sink
us single-handed.   It was the falling back of a hood
that had disclosed to me how precious a cargo the
little boat was carrying.   They were almost beneath
our bows, and was I mad or dreaming — there
stood Donna Maria, and beside her, the wind blowing her dark hair back from her face, was Inez!
Never did I let my voice out in such a shouted
order.

"Hard-a-lee! hard-a-lee!" I cried, and with a

roaring and shaking of our foresail, the ship came up into the wind. The shallop struck our starboard bow, glanced, half filled with water, swirled for a minute, and was saved. One of the men near me snatched up a firelock and laid it across the bulwarks. I dashed him to one side, and stopped another man as he was about to point a second. We came about on the new tack and left the little boat to be picked up by the on-coming Spaniard, and thus it was that I missed sinking one of the chief officers of the great Armada, but had saved myself from shortening my own life, for had I been late in the giving of that order, I should not have cared to live!

I marked well the vessel that picked them up. She was a great four-decked craft with a brilliant yellow stripe running her full length, a high, gilded stern, and bedecked with streamers and ancients. I would have known her anywhere. She let fly at us as we made off, but her shots went wide. At first I could not gather my thoughts together enough to reason as to what it would be best to do. I longed to tell some one — I craved advice. Had my eyes played me false? In fact, I was so taken aback altogether that if my second in command had not come to the front and assumed charge of the ship, I might have got into trouble, for we were holding on most dangerously close to the Spanish line.

I went on board the flagship that night and told
my tale to the Admiral, and what did he say?

"Look alive, Sir Matthew, or we will be thinking more of love-making than of fighting!" and
then he laughed.

"Never fear, Admiral," I replied. "I will take
care that there is no complaint forthcoming; all
I ask is that, if we lay them alongside, I be given
a chance to make fast to the big galleon with the
yellow stripe."

"You will get that," he said, "and I will be
with you; we will hunt in couples."

"Why won't the Spanish haul their wind and
fight us?" I asked. "What purpose have they
in huddling up the Channel?"

"I take it," Drake replied, "that they are acting
under orders to join with Parma off Dunkirk.
And it is not far from there that the great battle
will be fought. We have given them but a taste
of what is to come!"

We had drawn off for the night; the Spaniards
had extinguished the fire in the big galleon, though
in the confusion one of their large ships had been
almost dismantled by running afoul of their hulks.
They had gained their well-kept formation and
were pressing forward, their signal lights flashing
and dotting the waters to the northeast.

  * * * * * * * *

It is of the battle of July 23d that I intend to write. The day previous we had fought a fight almost in mid-channel and had taken a few ships, —among them the half-wrecked *San Salvador* and several minor prizes; but it was Tuesday's battle that will remain forever in my mind. I had kept as close as might be to the *Revenge*, and we were well up to the westward and partly in the rear, when Howard made his change of front and tacked on the new wind to the east. But he was fair to lose the weather gauge; and Drake, seeing this, held on, signalling his own ships for closer action. We bore up to windward, and soon were in the thick of it. The *Sparhawk*, having nimble heels, kept in the van.

The smoke hung over the water like a fog, and the first thing that I knew, we had sailed down into it, and the Spanish ships were to the left and right of us. It was give and take on every side. I had chance more than once to grapple and board, and was saved from destruction on more than one occasion by the very size of our adversaries, whose shot passed over me, while I raked them from beneath and sent the splinters flying. For more than ten minutes I had not seen an English flag. The wind had fallen somewhat, and the great, unwieldy galleons pitched to and fro, with their sails sometimes flat aback, hopelessly bewildered.

Their captains hailed one another, asking for orders like country bumpkins at a fire. I fain believe that, though some of their missiles failed to find lodgment in English oak, nevertheless they wrought great destruction elsewhere. On one occasion two great ships of Spain galled one another direly, not only once, but thrice! But I had failed to see what my eyes sought for most, — the galleon with the yellow stripe!

Suddenly, pressing along, wending her way skilfully through the crowding, blazing shipping, I saw the *Revenge*. Her men were cheering as they worked the guns. I kept in close to her.

"Well done, *Sparhawk!*" cried some one from the quarter-deck, and, looking up, I saw the Admiral himself. Our men responded with an answering shout. She swept by us, and at that moment the heavy smoke lifted, and right astern I saw the vessel I had been searching for. She was well handled and, unlike the others, had kept her sails filled.

"Admiral Drake!" I cried. "There she lies yonder!" I pointed to where the great ship lay. Whether Sir Francis had heard or not, I did not know, but taking it for granted that he had, I squared away, and, coming up astern, we fastened to the Spaniard's sides like a bulldog on the flanks of a baited animal. And now there followed some great fighting! She was over three times our size,

"We fastened to the Spaniard's sides."

and carried three times as many men. But twice my brave fellows gained her deck, only to be beaten back. Could she have depressed her guns enough, we would have been sunk by one discharge, but our small size favored us. At last, to my great dismay, I saw the case was hopeless, and, with my heart almost breaking, I cut away the grappling lines.

Just as we floated clear, up came the Admiral, and the English cheer rang out again! I can hear now the crash of the broadside! I can see the Spaniard leap and quiver, 'neath the heavy blow! And then a strange fear came over me. Would my loved one be safe from that storm of iron? Would I be in time to rescue her?

Calling all hands to make what sail we could, I tried to regain the position I had lost, but the rigging of the *Sparhawk* had been so shattered and so much top hamper had been shot away, that we were scarcely more now than a hulk, though tight and sound below. And then I saw the flagship strike the Spaniard's side, and I knew she was as good as taken. But out of the smoke came another great shape, with many decks, towering one above another! One of King Philip's royal ships upon whose stern I read *San Luis*, came roaring along. The *Sparhawk* was almost athwart her bows, and there was no way of escape! My men left their posts and came running aft! She struck us fair

and square, and we rolled over almost bottom upward. There came a great grinding, crunching
sound as the huge bows bore us down! But English ships are stoutly built, even if they be but merchantmen, and though, from our bulwarks to below
the water-line we were cut and splintered, we sheared
off and still floated.

As if disdaining to look and see what had become
of us, the *San Luis* held her course, straight for
where the *Revenge* was fighting the big galleon.
Close up she ranged, and almost with a cry of horror I perceived that the Admiral would be caught
between two fires! Either vessel was larger than
the flagship; each one must have rated at least eight
hundred tons; the *Revenge* was hardly more than
half of that. The *San Luis* closed upon her. It
appeared as if she would be crushed between them.
Drake saw his danger, but he had kept his sails full.
I heard a trumpet blow an English call, I saw the
larboard broadside of the flagship speak, and then
how it came about I could not tell, but the *Revenge*
slipped out from between them like a thing alive,
and the two huge vessels crashed together! I could
hear them roaring like great maddened beasts,—
foiled of their prey!

But the *Sparhawk* was settling deeper and deeper,
and I had to mind what went on about me. We
had one small boat left. It would not hold our

wounded or those of us that were left alive, so all of our energies were now bent to make a raft that would suffice to keep us on top the water, and we had no time to spare. We had but launched it and shoved off when the brave little vessel pitched forward and sank with a great bubbling moan.

We had come to a pretty pass, indeed. The little rowboat was crowded to the gunwales. With every dip we shipped the tops of the choppy seas and were forced to bail. The men we had saved lay on the hastily built raft, with the water dashing over them. The fight had drifted to the eastward where the smoke still hung thick. Suddenly there came a change of wind, and it appeared to be coming back to us. All at once out of the ruck and clamor, I saw the flagship come again. Drake, as usual, was taking advantage of the change in direction of the wind to keep upon the flank. He hove up short, and I saw three or four of his vessels gather near, in obedience to the signals he had given them. They were scarce a long-bow-shot distance. Even at the risk of foundering I called the men to lay back on the oars, and bailing and plashing, we gained the flagship's side. Somehow I scrambled up on deck. The Admiral looked at me as if he had seen a ghost.

"What, ho, Sir Matthew!" he cried, "art thou alive? God be praised! I thought I'd seen the last of you. We need officers," he went on, speaking quickly; "take charge there, off the forecastle."

I ran to my post, and within five minutes we were in the thick of it again. I kept a lookout for the yellow stripe, but could not see her, but soon I had other things to think of. We were close aboard a great galleasse, and, ranging up, made fast to her. I was one of the first upon her deck, and back of me were fourscore good English swords. She had been badly handled ere we found her, and her crew were in dire confusion. On her high poop a knot of officers were trying to rally some pikemen and musketeers. At them we went, and soon the blows and cuts and thrusts were passing. Some one parried a great stroke that I aimed and I saw before me a man in half armor, his eyes gleaming from behind a heavy vizor that hid his face. I thrust again! My point caught beneath his steel-clad arm, and broke short off. For half a minute with the hilt I managed to keep him away, but he would have borne me down had not something unforeseen happened at the instant. A great, bare-headed sailor-man pushed up beside me.

"I'm here, Sir Matthew!" some one cried, and though I could not glance about, I knew the voice for that of Roger Truman. He was armed with a great capstan bar that few men could have done more than lift to shoulder, but in his hands it might

have been a wand. The man with the steel head-
piece was so intent on getting at me, that he did not
see the coming blow. It struck him full and fair
upon the head, and, had it not been guarded by the
helmet, it would have crushed it like an egg. As
it was, it split his casque wide open, and before me
there I saw Don Lopez, the villain! He had
dropped his sword, and I leaped forward at his
throat. Down we went together, I cutting and
thrusting at him with the few inches of steel that
were left upon my hilt, but his armor saved him,
though once and again I almost reached his head.
Still clinging together, we got up on our feet and
staggered to the bulwarks, and there I had him, for
I got my point wedged in beneath his corselet!

"Dost thou know me?" I cried in Spanish, "thou
knave and thief! Remember how I caught thee
with the stolen pearls! Remember him thou saidst
had taken them! Now answer for thy sins!"

I was about to drive the short blade home, when
there came a great explosion in my ears that almost
stunned me. Don Lopez fell backward from my
arms! I turned and saw the smoking muzzle of an
arquebus, and behind it a tawny British face. So
close had the *Revenge* drifted and wedged herself to
the galleasse's stern that one of the musketeers seeing my plight had fired at close range from her bulwarks. My head still rang with the nearness of the

discharge. That Don Lopez would sin no more was now a certainty. I turned away from the ghastly sight.

The galleasse had surrendered, and leaving a prize crew on board, at the call of the trumpet we went on the flagship and cast off the grapplings. It was growing late in the afternoon, and we were well to the westward of the flying Spanish squadron, that was holding together like a mass of water-bugs in an eddy. The *Revenge* hauled off to reeve new running gear. I joined the Admiral on the deck. His eyes were bright and sparkling and his cheeks aglow.

"I have some news for thee, Sir Matthew," he cried; "look over the taffrail there, look in near shore!"

Pounding on the sands two miles to leeward (for we had worked in close to the shallows in the mist of smoke) lay a great vessel with a yellow stripe along her side!

"She's there for the plucking," he said, "she'll make no more fight of it! Take a boat and put off to her — that prize is thine. And hark'ee!" said he, "if the wind changes a few points at the turn of the tide, thou canst work her off and save her. I will order a pinnace to go to thy assistance. Come, bear a hand, make haste!"

In less than an hour I was under the quarter of

"A great vessel with a yellow stripe."

the great painted galleon. Behind me I could see an English pinnace working down toward us. There were with me in the boat an officer and thirty men, enough to take possession. But the Spaniards had no idea of fight. A man in a silver-gilt salet hailed me over the rail. "We have surrendered," said he. And I saw the reason why. When the great ships had come together, the same bows that had sunk the *Sparhawk* had crushed the sternpost and rudder of the *San Marcos*, and reduced her to a helpless, drifting hulk.

My heart was fluttering as I climbed the sides. There a grewsome sight awaited me. Her decks were littered with mangled and dying men! But I did not stop there long. Down I plunged into the cabin, and there I paused.

Laid out upon a hastily constructed bier, with candles burning at its head, was a figure robed in black. Fearfully I lifted the cloth, but drew back half in horror. There lay the body of Padre Alonzo —dead this time to a certainty! There was a round, smooth hole through his temples. To the deck below I plunged again, and saw how great had been the destruction. Handsome silk and satin hangings were torn and scattered in confusion. I paused. Moved, I know not by what impulse, I called a name aloud, —

"Inez!"

There came no reply, and then again I called. This time I heard a sound, and, turning quickly, there my dear lady stood! I stepped forward and stretched out my arms. She did not move, and there we stood silent.

"Don Marteo!" exclaimed another voice. From behind a hanging curtain stepped Donna Maria. She grasped her daughter's hand. "See!" she cried, "God has sent him to us! We are saved again!"

I saw the tall, slight figure swaying, but with an effort Inez kept herself from falling, and then, with a half cry, she stretched out her hand, and her head sank on my shoulder.

"Oh, señor," cried Donna Maria, "she would have made such sacrifice to save us, for she was pledged to marry a man that she detested,—one of Parma's officers, Padre Alonzo's nephew. We were prisoners here. She would have sacrificed herself, for the Black Wolf had agreed to spare our lives if she would obey him! Our lives were in his hands again."

Inez lifted her head, and her eyes sought mine.

"I thought I would never see thee more," she said.

"Thank God, who has watched over us," I replied. "We will not part."

That night was brilliant with the great round moon. As the tide turned, we worked the *San Marcos* off the shoal, and at daylight, towed by the pinnace, we dropped our anchor in Portland harbor. Drake and his Yeomen had taken a fair prize. But I had made a fairer — one worth to me more than all the golden galleons that ever sailed the seas.

www.ingramcontent.com/pod-product-compliance
Lightning Source LLC
Chambersburg PA
CBHW030941110726
47900CB00004B/1083